THE FLEET
BOOK 3: BREAKTHROUGH

Including . . .
Larry Niven and David Drake
THE MURDER OF HALLEY'S COMET

Khalian plotters destroy Halley's comet, not knowing that
they are pawns in an even greater conspiracy!

Diane Duane and Peter Morwood
LONG SHOT

Roj Malin, lieutenant commander, is about to experience
what it's like to work with a brainship!

Janet Morris
BAD LUCK

Space marines with X-weapons fight two deadly foes: the
Khalians, and the man in charge of their mission!

AND MANY OTHERS!

Ace Books edited by
David Drake and Bill Fawcett

BREAK THROUGH

THE FLEET

BOOK 3

Edited by

David Drake *and* **Bill Fawcett**

ACE BOOKS, NEW YORK

THE FLEET
Book 3: BREAKTHROUGH

An Ace Book / published by arrangement with
Bill Fawcett & Associates

PRINTING HISTORY
Ace mass-market edition / May 1989

Copyright © 1989 by Bill Fawcett & Associates.
"The Murder of Halley's Comet" copyright © 1989 by Larry Niven and David Drake.
"Suicide Mission" copyright © 1989 by Christopher Stasheff.
"Character Flaw" copyright © 1989 by Steve Perry.
"Long Shot" copyright © 1989 by Diane Duane and Peter Morwood.
"Battle Off Dead Star 31" copyright © 1989 by Trigee Inc.
"Double Blind" copyright © 1989 by Janny Wurts.
"Khasara" copyright © 1989 by Robert Sheckley.
"Indie" copyright © 1989 by S. N. Lewitt.
"A Family Business" copyright © 1989 by Karen Haber.
"Promotion" copyright © 1989 by Bill Fawcett & Associates.
"Crossing the Line" copyright © 1989 by Jody Lynn Nye.
"Bad Luck" copyright © 1989 by Janet Morris.
"Team Effort" copyright © 1989 by David Drake.
Interludes copyright © 1989 by Bill Fawcett & Associates.
Cover art by Jim Gurney.

Visit our website at
www.penguinputnam.com
Check out the ACE Science Fiction & Fantasy newsletter!

ISBN: 0-441-24105-0

ACE®
Ace Books are published by The Berkley Publishing Group,
a division of Penguin Putnam Inc.,
375 Hudson Street, New York, New York 10014.
ACE and the "A" design
are trademarks belonging to Penguin Putnam Inc.

PRINTED IN THE UNITED STATES OF AMERICA

10 9 8 7 6 5 4 3

CONTENTS
Book 3   Breakthrough

INTERLUDE

No one item is more ubiquitous than the omnivision. From tiny portable units less than two centimeters square to the massive units used at sports stadiums, it is estimated that there are 1.3 omni broadcast receivers for every resident of the Alliance. Of those shows appearing on the omni, few are more popular than the adventures of Captain Hawk Talon of the Fleet . . .

Millions watch as the 4,032nd episode of "Hawk Talon of the Fleet" begins. Our hero is poised over the port, staring down at the Khalian admiral. Behind him you can see the hull of the barbarously painted, mile-long Khalian superdreadnought.

"You've slaughtered your last innocent victim, Admiral Grrrh," Talon declares, smashing through the ship's view port. Shards of glass are everywhere. He lands on the bridge less than a meter from the hissing, growling, Khalian officer. The Fleet emblem glitters on Hawk's chest as the hero rips off his helmet and . . .

Suddenly the entire three-dimensional grid that projects over the top of the omni goes black. Just as abruptly, the actual Fleet emblem floats in the center of this new darkness. While less ostentatious than that worn by Captain Talon, it is somehow just as impressive. Martial music rises and then fades as a schooled voice explains, "We now interrupt this program for a special announcement."

THE MURDER OF HALLEY'S COMET

by Larry Niven and David Drake

EVEN WITH HALF a square kilometer of light-sail deployed, the Khalian projectile was an insignificant blip compared to the four-kilometer diameter of the comet's core. The entire unit weighed just under ten kilograms. There was a terminal-guidance system which incorporated a proximity fuse, a small bursting charge, a reflective shell, and tiny servomotors coupled to the spars of the light-sail.

The sail blazed with a terrible intensity, a tiny, peculiar star, brilliant green. It was traveling at almost 25,000 kilometers per second—8 percent of light speed—when the payload detonated. The cloud of shrapnel grew but continued with the same course and velocity as the missile had before exploding.

Its target was black with age, invisible against the sky.

The projectile had become a cloud over four kilometers across when it splashed across the ancient ice ball. Traveling at a significant fraction of light speed, the shrapnel's effect was that of a blast of gamma rays. Half of the comet's surface absorbed the impact and vaporized instantly. Stresses transmitted by flash heating shattered the remnant of the loosely compacted ball of snow and slag.

The comet exploded. Thirty-meter chunks of rock and finger-sized shards of ice drifted apart in millions of separate orbits.

The *Admiral Wilhelm Canaris* hadn't moved in nearly a decade. The huge spiky cylinder rested in unstable equilibrium in the L3 point of the Earth-Moon system, at the fringes of Earth's gravity field. Escape craft were positioned to serve as attitude jets. Their main motors fired now and then to adjust the big vessel's orbit.

The heart of the *Willy C.* wasn't the vessel's bridge, but rather the office deep in its interior where sat Sector Commander Lars Eriksen, the Fleet's highest ranking officer for thirty light years in any direction. The bridge only controlled the vessel's rare course adjustments: trivial matters to a sector commander.

A sector commander's business was politics.

The spymaster-class command and control ship circled Earth itself, where the Alliance Senate met and deliberated on the Fleet's budget. In an hour Eriksen would be meeting the Senate's Trade and Industry Committee. Deep inside several concentric metal shells within what could still be described as a tremendous warship, Eriksen sat within a ring of heads. He was choosing among the alternative hairstyles that his coiffeur had downloaded into his hologram projector.

Two of the three doors into his office burst open simultaneously. Eriksen looked up. So did six bodiless heads, each slightly different yet each his own, all rotating, all annoyed.

"Our telemetry links—," blurted Captain Crocker, head of the sector's Bureau of Military Affairs.

"On the omni—," said Captain Krasnowski, head of the sector's Bureau of Civil Affairs as he pointed to the omni unit beside the desk.

The captains were too agitated to notice one another's presence. The admiral gestured with his little finger; his desk's artificial intelligence shut off the omni hologram projector. The other heads faded.

"—on Halley's comet—," continued Crocker.

"—Noel Li says—," continued Krasnowski.

"—report that the comet has exploded!"

"—that the Khalians have blown up Halley's comet! Oh, sorry, Grig."

Eriksen pointed to the omni and said, "On."

The AI responded instantly to Eriksen's command. The omni's surface clothed itself in a three-dimensional image that appeared to squarely face every human in the room. Noel Li, Earth's top newsreader, was saying, "—however, Fleet sources have refused to comment—"

Somebody from Technical Affairs chimed for admittance at

the third door to Eriksen's office.

"Come!" the admiral snarled, his eyes on Noel Li.

"—on whether the comet's destruction was the first action of a Khalian armada headed for Earth."

Halley's had been visible when Eriksen's eldest son Mark was born; so his wife had told him. Thirty-four years ago. The comet must be almost at aphelion, near Neptune's orbit, Eriksen thought; better check when he had the chance.

Li's face was replaced by an image of what Eriksen took to be Halley's comet. The holocast showed it as a cold gray ball, dimly lit, lumpy. Steam feathered out from some surface crack. Above the image glowed the word SIMULATION—in English, because the men in the office had been speaking English.

Simulation. The real Halley's was black with comet tar, carbon and polymers and other solids left on the surface by evaporating ice. The astronauts had to wear Teflon boots. Water volcanoes peaked all around them, and tiny Jupiter rose every seven hours twenty-four minutes. Thirty-five years ago, when Mark was conceived, they'd left the omni on for the whole four days, with the Halley's expedition as background.

One side of the dark sphere suddenly glared flame-green. A moment later a bright cap of vapor exploded away from almost a third of the original surface. The dark side shattered, a snowball striking a wall. Ice fragments spewed one way, steam the other.

I'm watching computer-programmed guesswork. The map is not the territory. Simulation . . . but Halley's comet is dead.

"Ah, that's what it was," said Commander Mown, who'd entered the third door when the AI opened it. Unlike Crocker and Krasnowski, the head of Technical Affairs didn't have even the option of barging in on the sector commander unannounced. "Just a drive laser—so of course the modulation was random."

"What?" said Admiral Eriksen, twisting to look squarely at the ferally slender Mown.

"Whatwhat?" gabbled Crocker and Krasnowski.

"Do you mean you—" Eriksen began.

"Is this something—," said Crocker.

"How do you mean—," said Krasnowski.

Eriksen turned again and stared at his Civil and Military Affairs chiefs. They were not too flustered by the situation to read danger in the admiral's look.

In the silence, Commander Mown said, "Three days ago, a

courier on the Earth-Titan run, the *Sabot*, I believe, with three crew named—''

"Mown."

"Yes, of course, sir. The *Sabot* encountered what appeared to be a powerful laser signal directed inward, across the solar ecliptic. They recorded the data—as a matter of course—and passed them on to us for analysis.''

As Mown talked, he tapped the side of the multifunction helmet he wore even here in his superior's office. His eyes focused on the holographic display it projected—visible to the others in the room only as occasional flickers—and his fingers tapped a rapid pattern of keystrokes in the air. The nerve impulses rather than the 'touch' of Mown's fingertips controlled the data flow.

"We assumed it was a message. It was modulated. We found coded patches in Old French and English and Japanese. We wondered if the code was changing second by second. Truth was, there was nothing to analyze,'' Mown's voice continued while his eyes tracked information the others couldn't see. "We think the modulations are partly randomized and partly bits of old messages in obsolete codes, stuff the Khalians must have been picking up for a century. The beam's only a drive laser of considerable—

''*Here* we are. Yes, quite correct. The vector indicates that it was driving a projectile toward Halley's comet.''

Mown's fingers danced as though he were executing half of a secret handshake for entry to a lodge. The data terminal opposite the omni obliged: it switched itself on to project visions.

Admiral Eriksen watched a schematic of the solar system from behind the omni. Here was black space where reality held only his office wall. Planetary orbits showed in primary colors, each a ring with a cluster of lumps on it, wound tight around the white dot of the sun. Thousands of spacecraft showed as little vector arrows. Clusters of comets showed as clouds. A bright green path indicated the computed track of the laser beam.

Fury closed Eriksen's throat. *Halley's comet!* Without the capacity for berserk rage, he never would have survived his two decades as a warrior. He'd learned how to swallow rage. But: A thousand years ago, Halley's comet showed us that we can predict. There is more than caprice in the world; there is law.

The Weasels have murdered law.

"—listeners fully informed about the crisis," Noel Li's image closed primly.

"Off!" snapped Eriksen, pointing a finger toward the omni and wishing he had a pistol. He pointed at Mown and said, "Commander, stand in front of me where I can see you without pretending to be a contortionist!"

The admiral's tone cut through the hazy reality that surrounded the Technical Affairs chief. He hopped quickly around Eriksen's desk to stand between Crocker and Krasnowski.

Eriksen pointed to the green track of the enemy laser beam. It wasn't a line, it was a narrow fan of probable paths. "Why the blurring? Where's the uncertainty?"

Mown answered, "We don't know very much about the projectile, after all. We can guess how hard it hit, that is, how much kinetic energy it was carrying. We've seen the beam, so we know how much energy was in that. But we don't know the mass of the bullet, or the size of the light-sail, or how long the beam was on—"

A pair of panicked lieutenant commanders, the seconds in command of both Military and Civil Affairs, burst into Eriksen's office behind their chiefs.

"Sir!" blurted the officer from Military Affairs. It was unclear—perhaps even to her—whether she was speaking to her direct superior or to Eriksen himself. "The secretary of the Senate Liaison office just called. He's demanding we sound Red Alert and recall at least three battle squadrons soonest!"

"Sir!" said the junior from Civil Affairs, to Krasnowski. "The president of the Senate's on the line for"—his eyes flicked toward the admiral—"Admiral Eriksen. The president herself is on the line!"

Eriksen's handsome features were a requisite for his position, but there was nothing wrong with his mind, or his ability to act with decision. He pointed toward Krasnowski. "All right," he said. "I'll take President Ssrounish's call."

His finger twitched toward Crocker. He said, "Red Alert. Do it."

"And the recall?" piped Crocker's aide.

"I said alert! If I meant something else—" Keep it simple, especially when giving important orders. Keep it explicit, keep it simple. "Do not send a recall. I have not authorized a recall."

Nodding—both lieutenant commanders white-faced—all the intruders started to leave Eriksen's office. "Wait," the admiral ordered crisply.

He pointed toward Mown. "You," he said. "Can you locate the source of that drive laser?"

Commander Mown's lips pursed. "Very probably, yes," he said. "Yes, I suppose so."

"Make the attempt," Eriksen said. "And you"—Crocker snapped to attention, at the business end of the admiral's finger—"*take* his plot, and if it is Weasels, I want their ears! Dismissed!"

The office cleared. Crocker followed Mown. As they disappeared into the corridor leading to Technical Affairs, Mown was saying, "Actually, Khalians have very small external ears. It's my understanding that the field units take the tails as . . ."

"Why was I not informed of thisss . . . ?" demanded President Ssrounish. Her accent was normally flawless; she drew out the terminal *ess* of her question now to have an excuse to curl her lip above her fangs. "Why was no member of the Ssenate informed?"

The Alliance of Planets was denounced often enough—and with enough truth—as the Alliance of Human Planets. It may be worth noting that such denunciations came generally from humans and Hrrubans. Other species did not find it worthy of comment that a powerful race should favor its own.

But when a thoroughly acceptable nonhuman candidate presented herself for the post of president of the Alliance Senate, her colleagues had voted her in by an overwhelming margin. The duties of president were largely those of a figurehead—

And the head of Madame Ssrounish, the Hrruban senator, was fearfully impressive.

Ssrounish was intelligent by any standards, much less those of politicians. Her grace and beauty were remarkable; and in her social dealings she had invariably proved herself to be as gentle as a butterfly. Nevertheless, as Admiral Eriksen faced the holographic image of the catlike Hrruban, his insides twisted the way those of his remote ancestors had done when a saber-tooth stalked through the entrance of their cave.

"Madame President," Eriksen said with the dignity of absolute truth, "I believe you learned as fast as I did. I've just watched it on the omni. That is all I or my chief aides know about the event."

"What?" Ssrounish's jaws twitched as though she were trying to swallow a bolus too large for her throat. It was simply a gesture, but Eriksen's instincts told him to hurl himself through the doorway behind him.

"Halley's comet has exploded," he said calmly. "We know that much. We'll know more shortly."

Eriksen had commanded the *Tegetthoff* when plasma bolts killed fifty-eight of the seventy men with him on the cruiser's bridge. This wasn't the first time he'd had to function when he was scared green.

Ssrounish blinked but remained silent for a moment. "I don't—," she began. Then her eyes clicked into focus again, and she continued decisively, "What additional measures are you taking to safeguard Earth, Admiral?"

Superimposed over Ssrounish's image in the holovision tank were red letters reading SENATOR PENRYTH—another priority call that Eriksen's aides knew their chief would have to deal with personally. Hugh David Penryth's votes were so closely identified with policies emanating from Fleet headquarters on Tau Ceti that he was known—not to his face—as the Senator From Tau Ceti.

Penryth would be asking the same questions as Ssrounish, but his priorities would differ. Eriksen thought vaguely of merging the calls, but this was going to be unpleasant enough one-on-one.

"Earth's defenses—the Home System defenses—," Eriksen said, "are already sufficient to meet any potential threat, Madame President. Until—"

"You say that, wrapped in a Fleet dreadnought!" Ssrounish roared. She reared up on her hind legs; the sending unit in her holotank panned back automatically to show the august president of the Alliance Senate clawing strips from the three-meter ceiling of her office. "The Meeting Hall has nothing above it but clouds—and they are sparse enough in this damned bright atmosphere!"

Must I step outside to speak further? These days Eriksen rarely exercised his talent for sarcasm. "Madame President, the

Home System is more heavily defended—''

"I am old and perhaps ready to die!" Ssrounish continued, belying her words with the supple fury of her limbs. "But my colleagues—the senators who vote the Fleet's appropriations— they are perhaps not all so philosophical!"

But enough was enough. "One may hope they are less timid, also," Eriksen said. "Sol system is more heavily defended than Port Tau Ceti. Any monkey with a spacecraft can blow a snowball apart, but a real Khalian attack would require greater force than they've ever demonstrated . . . if the Khalians are even involved. We have only the news broadcasts to suggest even that."

"You said 'timid,'" President Ssrounish said.

"Have you remembered your dignity, Madame President?"

President Ssrounish settled back into her normal posture, bonelessly, like a house cat. "Admiral, you must be very sure of yourself."

"Why not? This is my skill."

"You say that we have only the omni newscasts to thank for any information about the attack. How is it that Noel Li knew about it before you did? . . . or the Senate either!"

"Madame President," said Eriksen grimly, "I hope to find you an answer very soon."

When Lieutenant Scarlatti's console began making busy chuckling sounds, Scarlatti stood, stretched, then leaned over the divider to see how Lieutenant Stich was doing.

Stich was rising also, sweeping her fingers across her scalp as if to straighten the hair that she'd had stylishly removed. Almost no one really looked good as a baldie, but Jenna Stich was the 'almost.'

"What do they have you on, Alec?" she asked Scarlatti with a smile that sometimes made him wonder what a female praying mantis looked like to a male. Beautiful. Worth whatever it took . . .

"Ah!" he said, snapping back to the reality of the two of them on duty, ten levels deep inside the *Willy C*.

Of course, their consoles were doing the real work.

Still.

"One of the courier ships tracked through a laser. Somebody's drive laser," Scarlatti explained, glancing back at

his console to be sure that it didn't require a human decision.
Nope. "I'm to calculate the probable track of the laser and come
up with a source . . . assuming it was ship-mounted. Max
priority."

Stich frowned and said, "But you can't calculate direction
from one point, can you?"

"Well, no, but it's *not* a point." Scarlatti gestured to his
console and muttered a command. Stich moved closer to see
over the divider; their arms were almost touching. "The courier
was in the beam for almost thirty seconds, so there's a good
long line to work with."

The ignorance implied by Stich's question bothered him for a
moment; it was as though she'd asked him how to turn on her
console. But though the units were identical, the operators and
their jobs were not. Jenna didn't do the particular sort of number
crunching that was second nature to Scarlatti.

The console obediently gave him visuals, a green line hanging
in the air. "The intersection line," he explained. The green
shrank to a mere dash, then extended in orange from one end, in
a narrow flattened cone that stretched to the limit of the
hologram display. "And a location cone, depending on the
sender's course and speed. I'm checking the extension against
known objects before I run a plot from what I have already."

Scarlatti knew that what he had so far wasn't enough to locate
the sender, unless a couple of battle squadrons were recalled to
the Home System to sift through all the possibilities; but Stich
probably didn't realize that. The bit of harmless boasting made
the young lieutenant feel good.

Beaming with his promise of success, Scarlatti said, "What
do they have you on, ah, Jenna? Not"—a cloud passed over the
sun of Scarlatti's hopes—"a cross-check on my, ah—"

"Oh, no, nothing like that!" Lieutenant Stich warbled in
amusement. "One of the omni newsreaders announced—"

Stich cued her console with a gesture Scarlatti failed to catch.
The unit said in Noel Li's dulcet, cultured tones, ". . . *the
Khalians have blown up . . .*"

"—Halley's comet blew up before anybody here knew about
it," Stich continued over the newsreader's voice. "I'm looking
for the source of their data—"

". . . *Fleet sources have refused comment on . . .*"

"What?" Scarlatti interjected, pointing as though the recorded words weren't utterly disembodied. "You mean they *did* report it to us before the broadcast and somebody—"

Stich's smile wasn't so much mechanical as electronic in its precision. She gestured again. Li's voice switched in midsyllable to a man saying, ". . . *Landhope, producer of the Morning News. We have a report*—"

"Assistant producer," murmured Stich coldly. "He's calling Commander Brujilla in the Public Information office thirteen minutes before air time."

"*—just been blown up by a Khalian armada incoming to attack Earth. Can you comment on that for the record, Commander?*"

"*What?*" demanded a female voice from the heart of Stich's console. "*Landhope, what are you on?*"

"*Commander Brujilla, I'm not going to be put off by pretended ignorance,*" the producer snapped. "*If the Fleet refuses comment on the biggest security lapse since Pearl Harbor, we'll run what we've got!*"

"*Well, run it and be damned, then, Landhope! And if you think your calls here'll ever be answered again, y—*"

"Ooh . . ." said Scarlatti.

"Yeah," said Stich. "Brujilla's got about as much chance of promotion as Ito van Pool." Van Pool had docked Admiral Ozul's gig three meters deep into his flagship's hull, sixty years ago. Such things are remembered. "And I'd have said the same thing if anybody'd called me with such an idiot story . . ."

"Sure, anybody would," Scarlatti agreed. The cold feeling in the pit of his stomach had crushed all the pride, all the sexual display, out of his voice. He'd just seen somebody's career get hit by an astrobleme.

Stich gestured again. "This is the call to Broadcast Towers," she said.

"How do you . . . ?" Scarlatti asked. "I mean, are you just pulling these calls out of a file, or . . . ?"

"Of course," Stich agreed. Her quizzical expression reminded Scarlatti of how he'd felt when she asked a ridiculous question about course computation. "They don't name these ships after spymasters and hang them over sector capitals for nothing, Alec. I told my console to sort message traffic to and from Broadcast Towers over the past three days, using the key phrase 'Halley's comet.'"

"*. . . Towers,*" said a voice from the console. "*Can I help you, please?*"

"*Record this,*" responded another voice, probably unnecessarily. "*I won't say it again. A—*"

"We don't have a match on the voice, at least yet," Stich explained in an undertone, "but the call originated from Dallas."

"*—Khalian armada is inbound toward Earth. They have already destroyed Halley's comet. Professor Sitatunga at Fermi-Geneva will confirm this.*"

"Thirty-seven minutes before air time," Stich added with professional appreciation. "They were cutting it close."

When Jenna Stich flicked her control hand again, the console generated a hologram of a man with implanted hair—a cheap job that looked as though the surgeon normally specialized in putting greens— oriental features, and a rich black complexion.

"*Yes, yes?*" a voice was saying; the image's lips moved, slightly out of synch with the words. "*I am Sitatunga, yes.*"

Noticing Scarlatti's frown, Stich said, "They didn't have enough warning to arrange pictures for the initial flash, but they got cameras on him later. I'm just manipulating those sends to fit the initial call."

"*. . . told me you'd be calling about my research . . .*"

"Told by the same guy as made the call to the station?"

Stich nodded absently.

"*Yes, Professor, but what about the comet exploding?*" The caller from Broadcast Towers was probably Landhope; Scarlatti couldn't tell.

Stich murmured, "Yes, he called Sitatunga from Dallas the day before, pretending to be Noel Li's producer himself."

The holographic face registered amazement and horror. "*Why are you saying this to me? This is no joke! The comet is not exploded, it—*"

"Told him they wanted a feature on Halley's comet, so he'd have the latest telemetry ready when the station called—"

"*See, right here!*" insisted Sitatunga, obviously pointing to a display terminal that would probably have been illegible even if he were on-camera during the conversation. "*It says . . . oh my God! Oh my God! Oh my God!*"

"*Professor?*"

"All my equipment! Gone! Gone! Exploded as you say! All my life!"

Stich gestured away the scientist's voice and the sight of his pop-eyed horror.

"He was the greatest authority on the comet in . . . I suppose the universe," she explained. Her mouth moved in what could have been a cold smile. "I suppose he still is, but there isn't as much now to know."

"Except who did it. And even that—" A pulse of red light and the beep in Scarlatti's mastoid implant warned him that his console needed a human decision.

"Go ahead," he ordered as he turned to face his equipment.

CONFIRMATION POINTS appeared in the air in bright amber letters. The heading lifted a hand's breadth. Beneath it—in red, indicating a high degree of probability—appeared MARS, followed by thirty-digit time-location parameters.

"Right," Scarlatti said. "Check it out."

Stich waited a decent five seconds to be sure she wouldn't interrupt further business, then asked, "Check what out?"

"Ah," said Scarlatti. "The calculated course suggests the drive beam may have intersected Mars before it hit the *Sabot*."

"Wouldn't that have been reported?"

"Sure," Scarlatti agreed, "but so what? A laser beam intersecting a Fleet unit is an incident that sets off alarms. But intersect a planet and that's just data . . . until somebody asks about it."

Lieutenant Stich responded with a smile that warmed Scarlatti all the way down to his toes. "My dad thinks my being in Fleet intelligence is exciting. I tell him I'm just a librarian: my job's information retrieval."

Scarlatti nodded toward his unit. "Yeah. Like I could call somebody on Mars myself . . . after the console told me who. But it's a lot simpler to let the console talk to the data storage site directly."

"Computers don't go out to lunch," Stich agreed.

Scarlatti's implant chimed pleasantly, alerting him that new data hung in the air, to replace the calculated parameters. "Three hours?" he said in amazement as he translated the digits into human reality. "The beam was painting Mars for three hours? That's absurd! Unless they were . . ."

Stich said, "And what were the chances that the beam would

intersect a Fleet courier by chance?''

Scarlatti pointed to key his console. He had his mouth open to request the calculation when he realized that the other lieutenant hadn't meant the question literally. "Oh," he said, covering his embarrassment with a fixed grin. "Tiny. Had to be an accident, Jenna."

"Maybe not. What about Mars?"

"Yeah. The Weasels meant to be noticed. Jenna, they kept a violently accelerating bomb between Mars and their ship for *three hours*. So people on Mars would look up. And see Halley's comet explode. And that tells me a *lot* about their course." His hands were moving.

At Scarlatti's mutter-gestured command, his console threw up a course calculated with the addition of the new hard data. The intruder's green line danced in the smoothly-perfect curve of masses in vacuum dancing through the sun's gravity well. The cone of extrapolated paths (orange) had narrowed considerably.

"—but we only know this because *Sabot* was in the beam. And that's four points on a line, Jenna. Couldn't have been planned."

A chime from Jenna's console drew the attention of both technicians. Scarlatti couldn't hear the question Stich's mastoid implant was asking her, but when she said, "Run," the console spewed out loud the recorded conversation it had retrieved from *Willy C.*'s files.

It made no sense at all. "What language is . . . ," he murmured, too lost in his own ignorance to notice the frown wrinkling his companion's forehead.

Stich crooked a finger at her console. It obediently threw a holographic caption in the air above itself:

> NO KNOWN LANGUAGE.
> POSSIBLE COGNATES:
> WESTERN EUROPEAN/PRE-EMPIRE.

No known cognates within the thousand years since the collapse of the first starborne human civilization.

The speech, unintelligible even to the SCCS *Willy C.*, stopped. Without prompting, Stich's console threw up an additional caption:

TIME TO NEXT PORTION OF TRANSMISSION:
FIVE HOURS, THIRTY-TWO MINUTES.

"Well, compress it, then!" Jenna snapped as though the console and not its programming had forced her to give that 'obvious' instruction.

"Five and a half hours," muttered Scarlatti, doing the computation for which he didn't need his console's help. "If the delay's due to transmission lag"—and he couldn't imagine it being from anything else—"it's originating from well beyond Neptune. From the inner comets. Of course."

Stich's console began speaking in a different recorded voice, though the language was at least putatively the same. "The console picked the call out on the basis of the voice print—one speaker's a good match with the man who called Sitatunga and Broadcast Towers."

"In Dallas?"

Jenna nodded. "Forty-three days ago. The other half of the circuit is supposed to be Gravitogorsk, Mars."

"Then why the lag?" her companion asked in puzzlement. "Mars should require only a few minutes' delay."

"Supposed to be," Stich repeated with a slight astringency for what she considered to be someone missing an obvious point. "With thirty seconds and a plot of comsat orbits, I can crash a Gravitogorsk circuit too, or any open circuit."

"But could you do it from five and a half light-hours out?" Scarlatti prompted.

Jenna paused, pursed her lips in consideration. She looked beautiful. "With the *Canaris*'s navigational software to steady the transmission beam," she said at last, "yes. Give me a starship's navigational equipment, and I could tickle an orbital satellite any way you like. I could make anyone think a call was coming from Earth instead of. . . . The Oort Cloud is what we're talking about, isn't it? But you normally wouldn't bother . . ."

"Unless you had an agent on Earth," Scarlatti said, taking the verbal handoff from his companion. "And you wanted to give him the details of your plans so that he could prepare the propaganda campaign."

Stich stared at the holographic solar system glowing above Scarlatti's console. "Alec," she said cautiously, "if you—"

"—factor in the distance and course calculated from the decreasing lag time between call segments. That's their velocity component toward the *Sabot*. Hee hee hee! We'll have their velocity vector. That's more than they wanted to tell us." Scarlatti's fingers danced. The unit began to chuckle as it processed data.

The orange cone was now on the outer end of the green line—the course the intruder might have taken after his laser beam intersected the *Sabot*.

"—then what's on the inner side of the plotted course?" Jenna finished.

The red pulse and mastoid chime from Scarlatti's console drew the eyes of both operators.

It was only a possibility, of course; a computer's estimate based on the assumption that the Weasel ship had a specific intended goal, and that the vessel's computer would choose the most elegant solution when it laid its course.

There was an event point from which a microwave beam from the Khalian ship would align almost align with Mars on its way to Earth itself. A later event point from which the beam of a drive laser would intersect the *Sabot* and Mars sequentially. There was an event-point beyond—

"Of course, they could've popped into sponge space and headed home," Scarlatti muttered. "They'd be crazy to do anything else."

"They haven't done it yet," said Stich. "An unscheduled sponge space entry within the solar system would've alerted the whole defensive array. If they stayed in normal space-time, they could assume no one would notice until . . ."

Scarlatti pointed, keying the console; then he paused while he decided whether to inform Commander Mown under the usual procedure, or to alert the Battle Center directly.

They'd have to be crazy.

Weasels are crazy!

"Battle Center," he said. Moments ago he had watched one Commander Brujilla blow her career in six hot seconds. Likely enough he had just done the same. But beside him, Jenna Stich's bald, finely formed skull was nodding approval of his decision.

Even if there were a ship prepared to take off at once,

star-drive required incredibly complex equations that took time to complete.

And if the computed guess glowing above Scarlatti's console was correct, the handful of scientists at Tombaugh Station on Pluto didn't have very much time at all.

"Look, this is really some kinda training exercise, isn't it?" said Pilot Trainee Rostislav. The fear was creeping up his spine. "Come on, Chalfond, a courier ship's too small a box for us to be gaming each other."

"It's no exercise, Rostislav," said Warrant Officer Chalfond, captain of the *Sabot*. "Shut up and worry about course coordinates."

Chalfond had been in charge of a destroyer's gun turret before a Khalian torpedo shredded her legs. Transfer to the command of a courier vessel on intrasystem runs could have been considered a promotion. At least it wasn't forcible retirement.

She hadn't considered it a promotion until now, when it seemed there might be a chance of action after all.

"Captain, the coordinates are set," Rostislav said in a frustrated tone. "They've been set for half an hour. It's the calculations to get there through sponge space that're the problem, and I can't speed them up by poking at keys myself." He grimaced at the blank, pulsing depths within his omni.

The *Sabot*'s command console was a meter-thick pillar in the center of the vessel's cabin. The console had three niches offset 120 degrees from one another, with seats facing inward. When the crew was at flight stations, they were almost touching—but they couldn't see each others' faces.

"Moggs, are your guns ready?" Chalfond demanded.

"Is a bear Catholic?" Rostislav muttered with another grimace. Couldn't she just keep quiet and let the software—

"Huh?" said Crewman Third Class Moggs. Moggs spent all his free time running training programs at the gunnery screen, zapping pirates, meteor storms, Khalians, and whatever else the computer chose to throw at him. "I don't get it, Rostislav."

Rostislav wasn't sure Moggs was bright enough to understand the difference between a training program and what was maybe about to happen.

"You know, Moggs," the pilot said. "Does the pope—"

"Shut *up,* Rostislav!" Chalfond snapped. "Moggs, are your—"

"Captain," said Rostislav. "The console is ready to start sequence."

"Action Stations," said Chalfond. "Pilot, start sequence."

"Sequence started." Rostislav tapped a key and waited for the shift. It always felt like being turned inside out. Captain Chalfond never reacted. She claimed that she had become used to it. Rostislav believed that the captain was lying.

"Moggs, are your guns ready?" Chalfond repeated in a calm voice. Rostislav could hear the tap of keys from by her side console, but his screen was loaded with flight data and didn't echo whatever Chalfond was setting up.

"Yes, Captain."

"C-captain Chalfond," said Rostislav. "What if it really is a Weasel armada we're jumping into the middle of? I mean, I know there won't really be anything there, but if there was . . . ?"

"Don't worry, kid," said the legless warrant officer in what she must have thought was reassurance. "They're scrambling everything in the system! All we gotta do is take the Weasels' minds off Tombaugh Station for a couple minutes."

It was a very short transit. The *Sabot* made a blurring lurch back into normal space-time. This time, Rostislav had too much on his plate to notice the momentary nausea.

"I have a target," said Moggs.

"Magnetics up," said Rostislav. The magnetic shielding that dispersed the effect of plasma bolts was one of his responsibilities at Action Stations, though he was only vocalizing what the green sidebar on the captain's screen told her.

"Unidentified vessel," Chalfond ordered over the tight-beam laser communicator. "Drop your screens and prepare to be boarded."

The *Sabot* gave a triple shudder. Its load of ship-to-ship missiles had toggled off in accordance with the engagement sequence that Chalfond programmed while they were still in sponge space.

"Chalfond!" Rostislav shouted. "We can't shoot before we know—"

Six screens, the outside views, flashed green and were blank. The data displays were unchanged, except that the ship's skin temperature was rising fast. High flux on that laser. A merchant ship would be boiling away. Rostislav recognized that shade of green from days ago and said, "Never mind."

"Stay alert," Chalfond said. "That green light can't hurt us much, but—" The *Sabot* shuddered again. A transient of orange light sparkled within the depths of Rostislav's screen, fogging the data there momentarily. Magnetic fields, *Sabot*'s shielding, twisted in the flow of plasma bolts.

"Taking evasive action," said Rostislav in a steady voice pitched an octave above his normal speech. Khalians. *Weasels*.

"Gunnery officer, open fire," Chalfond said.

Six-round bursts from the ball turret in the nose hammered the hull sharply. Training programs didn't duplicate the effect on the *Sabot* of miniature thermonuclear explosions, contained and directed by laser arrays in the breaches of the twin turret.

The outside cameras came back on.

Rostislav had brought the courier vessel out of sponge space at the rim of Pluto's gravity well, on a reciprocal course to that computed for the intruder by the *Canaris*'s Battle Center. *Sabot*'s real-space velocity was low, but somebody on the command and control ship had really been on his toes: the *Sabot* was headed right down the intruder's throat, and the Weasels' own significant fraction of light speed gave Chalfond's missiles a mere thirteen-second trajectory.

Another plasma bolt snapped close enough to set a relay in the *Sabot*'s guts singing, but that was chance. Rostislav had cranked in lateral accelerations that took the courier out of its ballistic path. The side-thrusters pulsed with computer-generated randomness. That was unpleasant to the crew—but not nearly as unpleasant as taking a direct hit that would flatten the magnetics and vaporize the *Sabot*'s forequarters . . .

The green light flashed and was gone, and was back, and held. Not much of a weapon, that, not to today's mirror-surfaced warships.

The red pip of the Weasel in the center of Rostislav's screen calved a trio of additional pips: missiles. They winked out instantly. Moggs couldn't have reacted to the actual target so quickly, so he must be firing at where and when he expected the Weasels to launch.

The gunnery training programs were worth something after all.

So was Moggs, despite his room-temperature IQ.

One of Chalfond's missiles vanished from the screen. The Weasels had switched their guns onto the missiles homing on them, but there wasn't time to—

The red pip blurred.

"She's trying to enter sponge—," Rostislav warned.

The pip sharpened, then expanded into a fuzzy cloud quite different from the blurring of a moment before.

"—space."

Ships had to lower their magnetic shields before entering sponge space.

"Game's over," said Moggs simply.

The two remaining missiles plunged toward the heart of the cloud. Chalfond detonated them with an abort command. There might be debris worth examining. "Gunnery officer," she ordered, "secure your weapons. Pilot, bring us around."

Pilot Trainee Rostislav found that his hands were shaking so badly that it was several seconds before he dared touch his controls.

Twenty years before, Commander Antonio Soler, a brilliant young officer, made a brilliant marriage and resigned his commission to follow a brilliant academic career. The marriage hadn't lasted, though friends argued about whether Antonio's drinking was the cause or an effect of the failure. The academic career went by the boards at about the same time as the marriage; and, though he dried out, the brilliance remained in eclipse.

Antonio Soler came back to the Fleet, to serve out the seven years remaining before he was eligible for a full pension. Few military positions require brilliance. The Fleet was glad to give the ex-commander warrant rank and command of Mine Warfare Vessel *774T*.

"Region Twelve cleared, sir," reported Yeoman Second Class Teddley as she began to furl the gossamer static lines with which MWV *774T* had cleared another assigned sweep area of debris from the Khalian vessel. There were a dozen ships involved in the hasty search, but only the *774T* and her sister ship MWV *301A* were really designed for the work. "Shall I proceed to Region Thirteen?"

Warrant Officer Soler was standing with his hands on hips, jaw out-thrust. Slightly tilted on Velcro slippers, he was facing but not really viewing the main navigational screen. He didn't respond to his subordinate's question.

"Ah," Teddley said. "Sir? Shall we proceed to Region Thirteen while we process the drag-load from Region Twelve?"

"What?" said Soler, turning with the confused embarrassment of a man caught viewing himself in the mirror of his mind. "What? Yes, yes, of course."

Teddley chimed a warning of the coming course correction. It was a moment—as Teddley expected—before Soler himself realized he needed to get into his own acceleration couch.

"Have you been considering the enigma of why the Weasels would attack Halley's comet, Teddley?" Soler demanded.

"Yessir," said Teddley. She programmed the burn. It was a rhetorical question; it wouldn't make the slightest difference whether she responded yes, no, or maybe.

"Let me postulate a plan," said Soler, "a plan for Weasels. I'm a brilliant Weasel, yes? I know I can't invade Sol system. It crosses my mind that I barely have the power to destroy an ice ball ten miles across. That shows no immediate personal profit, so as a Weasel I may well stop thinking at this point."

"But let me attempt to think like a human politician. We Weasels know that they're a cowardly lot." Soler smiled at Teddley; Teddley smiled back. *Burn in twenty seconds.*

Soler said, "If something as prominent as history's most famous comet is suddenly blasted into a vivid cloud of ice crystals, won't the human government panic? The results must be to our favor. Ships from the Fleet will be withdrawn to Earth for defense there, instead of patrolling regions we Weasels can raid."

"Yessir." The vessel's thrusters fired under orders of the navigational computer. The acceleration was mild, less than a tenth-G, as MWV *774T* eased through black sky, sifting vacuum.

"Well, but you see, the threat has to be credible," Soler continued. "The death of Halley's should look like the first move in an invasion. So my next move is to get my tiny ship out of the solar system, quick, before Earth's defenses can get to me. Otherwise—"

Teddley was intrigued despite herself. "Otherwise Earth's navy will find themselves looking at the blasted remains of one little ship—"

"Too small to invade a decent hotel!"

"Right. But they raided Pluto."

"Why?" Soler demanded. "They could have launched and disappeared. They could have been gone while the laser light was still in transit, and the message to their spy, too. Gone before the comet was even touched."

"Um. Well," Teddley said, "they thought they could get away with it. Immediate profit. The captain couldn't make himself go home without something for his trouble. Weasels are like that."

"And now we know there's no invasion fleet."

Teddley shrugged. "They got caught. *Willy C.*'s crew was on the ball. But they didn't expect to get caught."

"But Tombaugh Station is a trivial target," Soler protested, treating Teddley as one of his erstwhile graduate students rather than a military subordinate. "Pointless compared to the propaganda effect that was the object of the exercise!"

"Sir," Teddley said, "somebody who's embezzled millions doesn't pass up a wallet he finds on the sidewalk. A crook is a crook. A Weasel's a Weasel."

Soler's console pinged three times, indicating that Karelly, in the vessel's net bay, thought he had an emergency. Recalled to his duties, Soler grimaced and said, "Karelly? Go."

"Sir! We got something this load that I think you gotta see. I think the sector commander's gotta see it!"

"Calm down, man. You're carrying a camera? Show me."

Soler peered at the blurred, off-color image. "It's frozen," Karelly babbled, "and the blast has chewed it, but *look*—"

"Right. Thank you, Karelly. Teddley, do you see what I meant? No Khalian would have thought of any such plan. The rewards can't be eaten or worn or spent. Phone the *Canaris* for me, will you? Sector commander."

From the surface of Mars, from most of the moons of Jupiter and Saturn, from any worldlet with a black sky, a good eye might see the murder of Halley's comet. One would have to know where one was looking; and then the expanding cloud of ice crystals was a tiny pale smudge, quite different from the sharp point that would be a star or planet.

But beneath the murky atmospheres of Venus and Earth, or within the rock of Ceres and Vesta and hundreds of other asteroids, the pale cloud filled a billion omni screens. A million individual shards flowed twinkling toward the eyes of two billion voting citizens.

Noel Li spoke offstage in an edgy voice with precisely chiseled consonants. "The Fleet reports no sign of the invaders. But fourteen years ago, the Khalian invasion of Rand looked like this—"

Ten thousand individual ships flowed twinkling toward the viewer's eye. The fourteen-year-old omnitape of the invasion of Rand looked dauntingly similar to Halley's comet exploding.

Krasnowski of Civil Affairs was professionally calm, almost sleepy-looking, as he met Noel Li's huge dark eyes in the omni. He waited at the edge of the sector commander's office, out of sight of the cameras which would send Eriksen—as a hologram —into the Meeting Hall of the Alliance Senate, as soon as the sector commander has something to say.

Krasnowski's aide had less experience than his chief in the terrors of political brinksmanship. The lieutenant commander wrung his hands as he scurried in and whispered in Krasnowski's ear.

Krasnowski listened, then waved his subordinate back to the commo center where he would be ready to relay the next frantic message from groundside.

Eriksen cocked an eyebrow. Civil Affairs made another negligent gesture and said, "The natives are restless, Admiral. Perhaps you might throw them a few well-turned phrases while we wait for the—"

"Not until—," Eriksen said, turning toward Captain Crocker, who sat beside Krasnowski and Commander Mown.

Military Affairs met his superior's glance with a look of icy indifference. The expression was as false as a papier mâché cannon, but it was perfect in its artistry.

"Not until Captain Crocker reports," Eriksen continued. "We have one chance to retrieve this situation, and we aren't going to lose it by being—" Crocker's aide ducked in through the door, handed him a brief sheet of hard copy, and disappeared at once. "—overanxious."

"Thank God," Crocker muttered. "We're all right," he

added, rising from his seat to hand the flimsy to Eriksen. "There was only one small ship, as we conjectured, and it's been destroyed."

Eriksen waved the document away. Nothing would mar the serene polish of his desk when the cameras went on in a few moments. "There's no possibility of a garbled transmission?" he demanded.

Crocker shook his head with a satisfied smile. "None whatever," he said. "The ship that made the kill was a courier, the *Sabot*. They brought the news back themselves while later arrivals continued to check the area."

"All right," Eriksen said, composing his features into stern, fatherly lines. He stood; simultaneously, his desk sank until its top formed a flush surface with the decking. "I'll see them now."

The outlines of the sector commander's office vanished from his vision. He stood instead in an illusory hall large enough to hold the three hundred Senators and more than a thousand accredited Observers who deliberated on the course and finances of the Alliance of Planets. President Ssrounish faced him from her central dais, while rank after rank of seats mounted in curves to either side.

A surprising number of the seats were empty. Or not surprising, given the widely publicized belief that this room would be the first target when the Khalians' ravening armada reached Earth.

"His Excellency Lars Eriksen," boomed the hall's Enunciator. "Admiral of the Red and Commander of Sol Sector!"

Eriksen waited a three-beat pause. "Madame President," he began. "Honorable Senators and Observers of the Alliance of Planets . . ."

Pause.

"Today I come before you to admit error and apologize on behalf of the Fleet."

There were as many gasps as there were filled seats in the Meeting Hall. Several members rose and scuttled toward the exits, certain that they had just received confirmation of their blackest fears.

"For many years," Eriksen continued in rotund tones, as though he were unaware of the commotion he had caused, "the Fleet has maintained a secret testing facility on Halley's comet.

I must now admit to you that an inexcusable lapse in safety precautions occurred, causing an experiment to go disastrously wrong.''

Pause.

The hall gasped and burbled, like a catfish pond at feeding time.

"Through that error," Eriksen said, "Fleet scientists have destroyed Halley's comet."

Shouts of amazement.

"We must be thankful," Eriksen went on, knowing that the Enunciator would raise the volume of his voice to compensate for the ambient noise, "that no lives were lost in the occurrence . . . but I realize that this is small comfort to those inhabitants of Earth, and to their unborn descendants, who will lack forever one of the crowning glories of the solar system."

Several of those listening in the Meeting Hall were literally dancing in the aisles. A portly Observer attempted a cartwheel and wound up crashing into a desk three ranks below her own. No one seemed to care.

"There is only one recompense adequate to the scale of the error," Eriksen said. "I have contacted Fleet headquarters"—There hadn't been anything like enough time to inform Port Tau Ceti of the situation, but that lie would be lost in the greater one—"and have received the full approval of my superiors for the following arrangement."

He paused again, letting the room quiet to increase the impact of what he was about to say.

"We of the Fleet," the sector commander boomed, "at our sole effort and expense, will rebuild Halley's comet, using material from the Oort Cloud. The project is expected to take three years"—Eriksen could imagine Mown nodding approval at the fact his superior had remembered the correct figure—"but at the end of that time you will have a comet identical in orbit and composition, not to the Halley's of two days ago, but to a younger Halley's comet as it was seen four thousand years ago by the Chinese. A young Halley's comet with thousands of years of life ahead of it."

It was almost ten minutes before the cheers and clapping died down enough for Eriksen to signal an end to his transmission.

"God!" he said, flopping backward before he checked to be sure that his chair had risen high enough to catch him. It had.

"Brilliant, sir!" Krasnowski was saying. "Absolutely brilliant!"

"Monitor the omni," Eriksen muttered with his eyes closed against the memory of over a thousand politicians with their mouths open. Cheering now; but it could have been his blood for which they shouted.

When the admiral looked up again, he saw to his surprise that Captain Crocker was frowning, and even Commander Mown looked concerned as he read the sheet of hard copy Crocker had passed to him. "Yes?" Eriksen demanded, waiting for the worst, waiting to learn there really was a Khalian invasion force . . .

"There wasn't much left of the ship the *Sabot* nailed, sir," Crocker explained. "Some Khalian protoplasm. And they did find an arm in a uniform that doesn't match anything in our files to date. Here." Crocker gesture-muttered, and the picture in the omni blurred.

"I didn't think Weasels wore uniforms at all," Eriksen said carefully. What was he looking at? A jittery hand held something in front of an omni camera. Eriksen couldn't make it out. Double image?

A human hand held . . . held a human hand, pale with frost, and half of the raggedly torn forearm.

"Yes, that explains it," Mown muttered. "It bothered me that Khalians understood human psychology so perfectly."

Admiral Lars Eriksen's guts felt as though he'd just dropped into sponge space, except that the sinking sensation went on and on.

INTERLUDE

On the Earth of the Alliance there were only two means of communications more widespread or efficient than the omni. One was the ageless tradition of gossip, and the other the enlisted men's grapevine. Both had rattled for over a week that all was not what it seemed with the Fleet admission of the loss of Halley's comet. For weeks the Fleet was trapped into defending its own incompetence. Daily, the discomforted brass sent urgent directives to Port demanding something be done to restore their prestige. These in turn, gave rise to some very questionable missions. Surprisingly, one paid off.

SUICIDE MISSION
by Christopher Stasheff

THE BLACK PLASTIC ship nosed up alongside the Khalian frigate—black, so that light-based sensors couldn't find it, and it couldn't be detected visually as it drifted in between the ships of the Khalian perimeter; plastic, so that radio-based sensors couldn't find it. Darts sprang out from its side, darts tipped with synthetic-diamond covering explosive charges. They slammed through the Khalian's hull, and four explosions mushroomed their heads.

Inside the black barracuda, winches whined, reeling in line, pulling the two ships close together. Then a metal ring slammed into the Khalian, and current flowed, binding the collar to the Khalian while automatic screws dug into the ship's skin. A man sprang onto the mesh tunnel that joined the collar to the plastic ship and began slapping explosive gel onto the Khalian's hull in a widening circle.

Bound together in an embrace of hatred, the two ships floated in the void. Distant stars gleamed—Khalian ships and Terran ships, twinkling with death as they circled Dead Star 31.

When he was a kid, Corin had wished he'd had a brother. And sometimes he'd wished his father could stay home all the time, like other dads.

He wished he'd had anything but three older sisters and a younger one, and a mother who screamed at him all the time.

"It's a chance for a breakthrough," the captain said. "It'll only work once—but it only has to. Break through their line, and there's their home world, right in front of us. We have one

28

chance in a hundred of bringing it off, but it's worth the risk."
He raked the line of marines with his glare. "Any questions?"

Silence.

Then Sergeant Krovvy stepped forward. "Sir!"

The captain turned back, frowning. "Yes, Sergeant?"

"If the odds of success are one to a hundred, what're the odds
on coming back alive?"

The captain grinned like a shark. "How about one in a
million?"

That was when Corin stepped forward.

The captain turned to him, frowning. "Are you volunteering,
or just going crazy?"

"Volunteering, sir." Hands to his sides, eyes straight ahead,
face wooden.

"Should I call the medics, or should I ask why?"

Corin shrugged. "Anything's better than waiting through a
stalemate like this."

The captain nodded. "And . . . ?"

Corin grimaced. "I want to find out what the plan is."

"And you'll only learn that by volunteering." The captain
nodded. "Good enough." He turned back to the other marines.
"Anyone else?"

He looked up and down the long, silent row.

Sergeant Krovvy cleared his throat and took another step
forward.

The captain's grin touched his ear lobes. "Two out of fifty!
Not bad, not bad at all! But I need a dozen. One more! One
more to die for the glory of the Fleet! . . . No one? . . .
Dis*miss!*"

The corporals barked, and the marines marched away.

"You two." The captain jerked his head toward the airlock.
"Come on."

Aboard his courier, he told them the plan.

Which was great. Now Corin *knew* it couldn't work.

Daddy was away. Daddy was away, and when he was home,
he was in his room.

"I *told* him you shouldn't let him keep coming through our
yard," Mommy had yelled at him. "I told you and *told* you, but
you wouldn't even ask him to stop!"

"It's not that important," Daddy had mumbled.

"It *is* that important! I don't want some old coot walking

through my yard just any time, without even asking! That's why I went to the lawyer! And do you know what he said? The old man's got the town council declaring it a right of way! But would you lift a finger to stop him? Oh, no!''

And Daddy had gone to his room. Daddy always went to his room. And stayed there.

It was a dumb idea, but Corin had known that when he stepped forward, even though he hadn't heard what it was. But he knew that it couldn't possibly work, and that even if it did, it would get every last one of them killed. And when he found out what it was, he was sure.

But it would be worth it. Just to get this infernal waiting over with, he told himself. It would be worth it.

It was really very simple. Pick out the largest ship in the Khalian horde, find a frigate next to it, board that, and use its guns and torpedoes to shoot the other down. There were rumors the Khalians were using larger ships. Then the Fleet's dreadnoughts could bull through the gap, swatting lesser ships as they went—and the captured frigate could keep running interference for them, shooting down any other Khalian ships within range. It should be able to do a lot of damage, before the other Weasels figured out what was happening and blew it to vapor.

The trick was getting close enough to board a Khalian frigate without the Weasels finding out, by eye or by sensor, and being able to take over so fast that they couldn't call for help. Which they weren't apt to do. The Khalian ideal of cooperation being what it was, the Weasels would want to take care of their own interlopers.

Privately, Corin figured the captain's odds on coming back were a little high.

But that, he realized with surprise, was okay with him. In fact, it was just fine.

"Take out the garbage, Corey," Mom said. "Don't be like your father, always putting it off."

So he took out the garbage and came back in, and she said, "You missed the bathroom wastebaskets. Go do them all."

He hated the bathroom wastebaskets. Darlene made such a mess out of them, what with her makeup tissues and hair and all.

And when the wastebaskets were done, and dinner was over,

she came out screaming, "You didn't wash it out! Now go out there and take the hose, and wash out that wastebasket!"

It was November, and it was cold and dark, and his hands were blue when he came in.

Except for the long rows of facing seats, the ship was stripped to the hull, and the marines were stripped to raw emotion. They sat, belted in, tense and expectant. The ship rocked, and Corin knew they had fired their grapples. He waited, taut, till he heard the crash of the electromagnetic collar taking hold of the Khalian's skin. *What if it isn't iron?*

Just in case this Khalian's hull wasn't ferrous, the electromagnetic ring had borers built in. The grinding noise filled the Fleet ship as the long screws bit into the pirate's skin.

"Demolition!"

"Here!" And Valius was, as the iris dilated in the side of the barracuda. He leaped through and started slapping plastic onto the Khalian hull, building it out in a widening circle almost to the lip of the circular electromagnet—a shaped charge, strong enough to blow a hole in the side of a spaceship, strong enough to kill anybody who happened to be in the chamber it holed. . . .

Overhead, plastic vaporized in a long, wide, trough.

"Stand fast," the captain ordered. "He can't depress his cannon any more than that—and you're already breathing your own tanks."

The marines were all in pressure armor, of course, breathing bottled air. And by the time the pirates were suited up, the marines would be among them.

The barracuda's hull vibrated, but the humming of the pump dwindled quickly as it pulled air out of the ship's interior and into storage tanks.

Valius scurried back, a length of wire unreeling between himself and the circle of explosive.

"Blow!" the captain commanded.

And it did, incidentally, cutting the feeds for the frigate's artificial gravity.

Corin. It was a perfectly good boy's name; his father had told him so. It came from Shakespeare; it was the name of a shepherd or something. But there was a girl in school. She was named Cornelia but everybody called her Corey, so the boys called him Corey, too.

"Corey, Corey! Tell us all a story!" they'd yell in a mocking singsong.

And he'd come home with a black eye, still trembling, still angry, and his mother had started screaming, "Do you know who that was? That was your teacher on the phone! She told me she saw you picking a fight out there in the playground! Don't you *ever* do that again!"

And the anger had surged up, and he had shouted, "Mom! He hit me first!"

"Don't you *dare* shout at me!" *Crack!* The slap caught his face where it still ached from a punch, and she was screaming, "They *always* hit you first. I know your kind, you always find some way to make them hit you first."

"They were making fun of me. They were calling me 'Corey!' "

"There's nothing wrong with that, it's a perfectly nice name."

"It's not! It's a girl's name! I want a boy's name. Why didn't you give me a boy's name!"

"How *dare* you speak to your mother that way!"

This time, he saw the slap coming, and ducked.

"Oh! You little *monster!* Don't you *dare* try to get out of your punishment!" She grabbed him by the shoulder this time and boxed him on the ear, so his head was ringing with her screams as she slapped him and slapped him again.

They saw their own hull vibrate with the blast, saw the burst of smoke, saw the sudden hole where the explosive had been, saw the mist as the air exhausted from the frigate.

"In!" The captain's voice roared from his earphones, and Corin dived through the mesh tunnel and into the Khalian frigate, holding down the trigger button with his thumb, spraying slugs in a cone, all around him. Three of his mates jumped in with him, their cones blending with his. Who cared if the slugs pierced the Khalian's hull? Who cared if they lost air? They had their helmets on, and they were trying to kill the Khalians, anyway . . .

And they had. The hell with the bullets, too. Three dead Weasels drifted in the nets they used for bunks, half uncurled from sleep; one even had his sidearm in his hand. But little red globes drifted away from their noses and mouths. One had a big globe, as though he were blowing a bubble of death. Explosive decompression had done the marines' work for them.

As he reloaded, Corin stared at the dead, floating Khalians, and thought, *These were the easy ones*.

The other boys had found out about the old folk song and jeered after him all over the playground, but he didn't dare fight, or Mom would scream at him. His little sister, Snookie, had heard them and started singing it as soon as they came in the door.

"Wake up, wake up, darlin' Corey! What makes you sleep so sound?"

"Shut up," he snapped at her.

"I don't have to shut up. This is my house, too, you know." And she turned away, singing, "Now, the first time I saw darlin' Corey, she was sitting by the sea . . ."

"*Shut up!*"

"Why should she shut up?" Mom jumped on it even as she came into the room, glaring. "You don't give orders here, Corey. She can sing whatever she likes, in *this* house. And don't you *dare* try and stop her!"

So he had to swallow his anger and turn away, and after a while, Mom had tired of hearing the song and sent them out to play. It was catch, and she hadn't brought the glove up in time, and the ball had hit her cheek, and with a sick sinking in his stomach, Corin had realized what Mom was going to do to him when Snookie ran in screaming—

Unless he could make Snookie laugh it off.

So he shrieked in horror, "Snookie!" and dashed over. "I'm sorry. I didn't mean it. Did it hurt?"

She was still a moment. Then she laughed a little, blinked away the forming tears, and chuckled, managing a brave little smile. "Naw, it was just rubber."

And they had gone back to playing catch, Corin with the sickening knowledge that he had caved in, capitulated, chickened out—and before he was even challenged.

Corin glanced about the chamber, seeing the circular holes at fore and aft, either end—hatches, blocked now by steel plates.

The Khalians didn't waste money on anything inessential, but they had every safety feature in the book. Valius had placed his charge where the fo'c'sle was, to make sure they took out any crew who were off duty. It had worked; they had taken three out of six or seven—but as soon as the pressure had dropped, bulkheads had sealed off the fo'c'sle from the rest of the ship to limit loss of air and Khalians. Now the rest of the Weasels had had time to pull on their pressure suits or to call for help. Not both.

"Jakes and Boblatch, aft!" the captain barked. "Valius, make room for 'em."

Valius slapped a shaped charge on the aft bulkhead.

"But, Captain," Jakes objected, "there won't be anyone there."

"If there isn't, you can come join us fore. If there is, you can join us after he's dead. Blow it, Valius."

The bulkhead blew; air blasted out. Jakes and Boblatch dove through into the galley.

"The rest of you come fore." The captain turned. "That charge ready, Valius?"

"Uh . . . it is now, Captain."

"Blow it," the captain commanded.

Smoke erupted in the hatchway, awesome in its silence.

"Don't just stand there gaping," the captain bellowed. "Now!"

Sergeant Krovvy hit the trigger button as he pushed himself through the hatch—and his head exploded.

Corin stared at the expanding globe of red and gray, his stomach heaving.

"You were supposed to make the sale!" the sales manager snapped. "We don't keep you here just so you can walk around looking important!"

"I—I'm sorry." Corin lifted his chin and set his jaw, but he could feel his shoulders slumping. "He even had me chalking up the measurements, and then he just said that—"

"I *heard* what he said! I heard what he said to *me!* That you're an arrogant little twit who shouldn't even be working in the stockroom!"

"All I said was that he should wear the cuffs a little higher . . ."

"If they want advice, they'll go to a couturier! You're just here to sell the clothes, understand?"

"But, look! If he got 'em chalked up wrong, he'd be a dissatisfied customer!"

"Don't argue with me!" the sales manager bellowed.

"I'm not arguing, I'm trying to explain—"

"Don't." The boss's eyes narrowed. "Explain it to Welfare. You're fired."

Corin's mouth opened in a scream as he dove through the hatch, landing flat on his belly, slugs chattering out of his gun, the recoil kicking him back. But his heels butted against the bulkhead as two Khalians trained their own slug throwers on him. A ricochet smashed into the barrel of his rifle, stinging his hands as it wrenched the weapon away, but Lurkstein shot through to join him, as did Danvel and Parlan, their weapons shuddering. The Weasels had to split their attention, while Corin could pull his rifle back, check it, and aim, his stream of bullets sweeping across one Khalian, then the other. Danvel's body bucked, gouting redness, but the Weasles flipped backward, almost jackknifing. They were probably screaming, but they were wearing pressure helmets, and the atmosphere was gone, and they had a different com frequency from Corin's. Then Lurkstein's and Parlan's slugs caught them, and their bodies spasmed in a grim dance of death, but they wouldn't be screaming any more.

Then Morton and Dunscythe were in, racing past what was left of Krovvy, and Valius was slapping a charge on the forward bulkhead across the room, and suddenly, the cabin seemed to be filled with Fleet marines.

The captain was pulling Corin up by the arm. "Hurt, mister?" the voice demanded in his earphones.

"No, sir," Corin gasped, giving his head a shake. "I should be, but I'm not."

Catherine laid down the menu. "You could have let me order first!"

Corin looked up, startled. "I waited. And you didn't order, so I went ahead."

"And made it look as though I was just waiting to disagree with you. Honestly, Corin, just because we're living together, doesn't mean you get to run my life!''

"I didn't order for you."

"You could have offered. It just so happened that I *did* want the chicken Kiev, but I couldn't say that after *you* had ordered it.''

"There's no crime in our liking the same things,'' he protested.

"Look, if you think you're going to boss me around, you can just forget about this whole relationship!''

"But I *wasn't* trying to boss you around.''

"Well, just see to it that you don't.''

Corin finished reloading just as the deck lurched out from under him, and Dunscythe went cartwheeling across the chamber. All Valius could do was hang on for dear life as the gel he'd been applying flipped away off the bulkhead.

"The Weasel's taking evasive action!'' the captain yelled. "Grab hold!''

Marines grabbed for handholds wherever they could find them, and Corin grabbed an ankle and pulled himself up enough to grab someone else's arm, which he used to pull himself up some more. Then he got a hand on the fire-control console and pulled himself to his feet. It was like climbing a mountain with a hundred-pound pack, but he made it, pulling himself up and reaching out to grab the lump of quivering gel.

Then, suddenly, the bottom of the hill was its top, then its side; the pilot was tumbling to his left, and Corin slammed into the console. Pain seared through his hip, but he kept his holds on both console and explosive. Then he pushed himself away enough to get a foot against the console's side, and he flipped around enough to grab the T-handle the Weasels used for dogging hatches. He inhaled sharply, stiffening his muscles against the pain in his side, and hauled himself up to slap the lump of plastic onto the bulkhead.

"That's it, Private,'' the captain's voice said in his earphones. "Pound it out, now!''

Corin hit the lump twice before "up" suddenly became "sideways" again, and "down" was under his back. He hung on to the T-handle grimly, jackknifing to get a knee over one bar of it, and went back to pounding the gel.

"Shape the sides, now," the captain told him. "Make it a dome."

Corin pushed and prodded the material, wondering crazily if he was supposed to be a marine or a sculptor.

"All right, now, back off," the captain snapped.

Corin unhooked his knee and let his body swing out at right angles to the bulkhead, hanging by his hands. He checked below, saw empty wall, and let go.

He dropped like a rock, absorbing the impact with bent knees, and grabbed a stanchion.

Then the captain hit the button, and the hatch blew in.

"Look, I *like* Jody, and if I want to go out to lunch with her, I will!"

"All right, all right!" Corin turned away, raising his hands. "So we *don't* have a lunch date. So I'll see you this evening."

"Not 'this evening.' I have a sales meeting."

"All right. I'll be here when you come home." Corin wondered if he really should be. He wondered if he should ever have moved in with her.

"Oh, that's right, just load me with the guilt trip!" Ellen stormed. "Poor little Corin, who just can't stand to be home alone! Not a friend in the world—"

"That's enough," Corin grated.

"Nowhere nearly enough! Be a *man,* will you?"

Corin turned, frowning. "I thought that's what I was."

"You'd never know it at night." Ellen marched over to the door and yanked it open. "Try to get some rest when you get home, will you? Maybe things will work better."

"Down" ceased to exist; the explosion had rattled the Weasel pilot enough to make him let up on the acceleration. Either that, or he was bracing for combat . . .

"Get in there!" the captain shouted. He slipped a hand under Dunscythe's boots and threw the marine like a javelin. He flew through the hole, but he hit the trigger button too soon, and the recoil bounced him back out again. Just in time; Weasel slugs were hailing around the hole in the bulkhead, with the odd one careering through to ricochet among the marines. They took cover fast, but one creamed Dunscythe's knee on the way. He yelped and pulled himself into a ball as he bounced into a corner.

"Just two of them left!" the captain shouted. "They can't hold off seven of us forever."

But they could, and he knew it. They had one hell of a defensive position.

Then the pilot went back to playing games—but this time, he outsmarted himself.

Suddenly, the new hole was "down." Corin glanced about him, aimed his feet toward the gap, and let go. As he fell, he swung his rifle down to aim right in front of his toes. The Weasel let up on the acceleration, but Corin had a lot of momentum by the time he shot through the hole and hit the trigger, moving the rifle to make a cone.

Slugs spattered around the pilot's cabin as the recoil slowed him just enough for a safe landing.

A safe landing on nothing! Nothing under him at all, nothing but blackness filled with stars. There was a huge hole in the hull with a console in front of it, complete with two Weasels in pressure suits, pointing rifles at *him*. *Them or me,* he thought crazily, and swept the stream of bullets toward them.

A blur swept past him, and a spiderweb spread across the stars at his feet. Of course! It wasn't a hole, just a huge view port to give the Weasels 270-degree vision. They were still primitives; they still wanted eye contact, in spite of their screens.

He landed bending his knees to take up the impact against the solidity of the panoramic port that lay between him and the rest of the universe. He looked up to aim, just in time to see the Weasels go carwheeling away in streamers of red from holes in their suits. He glanced up and saw two marine rifles poking through the hole in the bulkhead, with helmeted heads behind them.

Then he realized there was pain in his rib cage, swelling and swelling until it engulfed him, till all the world was a sheet of bright pain that darkened, and was gone. . . .

"But he's my *father,* for crying out loud!"

"But I want to go see *Swan Lake.*"

"Well, if you'd just told me you had tickets for it, I could have—"

"What, am I supposed to report every little thing to you? Are you going to try to keep tabs on every little move I make?''

"Well, no, but I thought you were going to be out late again tonight, and—''

"And you could go slinking off to whimper all about me to your father!'' Ellen sighed and shook her head. "Honestly, Corin! You've got to grow up and get away from him some day.''

"I'm pretty far now! I only see him when he's in town, and that's only once or twice a year.''

"Real solid citizen, isn't he?'' Her lip curled. "Can't even hold a job in one town.''

"He's a *salesman!*''

"Yes, and after forty years at it, he still can't make sales manager. You shouldn't *ever* talk with that loser!''

The rage surged up, but so did the shame—and with it came the sharp awareness that he shouldn't pick on a woman. So he just stood there, growing pale and rigid.

"Look,'' she said, "if you know I'm right, just say so.''

Corin turned on his heel and slammed out of the apartment.

He went back the next day, packed his clothes in one suitcase and his books and knickknacks in another, and walked out. There was nothing left that mattered; he could buy a new typewriter easily enough, and he wouldn't miss any of the little presents she had given him.

All that was left was two months' rent on the lease. He sent it in a single check and didn't tell her his new address.

The pain was back, but it was dull, remote. Corin found his oxy intake in his mouth; he spat it out and cranked his eyelids open.

The captain's face grinned down at him.

Corin squeezed his eyes shut.

"Back on duty, mister,'' the captain said cheerfully. "I patched your suit . . . and you, too.''

"Set my . . . ribs?'' Corin opened his eyes again.

"Taped 'em. It'll hold you till we're through here.''

Corin looked down and saw a wide band around the abdomen of his suit. "What happened to . . . pain?''

"An anesthetic.'' The captain's grin widened. "Plus five shots of adrenaline.''

Just then, it bit. Suddenly, the mental fog cleared, and Corin felt fine, just fine, if feeling like a current was flowing through you was 'fine.' "I don't need that much, Captain."

"So pay it back when the battle's over." The captain jerked his head toward the console. "For now, get over there. Your buddies are having a great time blasting blips, but you're the only one who talks Weasel."

Corin felt the elation begin. He grinned, set his feet under him, and pushed off.

He grabbed the center of the console and swung himself down to stand behind Kank and Lisle. The screen was alive with green blips and red blips, and the two marines were each moving a set of cross hairs around the field, pressing trigger buttons and leaving bright spreading pools of yellow wherever they touched a green blip.

The com grid chattered crazily in Weasel.

"That's for me," Corin said.

Kank looked up, irritated, then reluctantly moved aside to make room for him. Corin swung himself down onto the odd contour that served as a Weasel chair.

The chattering went on.

Corin could just make it out; it translated roughly as, "What the hell is wrong with you, Frigate Thirteen?" He pressed the mike patch and shrilled back, "Control system malfunction. Beware! Move clear! Directional control system malfunction! Fire-control system malfunction!"

On the right-hand side of the screen, a larger blip was appearing, and in the view port, a disk was swelling, as Lisle nudged his joystick—the Khalian cruiser, such as it was. Corin realized he couldn't have been out for more than a few minutes. If he could just stall the Weasels for a little longer . . .

"Sheer off! Sheer off!" the Weasels were chanting frantically.

"Control system malfunction!" Corin yammered back, watching Lisle center his cross hairs on the biggest blip. "We have lost steering capacity! Acceleration is locked at full thrust! We are attempting to regain control! Stand by!"

"Cease firing!" the Weasels answered in a manic gibber.

"We cannot," Corin answered, and Lisle hit the button on his joystick. Corin went on, "Guns are locked at full fire. We are trying to cut the circuit, but it will not respond."

The laser beam was on its way, lancing out at the speed of

light toward the cruiser, invisible where there was no atmosphere, no dust. Corin locked his sights onto the cruiser, too, and hit his button, staring at the expanding disk of the cruiser, hoping, hoping. . . .

The next Weasel phrase translated roughly as, "They are mad, or their ship is!" And another gibber answered, "They must be destroyed."

Then light blossomed on the side of the cruiser.

"But you were so *right!*" Corin stormed, turning away from Nancy. "Everything was perfect while we were dating! You were so beautiful, and the music wrapped us up, and the two of us were all there was, just the dancing and your eyes—"

"*Stop it!*" she screamed. "Do you know what you're doing to me? *Stop it!*"

He turned back to look at her—eyes red and swollen, tangled hair hiding half of her pudgy face, bathrobe a little too far open, showing just a glimpse that was supposed to be tantalizing but was flat now, and sagging.

"Your friends would be my friends, you said." He moved back toward her. "And my friends would be your friends."

"If *you* think I'd be seen in public with that bunch of superannuated sociopaths—"

"All right, so we won't! Do you realize how long it's been since I've even *talked* with Sean or David?"

"Aw, poor little boy! Not a friend in the world!"

He reddened. "Not yours, certainly."

"You don't think I'd let them see me like . . . *this!*"

"Why not?" he flared. "You let *me* see you like this."

"But you're my *husband!*"

"So I deserve less than your friends?"

"You should be *ashamed* to let my friends see what you've turned me into."

"Oh, so *I* made you drink like a fish? *I* made you quit going to the health spa?"

"Yes! And I just can't *face* them now."

"I won't ask you to," he sighed, turning away. "But I did want to take you out again. We used to have such a good time."

"While you still had a job, sure," she snapped. "And you asked me to give up mine . . ."

"I didn't ask you to!"

"You did." Her lips thinned. "I distinctly remember you sitting there on the sofa nibbling my ear and saying, 'Give it up, honey. I'll take care of us both.' "

"I didn't! We were sitting there on the sofa, all right, and I *was* nibbling your ear, but you were saying, 'Look, now that you've got such a good job, I don't really need to keep working, do I?' And I said—"

"I did *not!* How *dare* you accuse me of lying! Just because you couldn't keep your 'good job.' "

"Look, the company went broke!"

"I should have realized you'd choose a loser!"

He looked up slowly, eyes narrowing. "What's that supposed to mean?"

She gave him an acid smile. "It takes one to know one."

He was beside her in a single stride, fists clenched, eyes glaring.

She flinched back, hands upraised. "Go ahead, hit me! I don't care!"

He almost did, just because she had said she didn't care. But he caught himself in time and stormed out the door.

He always did that. He always wound up doing that, somehow, whenever they had a fight—always going out the door.

Some time, about two hours later, he came out of a morose alcoholic fog to look up and see a sign that said JOIN—THE FLEET! with a picture of a marine in front of a spaceship.

He looked around and realized that it was the only lighted shop window left on the street; even the bar down the block had turned off its sign.

So he went in—just to get warm, he told himself. It was the only warmth in sight.

He never went back. He'd never even been within five light-years of Earth since then. But his paycheck went to her every month, and his letters went out every time they touched a Fleet base. She never answered them, though—until he received the letter from her lawyer with the divorce papers.

The beam didn't show in space, but its impact did. And Corin was one with the two sets of cross hairs: one with the particle beams that were burning through to the cruiser's control systems, and one with the torpedoes that sped toward it with warheads of nuclear death. He could finally kill everything in sight with a clear conscience—ships, Weasels, Khalians, bosses, lovers, wife, sister, mother! But Corin could see the sudden snowlike hail of blips that were torpedoes, moving outward from a dozen Khalian destroyers like hate and the consuming hunger that women called love, and coming finally to destroy him, as he had always known they would, to purge him in the fire of annihilation, but too slowly this time, too slowly . . .

Then the largest blip on the screen turned yellow, and in the view port, the expanding disk mushroomed, swelling in a moment to double its diameter. The five shots of adrenaline had Corin at threshold anyway, teetering on the edge, and the sight of that fiery blossom blew him over into the sheer, blinding ecstasy of fulfillment, the fulfillment of destruction. As he saw Lisle's cross hairs traversing downward to the swarm of torpedoes and as he moved his own joystick to follow, he knew they couldn't ever get them all, knew that even if they did, they couldn't stop the lasers that must even now be burning through the hull to crisp them all.

He hoped a torpedo would make it first.

Then one did; its warhead blew up in their power plant, converting their fusion generator into an H-bomb and, in the instant of life left to him in the midst of the nuclear flame, the consciousness that had been Corin knew it had all been worth it.

INTERLUDE

The omni screen was filled with a close-up of the disemboweled horse. Panning back, the scene encompassed a number of similarly treated humans. The effect had been carefully calculated to enrage the estimated two billion Earth citizens who were watching the special Fleet omnicast. The scene faded slowly, lingering just a bit too long, a move calculated to make the omni-conditioned audience even more uncomfortable. The crisply uniformed figure that rose in its stead was as reassuring as the earlier scene had been alarming. His craggy good looks and measured tones inspired almost instant confidence. The crossed-ships emblem of a pilot glinted below a line of decorations. Such a hero would not let you down, or lie.

"Never before has the Alliance faced so vicious an enemy," the Fleet officer explained for those too numb to have understood the earlier atrocity shots. "One with so little regard for sentient life."

Rising to reflect his concern, the hero's face took on a worried look. Spreading his hands, he intoned how the "soulless Khalia have never shown mercy. Our experts, in fact, have determined there is no such word in their language."

CHARACTER FLAW
by Steve Perry

THE DISHARMONIC SCREAM of a Klaxon warned the medical crew of the incoming wounded. Chief Healer Amani felt the muscles in his shoulders bunch with tension under his fur, not so much from the blare of the hooter as the knowledge of what was to come. The spoils of this glorious fucking battle.

"Shut that damned thing off!" Amani said.

Assistant Healer Vita was stupid enough to try and protest. "Chief Healer, regulations specify—"

"Stuff regulations into your left nostril! I said, 'Off!'"

One of the blood-soakers scurried to obey. After a few heartbeats, the obnoxious horn died. Amani regarded Vita with a cool glare. "Captain Damu's announcement that we have been cheated of the glorious and lucrative victory is certainly sufficient notice that we shall shortly be knee-deep in gore, Assistant. I do not need a mechanical noisemaker's verification."

Vita swallowed and nodded, properly cowed. "Sir."

Amani swept his gaze over the surgery, his personal dominance secure. Four assistants and four soakers stood rigid at his outburst, odors nervously high, submissive to his will. The tables were ready, the instruments sterilized, the alien machineries operative—if the poet master could be believed. They were as ready as they would ever be.

The surgery's doors popped open, sliding into their wall recesses, as the first stretcher blew in on its cushion of air, two frantic field medics guiding it.

"How many?" Amani said, his voice snapping like a whip.

"Fourteen," the shorter of the two medics said, his breath

coming fast from his exertions. The Khalian had sharp, ferretlike features, while his rounder-faced fat partner was easily twice Ferret Face's weight. Both wore the white kilts and cross straps of their professional clan.

"Triaged?"

"There wasn't time, Chief Healer—"

"Never mind. Chimsha, stack this one for triage."

Even before he finished speaking, other stretchers fanned into the room. The injured Khalian troopers fought the pain, of course, but some moaned in spite of their iron resolve; blood ran freely from shrapnel wounds and decompression injuries; energy burns oozed serum; splintered and broken bones protruded from torn flesh and fur. Death musk fouled the air.

"Chini, Tumbo, let's move it!"

The assistant healers sprang forward and grabbed stretchers. Here was his world, the seeds of battle sprouted and fruitful, the booty of a pirate medic. Amani permitted himself a single sigh, then went to work.

"Prepare this one for surgery; he's got a perforated bowel. Start a big bore plasmaloid IV, TKO, crossmatch and type, and lay out a set of deep-lap surgical claws, that's a fourteen, twelve, ten and needle point, stat!"

"Pross, Chief—"

Amani hurried to the next patient. This one's left leg was shattered but not bleeding much. He could wait. "Pump him full of dorph and put him at the end of the line."

Another trooper, this one with his chest caved in. Amani pulled one of the Khalian's eyelids back and looked at the dilated pupil. The healer flashed his penlight at the eye . . . no reaction . . . then did the same for the other eye. "Pupils dilated and fixed," he said. Amani reached forth and pinched the nearest eye. When he removed his grip, the orb stayed pinched. "This one's dead. Get him to the tubes."

Amani moved quickly to another patient, this one with a pumping red cavity in the right upper quadrant of the torso. The wound was easily the size of Amani's hand. Amani sponged enough blood away to see that the patient's liver was shattered. Damn! In a proper surgery with the right equipment, he could save him. Here, in the middle of this insane war, there was no chance. He might keep him alive for a little while, but it would cost blood and medicines he could not afford. He hated it, but there was no choice, not if he were to help others.

"This warrior is beyond help. Pop him with a charge of keph and move him to the outer room."

At his shoulder, Vita once again begged to differ. "Chief Healer, why waste painkillers on him? He's dying—"

Amani spun; were stares knives, Vita would have been flensed to the bone in a heartbeat. "Yes, he's dying, Assistant *Healer!* We can do nothing but ease his pain, and that is little enough! Question me again and you may join him!"

Vita's whiskers stiffened at this, and his eyes went wide. There was no doubt who was dominant here, even if the threat was completely idle. "S—s—sir."

Amani moved on. Fourteen. They were lucky. Some of the other surgeries closer to the main engagement would have more to do. Much more. And some would have nothing to do, having been roasted by human guns and then exposed to the hard vacuum.

Was there no way to end this madness?

Ah, Amani, he thought to himself, *no one thinks it madness, save you. Who are you to deny ten thousand seasons of tradition?*

"This one has a ruptured spleen and some internal bleeding. We'll do a splenectomy and patch him before we do the perforated bowel. Lay out a deep claw and plenty of six and seven oh dissolving suture."

He kept moving. Time was of the essence.

"All right," Amani said, slipping his right paw into the sterile surgical claws, "what have we got?" He wiggled his digits; his own claws fit snugly into the recesses in the bases of the blades. The knives flashed a blue glare in the brightness of the surgical lamps, lamps designed to kill pathogenic bacteria, assuming the poet master designated to keep such things functioning had said the proper prayers.

The humans used coherent light for their cutting, as did many of the so-called advanced races, so he had heard, but there was nothing like cold steel for a Khalian surgeon. Amani wore no blades in his chest straps, but he was a master with what he knew. An extension of the paw was the best way; in an emergency, one's own claws could even be made to do. Try turning your fingers into lasers. . . .

"Sir," Vita said, "a ruptured spleen, a perforated bowel, two amputations, a tendon reattachment, and reduction of two fractures. Assistant Healer Tumbo is debriding burns, and Assistant Healer Chini dealing with shock and assorted minor trauma.''

Amani nodded. How de-Khalinizing trauma surgery was. The patients were not known by their names, but by their symptoms: a ruptered this, a perforated that.

On the surgical table, the spleen patient was resisting the anesthetic mask offered by the soaker.

"T-take it a-away! I will s-s-stand the pain!''

Amani leaned over the trooper. He was hardly more than a youngling.

"What is the problem here, trooper?''

"I am K-khalian!'' the trooper managed. "C-c-clan Dihidi of the S-s-outh! I n-need n-nothing for p-p-pain!''

"You are going to bleed to death in another two minutes if I don't operate,'' Amani said, "and if you twitch at the wrong moment while I am cutting, you will also die. That is the reason for the anesthetic, not to alleviate your pain.''

"B-b-better to d-d-die than be sh-shamed,'' the trooper said. His musk was full of pain, but also of bravery and challenge.

Amani snorted. Enough of this! "Listen, trooper, I am Chief Healer Amani,'' he said, allowing the anger to fill his voice and musk, "Shichini Clan of the West, ranked second in a class of two hundred healers, trained by those who give, and ship's surgeon for six seasons! You will shut up and accept the mask and you will do it *now*, is that understood?''

The trooper looked at Amani through pain-filled eyes. Despite the fact that Amani was only a healer, this was language and commanding odor the soldier could not fail to understand. Impossible as it was, Amani was dominant, and that effectively ended any arguments.

"Y-yessir.''

Amani nodded at the amazed soaker, who shoved the mask none too gently onto the trooper's muzzle. Twenty seconds later, the injured Khalian was unconscious.

Amani extended his augmented forefinger to the trooper's shaved torso and made the initial incision over the spleen, a bold and sure cut. Skin and flesh parted, and another soaker leaned in to sponge away the welling of blood. This barely named child would argue with him even as he lay dying. Warrior stupidity, always! Lunacy! How could such foolishness be ended?

His anger did not extend to his hands. The cuts were smooth and precise. The surgeon's fingers danced, and the glittery steel flashed again and again in the germicidal light, cutting to heal and not kill.

Eight hours later, he finished the final operation. His shoulders, back, and hands all ached, but the last patient was stapled and stitched back together. He had not lost any of them on the table, and unless infection set in, all would survive. The bactericidal and bacteriostatic herbs that Khalian medicine used were perhaps not as efficient as those more complex chemicals preferred by other-worlders, but he knew his own compendiums of drugs and trusted them. Alien things, even gifts, were not to be trusted.

Amani stretched his sore muscles. The assistants could watch the patients while he took a few minutes to rest. The gods only knew when another load of wounded might arrive.

"Greetings, Chief Healer," came the powerful voice from behind him. The stench of command overrode even that of the injured troopers in the surgery.

Amani turned. There was no mistaking the speaker. Ship's Captain Damu stood there, radiating total dominance.

Almost total dominance.

"Greetings, Ship Captain," Amani said.

"You and your staff have performed well," the captain said, his voice stiff and patronizing. "You have saved valuable troops."

The tension between the two Khalians sang almost audibly. The assistants and soakers found things to do that would move them as far away from the captain and chief healer as possible.

"Thank you for your praise, Captain." His own voice was also stiff and formal.

The two Khalians stood a single body length apart, neither blinking as they fought for dominance. As a soldier and captain, Damu was twice superior, but in this case, it was not apparent. Amani felt the heat within himself, and he knew he should retreat, should blink and look away, should offer the neck and give the slight bow of obeisance. With any other soldier, he could do it, and he had done it before with Damu, but . . . it was hard.

One did not readily bow to one's own twin brother.

"I have another patient for you," Damu said.

"Fine. I shall attend him."

"He is no ordinary patient."

"It does not matter."

"This patient must be kept alive at all costs. He was onboard the frigate *Nasmyth,* which was destroyed in the battle."

"I shall endeavor to keep him alive as I do all my charges."

"Not good enough, Healer. This patient must not die."

Amani framed a biting reply to the affrontery of his brother telling him how to do his work, but Damu was not yet finished speaking.

"As healers go, you are considered one of the best."

Amani heard, 'As dung goes, you are a fine turd.'

"Whatever skill you have in your *profession* must be utilized to the fullest. If this patient dies, you will suffer greatly for it."

Before Amani could answer this threat, the surgery's doors zipped open, and the two field medics, Ferret Face and Fatso, entered with a stretcher. Amani's quick glance at the patient was enough to still any outburst at his brother's insult.

A Fleet human lay upon the stretcher.

Amani flicked a look at his brother, whose smile now radiated triumph. Off balance, the healer tried to recover. "I am not a veterinarian, Damu—Captain."

"It was *your* choice to be a healer instead of a fighter, Amani. The apes breathe the same air as we do, and they bleed red. This is Fleet Admiral Stone, captured during the battle of Castleton's World. He deliberately rammed his vessel into the *Silver Raptor,* destroying it, as well as his own. He was being transported back to home world when the frigate was destroyed. He is an enemy, but he is a *brave* enemy, though I doubt *you* can understand that. *Your* duty is to keep him alive until such time as you are told otherwise. Is that clear?"

Amani tried to lock his stare onto Damu's, but the strain of surgery and the surprise of a human patient were too much. He glanced away, symbolically offering his neck, as he had so many times before. "I understand my duty, Captain."

Damu's triumph was supreme, the scent of it practically oozed from him like liquid. "Good. That is all I require . . . for now."

The chief healer watched as Damu turned and marched away. *He got you again, didn't he, Amani? He'll never let you forget it, not if you should both live to be a thousand seasons. Recall the day when you announced your decision—*

"Chief Healer? What shall we do with the patient?"

Amani tore himself away from his bad memories. "Put him on the diagnostic table."

How in the nine hells was he supposed to take care of an injured human? It had been generations since the givers had trained the first healers. He had never seen a live one, much less treated one. Damn!

For all his arrogance, Damu was right about one thing. These humans were similar in construction to real people. Physical examination revealed that while the organs were placed somewhat differently, they were close in design and function, as nearly as he could tell. Most of the injuries the man had suffered were straightforward enough. Cuts, contusions, smashed limbs, and most of this damage was old. Amani wondered who had attended the wounds originally. He would give a lot for that healer to be standing here next to him. The human was missing both legs from the hip down, neatly amputated; and only one arm worked, the other having been broken in half a dozen places, orthobonded and encased in slunglas from the wrist to shoulder. There were fresh cuts on the face and body that Amani methodically sutured. There were no visible signs of internal bleeding, and he had no idea what the normal human hemoglobin or hematocrit was; the only way to check was to use the alien diagnoster, which he did not particularly relish. He did not trust the machine, even though he had learned the operational poetry and thus did not have to rely on the mumbo jumbo of the poet master.

The poet was an old Orthodox, mostly senile, and Amani had come to believe that the prayers he offered were not nearly so important as the hard-core poetry itself, despite the old Khalian's dire warnings of the dreaded System Malfunction. The verses for the diagnoster, for instance, were hardly heroic or epic; instead, they were very straightforward doggerel a slackwit could remember.

Enough of that. The patient was unconscious, and unable to aid him. And if he died . . .

Reluctantly, Amani called Vita to bring the diagnostic device to him.

"Begging your pardon, Chief Healer, but I do not trust that thing."

Amani was tempted to spare Vita, but he was tired, and it would not do to allow his dominance to fail even if he agreed, which he did. "You are not required to trust it, Assistant Healer, merely to bring it. Without the poet."

Again put into his place, Vita scurried to fetch the instrument.

The machine was mounted on a roller, and once it was in position over the recumbent form of the human, Amani recited the operational poetry to himself.

> Over the patient center the eye,
> push the button next to the sky.

Amani touched the topmost control on the device. A power hum began, and a bank of red diodes lit up.

> When the lights are all aglow,
> touch the button farthest below.

Amani thumbed the lowest control tab. The machine's hum deepened, and several clicks came from it.

> When the screen asks you the name,
> press the number of the same.

A holoprojic screen lit up in pale amber, and a list of species names printed out in the air, written in Khalian block letters. Each name was preceded by a single number. Next to the word HUMAN was the number 4. Amani sought the number on the key pad below the screen and pushed it.

> Now the rest is up to me,
> wait a while and you shall see.

Amani watched tensely as the holoproj ran with a crawl of values from the tests it was performing. In the medical training he had received, in which each movement was repeated over and over and over until it was understood and could be duplicated perfectly, he had never worked with such a machine before. He knew it was running dozens of tests upon the patient—blood values, deep axial scans, tissue soundings and more—that he could not understand. He did not have the knowledge to fully utilize the diagnoster, but he only needed to know one thing for sure, whether or not the patient was bleeding internally.

After a moment, Amani found that which he sought upon the three-dimensional screen. Normal blood values for a human, compared to those of the patient. Amani sighed. The patient's blood volume and density were both within normal limits, given that he was legless and battered.

Reciting the shut-down procedures to himself, Amani depowered the diagnoster and had Vita remove it. There was little else he could do at this point. The man—Stone, Damu had called him—would live or die. Amani had done all he could figure out to do.

The human awoke some hours later and, supposedly in flawless Khalian militaryspeak, asked for a drink of water. This was told to the chief healer by the soaker dispatched to awaken Amani from his restless sleep.

Amani approached the man, who showed his teeth.

While the chief healer was no expert, he was given to understand that such a display of teeth was not a threat as it was among the Khalia, but a sign of amusement. That in itself might be considered funny by some, since the man certainly had little enough to be amused about.

"I am Chief Healer Amani. How do you feel?"

"Like shit," the man said. "Admiral Ernest Stone, of the Fleet, late of the dreadnought *Morwood*. You want my serial number?"

"I know who you are."

"Ah. Well, I can't say I'm pleased to meet you, Healer Amani, but I suppose I should thank you for your efforts on my behalf, considering that I ought to be dead twice over."

"I only did my duty."

"Yes. We all do our duty, don't we?"

Amani did not feel that Stone really required an answer to that comment, and he offered none. But the human sounded bitter. Odd, from a military commander.

"So," Stone said, "what's the drill? Am I still being shipped off to the torture racks?"

"I cannot say what your eventual fate is. My job is to keep you alive. You are considered a hero, and as such, an important person."

Stone emitted a kind of bark—ha!—and showed his teeth

again. More amusement. "Your military is going to take me apart like a broken flitter engine, Healer. They want to know what I know, and they will do whatever they have to to get at it . . . with all due respect for my heroic deeds, of course."

Amani felt uncomfortable. He did not doubt that what Stone said was true. Torture. Even though it was not his doing, nor his business, it turned his stomach. Another part of his flaw, of course.

"Well, it doesn't matter. In their place, I'd do the same. War is hell."

Amani was surprised. "You know our Philosopher Dumo?"

"Can't say as I do. But we have our own philosophers. They pretty much came to the same conclusion about it."

"Dumo is not popular on our home world," Amani said.

"Seems like the peaceful ones are never as popular as the ones who sponsor war," Stone said.

"Is there anything I can do to aid you, Admiral Stone?"

"I don't suppose you'd consider spacing me without a suit?" Amani said nothing to this.

"I didn't think so. Some water would be nice."

"Of course."

Amani lay in his cubicle again, staring at the metal bulkhead above him. Strange that a human military commander would speak of peace in such a wistful tone. Amani's years in the military medical service had shown him that humans were every bit as bloodthirsty as the most vicious Khalians. He had patched up enough wounded troopers to know that for certain. Humans killed as easily as Khalians, they thought nothing of turning an energy weapon upon a ship full of people and blasting it to pieces. A killer race, fighting his own killer race, both sides laughing as they died. Were they all blind? Couldn't any of them see what the end had to be?

Amani sighed. He was ever out of place. Perhaps his brother and the majority of Khalians were right: anyone who would chose to be a healer over being a fighter must have a deep character flaw, some inborn sickness that could not be cured or even treated. Not that he thought himself a coward—he had once stood up to his brother tooth and claw for what he believed—but to experience the kind of . . . compassion Amani felt was certainly not normal. For a female with her kits, yes. A mother could bemoan the loss of her sons in war, but a male was expected to chew it up and behave with honor. Fathers did not weep for dead children, nor brothers for the loss of their siblings. It was not done. Even gaining a name required a dance with death—many did not survive.

Amani, on the other hand, had sometimes wept for dead patients who were not even related to him. He kept his tears in private, of course; there were some limits to shame. Even so, those who were real Khalia, fighters, felt nothing but contempt for white kilts like Amani. A healer, like a poet or a priest, was exempt from duels, and only a coward would hide behind his *profession,* a term his brother Damu never used without biting irony.

Amani had hoped at one time that by being the best healer he could be, his service would somehow alleviate the stain of having chosen it. But, no. He had finally realized that by being the best coward in a field of cowards he impressed no one. He might repair a hundred or a thousand Khalians who would have died otherwise, but there was no honor in that. Life had less value than death, for a warrior.

How odd it was to find that a human, one of the enemy, seemed to have leanings of compassion. Before the man was taken from him, he would have to speak to him again.

Damu's voice on the communicator was brusque. In the earlier face-off, he had left Amani dominated. He furthered his advantage by calling over the com instead of coming to the surgery in person.

"How is the human?"

"Alive," Amani said. "As you required."

"Yes. As *I* required. See that he remains that way."

"I know my duty, Captain."

"Oh, of that I am sure, *Healer.*" Always, the contempt. And now, the certainty in Damu's voice, at last. I have you where you finally belong, brother. Cowardly and subservient.

Amani shut off the com and turned, just in time to catch his assistants and soakers hurrying to move from his sight. He might be submissive to the captain, but they were under his claws, and they obviously had no desire to find those claws gripping their necks.

Amani moved to the private cubicle they had arranged for

Stone. It was as much for the other patients' benefit as the human's. It would not do to have a recovering trooper all excited and tearing stitches because there was one of the enemy in the next bed.

Inside the curtains, Amani stood alone looking down at the crippled man.

"Not much of me left, is there?" Stone said. "Of course, there's a lot more than I expected, after ramming my ship into your formation."

"Not my formation, Admiral. That was another time and place."

Stone moved his shoulders as a Khalian would shrug. The movement pained him. "Doesn't matter, I suppose."

Amani moved closer and sat on the stool next to the bed. "Admiral, is that a note of regret in your voice?"

The man stared at Amani. "You mean, don't I wish I had destroyed more of your ships? Sure. All of 'em."

Amani thought about the risk he was taking and decided it didn't matter. "No," he said softly, "I meant, do you regret having destroyed any of them?"

"Healer, I am—or was—an admiral of the Fleet, defending my species against unwarranted attacks by your suicidal pirates. I did my duty."

"As you said earlier, we all do our duty," Amani said. "But duty and desire are not always the same."

"I am a man of war, sir. I have spent most of my life in the military, fighting against those who would enslave or kill humans. It is a valid reason for my actions; I need not justify them to you, one of the enemy."

"No. You need not justify them."

There was a long silence, a kind of peace that stretched between the Khalian healer and the human admiral.

Finally, Stone said, "I have never enjoyed the killing, Healer, if that's what you want to know. It had to be done, but I took no pleasure in it."

"I understand."

"Do you? Your race seems to find a particular glee in death, giving or receiving."

Amani nodded, staring past the injured man through the ship's walls into infinity. "Yes. My race does. But I have a character flaw, Admiral, which is why I am a healer and not a soldier. I am a necessary evil to my race, but one that is tolerated and not respected. Were I the best healer to ever live, I would be less than the dirt beneath the feet of the worst soldier. Because I won't kill. I cannot even allow death if I can prevent it."

Another long silence flowed before Stone broke it. "Ah. There goes my chance for suicide. You have to keep me alive, even though you know what they have planned for me."

"Even so, yes."

"Duty, again. I respect that. Even the largest machine cannot continue to run without all of its parts in place. Every piece is necessary."

"How odd it is that you can see that. A warrior, and an enemy, besides."

"Soldiers do what they are trained to do, reasons come from elsewhere. What can a single man do to stop the killing? Not much. Perhaps you and I have more in common than you think."

"Perhaps." Amani stood. "Well. I have other patients."

"Of course."

"I shall check on you later."

"Healer."

"Admiral."

Again, the call on the com. "The human is well?"

"I would advise you of any change, Ship Captain."

"We shall be arriving at the Sharptooth Station within a matter of hours, Healer. Once there, the human will be transferred to another ship. Keep him breathing until then."

"I hear your command, Captain."

"I know you hear it, brother. See that you obey it."

Amani swallowed his anger. He had symbolically offered his neck yet again, as he had done so many times before. Cowards always did that, and momentary shows of defiance meant nothing in the long run.

What *did* mean something in the long run? As the human so aptly put it, what could a single man—or a single Khalian—do to change things?

The com had long since clicked off while he was considering this question.

* * *

"I appreciate your telling me," Stone said. His face was grayish in the dim light, but he seemed in no more distress than he had been.

"You were willing to die for your beliefs," Amani said. "It is the least I could do."

"I won't be able to resist," Stone said. "Too bad my people think I'm already dead; they could void some of the information I'll give."

"Military secrets?"

"Some. But like most such things, they will be outdated soon enough."

"Admiral, I—I am sorry for what you must undergo."

"I appreciate that."

In his cube, Amani punched in a call for Damu.

"Yes? What it is, Healer?" He was annoyed. "I've got a docking coming up and no time for your chatter."

"I hereby invoke my sibling privilege."

"*What?* Now?"

"Now." Amani felt a small surge of joy at Damu's reaction, but he kept the feeling from his voice.

"Damn you, Amani!"

"It is my right, under the law—"

"Don't tell me the fucking law! I know it's your right!"

"Well?"

"All right. Get up here, now! I'll give you the required time, no more. Discom."

Amani hurried to reach the captain's quarters. Between twin siblings, there was a one-time right of total free speech. It could be called upon any time and any place by either twin, and the law required that the other acknowledge it. It was a point of honor, and to ignore it was impossible. Amani had never thought he would use it, but there was something he must know.

The door to the captain's cubicle slid open. Despite his arrogance, Damu was obviously intrigued by his brother's request.

"All right. I'm listening."

"Do you really think me a coward, Damu?"

"That's it? You invoke the one-time for *that?* You needn't have bothered, Brother. I would have answered that one for nothing."

"Then answer it."

"Yes. You are a coward. You chose to hide from honor when you went into your so-called profession."

"Because I picked life over death."

"Yes. Because a Khalian who will not kill denies his heritage! It is our lot to slay those who oppose us! Our blood demands no less! None but the Khalia can be strong!"

"And there can be no change? No compassion? No strength without killing?"

"Stop sniveling, Amani!"

"Even if it means the death of our race?"

"No matter what it means! You don't understand about honor, about bravery! You staunch the blood of soldiers you aren't fit to touch!"

"We gained our names on the same day, Damu. We both survived the Wilderness Test."

"That was not war!"

"I see. To be brave requires war."

"Yes! And blood. I am dominant because my blood runs hotter than yours," Damu said. "That will always be the way of it. You cannot help but serve and obey me because you are flawed, Amani! Less than whole. A coward. You cannot understand what it is to face death and laugh at it."

Amani nodded, as if agreeing, but what he saw was something else altogether. A problem he had been avoiding for a long time. And it had taken one of the enemy humans to finally show it to him.

"Is that all, Healer?"

"Yes. That is all."

"Then get out. Go back to your cowards and whiners. I have a ship to run."

"Arriving pretty soon now?" Stone said.

Amani, seated on the stool next to the bed, nodded. "Pretty soon."

"Well, win some, lose some."

Amani reached into his belt pouch and removed a single surgical claw—a short, curved blade on the end of a socket. He held it between two digits and twirled it back and forth, watching the light glint from the razor steel.

Stone watched him with sudden interest.

"A thing of beauty, the surgical knife," Amani said. Almost idly, he laid the claw on the small table next to Stone's bed. "Dangerous in the wrong hands."

Stone stared at the claw for a moment, then looked back up at Amani. "Hypothetically speaking, Chief Healer, but . . . what would happen to you if one of your very important patients should up and die unexpectedly?"

"That would be unlikely to happen. I am a very good healer."

"But just to satisfy my curiosity?"

"I expect I might well be found derelict in my duty. A reduction in rank would likely occur, with appropriate loss of clan status. Just before I was executed, of course."

"I see."

"But being such a good healer, it is unlikely that one of my patients would die without my prior knowledge. And if one of them did, it might well be for the best."

"Even given your duty?"

"Sometimes, Admiral, one's duty must be to a higher purpose."

"Ah."

Amani stood. "I think I have misplaced one of my surgical claws. I had best go and see if I can find it. Someone might pick it up and accidentally nick his carotid arteries." Amani touched himself on the sides of the neck. "Such carelessness could result in a quick and painless death."

Amani turned to leave. "Farewell, Admiral."

"And you, Healer. Thank you. You are a brave man."

"Not a man. I am Khalian."

"Maybe that doesn't make much difference."

"Perhaps you're right, Admiral."

In his cube when the ship docked, Amani felt a sense of calm unlike any he had ever known. He had defied his brother and the order of things, and even the sudden frantic pounding by his assistant upon the door of his cubicle could not disturb his sense of peace. Perhaps the desire for peace was indeed a character flaw; if so, it was one his race would have to develop, sooner or later, or risk being destroyed. Khalians might defeat humans, though Amani did not think it likely, but what would happen if they should someday happen upon folk far more powerful, like the First Others? Aggression against such people would truly be suicide. How could his own race not see it?

"Chief Healer, it—it's the human patient!" The assistant's pounding grew more pronounced, but the healer ignored it.

For his act, Amani would pay an expensive price.

He shrugged to himself. In the end, it only mattered that he had done what he'd felt was right. And Stone had been correct. Even the loss of the smallest part might stop the functioning of a large machine. Who could say?

Even a character flaw might change a race.

INTERLUDE

Hawk Talon was in trouble. Having destroyed the secret Khalian base, he was trapped in a crater by over a hundred of the hideously tusked invaders. With near miraculous skill, Hawk had shot nearly half of the aliens when the Weasel battlecruiser rumbled over the crater.

Slowly, while the maniacal laughter of the evil Khalian admiral echoed, the barrel of a truly gigantic plasma cannon began to swing toward the Fleet hero. The sound of lightning crackled as the house-sized weapon charged. Valiantly, Talon stood, legs apart, his pistol raised in defiance. Behind him the senator's daughter he had just rescued from a fate worse than death cringed, clutching his leg.

Suddenly a familiar silver ship streaked over the horizon and in a single burst shattered the cannon and crippled the Khalian dreadnought.

"But you were alone?" the voluptuous female exclaimed in wonder.

"You're never alone when you are teamed with a brain ship like the *Derv*," the Hawk informed her as they climbed the wreckage of the fallen dreadnought.

Freeze and roll credits.

LONG SHOT
by Diane Duane and Peter Morwood

SHE WAS AT least one hundred meters from her blunt nose to the shielded drive-ports in her tail, but hanging in the two-thousand-meter shadow of a Fleet dreadnought, she was tiny. Her skin was a jagged alternation of mirror-bright and black, the reflec and absorp coatings of scan-dazzle camouflage that said "military" as plainly as any gaudy battle insignia. Her battle insignia, painted small and with their colors muted, said Khalian. So did her shape and the aggressive flight pattern in which she had approached her docking space in the lee of the gigantic battlewagon. But the voices inside her hull said Fleet.

"Status please, Minerva."

"Showing green-green-green all across the board, ten-ten constant." There was a brief pause while supercooled circuits spoke to each other, and then: "Why? What else did you expect?"

"Uh, nothing, really. I just . . ."

"Wanted somebody else to talk to. Yes, Roj, dear. I quite understand."

Roj Malin, lieutenant commander in the Fleet, was old enough and wise enough to know when he was being teased and could take it with the best of them, but he still wasn't quite accustomed to taking that teasing from his ship rather than from his partners. Even though olympus-class brainship *XM-14376*

63

was as much of a partner as any crewman he had served
with . . . probably more so. Usually the brainships carried
only their regular "brawns" as crew, but Roj was working with
Minerva on irregular secondment for a whole slew of reasons,
some of which they had been told and others which they guessed
at. The principal reason, indeed the only one worth noting at
all, could be summed up in one word.

Intelligence. His, hers, and Fleet military. They were "acting
on information received," as the jargon had it. Where the
information had come from, and who it had been bribed or
twisted out of, wasn't his affair; and Minerva had made it quite
plain during their brief shakedown that she didn't want to know.
That the information existed was enough, thank you very much.
While Roj had been settling into his quarters, and after she had
checked out what his responses might be with a few questions—
some subtle and others not—Minerva had spent a cheerful
quarter hour grousing about what had been done to her
just-completed and not-yet-flown new hull shell during a
high-speed refit at Port's orbital facility.

She had put on makeup. Not feminine, especially, but
theatrical, to make her look like something that she wasn't. The
olympus-class ships were cased in ablative armor both
for military purposes and to give them full atmosphere capa-
bility. That was why they had picked an olympus for this mission: the sturdy subframing which carried the armor enabled
Port's tech squad to fit what Minerva called "all that junk outside."

Roj had seen it and had known what it was. Makeup, all right.
And war paint. She looked, and they both knew it, like a
Khalian fencer-class frigate.

That brief, gossipy period while Roj and Minerva took each
other's measure was a crucial one for the mission about which
neither of them yet knew. In the first week of their acquaintance,
future tasking meant little either to them or to the Fleet rear
admirals who were watching the forced relationship. The human
mind that was Minerva, with emotions and opinions still present
no matter how well she had been schooled in the controlling of
them, retained the right to refuse this particular crewman and
insist that she be assigned a regular brawn for regular duties. Roj
was already a volunteer for CDR, covert deep reconnaissance—
occasionally known as NASDAQ, nasty and sneaky, don't ask
questions—and it was only right that his ship, since only a brain-

ship was truly fitted for such a mission, should also be a volunteer and satisfied with his or her partner.

Minerva was satisfied. The brain that had been born as part of a crippled body had been prime controller of three ships now, counting the new olympus. She had seen the retirement of many brawns and had borne the deaths of four; those, and many others, had served to make her cynical. Even judged by the unhuman lifespans of brain ships, she was an old lady—although if the thought of age and her own death ever crossed her busy mind, it was dismissed as something not worth wasting time on. She had always survived before. There was no reason why that shouldn't continue . . . until she grew tired, anyway, and chose her own time and place to find rest. But not yet. Not just yet. . . .

And then came mission briefing, and Minerva was no longer so sure that she would have a choice in her own passing after all . . .

". . . and of course you are both already aware of the structural changes made to the *XM14376*'s outer hull," said the commodore.

"That's X-*R*-14376, sir," Minerva corrected, and her voice was curt. Roj smiled with unabashed pride. "And yes, I am most definitely aware of the changes. The olympus-class is cumbersome enough, what with all the armor and atmosphere-entry shielding. When the transfer came up I hadn't anticipated that it would mean being dressed like one of these Khalian barges on top of all else." Her voice became speculative and thoughtful. "I wonder, do ordinary women feel like this when they're pregnant . . . ?"

Commodore Agato had been talking in vague generalities for half an hour now, and Roj could sense Minerva's impatience with the way the briefing was being conducted. The commodore had the look of a man whose present duty was making him uneasy, and who was hiding his feelings behind the stiff formality that went with the tabs of flag rank and the impassive face that went with his Nihonji ancestry. Roj glanced at Minerva's primary lens and winked quickly. Deep within the lens where only he could see it, an iris shutter contracted in response.

"Commodore, given my brawn's specialization and the quantity of navigational data which Central have been porting to my core memories"—Roj suppressed a smile at the tone of voice Minerva was using—"I have taken the liberty of extrapolating various matters in connection with the forthcoming duty. Feel free to correct any errors in my supposition."

Agato looked startled for an instant, then gathered himself together again and nodded. "Ahem," he said. "Very well. Proceed . . . and I shall interrupt as necessary."

There were few interruptions. Minerva's analysis was more accurate than the Admiralty office had been prepared for, almost certainly because someone much higher up had presumed that a new brain ship meant what it usually did, a new brain as well. They hadn't taken into account Minerva's years of experience on other ships or her increasingly cynical view of the Fleet, or . . . or any one of a number of things.

"I would presume, firstly, Commodore Agato, that I have been chosen to simulate the Khalian fencer-class vessels because of my own current size, which nonetheless," Minerva's voice, initially as flat and dry as that of some Tech-group scientist presenting a learned paper, took on the merest hint of smugness, "belies the power I have at my disposal. Even in my present cumbersome and underequipped form, I am more than a match one-on-one for any but the largest ships likely to be found at the Khalian home world—and those I can outrun."

"*Home world . . . ?*" The commodore said it before Roj, but only by the barest instant.

"Of course home world. After that debacle at Target the Fleet is more determined than ever to find where the Khalians come from, then go there and . . . pacify them. Come now, sir. Am I not correct?"

The commodore studied his anachronistic printed-paper notes for a few minutes, then folded them and returned them to the equally anachronistic briefcase lying on the flight-deck work top. Whatever information they contained was evidently of little help right now. "Yes," he conceded. "You'll be looking for the Khalian home world. And you'll have a better than even chance of finding it on your first pass if you leave it to the guidance system presently locked into the onboard INS suite. Let it run, and it'll take you right to their front door."

"I would sooner try the back door." Roj didn't like the sound of the whole operation, and though he took care not to say so directly, he let the concern come through quite plainly in his tone of voice. "Or an unattended window. If there is one. What say, Minerva?"

Minerva didn't like what she was hearing any more than her brawn did, and she wasn't so worried about letting it be known. "What I say is, the Fleet seems to have made all necessary arrangements to get us there. What about getting back with the information? What about getting back at all? You haven't mentioned that yet, Commodore."

"You'll be fitted with extended-range message torps," Agato began.

"Torpedoes, eh? I was half suspecting that already!" There was bitter triumph in Minerva's voice, and more venom than Roj had ever heard directed at a senior officer before. "So this is a one-way mission after all!"

"Let me finish, *XR-14376*. If you'd be so kind." There had been times in Roj Malin's Fleet career when he'd been caught in similar cross fire, and always the reaction was the same: an overpowering desire to be somewhere—anywhere—else straight away, at once and right now. Something of it must have shown, because the commodore's head came round to face him like a plasma cannon laying onto a target (the man was at least doing Minerva the courtesy of addressing her core, her "self," rather than just the nearest vodex pickup). "Lieutenant Commander Malin, stand fast!" he snapped.

Roj hadn't actually moved at all and now had no intention of doing so.

It was a bit much, therefore, when Minerva's voice told him to "stay put, Roj, right where you are," especially when that voice had been cranked up to 120 decibels. He stayed put, stood fast, and tried not to exist too obviously.

The commodore shook a few echoes of her blare of sound out of his ears and looked, somewhat shocked, back toward Minerva's brain core. "Was that entirely necessary?" he demanded.

"As necessary as sending us out on a no-hope mission," she replied, just as irritably, "although"—and her tone changed imperceptibly—"I doubt that *you* had anything personally to do with it. But Meier's department is notorious for that sort of thing."

"I can assure you that the Admiral of the Red—"

"Does whatever his planners advise him to do. That's why he

has them on staff in the first place.''

"Ahem."

"As you say, Commodore. Ahem indeed. And amen, too.''

"Minerva . . ."

"Keep out of this, Roj. Private fight—nothing to do with you. It's not the first time that Fleet planning has tried to—''

"It's got everything to do with me, damn it! I'll be coming too. Remember? With you? Or did that slip your so-powerful memory banks?''

There was one of those nasty little pauses when everybody who has said a word in the past hour wants to get up and leave before they're accused of something, and then Minerva made a multifrequency sound that was much more like the clearing of throats than her studied "ahem" had ever been. "Ah.'' Another pause. "Yes, actually. But if you'd been with me before, and seen some of the things I've had to. . . . Commodore, you look like a man with something to say.''

"Several things. First, that Lieutenant Commander Malin is not without experience, otherwise we wouldn't have short-listed him for this assignment. You should have his personnel record on file.''

"I don't.'' Minerva sounded grumpy. "There was an eyes-only restriction on it.''

"That's soon put right. Open a channel to IntelSec Prime: code clearance Delta Delta. Voice and vision.''

"Done.''

"Patch in all your data requirements; you'll get them, or I'll know the reason why.''

Once Agato had identified himself and expressed a few choice opinions of IntelSec's personnel, there were no further queries or restrictions.

Minerva was silent for the few seconds necessary to scan the incoming data. The loudest sound on the flight deck after that was the click as she cut the connection to the IntelSec computer banks, and there was a great deal more respect in her voice when she spoke to Roj again. "So you were *that* intelligence exec. On Stone's flagship at Freeborn. I should have found out before this, Roj. You should have told me.''

He shrugged, not wanting to think too much about that bloody business even at this remove from it. He had spent three days in his office aboard the dreadnought's slowly cartwheeling

hulk after she had rammed one ship and then was bracketed by a
salvo of plasma torps, her starboard side blown to drifting
shrapnel. Three days listening to his carefully husbanded air
whistling thinly into vacuum through ruptured seams and the
dozen splinter perforations that he hadn't been able to reach
with the emergency sealant. Three days in darkness, because his
power could go to light or heat but not both, and there was
nothing but space beyond his door. Three days, before the hatch
blew—

And a Fleet rescue squad pulled him, sobbing, from the
frost-encrusted, stinking cabin . . .

". . . and isn't quite the desk warrior that you might have
expected," Commodore Agato was telling Minerva when Roj
squashed his ugly memories and came back to the present on the
crest of a shudder. "Neither am I, and I know what you'll need
to get out of hostile space with a whole skin. You'll be carrying
rather more than just message torpedoes. We've already fitted
state-of-the-art electronic countermeasures, but just before you
leave the yards the R&D boys are going to install something new
that came out of the business at Bethesda."

"Why don't I like the sound of this?" Roj heard himself
saying, scarcely believing his own audacity. Acquaintance with
Minerva was teaching him bad habits; it was already eroding his
ingrained respect for anyone with more braid on their cuffs than
he had.

"I'm not expecting you to like it, Commander." The
commodore didn't even look in his direction. "I don't like it
particularly myself. But it's available for use, and you should
take whatever you're given and be thankful."

"And what is 'it,' if I may make so bold as to ask, since
they're fitting it to me and not him?" Minerva sounded waspish
and wary; Roj guessed that at some stage of her career she'd
already acted as a test bed for new equipment and hadn't liked
the experience.

"They call it a pulse transceiver," replied Agato, refusing to
let the pair of them needle him any further than they had
already. "According to R&D, it'll be able to analyze the
protocols of the new Khalian orbital-defense drones we found
around Bethesda and reprogram them to recognize your own
IFF/ID blip rather than the Khalians' vessels. If the situation

arises, you'll have more firepower at your disposal than a task force could carry."

"If." Roj sat back in his chair and steepled his fingers, staring thoughtfully at their interlaced tips. "Commodore, I may be sounding petty, but what sort of combat record does this system have? I mean, it was developed after Bethesda, wasn't it?" Agato nodded agreement. "So where was it tried out in combat?" Agato stopped nodding, and Roj glanced sideways at the lens where Minerva was watching.

"Uh oh." She didn't need to say more.

"The lab tests have been very favorable. They were working with genuine Khalian data cores recovered from the orbital platforms." He stopped, shrugged, grimaced in disgust—in that instant looking more human and less like a uniformed automaton than he had all day—and then smiled sourly. "It hasn't been field-tested at all. Of course not. But I'd still recommend that you take it. It looks very promising."

"And if it doesn't work, or if it fails deep in Khalian space . . . ?"

"Then, Commander Malin, you and Minerva will be just as dead as if you hadn't tried the system at all. Except that I think that it *will* work . . ."

"Minerva, what do you think?" Roj said it to the air rather than to the core, as he might have spoken while avoiding someone's eyes. Not that it mattered particularly aboard a brainship, since Minerva could see him quite plainly in any direction and was indeed inspecting him in visual, thermal, and ultrasound scan right now. For good manners' sake she cut the scan when he spoke to her, but she had already formed a fair judgment of what he would say if pressed.

"I think . . . I think we should, Roj. Let's do it. . . ."

Three weeks later they entered Khalian space. Roj had left piloting the *XR-14376* to Minerva and had concentrated on running repeated checks on the IntelSec survey systems that were more his responsibility than hers. Everything seemed to be working perfectly, even the disguise and the fake Khalian ID that they were running. Indeed, that part was working just a little bit too well, as they discovered when they were jumped by a formation trio of light cruisers just on the wrong side of the frontier. . . .

Granted, as Roj said later, the Fleet warships were just doing their job, and granted that the discovery of a fencer nipping back out of Alliance-controlled space must have looked just like a tip-and-run raider heading for home, but even so, being fired on by your own side was a bit much, especially when the weight of metal they were throwing was coming a damn sight too close. There had been a five-second period far too like Freeborn for comfort, when the lead cruiser's opening salvo straddled them and Minerva's on-board systems went momentarily crazy. The gravity grids slammed through a jagged ten-g fluctuation maybe a half-dozen times in those five seconds, and even as the restraint harness hugged him tight into his seat, Roj had the feeling he was going to bring up every meal he'd eaten since second grade.

Minerva's response was instantaneous, ferocious, and typical of any Khalian vessel ever flown. Even as she hit a three-way break that would have folded her small enough to fit in Agato's briefcase had her hull integrity given way, she emptied an entire rotary autoloader of torps from her ventral tubes and followed up with a vicious spatter of cannon fire from the three turrets that her present incarnation carried. Then, before the startled cruisers recovered from the shock of running into something half their size with a target-acquisition system that could and had just hit all of them, she dropped the hammer on her boosted main drive and streaked beyond light speed with a slick ease that left them gasping.

Roj had been watching the tactical-visual repeater screens and had seen Minerva's counterstrike detonate no closer to the cruisers than their perimeter shields. The blinding blue-white glare of multiple detonations might well have been no more than a very emphatic form of protective coloration . . . but he wondered just a bit. He looked over the encounter once or twice on the recorder to be sure of his grounds.

"Annoyed?" he said at last.

"Don't be ridiculous," she said. There was a pause. "Wretched trigger-happy blue jackets anyway. I hope I singed their trousers, or wherever else they keep their brains."

"You made me throw *up*, Minerva."

"You've been putting on weight anyway. You won't miss that breakfast."

"Then again, maybe it was your cooking. . . ."

"Brawns are replaceable," Minerva muttered.

"Minerva." Perhaps she caught the tone of his voice. At any rate, she held silent. "Too much method acting can trip you up after a while. Don't come all over Khalian with me."

"It may save *your* rear end," she said, but her voice was a touch more subdued, and thoughtful, and for quite a while she didn't speak, as close as a shell could come to "going away" to think. Roj, none too sure of his own feelings, decided to refrain from saying anything further until well into the next day . . . but by then there was no point in criticizing the playing of roles any more.

That was when the Khalians found them.

The incoming ship was a sunray-class rapid-response corvette, all weapons and power plant with a three-seat crew compartment stuck on top as an afterthought, looking like a crystal pimple on an oversized torpedo. The fencer-class of Minerva's pretense was considerably bigger, and in common with the rest of the Khalian navy, big-ship captains were correspondingly more pugnacious than those of smaller vessels. That was why the sunray's challenge, when it came, was couched in terms that were both diplomatic and (for a Khalian) almost polite. In other words, crude, rude, and pushy, but never quite insulting enough to justify an armed response.

Minerva chuckled to herself. "All right. So that's etiquette, is it? Then try this . . ."

Roj listened as she gave him an advance hearing of what her reply was going to be—before it went through the translation suite—and was appalled. Her normal vox-synth was indicative of her self-image—a dignified lady of mature years—and it had given him a mental image of the "person" behind the brain core: silver haired, staid, and mannerly. What that silver-haired lady planned to tell the Khalians. . . . "Oh, God, Minerva," Roj said when he heard it, "isn't there some other way to say that? Any normal male—"

"They're not normal. Put a sock in it."

She sent it, and after a twitchy second's silence the sunray acknowledged with a rather more cautious choice of phrase. Then it sheered off hurriedly, shortly accelerating away about its patrol duties at a speed that suggested Minerva had touched a certain chord of self-preservation in the corvette's commander. Roj watched them go until not even the augmented scanners showed any trace, then turned to face Minerva's primary lens and looked her in the "eye." He was trying to look disapproving, and at the same time, trying not to smile.

"Who taught you to swear like that?!"

The speakers cleared their multiquadrophonic throat at him, sounding just the merest touch like an embarrassed maiden aunt. "A-hem. Well, one here, one there . . . when I was much younger I wanted to learn everything I could about the people I met, and, er, once I learn something I don't forget it. Ever."

"I bet *they* won't," Roj said, his eyes flickering more or less in the direction the Khalian had taken. "What else did you tell them, besides what their pants—never mind. . . ."

He could feel Minerva smiling at him. It made him itch. "So far as they're concerned, we're a raider that crossed the frontier ten days ago, coming back with a hold full of booty—which is why I warned them off so, er, emphatically. Khalians are like that about plunder. Possessive. But their records will show that they counted 'us' out and then counted us back, so we're in the clear."

"And the original raider?"

"Blown to plasma by the same patrol that took a potshot at us. Fencer frigates slip in and out on such a regular basis that all I had to do was monitor the close-patrol bands, and sooner or later I'd pick up a genuine Khalian IFF/ID, rather than the fake one that I've been using. No wonder they were confused, poor boys. Fancy having to blow up the same ship twice in a week. . . ." Minerva chuckled again.

"Uh, Minerva . . . How long do you think this cover's going to work?"

She made an interrogative noise at him.

"I mean, the Khalians may be crazies as far as we're concerned, what with all that 'no dishonor, death and glory' stuff, but then so were a lot of people in the past, like the samurai. Agato should have guessed that one at least. But it doesn't mean that they aren't intelligent. There are brains in those toothy little heads. I've fought against them and I know!"

"What makes you think that I don't, then?" Minerva said, and her voice had that honey-with-the-bee-still-in-it sweetness with the sting waiting. "Roj, dear lad, I was fired on by a Khalian ship before you had graduated from school, much less from the academy. Of course, that was in a different hull, but

still . . .'' She broke off for the merest instant. ''Ah. The
long-range scanners have just cut in: they're in search mode for
traces of heavy traffic activity around any viable planet in this
system. However, since I estimate some five thousand bodies of
above seventy meter diameter in one form or other of stellar
orbit, this will probably take rather longer than those optimists
at Port projected. Sit back and make yourself comfortable. And
Roj . . . ?''

"Yeah?"

"Trust me."

He never had; he was going to have to. It came down at last to
that.

Even with on-board telemetry running as fast as Minerva
could handle it, analyzing input from so many potential targets
(Roj found his mind tended to spell that with a capital *T*, and
didn't much like the way his thoughts tended afterward) was
taking a lot longer than anybody had anticipated. Not long in
terms of time, since Minerva reckoned that she would complete
the task in about two hours, but long in terms of what it might
do to their cover. A skipping, uncertain transit of a supposedly
familiar sector of space was likely to draw attention—the one
thing they wanted most to avoid.

"Monitor any chatter, Roj," Minerva said suddenly as they
dropped back for the seventh time. "All frequencies. We'll want
advance warning if anyone starts to wonder."

"Been doing that," he muttered and returned to the multiple
layer of jabbering from the dozen or so Khalian ships in their
immediate area, a sphere maybe a quarter-million miles across.
One set of speakers, gain turned well down, was giving him a
mutter of Khalian intermingled with bursts of whispery garbage
from the nearer stars, and other sets, his earpiece included,
provided a verbal translation of the several squawks that
marched in variously colored letters across his repeater screen.
The translation suite, running on automatic, was keyed to give
him both audible and visual indication if any Khalian used one
of the several hundred keywords that might be the beginning of
something nasty. It wasn't exactly the way Roj might have
chosen to spend his time, but his stint was—hopefully—almost
over, and there had been no chimes, no buzzers, no flashing
high-visibility transcriptions. Nothing but the stars and the

Khalians, and unimportant private conversations from them both.

And then the horn went off, and for all his nonchalance and boredom, never mind his locked seat harness, Roj Malin almost had to scrape himself off the flight-deck ceiling.

"Oops!" said Minerva just a second later. "Too loud. Sorry. But I think I've got something."

"Me too." Roj wasn't amused. "Thunderclap cardiac arrest, thanks to you."

"I said I was sorry, didn't I? Look here. Tactical overlay one . . . and two . . . and three. Well?" Roj looked, and said nothing for a while. "Roj, you're too old for sulks . . . and I'd like a second opinion sometime today if that's all right by you."

"I'm not sulking. Just looking hard, as requested. Run those three past me again." The palms of his hands were beginning to sweat, and a set of the twitches the size of a battleship was coming to life in his stomach. "Yeah. There. Bull's-eye! So IntelSec was right after all. Either that's the place, or it's one hell of a big traffic junction. Nice going, me lady . . ."

"Maybe. I hope so." Minerva sounded uneasy for the first time since he had met her, and it was an experience so unusual—and consequently so unsettling—that Roj turned right around from his console and looked straight at her.

"You don't like this any more than I do." It wasn't a gloat or an accusation, just a statement that he hoped she would answer truthfully rather than with the evasions she used so adeptly.

Silence. Then, "No, I don't," she said. "When you've lived as long as I have, the prospect of the end starts getting . . . familiar at least. Sometimes inviting. 'A consummation devoutly to be wished,' if I was devout, which I'm not. But now . . . now I'm not in as much of a rush any more. I'd like to keep going a bit longer."

"Then log that planet's coordinates and let's get out of here. Or"—and he stared at the armor sheathing of her brain core—"are you thinking we should take a closer look?"

"We've come this far. Everything's working as it should. Shame on us if we turn back now."

"You sound like a Khalian."

"If you're going to insult a lady, you can get out and walk home. Roj . . . do we go in?"

"Er . . . Yes. We do. But very, very carefully."

"And quickly."

"And quietly."

"As a little mouse, believe me. Better run through the preapproach checks, Roj. Confirm for me. ECM—at standby condition; IFF/ID—holding constant; scanner suppression . . . ?"

"At readiness; tubes charged—standard spread; cannons— preheat cycle; shields—powering up, set to maximum." He paused to swallow what he could of the constriction in his throat, glanced down the remaining dozen or so very minor checks, then glanced at Minerva's primary lens, the one that to him always approximated looking her in the eye. "I guess we can finish the rest as we go, so . . . so you'd better take us in."

Their approach vector, all hundred million miles of it, was flown in a weird combination of tippy-toe caution and swaggering arrogance. At least that was how it looked to Roj, watching from the inside. To the occasional Khalian warship— and that "occasional" was rising in frequency at an alarming rate—they were just one more fencer-class inbound for a postraid refit with the crew making whoopee aboard.

"This is damned strange. This close to Port we'd have Fleet ships all over us. Why won't they come in for a closer look?"

"Simple." At least it was simple for Minerva; she had instant access to the great sheaf of intelligence data about the Khalians, while Roj had to sift through what he remembered reading. "We're coming home, we're in high spirits, we're cock-of-the-walk, and for all or any one of those reasons we might fire on them. Or just to prove how tough we are . . ."

"Crazy people . . ." He subsided into a data-monitoring slouch while the pods of IntelSec packs along Minerva's fake-fencer hull noted everything there was to be seen, heard, scanned, and speculated about the little blue-green world planet all those miles away.

"Passing through the outer perimeter globe." It was a dry enough statement, but various tactical screens blinked with windows indicating the position and the number of what made up that perimeter: little amber dots on an outline display, like beads strung on wire, six thousand of them according to the readout. Defensive platforms, each packing the firepower in torps and cannon of a heavy cruiser. "The inner perimeter is yellow and the orbital stations are green," Minerva continued blandly. The white circle representing the planet was becoming rapidly obscured by variously colored specks that interwove like fireflies dancing. "Do you want the ship traffic as well?"

"Oh, why not? Let's have the lot. But break it up a bit, will you? Individual overlays."

"All right. Here's the system and the outer sphere. The planet, its moons, and the inner sphere. The planet, and its orbital platforms. The planet again, and local traffic. Now all of it together . . ."

"Dear God." Roj stared at the main screen, gone gaudy now with a polychrome spatter of unsettling schematics. The planetary disc was lost somewhere at the core of it all—and they were intending to infiltrate *that?*

"I don't think there's any further doubt about it. This is either the Khalian home world or their main spaceport."

"And we're right on their doorstep."

"Not yet, but we will be quite soon. Stay on the recorders; I'm patching in for a long-range visual. You might want to look at this." Blue oceans, green-brown land masses, swirls and streaks of cloud in the atmosphere envelope, everything peaceful, pastoral, not in the least menacing. Nothing like the base and HQ of a navy which had been a thorn in the Fleet's side for far too long. "You see?"

Roj could see indeed. Their approach was a long parabola, curving against the planet's rotation, and as he watched and they moved and the world turned, what had been a preindustrial planet became a technological wasps' nest. There was only one spaceport and repair facility on the world, but it covered the surface of an entire continent . . .

"They didn't build that," said Roj. "Not with their cultural level. There isn't a trace of any city, any heavy industry, anything at all on any of the other continents. They're just forest, and plains, and—"

"And there's more to this than meets the eye. I don't like the feel of it, not one bit. But it's not our business right now. Let's finish what we came to do and get out of here."

"I'd second tha— Look out! Break right! *Incoming . . . !!*"

Minerva didn't quibble. She rammed all controls into the corner and racked around in a wrenching 90-right. A human pilot with human reflexes wouldn't have reacted in time to sidestep the Khalian destroyer barging into the disorderly conga-line that passed for a traffic pattern. Even then, an extra coat of reflec-absorp paint might have made the difference between being scared and being scrapped.

The destroyer, being the biggest thing in the vicinity and carrying presumably the meanest, toughest, most senior officer, trundled haughtily on toward a rank-pulling priority orbit while in its wake the smaller ships began to jockey back into some sort of favorable position for their own approach, their crews turning all frequencies blue with loudly expressed but carefully modulated opinions.

"Too close! Too bloody close by half! They tried to ram us!" Roj stared at a proximity gauge that was telling him the two ships had passed within six hundred yards of each other. He thought of what would have happened had they made contact, and then decided not to think thoughts like that any more.

"No. They did what they wanted, made us get out of their way. My fault." Minerva sounded genuinely apologetic for once. "It's one thing pretending to fly like a Khalian, but this lot do it naturally. At least they probably just think we were playing chicken—" Something bleeped, and a green light on the board began to blink amber. "Damn, not again! Glitch in the transponder, thanks to that hammering from the border patrol. It doesn't like violent maneuvers any more than I do. Look, Roj, warn that cretin off while I fix this, would you?"

"That cretin" was a Forger-class frigate trying to sneak into line ahead of them; standard Khalian base-leg behavior, just as not letting the Forger get away with it was standard response. Roj tabbed in manual override and moved closer, threatening, as the destroyer had done, to ram the smaller ship if it didn't give way.

Although it held position with laudable stubbornness, the forger gave way at last, moving aside reluctantly with the sort of foul-mouthed insults that Khalians of apparently equal status exchanged in such circumstances. These observations screeched and chittered from the Language-One speakers like poorly unoiled machinery, and the translator converted to an entertaining mixture of comments about the fencer captain's parentage and sexual proclivities, and invitations for him to copulate with various lower animals.

"Does all that refer to you?" Roj wanted to know.

"Huh?" Minerva left off her repairs for just the merest beat.

"No, you. I never had the parts he just referred to. . . ."

Grinning, Roj patched an open channel through the translator. "Vulgar enough," he told whoever on the Forger cared to listen, "but lacking the true creative spark. Better luck next—"

"No, Roj, not like tha—," Minerva began to scream from all her speakers. She was cut off by the static-screech and gravity-grid jolt of a close-range hit on her outer shields. "Oh, *damn!*" she wailed. "Why couldn't you have been like any other sailor and sworn at the bastards rather than trying to be so bloody clever! They don't talk like that! You heard them!" The deck under his boots began to rumble with main-drive subharmonics as Minerva accelerated. "If they insult you, you're twice as rude right back, or you say nothing and accept inferiority. You don't indulge in witty repartee or— Oh, Roj, listen. . . ."

"I hear it." He glowered at the translator speakers, furious with himself, with IntelSec, with the mission, with the Khalians for not acting like sensible creatures. . . . The only thing or person in the entire Galactic arm that he didn't hate right now was Minerva, and that was because he had gotten her into a no-hope situation through his own stupidity.

"Spies!" the forger was yelling. "Disguised enemies! Alarm! Alarm!"

"I should have blown them to atoms and claimed insulted honor," muttered Minerva. "But it's too late now to be of use."

It was; the reply from the home world's surface was crackling out even as she spoke, in a choral chant of many voices from whatever group ran traffic control down there. "Kill the spies! Kill the spies! None must escape! Glory to their slayers! Kill! Kill! Kill!"

A single stern-tube torp spat from the *XR-14376,* and the still-squawking forger erupted in an incandescing flare of slag and splinters. Roj drummed his fingers near the activated weapons-system master board and smiled ever so slightly at nothing in particular. "Never mind use, or even honor; general principles is a good enough reason for me. And I don't think they mentioned what ship we actually were, did they?" He looked at the tactical screens, each of them going berserk with readouts and schematics. "What sort of chance do we have . . . ?"

"Not much. I still don't know if the pulse transceiver is going to work or not."

"Then we'd better try it. Where to, ma'am?"

"Toward the planet. Let's see which of us the orbital platforms like best, shall we?"

"Sure. But first rig for an all-tubes salvo and . . . and launch the message torps along with it. Just in case."

"Just in case. Yes. Torpedoes away." The deck jolted at the soles of his boots again, once, twice, three times . . . and then kicked hard enough to knock him off his feet.

"That wasn't a standard volley, was it?"

"No . . . that was our old friend the destroyer. And he wasn't firing on us, not directly. . . ."

"So then what . . . ?" Roj pushed himself upright, flopped into his chair and secured the harness tight, wondering at the amusement in Minerva's voice.

"This." The big main screen lit up, and despite their hazardous position Roj began to laugh, grimly, but with real humor for all that. Space around the home world had gone mad in the few seconds since he had taken out the Forger, and all the ships that had been queued up for entry to parking orbits or to the landing fields had broken out of their never-very-orderly line and were all over the sky. Even as he watched, the biggest ship in sight—their "old friend," in very truth—raked a delta-class corvette with cannon fire and then trisected it with a pair of torpedoes.

"They're looking for us, Roj. They're trying to find us, and they don't know what to look for! The frigate's crew must have been so excited about finding us that they forgot to get off an ID fix before you— Oh, well done! Our chances have just more than doubled!"

"Minerva, twice not much is still very small indeed."

"It's going to get better. Don't forget the ships planet side. They'll want some glory, too, if there's any to be had right on their own doorstep, so it's going to get crowded up here."

"And if we—you—can reprogram the defense satellites. . . ."

"We, Roj, we. Both of us together. The way we started or not at all. Let's try, uh, this . . . ."

Minerva ran a jinking gauntlet course through the swirl of Khalians, screaming insults at all, launching an occasional torpedo from her recharged tubes, and generally behaving like every other ship in local space just then. Even when she wasn't being shot at, there was so much wild energy sleeting against her shields that keeping the viewscreens functional was sometimes as much as Roj could do from one minute to the next. The flight-deck gravity grids had shut down prior to combat maneuvers, and dull red emergency lighting was the sole illumination other than the coruscation of color glowing from the repeater screens.

"We've been spotted!" he yelled above the racket of engines and torp-tubes and cannon and Khalian squalling. "Zero niner seven, two delta-class cor— Wowee!! They just ran into each other! Will you look at that!"

The pair of corvettes, which might at a less frantic time have tried working in concert, had spotted the one vessel of all the milling throng that was trying to get closer to home world rather than farther away from it, and their captains had jumped to the same conclusion. Unfortunately for them, the scramble for a good attack position took both ships at high-g acceleration into a space that was really only big enough for one. . . .

"We're in trouble, Roj. This piece of lab-tested junk refuses to cooperate. I think that last jolt did it no good at all." Minerva managed somehow to sound no more than irritated, an unlikely and restrained attitude under the circumstances.

"Keep working on it." As they slithered sideways, impossibly eel-like for a rigid, cylindrical ship, Roj sent a spread of torpedoes into the thick of the swirling Khalian ships. Two flared with the brilliance of direct hits, and the rest scattered wildly, which was not a good move at all. "Ouch! Five-ship collision at two-one-seven, three totalled and two drifting. Are you close enough to the platforms yet?"

"Too close, if this IFF/ID crashes. And it's getting busy in the atmosphere; the ships that were scrambled are on their way up. Any who get there. Where *did* they learn to mistreat ships like that?"

"Never mind that. More trouble. Big trouble. That destroyer's taking too much of an interest!"

"Weapons onto full manual. . . . You deal with it. I can't take time away from this blasted transceiver to do anything myself."

"No! Firing would only confirm—"

"And just what have we—and everyone else up here—been doing to each other these past few minutes, that destroyer

included? Behave like a Khalian, man: shoot at it. But leave me
in peace right now!''

As Roj watched on the rearward screen, the destroyer blasted
two more of its erstwhile companions into drifting junk, then
turned with unpleasant slow deliberation toward Minerva.
Probably its captain was still no more than mildly suspicious,
but that hadn't helped the Khalian ships whose remains were
now searing across the outer edge of their home world's
atmosphere.

"Minerva—here it comes . . . !'' Silence. His fingers tightened on the fire selector, and a targeting display glowed into life
over the image of the destroyer. "Range thirty-two hundred.
Thirty-one hundred. Range three thousand miles, closing.
Target-acquisition engaged, locked and standing by.''

"Going to full evasive,'' she snapped, impatient with the
recital of what her tactical systems knew already. "Heading for
a close pass of the nearest defense platform—now.'' The
destroyer slid sideways off the screen as she accelerated down
and away from it, then drifted back as Roj corrected.

Minerva said something in perfect quad stereo that she must
have learned from her roughest brawn. "Give them some
cannon fire,'' she snapped, "and keep them off my back!''

Roj let go with the turrets that he could bring to bear, two of
them, and saw energy splash uselessly against the destroyer's
shields. It was, as he had guessed it would be, no more than a
gnat stinging a crocodile, and the crocodile had had enough.
The big ship was surging after them, and the readout along one
side of his screen was warning that the destroyer's target lock
was actively hunting them, defeated so far only by Minerva's
scanner suppression and the ECM jammers. But it would
be only a matter of time before it came close enough for blind
firing or visually backed approximation to be worthwhile, and
then . . .

Then Minerva said, "It works,'' like someone passing a
death sentence, and the destroyer blew up in a pure white
pyrophoric flash that dimmed all the screens to black.

The background keening of her main drive slid up the scale to
a banshee howl as it began the long, hard push to take them clear
of the Khalians and their base and this entire blasted sector of
space. Blasted was close to the truth; when the viewscreens'
phototropic shielding ran back down to normal, they revealed a

scene of devastation that shocked even Roj, who had seen the aftermath of Stone's miscalculation at Freeborn. Not merely the orbital platforms but both inner and outer perimeters had taken Minerva's reprogramming squirt without so much as a hiccup, and they had done what their designers had intended them to do. Except that they had done it according to the wishes of the Fleet. Fifty percent of the Khalian vessels in flight when their defensive net went rogue now tumbled or flared or hung most dreadfully dark and silent, while those who remained, fled to the empty places within the orbits of the world's moons, until someone far wiser than they could make the deadly platforms safe again.

". . . paid, and laid, and then get drunk. Roj Malin, I'd have expected higher ambitions from a man like you!"

"Give me time to think of them, will you! I've lived through something I wouldn't have given a snowball's chance in hell, so at least give me peace to celebrate survival in my own way." He sniggered, the last trace of what might have been a sort of mild hysteria. "What about you? What do brain ships do when they survive the impossible?"

"Sometimes they sing," said Minerva, very softly. "We can, if we want to. Any voice you please. And sometimes they just smile, down in here where nobody can see."

"I can see."

"Where nobody can see, except very special people."

Roj sat quiet for a few seconds, looking beyond the casing of proof armor. Looking at her. "They confirm that last IFF/ID squirt. The escort's on its way. ETA less than five minutes." More quiet, for a second or two, and another hard look. "When we get back to Port, and debrief, what'll you do first? Rest? Relax?"

"Undress. I want this stuff outside me off in jig time. I want to be me again, not whatever fake the Fleet thinks I have to be."

"And afterward?"

"I want a brawn of my own. Someone I can work with and rely on. Someone I can trust." Silence. "Someone like you."

"Me? After everything that happened?"

"Yes."

"They'd never allow it."

"Do *you* want to?"

Roj stared at the viewscreen, and at the eerily ponderous grace of the four-dreadnought escort that was closing in to take them safely home. "They'll never allow it," he said again.

"Listen to him." The smile in Minerva's voice was stretching into a grin. He glanced at her, smiled in his turn, and then began to laugh at what he knew was coming, at the one statement that he would never question or deny. There were those who later claimed that both ship and crewman laughed all the way back to Port.

"Roj—try it again. Trust me . . . ."

INTERLUDE

A circuit tracer from Toledo was just about to spin the Nebula wheel to determine her prize for successfully naming Tau Ceti as the location of Port when Galaxy Guess was interrupted for a special announcement.

As the Fleet eagle began to fill the screen, millions of viewers, recalling their last announcement three months earlier, braced themselves. Most relaxed when the now-smiling face of Admiral of the Blue, Tor Doherty, appeared. The Fleet brass only casted in person when there was good news.

"I am happy to announce," the big officer begin, "a smashing Fleet victory over superior Khalian forces." The former star slugball player paused as if awaiting applause.

"Alerted by settlers, the Fleet was able to act decisively to crush this latest Khalian incursion before it could strike a single planet. Facing enemy ships of unprecedented size, we have won a complete victory. Experts view this as a true turning point. . . ."

BATTLE OFF DEAD STAR 31
by E. Gary Gygax

PROLOGUE

"ALL HANDS TO BATTLE STATIONS . . . ALL HANDS
TO BATTLE STATIONS."

The voice was loud but as emotionless as the insistent
pe-beep, pe-beep, pe-beep coming from the computer system of
the big ship. For all I knew it might have been the computer
ordering all hands. It really didn't make any difference one way
or the other.

"General?" It was Major Brady sounding uncertain.

"Just like the drills, Doug," I said with a little smile to
bolster him a bit. "Get your crews into the hangar lock and
stand by. You'll probably have to wait, but hurry up now!"

"Aye, aye, sir."

"And, Major, I wish I were going out with you. Good luck!"

Brady grinned at me then. "Me, too, sir. I'll nail a Weasel for
you." He snapped a salute and left.

The silly bastard meant it. I guess I did too. He and his men
were going to putting their lives on the line in minutes. Most of
them wouldn't return. Yet he was proud and happy to do it, and
I wished I could too. Anything was better than sitting helplessly
inside this lumbering tub . . . Anything? No, not considering
the last few months.

"The latest intelligence from Verge, sir."

I looked up from the hooded omni on my desk with a scowl.

86

The new lieutenant took that to mean I was angry at his interruption. "The orders were to bring them to the general—"

I didn't let him get any further. "Thank you, Lieutenant Haake. That will be all." He came to attention with a snap, uncertain, for my face was a mask. It wouldn't do to have everyone know what was really troubling me, even at the expense of causing personal, unnecessary anxiety in a fine young officer. Haake turned smartly and left. Soon the outer offices would be buzzing with the latest word. Stay away from the Old Man; he's as irritable as a rogue griscat today. Well, let them all think that. I'd have to let them in on what was happening soon enough. Until it was absolutely necessary, though, their attributing things to my well-known irritability and bad temper was fine.

In truth, I *was* irritable and bad tempered. Who wouldn't be, planted behind a desk as I was. That came from being *General* instead of Lieutenant Hohenstein. I didn't want to be commander of the Freeborn Marine Division, but after twenty years of service, the commandant, and the navy too for that matter, thought otherwise. I became General Franz Hohenstein, and that was that. No sympathy from Downing either. Colonel General Downing had been a field officer, too, my immediate superior in many an action against the Khalia, before being kicked upstairs himself. He probably wanted to be back aboard a ship as badly as I. Feeling small satisfaction at that thought, I gritted my teeth and went back to work. The Independent Confederation of Planets had been formed only fourteen years back. That was seven years after Freeborn had withdrawn from the Alliance. Despite that, and its attendant hardships, we had more than managed. Besides Freeborn and the Brigit system with its various colonies of miners on the outer moons, there was Liberated, six light-years distant in the Teelmon system, and Verge, nine light-years off in the direction of deep space where our little arm of the Milky War petered out toward the intergalactic reaches.

You probably don't know much about us. Alliance history barely mentions Freeborn and so far ignores the Confederation entirely. Possibly it's due to the bureaucracy, no matter. Freeborn withdrew because we believe in the right to do as we choose. That includes building and maintaining our own space-craft and war craft to ensure our safety against pirates and raiders. Those are mainly Khalian vessels, but sometimes there are non-Weasel enemies out there too. Liberated is a newly settled planet with a thriving population of some five million already. Quite a few of them come from Freeborn, in fact, because it's getting pretty crowded here. With just over one hundred million square kilometers of habitable land and nearly forty million people, quite a few folks felt it was time to move to a less congested planet. The same is true of Verge. The Freeborn frontiersmen simply don't like having neighbors too near, so when things opened up on Ito IV, they moved in and renamed it Verge. They have about three million rugged individualists roaming around on three hundred million square kilometers of virgin land, and they think that's just about enough breathing space.

The Khalia and the Fleet's demands for punishment—because Freeborn dared to build its own warship—were the real causes of our secession from the Alliance. We blasted and took a Weasel *raider*-class vessel by boarding. That was considered contravention of law by the star admirals. So we declared our independence and they were too busy to care. Ever since, we've been careful to avoid confrontation with Fleet squadrons even as we cruise the spacelanes to keep off Khalia pirates and other hostile vessels.

The confederation now boasts a fair little navy. The single liner is somewhere between a Fleet battleship and a Khalian armored cruiser. The six big frigates which are the real heart of our navy stack up about on a par with the cruisers of the Fleet and are better than the Weasel's raider-class ships by far, just as our corvettes aren't as big as Fleet destroyers but more than a match for Khalian probes or Fleet scouts. For patrol we use cutter-class vessels. They're tough and fast. Good enough to take an armed merchant pirate, but probably in trouble in a duel with even the smallest *frigates* sent out by the Khalia. The liner *Retaliation* stays in Freeborn's space, but the rest of our navy is spread about evenly among the confederacy. That's because the Weasels don't discriminate when they decide to raid. Even the presence of *Retaliation*, in Brigit's system isn't due to selfishness on Freeborn's part. It guards the spaceyard on Oghma, the fifth planet out. There's a very special new spaceship being built there.

Under the circumstances, it wasn't surprising that the Confederation was liberal in its issuance of Letters of Marque. Privateers commissioned to attack the attackers, as it were.

Thus, the unofficial navy amounted to another twenty vessels of all sorts, from fast little yachts to corroded old freighters, buckets once used to haul ore. Such ships, along with the merchant craft which plied the routes to a score of neighboring systems and beyond provided us with a good intelligence gathering network. Information, computers, and native intelligence put the Confederation in a very good position *vis-à-vis* the Khalia, Fleet maneuvers, and just about everything else happening within fifty or so light-years of Brigit. You see, the only way to get data from one place to another is by courier vessel using FTL drive. Our navy could manage speeds in FTL at least as fast as the Weasels could; we stole the technology from them. Fleet scientists had the same information, but there were too many departments to clear things through, too many committees, and too much cost. I'd heard that the new hulls laid down were now sporting ungraded engines, but the Fleet was still slow. We had the designs weeks before they did. We acted on it months sooner.

The incursions of the Khalia were the reason why Confederation marines existed. Mostly, anyway. Freeborn supplies what amounted to a reinforced division, plus some special battalions, to the Confederacy. Liberated put up an understrength division as well. Verge, being different, supplies Verge Rangers. That regiment is a crack one, even if there is always rivalry, shall we say, between them and the marines, worse rivalry than between grunts from Freeborn and those from our other sister planet, Liberated.

When Weasel attacks in our sector became more regular than ever, we fed everything to Intelligence and they told us to start looking for a base nearby. In a few months we located the place the Khalia were using. There was a dead star between us and the Alliance's sectors, an out of the way place, actually, and not on the usual in or out spots for blinking from FTL to normal space drive. Look on your charts for Dead Star 31; you'll see it. There is a hydrogen cloud nearby and lots of asteroidlike debris in the vicinity. Naturally it was a place to be avoided, so it was just as natural for the Weasels to set up shop there. We spied on those alien buggers for a long, long time, and they never caught wise. The cutter nearest to their "secret" base actually used ancient signaling techniques to relay its messages. Would you believe a low-powered laser? It worked. Another disguised-as-an-asteroid cutter then radio-relayed on tight beam, and a series of courier boats took it from there. The chiefs of staff actually planned to hit the Khalian base, but then the Weasels sent in the big boys.

The Weasels never had *big* starships. Now they did. The Fleet calls these new Khalian ships dreadnoughts. They're bigger and more heavily gunned than the battleships of the Tau Ceti bunch. I'd be willing to bet that *Retaliation* could handle any one of the Weasels' new heavies, but not two. The Dead Star base suddenly sported a half-dozen of the huge warships. Our plans went out the window. Now we were *really* careful about our observation post. A score of Khalian warships within fifty light years of our three inadequately defended systems was grim. The Fleet wouldn't come to our aid. All we could do was hope the Weasels were where they were for some other purpose than making the Confederation part of history.

We'd already broken the Fleet codes, at least the older ones. They used tight-beam radio too, of course, to relay information from planetside to waiting couriers, vessels positioned to gather the intelligence messages and go into FTL immediately. Because of this, we picked up a good bit of their stuff. Now we were getting information from the Khalians too. It was credited to sheer luck when we managed to discover their cipher pattern and break their codes so quickly. I think it was a combination of what makes the folk of our confederacy so successful and the hand of some greater being. Who can say? In any event; the chiefs back at Patrick Henry on Freeborn were really placed between the rock and the proverbial hard place. The Weasels were about to fry far bigger fish than us. They were out to trap the whole of the Fleet in the sector!

In the great days of sail, enemy fleets groped about the seas, trying to find the other ships and fight. Actions were thus usually fought off some port city. Later, when aircraft and radio came into being, fleet actions were fought in more open waters, often without the combatants seeing each other's ships except via airplane or radar. Now we are back to the former situation. Spaceships travel faster than light, so communications are uncertain. Reports come in stating when and where the enemy has been spotted, and in what numbers. Then a squadron or task force, or whatever, is sent off in the direction which seems the most likely place the enemy will be. The alternative is for you to lie outside an enemy starport and wait for his ships to come home.

The Weasels had worked it out pretty carefully. They became active in the general area of the Confederation. They don't know that we aren't a part of the Alliance. Khalian raids upon Alliance territory were sufficient to draw a larger and larger number of vessels from Tau Ceti Fleet Base anyway. Then they allowed intelligence to fall into the hands of the Fleet. That bit of information revealed the number of warships the Weasels had gathered in the area, where they were going, and what they planned to do. The bait was a fair sized one: three of the new dreadnoughts, a dozen of their big armored cruisers, and the usual school of smaller craft. It was to be a full-scale attack on a major planet of the Alliance as far as the Fleet knew. Of course they took the bait and were putting together a force to engage and destroy the Khalian vessels. Because of our own information gathering, we knew that the Fleet force was composed of nine battleships, two of the new battlecruisers just out of the spaceyards, and sufficient cruisers, destroyers, and scouts to manage their counterparts in the Weasels' armada. They were really anxious to knock out those new Khalian heavies. The Fleet wasn't worried, and I personally think that they could have pulled it off. All except for the Weasels' ambushing force, that is.

The squadrons at the Dead Star 31 base were their ace in the hole. As soon as the Tau Ceti boys started grappling and moving for position, the Weasels would spring the trap. The other dreadnoughts, plus a few light vessels, would come in by surprise. Then there would be one of the bigger Khalian dreadnoughts for each of the Fleet's battleships, with enough armored cruisers left to handle the rest of the Alliance's navy there and to spare a heavy cruiser to assist each of their main starships. It would be a debacle, and the whole sector would be laid open to whatever the Weasels cared to do for the next few months . . . or forever!

The comm buzzed. "Another urgent message for you, General."

"Put it through, Lieutenant."

"Yes, sir. Scrambler omni line, General."

"I see. . . ." I hastened to switch from memory to incoming on my unit. There was my old friend Colonel General Downing. Under the circumstances I forgot about old times and greeted him formally as commandant and my direct superior. He didn't bother with such trappings.

"Haul ass over here, Franz." Still the same old Chauncy after all.

It was evident that he wasn't in his own office. "Where's here?" I asked with a smile.

"Oh, sorry! I'm at the Grand Pavilion. Get here immediately."

A quarter of an hour later I was there. So were a lot of others. The chiefs of staff, commandants of marines and planetary guard, and minister of defense were seated round a long table. In a few minutes a dozen admirals and generals joined the throng.

"Gentlemen, this is an official meeting," Minister of Defense Rudilsky said. "I am here to preside, but the matter is up to you. Each of you has been fully briefed on the situation. What is the Confederation going to do?"

That's the way things operate here. Once a course of action is decided upon, superior rank and reporting come into play. Until then, though, each of us is an equal citizen. Even as a mere general, I could vote along with any other officer at the table. The various officers spoke in turn. Soon it became evident that there was a strong current of anti-Alliance feeling running through the group. When Khalians fought the Fleet, the opinions went, then the Independent Confederation of Planets could only prosper. Admiral Schley objected, pointing out that the Alliance at worst left us on our own, while the Weasels were aggressively involved in all manner of things which brought grief to us.

"There won't be enough of either side to bother anyone for a long time after they get into action," opined Marshal Evereaux. Indefensible logic, but shared by Liberated and Verge alike. Finally it was my turn to speak.

"My boys just sort of go along for the ride, I guess," I quipped, "and I'm no expert on warships and naval tactics . . ." Laughter and a couple of jibes interrupted me there, for everyone at the table knew damned well that I had written a number of papers for the institute and was at work on a volume dealing with spacepower and its influence on events. "Okay," I continued after the room quieted down. "It isn't much of a matter either way. The only question we have before us is whether or not the Confederation jumps into the fight.''

"Risk our only means of defense to pull the Fleet's fat out of the fire? Not bloody likely!'' That was from Admiral Cunningham of Liberated. He got a murmur of approval from that.

"Your point is well taken, Ted,'' I said slowly. "There is something wrong with your logic, though. If the Tau Ceti bunch isn't around to counterbalance the Weasels, our navy just isn't big enough and strong enough to defend us. The Khalia can come in and gobble us up, one system at a time.''

"*Shotgun* is ready if the Weasels try that,'' Ted Cunningham said with pride. He was commander of that vessel.

"Fat lot of good one launcher, even a supership such as yours, Admiral, will be against a dozen capital ships.''

"You don't know that! I say that she'll be able to get in and deal with that many easily.''

We were about to get into hypothetical stuff now. "Shotgun'' was code name for the Confederation's secret weapon, the torpedo craft launcher *Hydra*. It was a huge starship designed to launch and recover a swarm of little boats while defending herself from enemy fire. The concept was certainly not new; it was that of Terra's ancient aircraft carrier moved ahead a few centuries with hyped-up FTL engines. *Hydra* launched her vessels while dropping back from FTL. The boats were then theoretically so close to their targets that it would be impossible for the enemy to react in time. Mines, missiles, and torpedos fired off, the little craft would hightail it back to the mother ship, be taken in quickly, and in minutes the launcher would drop back into FTL, jockeying for another pass. In tight situations, the launcher could get back into FTL sans boats, then come back for them later. The whole process relied on a refinement of the detectors used while in FTL drive. Moving thus, a vessel was blind to what was around it, but mass detectors prevented annihilation by impacting some planet or sun. Our scientists had worked up a version of this standard equipment which could give a readout on something as small as a destroyer, for instance, at a range long enough to be able to blink into normal space no more than five million kilometers from it, tops. At sublight speed of 200,000 kps, the launcher would match course with the enemy, the boats would be away, and the attack made in less than sixty seconds. Even the best of computer-operated defense systems, whether Khalian or Fleet, wasn't able to cope with such an unexpected attack as that. Later, maybe, after exposure and knowledge, there would be developments to counter our new weapon, but defense is always a game of catch-up.

"With all due respect, sir," I said slowly, "a hundred of the best attack boats can't manage more than four, possibly five, capital starships. That was pretty clear from the computer simulations. It takes from twenty to twenty-five of them against a single battleship to ensure they stop it."

"Simulation, hypothetical, worst case. . . . Nine are sufficient. My own staff has run countless exercises and checked them out—"

"And you always used best case," I countered.

Now Admiral Vandervoort chimed in. "So what is your point, *General* Hohenstein?"

"There are several, and one conclusion. The points are: One, we have to make certain that the Khalia don't win, because the Weasels will then hit our systems. Two, we can't take on a whole fleet of dreadnoughts, and we know that if the aliens win, they'll do space repairs and come in again for seconds. Three, we have the golden opportunity to hit the Weasels by surprize while they're lying in ambush for the Fleet, and taking out just four of the Khalian dreadnoughts will balance the contest between them and the Alliance's navy. Four, with a fairly even battle it won't matter which side wins, for it will be a Pyrrhic victory—won't matter that is, except that it's fellow humans against those bloody bastard Khalia. Five, we have to help other humans, even if it is the Fleet. Six, the Confederation will pick up invaluable prizes in the action, and we all know that even one salvagable dreadnought hull would bring us into position to convert it into a launcher. Think of three or four such prizes in tow! Seven, my men, and the marines and rangers under General Flaherty and Colonel Arlove too, of course, can board and take those Weasel ships if the navy gives them the opportunity to."

"Seven points well spoken," the commandant said. That could be expected, after all; but there was similar agreement from most of the others present, including the minister of defense. He asked, "And that brings up your conclusion, General Hohenstein—"

"What if the Tau Ceti boys decide to attack us afterward?" interjected the florid-faced Admiral Vandervoort. He was definitely a liner man, with little faith in the capabilities of a launch vessel. "They may just decide to get rid of another threat, especially if the torpedo craft are as effective as you seem to think!"

Ted Cunningham spoke up then. "If we do as Franz suggests and hit four of the Khalian heavies, that leaves the Weasels with a bigger force than the Fleet's, pretty fair superiority. The Tau Ceti boys won't be in any position to do more than limp home, if they win. More likely, the Fleet'll have to break off the action and retreat. It'll be the Weasels we'll have to worry about then."

"My conclusion exactly, gentlemen. Ted is right. That's why I think our whole navy will have to engage the Khalia as soon as the torpedo craft have done their work. *Retaliation* and one of the frigates have to take on one of the remaining dreadnoughts; three frigates alone on the other, and the remaining frigate and the corvettes keep the light stuff of the Weasels busy until the bigger Khalian ships are wasted." I paused, and there was an unkind comment about grunt generals writing space tactics for the navy. "I went to the same academy you did, Admiral. I get refresher courses, study, and have been on fighting bridges during the heat of action."

"Only you don't command," Vandervoort said loudly.

"Not the vessel, only the men aboard who have to go out and take the enemy where they are—starship or planetside. If we want to be rid of Weasels, help humans to survive, and come out of it all with prizes in tow, there is only one course to chart." That was all there was for me to say, and I sat down.

After the rest had their say, we put it to a vote. Nineteen were present. Nine were for, nine against. The minister of defense cast the deciding vote in favor of my plan. Naturally, once it was decided, all present were fully committed to developing it into a successful one. Staffs were assembled, and work on a formal plan was begun immediately. We had only a few weeks to put it all together and strike. Estimated collision time between the Fleet task force and the Khalia was between three and five weeks away. We had to be ready to move the moment the Tau Ceti ships disappeared in search of their foe.

As the plan was being drafted and refined, all leave was

cancelled, and reservists were called up to bring every vessel in the Confederation's fleet to full complement, Freeborn's and Liberated's, too. They took off for the vicinity of the Ito system where they would rendezvous to form a united fleet. *Hydra,* with me and a bunch of my own boys inside her bulbous hull, was lead starship.

"Welcome aboard, General."

"Compliments, Admiral," I replied.

Ted Cunningham grinned. "You got your way, and I got mine, too, sort of."

"That's true, and it gives my troops a chance to show their mettle in a new way." I was referring to the company of torpedo vessel pilots and crews aboard, *marine* pilots and crews, that is. Pilot, defensive systems, man and weapons chief were all the crew that an STC carried. The admiral had talked up things so much that the chiefs had decided to allow him to launch twice. There were twenty back-up craft aboard. The *Hydra* would come in, launch, and then drop back into FTL while it readied its second force. Cunningham would bring the big starship back again just as the rest of the ships were closing on the Khalian vessels. The extra twenty STCs would be launched into the fray, and then *Hydra* would sit around waiting for its hornets to come back to the hive, so to speak.

"How about a bet between us on which pilots get a better hits ratio, mine or yours?"

"Too grim, Ted. Both are nothing but green kids. I want 'em all to get back alive."

"I take your point, Franz," the dark-skinned starman said, "but you and I both know there'll be losses. If those young men do their duty, the enemy will suffer, but a lot of STCs won't be coming back here. I just thought a little competition might help us both take our minds off that and put them where good officers' thoughts should be—engaging and destroying the enemy."

I cocked an eyebrow and gave my head a little shake. "History & Mission briefing comes next. . . . You're right, though, you space buzzard. A month's pay on my boys, even odds?"

"You've got it."

* * *

Two days later we were on a station a few million kilometers from the secret Khalian force. Now it was all a matter of timing and good aim. Our cutters would come soon, carrying word that the Fleet task force had left in FTL mode to seek out the Weasels. We were faster than they were, so that would give us the time we needed to get ready for battle ourselves. We knew where the Khalia were heading, and it was necessary for us to arrive there at just about the same time. If we were early, then there'd be no launching of STCs—and the Confederation's navy would be no more! If we came too late, the Weasels would be mixing it up with the Fleet's ships, and we'd be unable to carry out an effective attack. In strictly ship-to-ship terms, our little navy wouldn't have much effect, I supposed. Perhaps our being there would enable the Fleet to withdraw without crippling losses, but our own ships would take a beating in the process. That we certainly couldn't afford, not just to save some star admiral's bacon.

Then again, too late was better than too early. If the Tau Ceti ships pulled off without severe losses, that is. They would hang around the Khalia awaiting reinforcements, and the alien combined fleet wouldn't dare risk diversions under those circumstances. The Weasels would either beat a retreat or else see about their own reinforcements. It wasn't likely either side wanted an even slugging match. Then one or the other would lose its fleet in being. The Khalia certainly had an empire of sorts, just as the Fleet had to be around to hold the Alliance together. Perhaps the Weasels had weasels of their own to raid 'em. Too early, too late, too nothing. We just had to be on time!

Because the *Hydra* had the best sensors, she led the way. She dropped back into normal space and shot out a beacon buoy even as the crew maneuvered the ship into the proper position and spun her so that the launch tubes would come on line. Every three seconds and another wave of twenty little STCs were sent arrowing toward the black hulks which were the Khalian dreadnoughts. The whole process was over in thirty seconds, and the *Hydra* was back into FTL under a minute later. Just before that happened, I saw the little specks of the rest of our ships suddenly appearing on the screen. Too bad.

The *Hydra* had come in about a million kilometers too far out. There'd be some long-range exchanges after all.

My personal intercom clicked, and I switched to command channel.

"Care to join me on the quarterdeck, General?" Cunningham had a fine sense of the anachronistic.

"I'll stay here with my men, thanks, Ted. As soon as they go to quarters, though, I'll take you up on your offer." In just a couple of minutes the second call to battle stations sounded, and Major Brady, CO of the marine spacecraft teams, led the ten crews to their boats. I watched them seal up, then headed for the forward elevator.

"Permission to come on deck, Admiral."

"Permission granted, General. Just take a spare seat and lock in. We're dropping out again in . . . forty-four seconds now."

A blur, then streaks, and suddenly the whole of space appeared on the huge viewscreen. Magnification brought what was happening up close. When we had first come into the space where the two forces were moving to engage, the Khalian main body had been in line ahead, a division of their supercruisers fore and aft the line of three lumbering dreadnoughts. A half-dozen or more smaller vessels were scattered around the line in a screening formation. It appeared to be a perfect opportunity, and the commander of the Fleet task force had taken it thus. His array was arrowing toward the Khalia in five columns. On the far right and far left of the formation were flotillas of destroyers led by the small cruisers from Tau Ceti. The right-hand group was echeloned so as to cover any move which would involve a turn of the Weasel line ahead to hook to their left to hit the flank or rear of the Fleet vessels. The other flotilla was in line with the three main columns moving to attack. Farthest right of these heavies was a division of four of the Fleet's grim battlewagons. Next to it, in the virtual center of the formation, was a division of five more of these big starships. The first four were evidently meant to tear up the leading cruisers, while the five battleships to their left hit the three dreadnoughts. There was also a column of smaller ships, the two new battlecruisers, and a pair of the Fleet's heavy cruisers trailing them, meaning to mix it up with the trailing divison of six Khalian attack cruisers.

It was a very sound bit of tactics. The right-most divison of four of the Fleet's battleships would savage the attack cruisers in the Weasels' lead with ease. The flotilla echeloned rearward would then run in and finish cripples, while one or more of the big ships turned to aid the center division of five battleships, which would by then be locked in combat with the dread-noughts. That would give the Fleet at least two-to-one on the Khalian big boys, and the Weasels could kiss it good-bye. The action at the tail of the line would be the hottest for the Tau Ceti bunch, no doubt. There the match was about even, and both sides would take losses. No matter. With the head stopped and lopped off, there would be plenty of time to work on the mid-dle and then get back to the tail to make the action a defeat in detail.

That had been a few minutes earlier. Of course the star admiral of the White commanding the task force about to engage the Khalian fleet was unaware of what else I had seen as the *Hydra* blinked in and out. Moving at full speed in line ahead was another formation of Weasel ships. A division of six dreadnoughts was coming up so as to be in position behind the attacking columnns of Alliance vessels. They would be the hammer for the anvil of the other line of Khalia. They had a flotilla of screening raiders with them, but these attack destroy-ers were really along for the ride and the mop-up after the main action. The three football-like raiders were in line ahead to the left flank and rear of the dreadnoughts, already beginning to maneuver off toward the left so as to catch the Tau Ceti boys' smaller destroyers.

What had happened with our STCs in the interval? Now we'd know. All sorts of alarms were hooting and wailing, and the com channels were going crazy. Nonetheless, the *Hydra* spun and the last twenty of our little boats were launched in two waves of ten—marine first, naval second. It was no wonder that the ship and its crew were making a bedlam of it. We'd come into normal space between the two columns of Khalia hot-rocketing it to the engagement. Streaks and flashes from plasma cannons and exploding missiles showed that there must still be some of the STCs in action against the six dreadnoughts. No! There was the whole of the Confederation's navy swinging to cut ahead of the Khalian column in a classic in a classic T-crossing maneuver. Then I got a good look at the division of big Weasel battlewagons. There were only three in proper order. Two others were straggling and out of position, and way back was the sixth, dead in space.

"Bravo niner, you just put that one into the bastard's ear!" It was one of my boys cheering. I'd switched to their com channel, and the STCs' crews were chattering like a band of monkeys as they fought. About that time I saw one of the straggling dreadnoughts shimmer, and there was a sudden sun glow near its stern.

"Aww . . . shit," another voice cried over the channel. "Those bastards just got Charlie! Look it. That little streak of molten stuff is all that's—" Then there was a sudden silence, and I saw another tiny bright spot fade away on the viewscreen. I couldn't take more of that, so I turned my gaze to the duel going on between our lone capital ship and the four frigates supporting it.

Not much better viewing there. Just as I focused on that engagement, one of the frigates was bathed in a hellish fire and fell out of line. The leading dreadnought was taking a real pounding, though. Its screens were glowing where they were taking hits from missiles and cannons. Quite a few were getting through, too. I wondered when it would have to drop its defenses. Soon, I thought, and then you could scratch one Weasel battlewagon for sure. Already the *Retaliation* was switching its concentration of fire to the second Khalian dreadnought, leaving the lead vessel to be pounded by our big frigates. This wasn't so bad after all. The captain of our liner knew something I couldn't see, or else he'd never have redirected his fire. The first dreadnought began to glow, its outer hull incandescent forward. That was it for him!

The *Retaliation* was coming about, tacking so as to get into position to pass down the enemy column, her escort of three frigates following bravely. I didn't want to think about the pounding all five ships were taking from the Weasels' big vessels, the casualties mounting and damage sustained. Where were the other frigates? Then I saw them. It was crazy. The two other cruisers, along with our four corvettes, were coming into position on the other flank of the Weasels' dreadnought division, popping away at those big starships as if they could seriously harm them. They were supposed to be after the escorting raider-class vessels, not mixing it up with heavies!

"Wham-wham-wham!" The deck vibrated, and the air compression hurt my eardrums. We'd taken hits there for sure. I'd been so wrapped in watching the action elsewhere that I'd ignored the screens showing what was going on around the *Hydra*. Now I understood why the second squadron had gone in after the Khalian dreadnoughts. All three of the escorting raiders were well away from them and coming in after the *Hydra*. I was going to see firsthand just how accurate Ted was in his claims that his ship could fight as well as tote around STCs.

"Damage report."

"Starboard seventy-twos hit, sir. Two launch locks destroyed, three seriously damaged. Casualties not fully reported sir, but as soon as they're in I'll feed 'em to Myrtle." The officer reporting referred there to *Hydra*'s computer. The damned thing was near sentient, and I could understand the personification, especially since "her" voice wasn't very sonorous. . . .

"Launch those Stonewalls, Commander, and get those cannons into action!" Cunningham sounded angry. He had reason to be. We shouldn't have taken those hits. "What's wrong with Myrtle?"

"She's overloaded, Admiral. Trying to keep track of the STCs, the actions around, and handle all the rest of what's going on has slowed her down by a full second!"

That was heartening at least. There were still STCs out there, a lot of 'em in fact, or else the computer wouldn't be in trouble. Ted's instructions were simple enough. Manual override whenever a missileer officer or gunner felt like it. The *Hydra* immediately began humming and giving occasional lurches. Cannons and rockets were shot off; incoming stuff was being fired at or screened out. Her armament wasn't particularly heavy, but the *Hydra* had a lot of small stuff. I watched a whole flock of glittering specks impact on one of the Weasel raider-class destroyers, and another, and another. In a minute or two there wasn't a Khalian ship there anymore, although in the meantime the *Hydra* took more damage. It was going to be a rough go, but I was sure that Ted was right about his baby. The *Hydra* could take it—and hand a lot back too. The launcher was being conned around so as to head back our fleet. That was also where the STCs were.

Spaceships don't just stop dead when they've been put out of the fight. Velocity remains constant, of course, in near-frictionless conditions. Disabled craft are a handicap, though, so Fleet, Khalia, or Confederation SOP is to use retros and bring the disabled vessel to a halt so as to keep her out of harm's way and not interfere with those ships still in fighting trim. That applies only to the severely damaged craft, naturally, those ships virtually powerless to defend themselves any longer or get off any fire. Happily, I now saw that three of the Khalian dreadnoughts were in just such condition. No—make that four! The lead ship had just broken in two parts. That left only two of the Weasels' big boys. Then I got a look at our own losses and felt sick.

The *Retaliation* and a pair of our frigates were still in there slugging, although all three were battered. The squadron on the other flank of the Khalia was in worse trouble. Of the two cruisers and four corvettes which had been in line, only the last little destroyer and the tail-end frigate were still firing. How the corvette had managed to survive until now was in itself something of a miracle. Not only had those two survived, but they were closing on the dreadnoughts before my eyes! Then another of the Khalia went off course, and I could see the little flashes which indicated STCs in action. The dreadnought must have been caught by a cluster of stalker mines dropped earlier. Those deadly canisters would move toward any mass which didn't broadcast on a set frequency to warn them off. With their fifth battlewagon out of commission, the Weasels were just about finished.

Their raiders weren't about to have done with the *Hydra*, though. The exchanges of salvos and cannonry continued unabated, with the *Hydra* taking a whole lot more damage than any ship should. About half of her launch locks were out of commission now, as were the cannon blisters and missile ports. Ted had been a little overconfident about his baby after all. I began to wonder if he and I would be around to celebrate. There wasn't time to worry about that sort of crap, though. I actually had a function other than supercargo. Cunningham was frantic, trying to deal with the attacking heavy destroyers while having to begin the process of recovering his boats on the side away from the action. Only a handful were now trying to come home, but that was sufficient. The little STCs hadn't fuel or anything else for extended operations, and they had to be taken in soon.

The *Hydra* was moving into the fray, however, and it was time for me to act. "Admiral Cunningham, permission to launch boarding parties?"

"Take your boarding parties and—" Ted snapped his mouth shut, realizing that he was beginning to lose it. This was his first major action, too, and I understood. "Sorry, General Hohenstein. Commander Jensen is in charge of that. If he can get those longboats into a launching lock and get them away, without interrupting STC recovery, you have permission."

I hurried below to where the companies of my grunts were packed into the boarding craft, waiting their turn. Each stripped-down company occupied one of the so-called longboats. The boats were actually specially built boarding craft, complete with heavy-duty, short-range laser and nitroplast application arms. Flat-nosed and blocky, these were good for only unopposed approaches, which we had, almost. Four boats were still only enough for a single dreadnought. Then these tubs would have to head back to the *Hydra,* load fresh troops, and set out again. The rest of the boarding craft were scattered around among the other ships in the Confederation's little navy, and it wasn't likely that many of them would be able to get away. Maybe those from the *Retaliation* and just possibly a couple from the frigates . . . if any survived intact when the Khalia were finished. I was too busy with my own worries now. Colonel Keogh was going with the first wave, so I gave him final instructions and saw the four longboats off.

"Why's there so little incoming stuff?" I asked the launch officer.

Commander Jensen was sweaty-faced and grim, but at that he managed a weak smile. "I just heard the admiral say that the last of the Weasels' raiders had bought it, General," the fellow said with a lot of pride in his voice. "*Hydra* isn't a ship to mess with and has now proved it!"

I bit my tongue, not mentioning the terrible pounding we'd taken in the process of getting rid of what amounted to only a trio of upgraded destroyers. "I'll be damned, Commander," I grinned in reply, then I was all military again. "The next companies of marine boarders will be assembling here in a couple of minutes, Mr. Jensen. Tell my officers where to stow their men so that they don't get in your way until the longboats return."

"Aye, aye, sir. I'll keep those gr— your troops safe and sound until the boats are ready for a second wave, General. Sorry we couldn't manage more than four, but . . ."

"Understood, Commander," I said, half turning to head back to the fighting bridge.

"Pardon, sir, but I did want to say that you marines are all right."

"Eh? What do you mean, Commander?"

"It was your bunch that got the fourth Weasel big boy, General; but the cost . . ." He trailed off, seeing my expression.

"I hadn't picked that up, Mr. Jensen, what with all that's going on."

"Oh. . . . Sorry, sir. I just heard myself, actually. We just took in the only remaining STCs, sir. Only three of your crews came back."

I turned without a word and left, making my way forward and above with a dragging step. My feet felt as heavy as my heart. This was a bitter victory. Still, it was a victory, no doubt. That was evident from the faces, the voices, and the viewscreens on the bridge. Ted Cunningham was too busy to notice me when I returned, so I slipped back into my seat without formalities. Donning the com gear, I switched through the various channels as I looked around to see the results of the action on the many screens of the big compartment.

The *Retaliation* had locked herself to the single active Khalian dreadnought. There would be no need for boarding by longboat there. I wondered how the Liberated Marine Division units who made up her marine complement would do in the ensuing melee. The 2nd Division was a tough lot. What price the Weasels would make them pay was the only question. The *Hydra* was limping toward the liner to join the pair of covering frigates with her. The bold little corvette and its frigate companion were amidst the others of their group. They were going to render assistance to their disabled comrades. Some of the damaged ships could be jury-rigged and operational again in a few hours, especially if they had spare parts and help from their more fortunate sister vessels. Some were expanding clouds of radioactive gas.

"Longboats returning, General. Permission to scrub the next wave of boarders and use them for STC crew rescue, sir." Jensen's tone was perfunctory, as if he was certain that there was no question of the matter.

"Permission denied, Commander. There's a Weasel dread-nought out there, and it's our duty to see that she's boarded and taken as a prize . . . survivors will have to wait."

"But they have only an hour's oxygen at best, General. Your own—"

"That'll do, Mr. Jensen. Follow orders."

"Aye, aye, sir!" Commander Jensen said with a grim face. He began issuing orders over the communications band assigned to grunt work. In minutes the second wave would be off, so I scanned the screens quickly to assess what was happening.

The *Hydra* was moving in a slow circle which took her through the areas where the first and second groups of STCs had been launched. All operational boats had been recovered, but there was still the likelihood that amidst the debris littering space here, there were living crewmen awaiting rescue. Only a pair of tiny rescue craft was available. But they gave the poor beggars drifting out there at least a glimmer of hope.

There was virtually no firing in the immediate sector. The action here had changed from missile and cannon to close-quarters and boarding. Everywhere I looked I saw Confederation ships locked against Khalian vessels, or else assisting their own. We had met the enemy and they were ours. What about the battle between the second bunch of Weasels and the Tau Ceti task force? It took only a second to get that picture on a screen. The two groups were all mixed up, and I could see occasional flashes and eye-searing streaks there. Some firing was still go-ing on, but the action was in its last stages. I couldn't be sure, but I thought that the Fleet had managed to do what it had set out to accomplish. Of course they wouldn't have without our jumping the ambushing force of Khalians, but what the hell.

"Ten seconds to longboat launching," Jensen informed me.

"Belay that, Commander! I'll be going in with the second group, and I'll need thirty seconds to get aboard."

"But—"

"No buts, Commander. My authority, and my responsibility," I snapped. Then I was out of there and heading for the stubby little boats. The grunts gave a cheer when I came aboard, but the spacer crewmen seemed uncertain. A very junior lieutenant seemed about to pipe up, so I tossed a salute. As soon as he returned it, I said, "Very good, Lieutenant. As you were." Then; "Carry on, Cox'n. Get this bucket on over to the Weasels' ship so we can do our duty." That was that.

Every boarding operation was one with a mixed crew involved. The marines went there to eliminate enemy resistance, the spacers to get the vessel boarded operational and underway. Prize crews were of necessity skimpy and makeshift groups.

I was webbed in and watching the forward viewscreen as the longboat sailed out and headed for the drifting Khalian dreadnought. It didn't take very long at all for us to match velocities, close, and lock to that leviathan. I felt like a flea on a rack bull's ass, let me tell you. Size alone was intimidating enough, but the vivid lines from the tertiary laser turrets of the dreadnought coming at us just moments before had generated a pint of palm-sweat on the way in.

We burned a lock open. The longboat was glued fast, and for the next minute or two the nyloplast foam would make an airtight way between us and the Weasel battlewagon. Once we were all inside the enemy, the same stuff would be used to seal us inside, the longboat would burn herself free, and we would be totally on our own.

"Let's kick some butt!" It was the NCO in charge of the unit, a grizzled old hand who had been with me in my very first action. As I looked on, he gave me a tense nod, saying, "We'll take 'em out, General. Don't worry!"

He had misinterpreted my expression, but I only said, "Thank you, First Sergeant McDonnel. I never expected otherwise." In fact, my concern was elsewhere. With an effort I cleared it from my mind and blanked my face. The marines were already plunging into the interior of the Khalian dreadnought, armed spacers following hard on their heels. As befitting one of my rank, I brought up the rear. Bah!

The action was removed from me thereafter. I picked it up on the comband and that was it. We were in trouble. The Weasels had lost their drive and their main armament, but not many of those furry sons of bitches had bought it in the process. My men were taking heavy losses, and their advance had been halted after gaining only a toehold on a couple of decks. I hated to do it, but I had to: "Get on that communicator, Ensign, and get us some reinforcements fast!" He beamed the message out as if his life depended upon it. It did. It was touch and go for longer than I cared to think about; then the frigate *Frontiersman* locked on, and a swarm of wild rangers poured out of her hold. It was still a murderous fight, but from that point on it was all over for the Weasels. As usual, not one of the Khalia surrendered. That was just fine. Something unusual happened, too. Ever since that battle there in the Khalian dreadnought, no Freeborn marine has ever said anything disparaging about Verge rangers—at least not within earshot of any veteran of the Battle Off Dead Star 31, that is.

The prize crew was getting the captured dreadnought into operational mode, so I hitched a ride to the *Hydra* on the Verger corvette. When I got to the big compartment where all of us brass were assembled, there was a new feeling evident. The air was supercharged with it. We had come into the battle as a disparate collection assembled under a common banner. Now the Confederation was truly an entity. The Khalia had welded us into a solid unit.

A staff officer was giving the group a rundown on the battle between the Fleet task force and the Khalian main body. As I had thought, the Tau Ceti bunch were more than good enough sailors to handle the Weasels. They'd blasted half of the Khalia to atoms and routed the rest. In the process the Fleet had managed to grab a half-wrecked dreadnought, a pair of the big armored cruisers, and a Weasel attack destroyer. The signals flashing around the force from Tau Ceti had been filled to the brim with self-congratulations. Then somebody there got wind of what the Confederation's navy had pulled off. That news made the flames die in their tubes pretty quickly. We'd taken three of the Khalian monsters, had a fourth one, mostly wrecked in tractors, and had also managed to capture one of the three raider-class destroyers, too. In the process two of our frigates and three of the corvettes were lost. There wasn't a single vessel in our fleet that wasn't battered. Despite this, it wasn't a Pyrrhic victory . . . unless.

"Message from Star Admiral Duane of the Fleet." That sent a chill down my spine. The Alliance didn't recognize us as a political entity. Naturally, the officers of the Fleet, who liked us even less, had a policy of regarding the Confederation's naval force as a collection of pirates. According to their standing orders, the Tau Ceti boys would now be obliged to demand we surrender our prizes, if not our own vessels, to their authority. We were outside Confederation limits.

The old man growled. "Patch it through to the main screen, Captain. This is something we all have to experience." It was damned obvious that he was prepared for the worst.

The dark face and hard eyes of Admiral Duane were suddenly before us all, about ten times life size. The thin lips opened, and the star admiral said, "Well done, Galactic Admiral Weygard." There was a rush of expelled breaths at those words. The commander of the Fleet task force wasn't finished, however. Could there be more? You bet. "I'm requesting permission to come aboard your flagship, Admiral, for a conference . . ."

"That you have, Admiral Duane, that you have," the old man said without a flicker of expression. "We are ready when you are."

I was on hand less than an hour later when the group of Fleet brass was piped aboard the *Hydra* with full ceremony. It was a banner event indeed. What Duane was risking by paying this call was incredible, but I don't know anyone who has ever said that the *combat* officers of the Fleet weren't iron men. After formal exchanges, we all sat down and did some hard talking.

"Congratulations on your victory, Admiral," the old man said with sincerity.

"It was a good engagement," Admiral Duane replied, "but the scope of our victory can't compare with your own, sir," he added. "It is also evident that my force would have suffered a crushing defeat had not your own intervened."

"Well . . ." Admiral Weygard let the rest go unsaid.

The Fleet's task force commander nodded. "I've already dispatched a preliminary report to Tau Ceti. There's a lot of unusual things about this action which HQ will have to investigate and explain. Just how your ships just happened to be here at the right time and place, for instance." The Old Man had to grin hugely at that, and Duane returned a somewhat wan smile. "It is fortunate that there were no hostile 'pirates' on hand—only a very fine navy!"

"Thank you, Star Admiral."

"No more than plain truth, Galactic Admiral."

That sort of exchange went on for a little while, but my attention was distracted. I'd been surreptitiously listening to the rescue band all the time. There were still boats cruising the vicinity, sweeping for survivors, recovering bodies, sorting through the flotsam and jetsam of the battle for important bits of wreckage. Excited voices had caught my ear. Another crew from a blasted STC had been recovered. I excused myself quietly and left, hitting the double as soon as I passed the hatch and was out of sight in the companionway. Startled naval personnel hastened to get the hell out of the way of a running marine general. I would have laughed, only I was too sick inside.

"Who did they recover, Corpsman?" I asked.

"Three grunts from one of their TCs," he said, then turned to see whom he was answering. He nearly fell apart when he caught sight of me, came to attention, and saluted with ashen face. "Sir!"

I didn't bother with any of it. "Names?" I demanded. He didn't know, but told me that only two of the three were still alive. I went past him without another word.

Karl had lost an arm. It was his right one, in fact. That was bad, but a whole lot better than dead. Prosthetics would have a computer-linked electromechanical limb on him in a few weeks. Not only would it be nearly indistinguishable from a flesh-and-blood arm, but it would operate a whole lot more efficiently. I know because I have an earlier model leg which works just fine. He was in sick bay but conscious. "Nice to have you aboard, Karl."

He managed a faint grin. "Thanks, Dad. It's sure good to be here. Have you seen Harry and Juker?"

"Thought I'd check in on you first, if that's all right with you . . ." I trailed off because Karl was asleep. They'd surely injected him with enough narcotics to have him stay that way until surgery was well behind. The arm of his escape suit had been shredded, and self-sealants alone had saved him from instant death in space. The boy deserved a little rest. Boy? He was a graduate officer and had a pregnant wife back on Freeborn. I was getting *old*.

After stopping by to check on Juker, the other survivor from my son's crew, I hastened back to the conference. It was all over, and the Tau Ceti brass were on their way back to their ships when I arrived. I thought I'd come in unobtrusively, but there was a cheer when I sat down. Backslappings and hand pumpings concluded, someone broke out a real bottle of genuine bourbon whiskey. I mean Kentucky sour mash. We all toasted to the victory, and I drank my share—both for the boarding actions and for the fact that Karl had hit the Weasels and lived to tell about it.

The *Hydra* had launched one hundred twenty STCs. Sixty-three came back more or less intact. Five more were recovered with crews alive and boat salvageable. Sixteen more crews—or surviving crewmen equaling that number—were rescued. All told, about one-half of the boats had been lost, with crew losses at one-third. That was a terrible price. Losing almost half the STCs was negligible. The little vessels were relatively cheap and easily manufactured. The lives of their crews were another matter. Analysis turned up the fact that the *Hydra*'s STCs had accounted for three of the Khalian dreadnoughts. You didn't need a twenty-to-one ratio at all. Double it and add a lot of luck. Also, add more shielding to *launchers* and up-gun them. The *Hydra* had taken too much punishment from light spacecraft. Ted Cunningham was jubilant on the one hand, chastened on the other. I commiserated as much as possible. Even winning my bet was no joy. Marine losses in the boardings had been heavy. That was expected. Thanks to the Vergers, the actual casualty rate had been a bit lower than anticipated. Somehow, now that it was all over, I thought it was worth it. The Khalia had done us a favor.

Without their alien menace, there probably would have been shooting between us and the Fleet, later if not sooner. Star Admiral Duane would probably be in retirement sooner than I could sing the Alliance anthem, but his courageous gesture, his acknowledgment of the Confederacy's crucial part in the victory over the Khalia, spelled certain détente, at worst, between the Fleet and our navy. Men killing men in a major war could be ruled out in this sector of the galaxy for a decade or two, at least. That wasn't an insignificant achievement.

"Isn't that the *General Hohenstein?*"

"Home for the duration, Ensign," the scarred bo'sun's laconic answer came.

"She's fitted out from the hulk of a captured Khalian dreadnought, captured four years back at Dead Star 31 you know," the newly commissioned pilot said seriously to the spacer who was guiding the launch toward the vast starship. "They rebuilt her as a launcher because we don't need more than four liners in the navy. Now that Colonel General Hohenstein has been retired, they went back to some old tradition and named a ship after a dirtballer."

That made the veteran spacer lose it. "Look, sonny! I happened to be with the general when he boarded that Weasel dreadnought in '09. He spent more time in the chow lines of starships than you've put in since enlistment!"

The young ensign stared hard at the man, disbelief etched on his clean-shaven face. He shot the spacer a wry look and finished that with a little salute. "As you were, spacer. I stand corrected." Then he turned to watch the gigantic hulls of the new liners *Freeborn*, *Liberated*, and *Verge* drift past.

INTERLUDE

Broadcast from satellites, all one hundred and seventeen omni stations located on the earth are required to fill a twenty-four-hour schedule. This does not mean that every station is capable of programming each hour with interesting entertainment. Even over six hundred years worth of reruns has a limit. To fill the empty hours, many of the smaller stations use interviews with local personalities or heroes provided by Fleet Information.

"Tonight"—the slick-haired host of "Hoy's Hour" opened his show in a bored voice—"we have an officer who's rapidly becoming one of the most decorated men in the Fleet.

"Lieutenant, can you tell our listeners a bit about how you earned your last decoration?"

DOUBLE BLIND
by Janny Wurts

THE ENCOUNTER HAPPENED entirely without warning, in the thick of battle at Dead Star 31. As if by design, the Fleet's most junior lieutenant sat drumming his fingers at the controls of a state-of-the-art Fleet scoutship. Light from the monitors silvered his aristocratic profile, which expressed bitterness, frustration, and longing. The scout craft *Shearborn* was commissioned as a chaser, handily styled for concealment. She carried just two plasma canon. Hit and run, or follow and hide, had been her designer's intentions; "mop-up following engagement" read the bottom line in her battle orders. Last month, even yesterday, Commander Jensen had burned for a small part in the Alliance offensive at Dead Star 31. Today, while others were earning advancement and citations of valor for crippling the new Khalian dreadnoughts, he ached for action.

The firing studs so near his tapping fingers were dandy, except there were never going to be enough of them to satisfy the ambition that smoldered beneath the lieutenant's faultlessly correct Fleet bearing.

Across the cockpit, Harris slouched in the untidy gray of his pilot's coveralls. The wing patch at his shoulder crumpled under his fingers as he scratched himself, paused, then whistled as if at a woman. "What the hell?" His eyes widened, bright with the reflected flashes of battle off the analog screens.

Jensen spoke frostily from his crew chair. "Have you something to report?"

The pilot raised his eyebrows at the reprimand. His most insolent grin followed, as he banged a key for redefinition, then added in lilting admiration, "What the blazes is a tub-engined

113

private hauler doing blasting ass across a battle?''

Narrow-eyed and intense, Jensen regarded the offending speck on the screens, hedged now by flashes of plasma fire as she sliced through warring factions of Khalian and Fleet dreadnoughts. Overhead, the monitor on citizen's frequency blared a curse and a startled challenge; the tone of the officer who hailed the offending merchanter matched that of Harris, exactly.

As the civilian vessel continued to hurtle across the lines, a prickle of intuition touched Jensen. His gut went cold and his fingers clenched. "That's nobody's merchanter."

He keyed his board for more data. At once the craft's configuration flashed in design graph on his screen, ugly and ungainly as a toy assembled by a kid from unassuming bits of junk. Recognition struck Jensen like a blow to the vitals. He knew that craft, would remember her anywhere, from any angle, even to his dying moment. What could the *Marity* be doing carving a line across a Fleet offensive? It meant nothing but the worst sort of trouble; her captain happened to be the craftiest skip-runner in the Alliance.

Harris stared, captivated at the analog screens. "Bugger, that pilot's got the gift. Will you look at that evasion?"

Jensen needed no proof of the *Marity*'s maneuverability. He had personally experienced MacKenzie James's corkscrew style at the helm. Recall left the young officer sweating, not out of nerves but in memory of the aftermath, and a degrading depth of humility a proud man would kill to erase. Jensen reacted this time without thought. "Follow him."

Harris looked up from the screens. Blank with incomprehension, he said, *"What? Are you brain-shocked?* That guy's Weasel steaks in the making, mate. He's ducked into the Khalian lines.''

"I saw." Jensen turned his chair away. "I ordered a chase on that hauler. Section seven, bylaw four sixty two point zero, punishment for insubordination—''

"Courtmartial, followed by death without appeal at conviction. I know." Harris flipped off his pilot's beret and scratched his red-thatched scalp. The hair sprung in snarls beneath his fingers. Challenge lit his eyes, which were blue, and about as innocent as a thief's. "Your faith in my ability is a compliment, mate. What I'd kiss fish to guess, is what excuse you've got ready for old by-the-book and his-grandpa's-an-admiral Meier. Because if your joyride doesn't get us slagged by Weasels, the commodore's surely going to sling your ass on a plate. Remember section seven, bylaw four sixty five point one, punishment for disregard of standing battle orders and leaving assigned position?''

Jensen said nothing. He sat straight in his chair, his hair was like combed ebony, and his fingers trimmed short like a model's. Harris pressed switches and sequenced the *Shearborn*'s condenser coils into recharge for FTL. Then Jensen fussed with the adjustment of his chair belts, as Harris shrugged, punched up the gravity drive, and wrenched their little chaser out of station.

Immediate protest issued from the ship-to-ship com speaker mounted above the controls.

''Commodore Meier, howling for both your balls,'' surmised Harris. His fingers hesitated ever so slightly above the flight board.

''Just carry on!'' Jensen tripped a switch, and the angry voice of their superior became buried in background noise as the power banks gunned maximum thrust into the engines.

Harris grinned in that cocksure manner indigenous to pilots. Skill of his caliber was too scarce to waste; when the boom came down, he could count on some measure of immunity.

Against the wrath of irate brass, Junior Grade Lieutenant Michael Christopher Jensen, Jr., had only the far-reaching influence of his politician father; if, that was, Jensen senior chose to bend his public stance of calling no favors for his son. Harris preferred to believe that paternal sentiment would prevail as he spun the chaser in a neat turn and opened throttle.

The lieutenant in command knew otherwise. Heart pounding, Jensen expected that hell would freeze before his family would bail him out of trouble. It had been his father's imperiousness about carving his fortune on his own that had tangled his fate with that of the skip-runner captain in the first place. The *Shearborn*'s pursuit simply resumed unfinished business.

Vigorous protest arose right on schedule. Commodore Abe Meier's voice barked angrily on emergency interrupt. ''I'll have your officer's bars, boy, and a mark for desertion on your record that even God can't erase.''

Slammed back into his crew chair by inertia, Jensen laced his fingers to stop their shaking. No threat could make him reconsider; by now, their course was committed. Harris's cocky grin was gone, dissolved into a frown of sweaty concentration.

"Snarking game of live pool," the pilot murmured, and intently slapped a control.

The *Shearborn* veered, narrowly missing the expanding nebulosity of a plasma burst vessel. Debris pattered against the hull, and something clanged against the port gun housing. Then they were past and screaming a tortuous course through the flank of the Fleet offensive.

Jensen barely noted the glittering bursts of fire on the analog screens. Harris's wizardry at the helm escaped him utterly. He saw only the white streak that was the *Marity,* twisting now with the immunity of a miracle through the thick of the Khalian fleet. Dead Star lay beyond, a disk sharp as a compass cut through a backdrop of scattered stars. As if that dark body were a magnet, MacKenzie James steered his craft for the core.

"Crazy," Harris muttered over the scream of the gravity drive. "Slag his coils for sure, if he doesn't slow down to shed heat."

Jensen sweated with his uniform fastened to the chin. The course Mac James had chosen was too predictable not to be deliberate. The lieutenant reaffirmed his intent to capture the space pirate. No price was too great to see the *Marity*'s captain brought to justice. "Don't lose him, Harris."

The pilot half spun from the controls. "I won't melt down an engine for anybody's pleasure, *sir*. Not to capture the devil himself."

Jensen knew *Marity*'s master was the devil incarnate. His shout for Harris to continue was cut off by the rising wail of the proximity alarm.

The pilot shrugged, stabbed the switch to raise the chaser's shields. The alarms went silent. Seated like a stone image and half-lighted by the angry yellow glitter of the monitors, he continued his silence, clearly challenging his superior to pull rank.

Jensen refused argument. Ruled by the need to evade the fire of Fleet and foe alike, Harris could not abandon their new course all at once; and a slight change on the analog screens offered a telling reason why the *Shearborn* should continue.

Absorbed with planning an evasive maneuver, Harris took

longer to notice that the *Marity* appeared to be braking. If the skip-runner captain who flew her intended to slip pursuit, deceleration cost him the chance. Past Dead Star and the forefront of the battle lines, the Fleet chaser would be on him like a wasp.

Mac James never made stupid misjudgments.

Convinced that he witnessed the power lag as the *Marity* charged her coils for FTL, Jensen grinned with a candor normally kept hidden. The *Shearborn* was newly commissioned; fitted with gadgetry hot off the design boards, she was capable of following her targets through FTL. "Harris, close in tight. We're going to trace the *Marity*'s ion trail."

"Just a snarking minute!" The pilot shot a glare at his superior. Giving a skip-runner chase across a battle line was a lark he could boast of to buddies, a daredevil affirmation of skills that might bring the customary slap on the wrist for high jinks that tradition accorded a gifted pilot. Deserting the scene of a battle was another thing, a speed-class ticket to courtmartial and a firing squad. Left grouchy by the risks just taken, Harris ended with a gesture that brooked no argument. "Forget it, sonny."

Jensen's amusement vanished. His obsidian eyes never left the analog screen, where a tiny fleck of light winked into being. It blinked once, then steadied onto a vector that bent gently and matched course with the *Shearborn*. The lieutenant keyed for additional data and almost laughed outright in satisfaction. "We've picked up a stalker mine," he announced. Even his recalcitrant pilot must now bow to expediency; the only effective evasion was to transit to FTL before the missile closed.

Harris scanned the readout without alarm. "Stalker mine's a damned lousy reason to go AWOL, sir, when we carry the coded disarm frequency."

"For Fleet any offensive," Jensen responded. He sounded smug. "This one's manufactured by the Freeborn. Check your screen, pilot, only do it fast. If you hesitate, *Marity* escapes, and we get convicted posthumously."

Harris shot a withering glare, fingers flying over the controls. "What's Freeborn hardware doing crapping up this sector, anyway? It might just get us killed."

Jensen answered with a confidence born of ruthless networking. "Fleet intelligence scoped a Freeborn plot to slam the

Khalian rear wave. But the codes for rebel stalkers weren't part of the package.''

Harris cursed. Jensen's explanation made no sense whatever; since secession from the Alliance, the Freeborn were hostile to the Fleet. But dispute of the fine points made a fool's errand. The damnable fact remained: a stalker mine of enemy manufacture had locked onto the *Shearborn* as a target. Either Harris abetted Jensen's craziness and punched into FTL, or two million credits worth of chaser got cremated. The reasonable alternative was to commit desertion in pursuit of a recognized criminal, except that the pilot would need to fly a course like macramé to make transit before the stalker took the *Shearborn* out.

Harris tripped the controls with an attitude of reckless abandon. Spun hard against her limits, his spacecraft flexed and groaned under the stresses of centrifugal force. As a grade-one test pilot, Harris had survived a lot of mistakes; he had a sixth sense for gauging tolerances. The chaser might protest, might develop a stress shear or two, but her tail pins would stay tight as she twisted and spun to gain distance from the less maneuverable mine. Harris caressed the machinery, wooing the electronics as he would a lady; the wail of the alarms and the digital display showing the stalker's course of intercept made him itch, as if the hot breath of the hardware fanned the back of his neck.

Jensen followed only the skip-runner ship that drifted like a lopsided jewel at the rim of Dead Star's disk. Apparently nerveless, he cared for nothing beyond the moment when *Marity*'s image flashed and vanished from the analog screens.

By then *Shearborn* was barely inside the requisite radius for an ion trail fix, with the stalker closing fast.

A green sequence of numbers flooded the navigational screen. Harris waited a panicky moment for resolution of a course readout. When the figure stabilized, he hammered the lever down and blew a kiss in sheer relief. Never in life had he been happier to suffer the queer hesitation in continuity that marked the transit to FTL. He blinked, elated that no explosion had erased his existence. The next instant, triumph died, quenched by the realities of the moment. Harris unclipped his seat restraints and rounded angrily on his superior.

"Snarking hell, Jensen. You damned near got us roasted. You *knew* Freeborn stalkers were loose out there! For that I'd like to push your face in. I wonder if you understand how close we came to being ionized?''

Jensen swung his crew chair from the screens. His dark eyes showed not the slightest trace of regret. "Try to remember how close," he said. "If you lose *Marity* on me, that stalker mine will be the only excuse we have to offer at our defense briefing.''

"And may you shrivel in front of the ladies for that,'' snapped Harris. He wanted a drink, and a chance to take a leak in real gravity. What began as a lark had turned seriously sour; until the sensors signaled *Marity*'s transit from FTL, nothing remained but to wait and brood, because certainly no sane man was going to fathom the intentions of Lieutenant Jensen.

The transit lasted days. Harris slept, or banged about in the chaser's tiny galley unearthing the beer he had stashed where he swore no Fleet inspector would check, never mind that access to his cache took most of his off-watch time. He needed his comforts. A man couldn't get booze in detention; to Harris's thinking that was precisely where *Shearborn*'s hare-brained officers would be headed.

"Autolog won't lie for us,'' he carped when the lieutenant in command crossed paths with him at meal time.

Jensen refused to debate.

Harris parked the heels of his boots on the table and cradled his mug, which untruthfully read COFFEE, between his knees. But even a barbarity of this magnitude provoked no reaction. Nettled by the lieutenant's secretive silence, the pilot added, "A leap this long could send us clear to Halpern's.'' Which was about as far from Khalian raid sites as a ship could go, and stay within charted Alliance space. "You better think up a very fancy alibi.''

Jensen sat down opposite, drank his orange juice in chilly stillness. His uniform looked as if he had just stepped off parade. No stubble shadowed his chin. Just when had he taken time to groom, Harris wondered. Since the jump to FTL, the man had done little else but pace before the analog's blank screen, brooding over the unguessable motives of *Marity*'s skip-runner captain.

Despite such fanatical vigilance, the tracking alarm caught *Shearborn*'s crew of two napping. Harris shambled from his bunk, stretching like a bear and complaining of a hangover. As always, he slept in his uniform. Jensen had not. He bolted without ceremony from his berth, clad in fleur-de-lis pajamas that looked like they had been starched with his uniforms.

"You guessed right," he announced when Harris reached the bridge. "*Marity* broke light speed in Halpern's Sector." He flicked irritably at his uncombed hair and killed the FTL drives. The *Shearborn* abruptly ended transit, underwent that unnerving blurring of edges that heralded return to analog navigation.

Harris winced as his hangover flared in sympathy. Once reality stabilized, he laid his cheek against the cowling of the companionway and muttered something concerning martyrs and zealously sober commanders.

Jensen ignored the comment, fingers drumming impatience while the sensors assimilated data and the screens flashed to life.

Visual display revealed the dim red disk of a dwarf star, a strangling haze of interstellar dust, and no immediate reason for *Marity*'s choice of destination. Jensen chewed his lip. "Why should a planetless star in Halpern's interest MacKenzie James?"

Harris pitched himself into the pilot's chair, his coveralls halfway unfastened. He studied the readouts, then shot his companion a look of surprise. "That's Cassix's star." The lieutenant continued to look blank, which proved to a certainty that his source network had not included scientists. Harris explained. "Any test pilot knows. That's the site of Fleet's classified orbital R&D lab—the deep-space flight-and-weapons division, where the fancy new gadgetry gets prototyped. Security like a church vault, though. A skip-runner shouldn't be able to get close."

But along with gunrunning, MacKenzie James's speciality was trafficking military secrets; he'd stolen records from Fleet Base once and gotten away clean. Uncomfortably, Jensen considered implications. The skip-runner was a dangerously subtle man. If the *Shearborn*'s crew caught him attempting a raid upon the Cassix base, they would instantly become heroes.

Jensen thought quickly. "Where's *Marity?* Have we still got a fix on her?"

Harris raised his brows with dry sarcasm. "You haven't looked through the tail port?"

Jensen did so, and colored as if caught in a gaffe. The *Marity* drifted off the *Shearborn*'s stern, so close that the scuffs of every careless docking could be counted in her paint. To the last worn strut, the craft looked her part; that of a privately owned, hard-run cargo carrier that had suffered and survived a succession of mediocre pilots. Scratches to the contrary, the man at the *Marity*'s helm had to be Harris's equal or better to have achieved her present position with such delicacy. The chaser's most sensitive motion detectors had tripped no alarm.

"Serves you right for leaving FTL without taking precautions," muttered Harris. "That merchanter's inside our shield perimeter. If Mac James is inside, he's certainly laughing his tail off."

Yet Jensen surmised that the truth was very different. MacKenzie James had a smile like crystallized antifreeze; his eyes could be unnervingly direct, but no man in Fleet uniform had ever known the skip-runner captain to laugh.

When the *Shearborn*'s lieutenant offered neither comment nor orders, Harris's annoyance shifted to suspicion. "Why should a criminal of Mac James's reputation lure us out here in the first place? I say you've played right into this skip-runner's hands. Or did you maybe agree to collaborate with him beforehand?"

Jensen spun from the analog screen, furious. Whatever rejoinder he intended never left his lips. That instant the communications speaker crackled crisply to life.

"Godfrey, but you boys like to bicker," drawled a voice. The accent was vague and untraceable, trademark of any operation engineered by MacKenzie James. Harris swore in astonishment, that any skip-runner alive should brazenly comandeer a monitored Fleet com band. Across the compartment, Lieutenant Jensen went threateningly still and cold.

Incisive as always, the skip-runner captain resumed. "If your pilot can fly covert, and if between you the initiative can be gathered to eavesdrop on local transmissions, you'll discover a terrorist action in progress. The director of research on Cassix is being coerced into breach of Alliance security. Now it happens that the *Shearborn* is the only armed vessel on patrol in this system. You'd better prepare to intervene, because your course log can't be erased, and your careers will both be stewed if you can't justify your precipitous withdrawal at Dead Star."

Harris slammed a fist into his crew chair and wished he could kick flesh. "Well, happy snarking holiday! Just who in *hell* does that arrogant sonuvabitch think to impress?"

But MacKenzie James returned no rejoinder. The *Marity* vanished, dissolved from continuum into FTL, leaving the *Shearborn* drifting unprepared. The instruments which flagged ion trails were not yet reset; neither Fleet officer had thought that a necessity, since every current theory assured them that the departure of the skip-runner's craft should not have happened solo. Within such close proximity, *Shearborn* should have been swept along as the coil fields collapsed. Yet *Marity* went FTL without a flicker of protest from the instruments.

"We've lost him." Harris lifted his opened hands, his light eyes bright with disbelief. "That rumor must be true, then. The bastard buys technology from outside."

"Maybe something an Indie found," Harris speculated.

But the whys and hows of *Marity*'s systems were suddenly the least of the issue. Hunched in the command chair with a frown of obsessed concentration, Lieutenant Jensen rose to the challenge. Cassix Station lay on the far side of the dwarf sun from their current position. If a raid were in progress, and if skip-running instigators had jammed communication by translink, they would be forced to coordinate their operation through local transmission. Temporarily they would be blind to more sophisticated sensory data, which meant everything scoped by deflection imagery. The *Shearborn* was shadowed by Cassix's star. She would not yet be noticed; but to stay that way and eavesdrop on the terrorists, she would have to launch a probe to relay signals from the dwarf's far side. Crisply, Jensen listed orders.

His pilot responded with indignant disbelief. "You aren't going to believe that criminal!"

"I never knew him to lie." Jensen gestured with extreme irritation. "Carry on."

Harris fastened the front of his uniform with uncharacteristic care, then entered the codes for navigation access. "Well, the society releases on the news bulletins don't cite that guy for humanity idealism. If I wore the stripes on your jacket, I'd be wondering what's in this for MacKenzie James."

But that was the uncomfortable question Jensen dared not ask. He had sworn to escape his father's shadow by outwitting and bringing to justice the most-wanted criminal ever to work

Alliance space. For that he would have to beat the skip-runner at his own game, and the necessary first step was to play along. Jensen said, "I want surveillance on that station, and quickly. Secure trajectory data and sequence ignition for launch of a relay probe."

Harris could be strikingly inefficient when pressed against his will. But driven now by pique, and a morbid desire to humor Jensen until the young officer screwed himself through the folly of his own arrogance, the pilot donned his headset and applied himself to the navigation console.

The probe launched with a minimum of kick. No trail showed on the monitors. Satisfied only momentarily, Jensen hastened off the bridge to don his uniform before his coveted data started to arrive.

Harris bided the interval by plucking loose threads from the cuff of his coveralls. Upon Jensen's return, he had fallen asleep in his headset, his large hands loose in his lap, and his mouth open with snoring.

The *Shearborn*'s officer in command spared no attention for annoyance. Tracking monitors showed the relay probe carving a wide parabola around Cassix star. The moment the light flashed green on the signal board, Jensen reached without ceremony and stripped the headset from his pilot. Harris woke with his customary hair-trigger reflexes and banged his head on the bulkhead as he rocketed out of his chair.

"*Damn you,*" he growled at Jensen.

Finding his fanatical commander absorbed by the new transmission, Harris stalked off to the galley.

He came back after an interval, munching a dessert bar. Jensen had already assembled details enough to confirm Mac-Kenzie James's assessment. Harris stopped chewing as his senior recited the facts.

Trouble had found opening because the fleet which normally patrolled Cassix had been pared down to one ship, in support of the offensive at Dead Star. That cruiser had fallen to skip-runners who by long-range design had kidnapped the director of research's two infant daughters from an earlier raid on a passenger vessel.

"A straight-forward case," Jensen reported, "except for their bent for terrorism. The bastards killed the director's wife to prove themselves capable. The two little girls they hold hostage will be spared, provided the staff at Cassix surrenders a working prototype of the new laser weapons system.''

Harris stood for a moment, crumbs from his snack falling unnoticed down his chin. For once his blue eyes were direct. ''Who hired the talent for this? Indies? Junk freighters equipped with that scale of armament could make for a very ugly mess.''

''Indies, or rebels, or some independent faction who buys through skip-runners, does it matter?'' Jensen yanked off the headset, then reflexively smoothed his hair. ''I want data on that station, as quickly as you can manage.''

Harris sank mechanically in his crew chair. He shoved his last bite of cookie in his mouth by reflex, while the headset between his hands repeated in precise and ugly detail just what would happen to the director's little daughters if the terms of their kidnappers were not met. He swallowed with difficulty, for his mouth had gone dry. ''I can't,'' he said finally. ''The specs on Cassix Station are one hundred percent classified.''

''But you flew test runs there,'' Jensen argued. Mac James had offered him a challenge he intended to win; and as a Fleet officer his duty was explicitly clear. ''Reconstruct what you can from memory. The skip-runners intend to exchange the children for the weapons system by cargo cable at 2000 hours, which leaves us very little margin to prepare.''

Harris looked up sharply. ''Cargo cable? We have a chance, then. Security might be recovered, but only if we write off the lives of two kids.''

''Just carry on!'' Jensen added no promises. Ruthless as his choice seemed, in this case Harris knew the young officer was not playing for heroics. If the weapons system currently in development at Cassix fell into Indie hands, far more than two little girls would suffer.

The *Shearborn* prepared for intervention. Jensen activated the cloaking devices and ran checks on shields and weapons. Harris applied himself to navigation and mapped a course calculated to conceal their approach behind the mass of Cassix's star until the last possible moment. Neither man spoke. Harris held singlemindedly to duty for reasons of conscience; Jensen's penchant for advancement promised that his record in a crisis must be impeccable.

Presently, the *Shearborn* hurtled on a meticulously arranged course around Cassix's star. At the precise instant she crossed into scanner range, Harris kicked the attitude thrusters, killed her drives, and made a face as the snack in his stomach danced flip-flops to the pull of inertia. Tumbling with the random majesty of an uncaptured asteroid, the scout craft he piloted went dead to observation.

"Nice work," said Jensen. Awkwardly stiff in his command chair, he smiled. Their timing was perfect, a clean thirty minutes before the scheduled exchange between skip-runners and station. As the scopes resolved data, the lieutenant leaned anxiously forward. He expected the spider-armed sprawl of an orbital station, gravity powered, and glittering with the lights of habitation.

What he saw was deep-space darkness, scattered with distant stars.

His blank-faced dismay raised laughter from Harris. "Well, what do you want for a security installation? Billboard lights and a docking beacon?"

Jensen shut his eyes, opened them, and tried not to blush at his foolishness. Like the chaser he commanded, Cassix Station would be surfaced in camouflage. The complex would be dark except for lighted pinpricks that simulated stars. Her deep-space side would be painted in reflective, and unless a ship chanced to cross her orbital plane and catch her in occultation with her parent star, she would be invisible to passing traffic.

Jensen bridled rising annoyance. He dared not use the *Shearborn*'s fancy surveillance equipment. Without knowing how sophisticated his adversary's gear might be, he must assume that deflection beam interference would warn an already wary skip-runner that his activities had drawn Fleet notice. There were other ways to locate an orbiting body. The simplest involved time-sequence imaging, then a comparison of star fields to determine which objects were artificial by drift; except time was the one most glaring commodity this blitz operation lacked.

"There," Harris said suddenly, startlingly loud in the silence. "I've got a fix on the target."

His experienced eyes had spotted the skip-runner craft. A flat flash of reflection confirmed his sighting, as a shiny surface on her hull caught reflection from the dwarf star. Jensen turned up the resolution enhancer on the analog screen. Though his pilot patiently informed him that the hardware would not perform under *Shearborn*'s erratically violent motion, the lieutenant continued searching until his eyes burned.

Hope of coherent conversation seemed nonexistent; Harris shrugged and made a show of initiating a star-field comparison search. Lights flickered on the control panels as computer circuitry normally reserved for navigation diverted to speed his results. The pilot laced blunt hands in his lap. Wearing the cynical expression he practiced for women who pressed him for marriage, he stretched back in his crew chair, adjusted his headset, and wished he could watch a porn tape. Sex was a better sweat than listening to the terse exchange between a desperate parent and an equally nervous skip-runner who doubtlessly wondered whether any Indie contract was worth taking risks of this magnitude.

Suddenly Harris shot upright, the mockery gone from his face. "Sir, your plan won't work."

Jensen held his focus on the analog screens, where, faint against the deep of space, a spider-filament of cable arced out, then ever so gradually drew taut.

"They're sending the babies down, linked to a timed explosive," Harris continued vehemently.

This time Jensen answered, very bleak. "Linked? How? To the carrier capsule, or the cable itself?"

Harris listened. "Cable," he replied after a moment. "The detonation code will be kept by the skip-runner. Which means the scum will skip system, leaving station personnel fifty-five seconds to reel that capsule in and cut those kids free before the charge goes off."

Jensen became very still.

Harris showed a rare mix of deference and regret. "I'm afraid we're shut down, sir. Best we can do is record data that might help an undercover agent round them up."

"Which will be impossible to manage, not before the Indies have replicated that laser design." All nerves and anger, Jensen flexed the fingers of his right hand. "I'll shoot out the cable link between the explosive and that capsule, first."

Harris grinned, sarcasm restored. "Boy, we're in problems up to our nuts already. Brass won't award a winning ticket for blowing two babies to bits. You'd have to be marksman elite to maybe hit that cable at all, far less the connecting link between a carry capsule and an explosive charge."

Jensen returned a nasty smile, then drew a chain from his collar. He dangled before his pilot's insolent gaze a medallion of skill that not one man in ten thousand held the privilege to wear.

"Shit," said Harris. "How was I to guess?"

"You couldn't," Jensen shot back. He was the youngest, by nearly a decade, ever to obtain the premier marksman's rating, but this once pride did not prompt his temper. The mission chronometer by his elbow advanced another fraction. A margin of minutes remained if the *Shearborn* was to foil the kidnappers.

The problems ahead were formidable, as Harris was quick to point out. "You can't hit that small a target without an attitude adjustment. *Shearborn*'s still tumbling, remember?" The pilot slashed a finger beneath his chin in graphic pantomime. "We break cover, and the little girls die. We're shot down the second we fire our gravity drives."

Jensen made contingency for that. "We wait," he said, an intensity about him that Harris had never seen. "After station personnel cable the plans up to the terrorists, the kids start down in the capsule. We stabilize our attitude then. Surprise will be in our favor. I shoot out the linkup. The kids and the charge are in free-fall but recoiling away from the break in the line. Station personnel will reel the babies in, bet on that. And with an enabled charge drifting back toward its point of origin, the skip-runners will have their hands full cutting loose that trailing cable. That gives maybe ten seconds for us to blast their ugly presence out of space."

"Clever." Harris scratched his chest in that thoughtful manner his drinking cronies would have recognized for a warning. "But your range is extreme. You haven't allowed for drift, or for the proximity of Cassix's star. Gravity will pull your shot off target."

Jensen reached out, gently smoothed the wing insignia on his pilot's coveralls. "That's where your part comes. You'll plot my aiming point. If my shot were treated as an exercise in drive ballistics, you and that computer would have no trouble getting it right."

Harris felt sweat spring beneath his collar. The accuracy required would likely be past the limits of the technology. Though the more brilliant pilots did such things in the course of test-flight emergencies, this was another matter. A man had no

business risking the lives of two little girls to instinct, the
reflexive style of hunch which routinely carried a badly drawn
design through without mishap. Harris had no grounds—but his
wilder nature was piqued. Here was a daredevil stunt like no
other; if he pulled it off, there would be accolades.

Harris set steady hands to the keyboard. "Give me the specs
on your pellet rifle, and may the god of foolish ventures smile on
us both."

Jensen grinned for the first time since the start of the
operation. Whatever queer challenge MacKenzie James had
handed the crew of the Fleet chaser *Shearborn,* one of his
skip-running breathren was about to get hammered out of space.

The inner lining of the pressure suit wicked away the sweat
from Jensen's skin. Doused alternately in shadow, then the
burnished, bloody glare of Cassix's star, he belted himself into
the service niche by the forward air lock. The state-of-the-art
gauss rifle cradled on his arm hindered his movements very
little. The *Shearborn* tumbled dizzily underneath him. Yet in
null gravity, as long as Jensen did not fix on the scenery, the
radical attitude of the hull did not disorient him. Any nerves and
tension he suffered stemmed from the unrevealed motives of
MacKenzie James. That point preoccupied the lieutenant to the
exclusion of all else. The children and the laser prototypes
Jensen currently jeopardized his career to save had become
prizes in a ritualized duel of wits.

Jensen checked the time. The suit chronometer read 2012. By
now, the crate with the laser prototype lay in skip-runner hands.
During the ascent, the speed of the cable's drive motor had been
measured and recorded into Harris's flight computer. The
lieutenant braced his rifle . . . and waited.

In the darkness beyond Cassix, the lift motor hummed and
reversed. Cable turned through frictionless gears, and a capsule
bearing two children and an attached packet of condensed
explosive began the kilometer-long transit toward the waiting
arms of the father. Harris finalized his calculations.

The chronometer read 2026. A buzzer trilled in Jensen's
helmet, and the pilot's voice read off coordinates.

Precisely on signal, the *Shearborn*'s gravity drives kicked
over. Centrifugal force slammed the lieutenant against his belt
restraints; stars spun like a pinwheel around him as the

Shearborn's attitude corrected with vicious and vengeful precision, compliments of pilot Harris in sharpest form.

The scout craft stabilized.

The parting kick of inertia was punishingly severe. Jensen's helmet struck the hull with a clang that made his ears ring. His head spun sickeningly and he cursed. If his vertigo did not stabilize fast, he would be unable to orient and take aim. Obstinacy born of exhaustive practice allowed him to slot the rifle stock into the connector which linked to the suit's visual display. At a second signal, he switched on the targeting scope.

On the *Shearborn*'s bridge, the monitors would be screaming, one red alleyway of warning lights as the skip-runner ship trained weapons on the chaser which dared an intervention. Both ships had their screens down. On Cassix Station, speakers blared as personnel shouted in dismay . . . too late. The integrity of the exchange they had promised the skip-runner was disrupted now past mending. No last-minute plea would convince a ruthless band of criminals that this rescue had not been betrayal. A father wept while a skip-runner's mate with shaking hands stabbed the detonation codes into a keypad. All men waited—one of them grim and another in tearful anguish. In under sixty seconds the silvery capsule on the cargo cable would explode in a coruscation of light.

Jensen raised his gauss rifle in the absolute silence of vacuum. With a clear head he locked the targeting scope onto coordinates, then cool-handedly squeezed the trigger.

The rifle kicked. Very far off, tiny to insignificance, a pinpoint of light crawled along a fragile thread of cable. The pellet which raced to intercept sped unhindered through vacuum, its course bent gently by the pull of a red dwarf star.

Sweating freely now, Jensen counted seconds—five, six— the marking tone sounded a final time. The lieutenant gripped hard to the combing. The reflective markers on the cable glistened like dewdrops poised on spider silk. By now, the magnetized pellet should have cut through. Jensen felt an ache in his chest. Along with the possibility of defeat, he realized at some point that he had stopped breathing.

Then the cable parted. Jensen shouted in relief as the tiny fleck that was the children's capsule drifted in a graceful arc against the stars.

A flash answered almost immediately, as the skip-runner ship

fired gravity engines. The technician in her hold abandoned his
keypad. Cursing and furious, he wrestled into a pressure suit,
desperate to free the locking clamp that secured the trailing
cable that now rebounded treacherously under recoil. Jensen's
marksmanship had brought havoc, for now the fully enabled
plasma charge drifted straight for the kidnapper's cargo bay.

"Now, Harris, now," shouted Jensen.

His helmet went black. Reflex shielding protected his vision
as Harris manned the weaponry, and both of the *Shearborn*'s
cannons opened fire.

The helmet's shielding stayed opaque for a long and madden-
ing interval. Jensen fidgeted like a child, cursed like a dock
worker. His visor cleared finally to reveal a spreading, glowing
curtain of debris that had once been a skip-runner ship. The
moment warmed like vintage wine. Jensen smiled. He stroked
his rifle like the thigh of a naked woman and said softly, very
softly, "Up yours, MacKenzie James."

Jensen tugged the sleeve of his dress whites from the grasp of
yet another congratulatory technician. The lieutenant had received a hero's welcome the moment the *Shearborn* touched the
dock. Every member of Cassix Station personnel had come
forward. They had shaken his hand, thanked him, and insisted
upon an impromptu reception to meet the key administrators.

"Just coincidence we happened into this sector at all,"
Jensen said in answer to the technician's question, the same
question he had repeatedly fielded over a three-hour supply of
coffee and cakes. "The *Shearborn* was in pursuit of another
suspect. Yes, that one got away, but his escape turned out to be
fortunate. No Fleet scout would have entered this system if that
chase hadn't gone sour. Yes, it was risky to shoot out that cable,
but the children were unharmed. Now, if you'll excuse me? I've
a promise to keep." He hefted the gilt-papered bottle he had
cadged for his pilot. An unwilling victim of regulations, Harris
had been forced to remain on duty aboard the scout.

The technician smiled and shook hands again. "You're a
brave young man, sir, and a pride to the Fleet. You've saved the
Alliance more than you know by keeping those weapon prototypes from the Indies."

Jensen smiled back, raised the bottle apologetically, then
dodged another wave of admirers. Any other time the lieutenant

would have reveled in public adulation; but not here, not now. A most telling question remained unanswered, one detail left loose to rasp his nerves. MacKenzie James was nobody's humanitarian. A criminal of his caliber was unlikely to act out of pity for a father's little girls. Jensen dared not consider the incident finished until he was back at his post on the *Shearborn* and out of the Cassix system altogether. The fact that Harris could not share the celebration became his only excuse to slip away.

The docking hangar was very dark. After the brightly lighted access corridors, Jensen found it difficult to adjust. Strange, he thought, that the overhead floods should be switched off. On the heels of a major crisis, he would assume a conscientious staff would take extra precautions.

But when Jensen queried the guard on duty, negligence proved not to be at issue.

"Damned skip-runner blasted the communications turret." The security man gestured in resignation. "Lights in here run off the same solar banks, and we'll need more than one shift on deep-space maintenance for repairs."

Though the explanation seemed reasonable, Jensen's nervousness increased. He crossed the echoing expanse of hangar with swift steps and hurried up the *Shearborn*'s ramp.

Instinct caused him to hesitate just inside the entry. He sensed something amiss, perhaps from the conspicuous fact that Harris was not at his usual post in the galley with a row of empty beers for company. Jensen paused midstride, almost in the corridor to the bridge. That moment, a shadow moved just at the edge of vision.

Jensen ducked. The blow that should have felled him glanced instead off his ribs.

It knocked the breath from his lungs nonetheless. The bottle spun from his hand and smashed in a spray of glass and spirits. Jensen bent double, whooping for air that tasted sickly of whiskey. He snatched by reflex for his side arm. But the shadow moved ahead of him.

It proved to be a man, a large man who already dodged the shot he knew would follow. A Fleet officer accomplished enough to earn marksman elite could be expected to handle his gun as if it were an extension of his living flesh.

Jensen's shot crashed into the bridge-side bulkhead. Padding exploded into fluff where the intruder's head had been but a fraction of an instant before. Cursing, the lieutenant shoved another round into the breech. He hastened forward, skidding over the puddle of alcohol and glass. The cold portion of his mind wondered why the intruder had fled. A second blow, better placed, might have killed him in that instant before surprise kicked into adrenaline surge.

Jensen whipped around the innerlock, slammed shoulder first into a stowage locker. He trained his pistol squarely upon his quarry, only to flinch the shot wide. His curse of white hot anger blended with the clang as the pellet hammered harmlessly into high impact plastic.

Over the heated end of his gun barrel, Jensen beheld the limp form of Harris, gripped like a shield in a pair of coil-scarred hands.

The name left his lips, unbidden. "Mac James!"

"Godfrey," came the muffled reply. "Tired of the party early, did you?"

The face, with its icy gray eyes, stayed hidden. Jensen was given no target for his murderous marksmanship, which was a feat. Mac James outweighed his unconscious hostage by a good sixty pounds. As to how the skip-runner had stowed away, Jensen recalled with sinking recrimination that the *Marity* had passed close enough to plant a boarder on the *Shearborn*'s hull. The stowaway's life-support of necessity would have been limited to the capacity of his suit pack, which meant that Mac James had gambled his life on the lieutenant's subsequent behavior. Had the *Shearborn*'s crew backed down, returned through FTL to Dead Star, the skip-runner would have been fried in the coil field. Instead, the heroics which had preserved the station's integrity and the lives of two children had earned the *Shearborn* a warm invitation, without security screening, into a classified research installation. With a dawning stab of outrage, Jensen understood. He had been nothing more than a pawn. His triumph over the terrorists had provided the linchpin of a plot for MacKenzie James.

"I could kill Harris to see you dead," Jensen said thickly. Certainly he was ruthless enough, MacKenzie James should recall.

But with insight that bordered the uncanny, the skip-runner sensed why the lieutenant dared not fire to kill. "First you'll want to know just what mischief I've set loose while you were celebrating, boy.''

Jensen's fingers whitened on the grip of his pellet gun. His thoughts darted like a rat in a maze but found no opening to exploit. He had visited the control bridge on the *Marity*. Her captain's ability to manipulate hardware was real enough to frighten; and if Harris had slugged down drugs with his beer, the *Shearborn*'s systems had been open to sabotage for something close to three hours. Any havoc was possible.

Mac James's laconic observation interrupted the lieutenant's thoughts. ''Now, I see you have two choices. Murder your pilot to get me, and you've got a Fleet investigation on your case. You can bet they won't send a lightweight to chew your ass. Not if you kill without witnesses and a suspect like me turns up dead on your chaser, smack in the middle of a classified installation.''

''That won't save you,'' Jensen said quickly.

''Maybe not.'' Harris's head lolled to one side as Mac James shifted his grip. ''But a review of *Shearborn*'s flight log will uncover a coded file, accessed through stolen passkeys. The data list includes plans for every project Cassix Station personnel have going on the drawing boards. Fleet court martial will nail you on theft of military secrets, without appeal. You need me alive, boy. Unless you know enough to go into that system and monkey that file out of existence without leaving tracks.''

Jensen felt shaky down to his shoes. He lacked the expertise to clear the encoded locks on the *Shearborn*'s software, much less to alter records on the other side. His helplessness galled doubly. In the event of a trial, the very ignorance that ensured his innocence would be impossible to prove.

''You're much too quiet, boy.'' Mac James shifted his weight with sharpening impatience. ''Why do you think I've been so *busy*?''

Rocked by a stab of hatred, Jensen perceived more. ''You sent that other skip-runner in, pitted me against him specifically to gain entrance to Cassix Station without leaving traces. The Indie contract on the kidnappers was only a cover.''

A strained silence followed, broken gruffly by Mac James's reply. ''A man lives according to his nature, you for pride and advancement, and Captain Gorlaff for his bets. That one buried his future permanently because he neglected to watch his odds. You can, too, boy. Or you can lift off Cassix and rendezvous with the *Marity,* where I can transfer that incriminating file without leaving traces in the system. I'll return Harris in a cargo crate. When he recovers from his hangover, he can fly you back to Commodore Abraham Meier for the commendation and promotion you both so richly deserve.''

Jensen steadied his grip on the gun. His hand trembled, and his face twitched. A single shot would restore his inner pride but shatter his public career forever. Swept by rage, and by a desire like pain to see the skip-runner captain who had manipulated him end up cold and bloody and dead, Jensen shut his eyes. Cornered without recourse, he made his choice.

Commodore Meier stepped forward on the dais, and stiffly cleared his throat. ''Each man lives according to his nature,'' he said in official summary. The medals in his hand flashed brightly in the lights of the vid cameras. ''May others draw inspiration from the bravery and initiative cited here.''

Jensen held very still as the precious medallion was affixed to the sash on his chest. Like MacKenzie James, he never gambled; there had been no allowance for doubt. A Fleet officer with a future might pursue a skip-runner to the death. The duel of wits would continue. Reveling in his promotion and his honors, the newest Lieutenant Commander in the Fleet promised himself victory at the next pass.

INTERLUDE

The rich, blue world shrunk in the background as Hawk Talon blasted away. Martial music played faintly in the background.

"Another lost world found for the Alliance," he intoned, satisfied. For the last hour Hawk had outwitted grasping politicians and outfought two Khalian cruisers. Finally he led a revolt by the general populace that had forced the corrupt planetary government to apply for membership in the Alliance, demonstrating once more how every right-thinking planet would rush to join.

Music swells and fade to crowd of cheering new citizens.

KHASARA

by Robert Sheckley

I.

WHEN BRODSKY ENLISTED in the levy from Perdido, he was sent to the planet Target, the Khalian staging ground which the special forces from Perdido, with a little help from the rest of the Fleet, had conquered some two years previously.

By the time Brodsky got there, the fighting was over and there was nothing much to do. So Brodsky had proceeded to do nothing.

Then one day, his platoon sergeant came to him and said, "The company commander wants to see you."

At the time, Brodsky was off-duty, sitting under a tree watching two crickets watching each other. He'd learned a lot from watching insects and small animals while on Target. It was funny, but when you really watched them closely, you saw that they did stuff the textbooks never mentioned. Individual variation. Despite their lack of personality, their behavior was never quite predictable.

"What does the company commander want with me?" Brodsky asked.

"No doubt he would prefer to enlighten you as to that himself," the sergeant said. "Are you coming?"

"I suppose so," Brodsky said.

"Can't you just say 'Yes, Sergeant,' like everyone else?"

"I suppose I could," Brodsky said. "But I'm not like everybody else. Nobody is."

* * *

II.

Brodsky was tall, gangling, awkward, and poorly coordinated. He had an IQ that registered around 185, genius level, but he didn't seem to have any aptitude to do anything with it. This provided a challenge for his company commander, James P. Kelly from Carthaginia II in the Eastern Ridge Star Sector CJ.

Captain Kelly was perfectly charming in a sarcastic way. "So here is Brodsky, the company philosopher!"

"You do me too great an honor, Captain," Brodsky said. "I am a mere seeker after truth."

"Is that why you invariably screw up our close-order drills?"

"I don't do it on purpose," Brodsky said. "I'm not rebellious."

"Except unconsciously?"

"Perhaps. But I submit, Captain, that a man is not to be held accountable for the actions of his subconscious, which is, by definition, unknown and unknowable to him."

"If you'd just pay attention," the captain said.

"I beg your pardon?" asked Brodsky. He had been staring out the window, wishing he were somewhere else.

"Brodsky, sometimes I wish we were in one of the old-fashioned armies of the bad old days. Back then, when soldiers screwed up, do you know what their commanding officers did?"

"Scolded them?" Brodsky guessed.

"A lot more than that. They punished them."

"I don't understand," Brodsky said. "What has punishment got to do with screwing up?"

"Nothing. We know that now. But in the ancient time, they thought they could correct behavior by punishing it."

"What a peculiar notion," Brodsky said.

"Quite unscientific. But can you imagine, Brodsky, what gratification it would be to me to be able to punish you after all the anguish you have caused me?"

"Sir, if it will help your state of mind," Brodsky said, "then by all means punish me. I won't hold it against you, and I'll never tell anyone."

"I may have emotions," the company commander said, "but I'm not an old-fashioned thinker. No, Brodsky, I'm not going to punish you, though my heart would delight in giving you pain. On the contrary. I am going to reward you. Is that modern enough for you?"

"I don't know if rewarding behavior you despise is really a

good idea," Brodsky said. "And I also have the feeling—call it a presentiment—that I am not going to like this reward."

"You can call it a presentiment," the company commander said, "or you can call it grape jelly. No power on Earth, and certainly no plea on your part, is going to prevent me from rewarding you for your miserable and vile performance ever since you joined my detachment."

"Detachment is something you have too little of," Brodsky said. "But if you're determined to reward me, let's get it over with. What's it to be? A three-day leave so that I can get disgustingly drunk in the horrible little town filled with sarcastic six-foot birds outside of our post?"

"No, it's better than that," the company commander said.

"Sir, I can't imagine what it is."

"Then I will tell you. Private Brodsky, you are hereby promoted to the rank of first lieutenant."

"That's it?" Brodsky asked. "That's my reward?"

"Only part of it. Aren't you curious why I've promoted you?"

Brodsky shrugged. "Maybe you have a daughter who has seen me and found me desirable and insisted that you give me enough rank so that she can be seen with me socially."

In a low, deadly voice the captain said, "Brodsky, have you been seeing my daughter?"

"I didn't even know that you had one. My supposition was purely hypothetical."

"I have promoted you," the company commander said, "because, according to the new directives, lieutenant is the lowest rank permitted to operate a scoutship."

"A scoutship? Me fly a scoutship? Sir, I can't even drive a car!"

"They are simple enough to learn. Intelligence is the magic key that unlocks all techniques. You told me that yourself."

At this time the search was on for the missing planets of the old empire. Two thousand years previously, the First Empire had come to an end. Its original nucleus had been thirteen planets, one of which was Earth. In the days of the last emperor the empire grew to encompass one hundred thousand planets. Power was in the hands of the Fleet, which headquartered at Tau Ceti, the Port.

When the Empire broke up, many records were lost, and

many planets went entirely out of communication. It was a time of dark ages. Part of the present day work of the Alliance was to find these planets, reestablish contact, bring them back into the Alliance.

Brodsky hadn't thought the exploration program would affect him. He was not an explorer type. He was not even a military type. In fact, he had good reason to suspect that he wasn't even a type at all.

"I don't know anything about piloting," Brodsky said.

"There is an instruction manual on board the ship. You will have several hours to study it. Also, you will have a partner, no doubt more technologically competent than you."

"Why me?" Brodsky asked. "And why a scoutship?"

"Scoutships," the company commander said, "are the ships of choice in the locating and contacting of civilizations."

"You want to send me out exploring?"

"It's important work, Brodsky. Two thousand years ago we were part of an empire of a hundred thousand planets. Think of it!"

"Unwieldy," Brodsky commented.

"Lofty. Noble. A grand conception."

"To each his own. I personally think there's entirely too much nostalgia for the Old Empire. The dark ages sound like much more fun."

"We need to find those planets," Captain Kelly said. "We need them back in the Alliance. We're at war, in case you forgot. The Khalians, remember? And the sinister intelligences behind them. Enormous forces are moving against us, Brodsky. We need everyone and everything on our side. And if self-interest doesn't move you, think of someone else's problems for a change. Do you know what the enemy does to unprotected civilizations?"

"I don't want to hear about it," Brodsky said.

"These planets are defenseless. Most of the planets have not been able to sustain an interplanetary civilization on their own. After a few generations of isolation, space flight is forgotten, or remembered only as a possession of some godlike race that once came and went. When the Khalians and others come across such people, it's easy enough to enslave them, or to kill them off, or have them quick-frozen for meat supplies."

"Please," Brodsky said, "I've got a sensitive stomach."

"I've said enough," the company commander said. He rummaged in his desk drawer and found a shiny ornament. "Here is your lieutenant's medallion. Put it around your neck. That's it. Welcome aboard, Lieutenant Brodsky."

Brodsky fingered the ornament. "Honestly now, sir, all humor aside. Is this really such a good idea? Sending me out in a scouter to explore alien worlds? I mean, that's work for an expert, isn't it?"

"Indeed it is," the company commander said. "We have considered carefully the ideal requirements for the job. You should be a trained linguist, of course, and quick at learning new languages and understanding dialects. A knowledge of chemistry will help you stay unpoisoned when you try to eat on your new planetary home. You should have some training in various disciplines—economics, politics, technology of all sorts—so that you can determine how important this planet might or might not be to the Alliance. It would help if you were a geologist, because there are still rare earths and metals to be found . . . a botanist and biologist, because some of our best cultures for a variety of things come from alien platforms. If the place has an ocean, as most oxygen-rich worlds do, it would help if you were an oceanographer. We'd like you to be a zoologist so that you could tell us something about the animals you encounter. If you were a sociologist and an ethnologist you could make some guesses about the various cultures, because the cultures we have come across so far have been anything but homogeneous, and they tend to have as much variation or more as races, groups, clans, religions, on Earth. It takes a trained man to deal with all this without giving offense. Maybe we'd better add psychologist to your list of credits. It stands to reason that you should be a doctor, if for no other reason than to heal yourself when you fall ill far from home and don't care to rely on the local methods, steeped as they are in alien physiology and alien nutrition. As a matter of fact, it wouldn't be bad if you were also a nutritionist."

"Well, I'm not any of those things," Brodsky said.

"I know. None of our explorers has the necessary requirements. They wouldn't do."

"That's contradictory. Why?"

"Because the explorer would be so burdened by knowledge that he wouldn't know how to respond to a new situation. It happens all the time in exploring. On these worlds, nothing is like you were taught, your analogies are imperfect, your inferences are incorrect, and, all in all, you're best off just playing it by ear."

"So how do you choose your explorers?"

"We take the ones we think will be pretty good at adjusting to weird situations. Misfits and oddballs, that's what we usually get."

"And you think that I fit?"

"Oh, yes, Brodsky, do you ever fit."

"Captain, if I didn't know better, I'd suspect you of having a sense of humor."

"That's probably a compliment, coming from you. But don't worry, Brodsky, I'm not being funny. I honestly think you might be well suited for this work."

"I can't imagine why," Brodsky said. "I don't know a thing about alien civilizations or how to greet our long-lost brothers from the old empire."

"True, but you have one big thing going for you. You always expect the unexpected."

"Of course," Brodsky said. "What else is there to expect? Doesn't everybody?"

"Most people," the captain said, "expect only the expected, and are very surprised when matters turn out otherwise. You will never have that failing, Brodsky. Now let's go out and inspect your new ship, and I'll introduce you to your new partner."

III.

The scoutship was fifty feet long. That seemed generous in a ship designed to carry only two or three people. But most of the narrow hull was taken up with the engines, operating and navigational equipment, and stores. There was a tiny bathroom and shower, a galley and a small recreation room with a sofa and armchairs and entertainment center. The control room was up in the bow, small and cramped and covered from floor to ceiling with instruments.

Somebody was sitting in one of the command chairs, idly tapping the computer keyboard.

"Who's that?" Brodsky asked.

The occupant of the command chair turned around. She was

about seventeen years old, dark skinned with delicate features. She had long lustrous black hair, which she wore down her back in a thick braid. She was small, and she looked fragile. She wore heavy gold bracelets. There was a small caste mark on her forehead.

"Lieutenant Brodsky," the company commander said, "let me introduce you to your partner in exploration, Lieutenant Muckerjee."

"Are you from India?" Brodsky said. "Or do you just wear a sari for kicks?"

"Neither," Anna said. "I am from Khali Twelve, originally settled from India and Pakistan."

"I had always been under the impression that Indian women stayed at home and left the fighting to the men."

She shook her head firmly. "On Khali Twelve the women are the warriors. I am fully qualified to fly spaceships of this size. What do you specialize in?"

"Goofing off," Brodsky said.

"I'll leave you two to get better acquainted," Captain Kelly said and left, grinning to himself.

IV.

Their first argument took place on the first day of their flight. That made it easy to remember.

After blastoff, when the ship had moved beyond the effective gravitational pull of Target, and while they were waiting for the computer-predicted moment to switch to FTL drive, Anna took out several large spiral-bound volumes, opened them, and began to study the contents.

Brodsky had watched without comment as she had done the entire liftoff herself. She was a trifle unfriendly, perhaps. But nice looking. He liked her eyes, which were long and almond shaped. Her head was well-shaped on a long, graceful neck. She seemed very competent. Brodsky liked that. Or at least he thought he liked that. Brodsky didn't always know what he liked until later.

"Nice takeoff," he told her.

"Thank you," she said. "It was just a standard takeoff spiral as prescribed in the manual. I tightened it somewhat in response to reports of approaching traffic from the control tower."

"That was clever of you," Brodsky said.

"But of course it was still within regulation parameters."

"Hey, that's good to hear," Brodsky said.

She frowned slightly. "They warned me about you. They said you liked to do things in your own way."

Brodsky nodded. "To put it mildly."

"But in takeoffs, there's not much room for self-expression."

"I know. That's why I let you do it."

"You let me? I wasn't aware that you were in charge of this expedition."

"I didn't mean to imply that," Brodsky said. "What I'm trying to say is, if I'd felt that takeoffs were something I did well, I would have done it."

She turned to face him. Brodsky noticed what a nicely shaped mouth she had. But he didn't like what came out of it.

"Lieutenant Brodsky," she said, "let's get something straight right away. I've got the technical skills for this job. You do not. As far as I can see, your commander put you here just to get rid of you. You're dead weight. Okay, I can live with that. I know what to do, and I can do it whether you're here or not. But I don't want you interfering. I believe there's an ample supply of comic books in the ship's video library. They should keep you occupied while I get on with this job."

Brodsky stared at her. He was starting to get angry. And then the absurdity of the whole thing got to him, and he had to smile. Here was this woman volunteering to do this job he hadn't even wanted in the first place. What was he complaining about?

"You go right ahead and do your thing, sis," he told her. "When my advice isn't wanted, I have no desire to volunteer it. But if you ever think I can be of assistance, feel free to call on me."

"Thank you, Lieutenant Brodsky," Anna said. "Your attitude is entirely appropriate for the situation."

"Well, it's a relief for me to know that," Brodsky said and went back to the galley. Just his luck. A long trip in space, alien explorations, the whole bit, and here he was, stuck with a woman who went by the rule book and seemed to have a chip on her shoulder. It would be interesting to see how long that would last.

After setting a course, Lieutenant Muckerjee came back and cooked lunch. Chicken curry. A little spicy, but nice for a change. Brodsky wasn't to know that this was what he was going to get for dinner every day until the end of the trip.

At the end of nine days shiptime, Anna brought them out of FTL drive. She had a promising planet lined up. It might even be Khasara, one of the important worlds of the First Empire.

V.

Antonin Huue, known as Leo, was a watcher on the upper summits of Mount Forgetful, highest peak in Khasara's southern hemisphere.

The watchers were elected by public lottery every year. It was their task to stay on Khasara's highest mountains, where the air was thin and telepathic telemetry was unimpeded. They were supposed to keep an eye and an ear turned toward space, and to give warning when an alien spaceship approached Khasara.

It had been a very long time since the last alien ship had come. Things were quiet on the alien front nowadays. But there had to be watchers anyhow because you could never tell about aliens: they always came back, and they were unpredictable and dangerous. It would never do to let them sneak onto the planet without advance warning.

The year's solitary duty gave Leo a chance to practice his three-pointed concentration, control his body heat by yogic means, and convert sunlight into sustenance. There wasn't much practical need for that sort of thing, but Leo liked doing it anyway.

It came as a nasty surprise when, one stormy morning, immediately after finishing his morning tea, his daily routine was broken by a weak signal from space. Leo hoped it would turn out to be a meteorite, or maybe even a stray comet. He locked on it, and within an hour the signal had resolved itself into an energy pattern that showed it to be a metallic body propelled by magnetic drive. There could be no doubt of it: it was a spaceship. Somebody was coming to visit, and that was never good news. The lord of the planet would have to be notified immediately, and that meant Leo would have to descend from his comfortable hut on the summit of Mount Forgetful to the tree line in order to send the message via tree network.

Leo packed a light lunch and put on his warmest clothing,

because he was tired of controlling his body temperature, and set off at once.

His way led downward between precipitous cliffs overhung with heavy accumulations of snow. It was the sort of place where a man had to exercise extreme caution, extending his radar sense to the uppermost and being ready to respond quickly to the slightest hint of danger. But Leo was thinking so hard about the message he was to deliver that the first warning signal he responded to was a roaring sound from just above him.

Avalanche coming right at him! And it was too late to take evasive action. Leo remembered now, too late, his father's final warning before his death—never trust nature, the old man had wheezed—and then Leo was engulfed and tumbled and turned, and somewhere along the line consciousness was lost.

When he came to, he found that he was tied hand and foot to a bed. With this as a clue, it was easy for Leo to figure out that he must have been rescued by a member of the Guaschi clan, hereditary enemies of his clan, the Huue.

A large, middle-aged man, holding a knife and clad in ratty furs, came forward from the shadows and nodded. "Yes," he said, "you have inferred correctly. I am Ottoline Guaschi. I am, of course, going to kill you."

"Why didn't you do it already?" Leo asked. "I mean, why bother rescuing me in the first place?"

"My dear fellow, rescuing snowbound strangers is incumbent upon us all. In any event, I bear you no enmity."

"Glad to hear that," Leo said.

"Or rather, I *do* bear you enmity, since our clans are mortal enemies, but the enmity I feel is purely formal—it is what goes with the role rather than being a true reflection of what my emotions actually are toward you."

"What are your emotions actually toward me?" Leo asked.

"Profound indifference," Guaschi said.

"I'm very glad to hear that."

"But I do have a formal role to perform. One is supposed to kill enemies."

"But you saved my life."

"Well, that's the sort of thing one does anyhow, isn't it?"

"I suppose so. But it's inconsistent, this saving me and then saying you're going to kill me."

"Inconsistent? I should think not!" Guaschi said with some

heat. "These contradictory actions are entirely consistent with my role, which is that of one discovering and-dealing with an ancient clan enemy."

"Well, all right," Leo said. "But before you take any drastic action, I have a favor to ask."

"Sorry, no favors," Guaschi said. "It complicates matters."

"This favor will do me no good," Leo said, "since I'll be dead. But it will be of considerable benefit to you and the rest of the Eleroi."

"Well, I suppose I must grant it, then," Guaschi said, his tone somewhat peevish. "What is it?"

"Please go down to the tree line and send a signal to the planetary lord. Tell him that an alien spaceship is approaching our planet."

"This is not some kind of joke?" Guaschi asked.

"Note my insignia. I am an official watcher, duly elected by the lottery. I detected an alien ship some hours ago. That is my last word on the subject."

"No need to get huffy about it," Guaschi said. "I had to express some degree of incredulity, didn't I? It's been a thousand years since the last alien showed up, hasn't it?"

"About that," Leo said. "But before that they used to come here quite frequently, sometimes to settle, sometimes to conquer, sometimes to explore, sometimes for no reason at all. In the end we always got rid of them, of course."

"Of course," Guaschi said. "And we shall this time, too. Shan't we?"

"Well, one hopes for the best," Leo said.

"Do you think they'll give us trouble?"

"They're certain to if you don't get on with killing me and going down to the tree line to send the signal."

"You can go down to the tree line yourself," Guaschi said. "It's a nasty bit of slippery climbing, and I don't fancy it."

"Then you're not going to kill me?"

"I didn't say that. You jumped to a conclusion." Guaschi smiled. "That's a good one on you."

"Yes, all right, it is," Leo said. "But you did say I was to go to the tree line and give the message?"

"Correct."

"Then I'll be on my way."

Guaschi drew a small revolver out of his pocket. "Not until you promise me to return after giving the signal."

"Of course I promise," Leo said. He walked off, thinking, *Simple-minded sod*.

"Hurry back," Guaschi called after him. "My daughter will be impatient to meet you."

Leo stopped and turned around. "Daughter? How does your daughter come into this?"

"I would have thought you would have inferred the answer to that very question by now. Quite obviously, I thought up an alternative to killing you. Instead, you can return and marry my daughter. It's dramatically acceptable, uniting the two opposing families and thereby resolving the ancient conflict. An admirable resolution every bit as acceptable as killing you."

"Of course, it's obvious enough now," Leo said. "Tell me, what does your daughter look like?"

"Come back and find out."

VI.

"Good afternoon, Lord Aftenby," Denton said. "I have something rather unpleasant to report."

"Have you indeed?" Lord Aftenby said. He was upset. He permitted Denton to see this by a very slight frown. A frown which said, "You know this is my last day of being lord of the planet, couldn't you have waited until the next lord was selected by lottery?"

"No, I couldn't," Denton said, cognizing Aftenby's thoughts by the rapid reading of a multitude of facial sub-cues. Learning this sort of reading was one of the main educational features of the Eleroi race. Anybody could punch up information on a computer. The real question was, did you know what's going on around you?

"All right, if it's so important, I suppose I should attend to it." Aftenby practiced a sort of offhandedness in his manner which was one of the accepted norms of Eleroi protocol.

Denton had opted for casual but firm directness in his manner. It was really the best personality for the job of prime minister, which was the position the lottery had won him this year.

"To get straight to the point," Denton said, "Leo Huue, the watcher on Mount Forgetful, just signaled. He has picked up a spaceship coming straight for our planet."

"A spaceship?" Aftenby said. "An alien spaceship from outer space?"

"Well, obviously," Denton said. "Since it's not one of ours it must be alien, and since it doesn't come from here it must come from there. The fact that we have no spaceships of our own also inclines me to the belief that it is, at least from our point of view, alien, though from its own outlook quite human, no doubt."

"I know all that," Aftenby said crossly. "I was simply expressing an appropriate amount of surprise. After all, it's been over a thousand years since the last one, hasn't it?"

"Something like that," Denton said. "And I knew that you knew that, but I made my speech anyhow to practice didactics. No offense meant, I assure you."

"And none taken. I suppose I had better get things going. The procedures are clear. We must go into defensive mode, first degree. Come with me while I broadcast the message."

Denton accompanied Aftenby across the broad Lord's Room to the open mullioned window. Outside the window were small red-and-white blossoms that hung on the tips of a tall multi-branched tree.

Aftenby reached out and grasped one of the branches. "Priority message," he said. "Clear the track."

He waited until the network was clear, then announced, "There is an alien spaceship approaching our airspace. Please notify anyone around you who is not interfaced with the biological network. We are going into Defense Procedure A immediately."

Aftenby could feel his message going out along the tree's roots and branches, entering the nearby forest, from where it was rebroadcast by vines and creepers and grasses until it had completed a circuit of the entire planet. Wherever an Eleroi was in contact with tree or vine, the message was received.

He turned to Denton. "That ought to do it."

"Shouldn't you tell them who you are?" Denton asked.

"I clean forgot." Aftenby grasped the branch again. "This is your lord speaking. Aftenby. The ruler of the planet, you may remember. Duly elected by lottery last year."

Aftenby turned to Denton. "How's that?"

"Pretty good," Denton said. "But shouldn't you say something to pick up their morale? I believe that is one of the functions of the head of a planet."

"Oh, very well, if you really think I ought to." Aftenby grasped the branch again. "It is usual in times of danger for your leader to speak words of comfort and wisdom. But the fact is, I'm scared as hell and you should be, too. Aliens are bad news. But we'll cope somehow, never fear."

He released the branch and turned to Denton. "That ought to buck them up, eh?"

"It certainly had its effect on me," Denton said. "Come on, let's get down to the operations room."

"What on earth for?" Aftenby asked.

"Because that's where we plan how to deal with the aliens. You as lord of the planet and me as your prime minister."

"It's a comfort to have you," Aftenby said. "You always know what to do."

"Just as long as I don't have to bear the responsibility," Denton said. "That, my lord, is your lot."

"Don't think I don't know it," Aftenby said. "Let's get to operations."

VII.

The ivy tickled Tony the Contactman into wakefulness. Probably not on its own, of course. Not enough internal musculature. Aided no doubt by the breeze. And the breeze directed by the universal interaction of the Eleroi intelligence with Gaia, the gestalt composed of all the subsystems of the planet and its ethereal surround. Or so Tony the Contactman surmised.

It could have been no more than a happy accident—fortuitousness—or did he mean serendipity?

The vine tickled his foot again. "Damn your impudence," Tony said in the tone of a man speaking to his beloved cat. He stretched, put on a light robe, and made himself a cup of tea. The vine was tapping impatiently against the wall. "Wait a minute," Tony called out. "I'm no good till I've had my coffee." But the vine couldn't understand. It had no ears and not much intelligence, either, despite the latest boost from the Universal Intelligence Upgrade Program, whose existence could be inferred but not verified.

Tony the Contactman was about to lose himself for an hour or so in speculations about cosmic upgrading. He was fat and physically lazy and less inclined toward kinetic activity than his fellows and very fond of thinking about generalizations. Of course, he was only fourteen; he might outgrow it. You could never tell what the Universal Program had in mind for you next.

Tap tap tap.

"All right, I'm coming!"

Without haste, Tony walked into the living room and crossed it to the open window, through which the ivy had thrust green fingers. Tony took one of the green fingers in his own and was immediately patched through to the headquarters of the lord of the planet. It was Aftenby this year, he remembered, and Denton was his prime minister.

Aftenby, himself, was on the vine line. "Tony! How are you?"

"I'm very well," Tony replied. "What's up?"

"Brace yourself," Aftenby said.

"I've already inferred what you're calling me about," Tony said. "It was simple enough, especially with the additional clue of your admonition, or should I call it an exhortation. It's aliens, isn't it? Are they on the ground yet?"

"Not yet," Aftenby said. "They will be soon."

"What bloody luck!"

"Well, it has been a thousand years since the last one."

"I suppose so," Tony said. "Well, what have you done?"

"Initiated Defense Procedure A. We've set up signal flares so that when the aliens are close enough for visual contact, they can see where to land."

"Where we want them to land, you mean," Tony said.

"Well, of course. But they usually tend to follow our landing suggestion. We bring them down in the north bay flats, close to the city of Dungruel."

"Dungruel? I don't seem to remember any place of that name."

"That's because nobody lives there. Don't you read the 'Procedures for Dealing with Aliens'? Dungruel is the model city left us by the ancients. It's where we show the aliens the tawdriness of our civilization."

"How will you explain the lack of people? Can't have much tawdriness without people."

"Stop being silly. Of course we're sending a population over right away, and they'll be in place by the time the aliens get here."

"Cutting it a little fine, weren't you?"

"Our watcher had a little trouble with an avalanche and a blood feud, and there was some delay getting word of the sighting back to us. Don't worry, there's time. You know what you have to do?"

"Yes," Tony said. "But must I? I mean, isn't there someone else around who'd really get a kick out of doing it and would probably do it a lot better than I would?"

"No. Anyhow, it's your job. The lottery selected you as contactman for this year. Don't try to weasel out of it."

"Of course I'm going to do it. I was just complaining, that's all. I'm leaving right away. Is that fast enough for you?"

"Just a minute. Do you know what to do?"

"Of course I don't know what to do," Tony said. "Do you think I lie around all day studying up on what to do in case aliens show up? When they haven't been around in a thousand years? But of course I'll access the information before I leave. When I said I was leaving right away, that was a metaphor for leaving as soon as would be consistent with the necessary preparation for doing the job right. Or perhaps you missed the inference."

"It'll be a cold day in hell when I miss any of *your* inferences, kid," Aftenby said. "I asked if you knew what to do, knowing beforehand that you didn't but were planning to learn; but I wished to underline the importance of taking more than a cursory glance at the material. Or did my tone of voice fail to make that clear?"

"Aftenby," Tony said, "you have succeeded in making me lose my temper. Thank you. I needed that jolt to my constitutionally phlegmatic system to energize me to where I can deal adequately with what is happening."

"Good luck, kid," Aftenby said. "Go out there and contact those aliens. Remember, we're all counting on you. But don't let that get you nervous."

"I won't," Tony said. "After all, the worst they can do is wipe out our entire race. But considering the ancient and well-accepted doctrine of the eternal recurrence of all things, that's not such a big deal, is it?"

"No, it's not," Aftenby said. "You are to be commended for the broadness and dispassion of your overview. But despite that, please try to keep our race going a little longer, okay? Now go out there and deal with those folks."

VIII.

It was only about an hour after landing. Brodsky and Anna were having a light curry dinner, when suddenly there was a knock at the spaceship's port.

"Who do you suppose that is?" Brodsky asked.

Anna looked up from her *Alien Primary Contacts* manual, which she was reading propped up on the table in front of her. "One would infer," she said, "that it is an intelligent alien."

"How do you figure intelligent?"

"It takes brains to know enough to knock. Not even the cleverest dog on Earth can do that. They bark, you see. Not even our nearest cousins, the big primates, can be trained to knock before entering."

Brodsky wondered how she knew that. Had a giant ape, trained but not reliable, walked in on her once? There were a lot of things he didn't know about Anna.

"Might as well see who it is," Brodsky said, then he undogged the port and pulled it open.

A small, fat boy in his early teens walked in.

"Hi," he said. "You must be the aliens."

"Yes, we are," Brodsky said. "And you must be one of the Khasarians."

"We don't call ourselves that any more," the boy said. "We call ourselves the Eleroi. Welcome to our humble planet."

"How come you speak English?" Anna asked.

"I'm a telepath," the boy said. "My name is Tony. I'm the contactman."

Brodsky stood up, looked at Tony, and shook his head. "Aren't you a little young to be a contactman?"

"Not at all. We Eleroi assign responsibility on the basis of intelligence and motility, not age."

"That makes sense," Brodsky said. "I'm Brodsky and this is Anna."

Anna shook the contactman's hand. She said, "Having a language in common makes it much easier. We want to know all about your civilization. And we want to tell you about ours.''

"Yes, that's the usual form, isn't it?" Tony asked.

"And we want to go sightseeing," Brodsky said. "Visit your major cities, look into the music scene, that sort of thing."

"Yes, that's what visiting aliens usually want," Tony said. "Come, let me take you to Dungruel."

"Delighted," Anna said. "Will we meet your leader, president, secretary-general, or whatever you call him, there?"

"Actually, he's rather busy," Tony said. "I'm supposed to fill in for him."

"We shall have to see him before we leave," Anna said. Her tone left no doubt that this would be accomplished in one way or another, peacefully, if possible, but any which way if necessary.

IX.

The Eleroians know all about alien invasions. They have had a lot of them. So many that when aliens land from other planets, the Eleroians just shrug their shoulders and say, "Oh, it's aliens again, trying to involve us in their fugacious embranglements."

It's all right if the aliens were just coming for a visit. Curiosity is understandable, though deplorable. Usually they go away if not encouraged. All you have to do is talk to them and pose for photographs and wave when they fly away.

But all bets are off if the aliens find fascinating ruins. Most aliens are crazy about old ruins.

The Eleroi take care to hide their antiquities underneath reservoirs and landfills. Even so, some especially pertinacious races have discovered them.

As often as they have been invaded, even more often have the Eleroi been sent gifts by soft-hearted peoples. The Eleroi have no prejudice against taking things. It makes the giver feel good and does no one any harm. But the gifts pile up in carefully camouflaged warehouses because the Eleroi don't need this stuff.

Some explorers come to Khasara in order to study Eleroi culture. These aliens tend to be earnest, honest, erudite, and very dangerous, because they often stay on for years and years asking boring questions and bringing in many assistants. The Eleroi try to discourage cultural curiosity by displaying only art objects that a Matagalpan Indian with a bone through his nose wouldn't spit on, and passing off these monstrosities as their highest cultural treasures. In fact, the Eleroi have learned to produce the sort of painting no intelligent being in his right mind would dream of hanging in his house. It's the only defense against alien collectors, and a lot of the time even that doesn't work.

The Eleroi are naturally weak, shiftless, lazy, and too clever by half. Their fatal flaw is the inability to resist leaving clues of their cleverness—tipping off their game—because to be appreciated is the highest reward. Luckily, most invaders are not intelligent enough, or are too opinionated and set in their views to pick up the nuances.

The Eleroi system usually works. Aliens land and stay for a while and then go away again, leaving the Eleroi to their immemorial pursuits. But sometimes fate or chance steps in; something you can do nothing about.

It had to be fate that brought people like Brodsky and Anna to a place like this.

X.

"How far is it to Dungruel?" Brodsky asked.

"About five lii," Tony said. "Our lii equals 1.002 of your standard kilometers. I'm afraid we'll have to walk."

"Don't you have any transportation?" Anna asked.

"We just haven't gotten around to inventing any yet," Tony said. "We were late discovering the wheel, you know."

"Luckily we brought our own vehicle," Anna said. "Brodsky, why don't you show him the altersoar?"

Brodsky went to the storage hold and brought out a large box about the size of a standard Terran coffin. He pushed it outside—it had wheels—told everyone to stand back, removed the safety interlock, and pushed a button marked ARTICULATE. The box exfoliated, revealing itself to be a collection of memory-tagged aluminum struts and a small central driving unit. These quickly assembled themselves into a vehicle.

"Pretty neat," Tony said. He followed Brodsky and Anna into the vehicle. It was a tight squeeze, but they all made it. Brodsky set the controls to lift, leveling off a hundred meters or so above the ground.

"Dungruel is right over there," Tony said. "You can steer by the pillar of smoke."

"What causes that smoke?" Anna asked.

"That's the new Smoke Factory."

"What does the factory produce?" Anna asked.

"Nothing. Just smoke."

"That doesn't make any sense," Anna said.

"It's perfectly reasonable," Tony told her. "You can always decide later what a factory should make. The first step is to find out if you can stand the smoke."

XI.

Dungruel was a large, shabby place of low ramshackle buildings and dirty streets. Tony pointed out the main sights— the Beggars' Guildhall, the Ministry of Handouts, the Pigout Restaurant. The few people in the streets were mean-featured, loutish, dressed in filthy rags, and sporting an impressive collection of running sores.

"Very interesting," Anna said at the conclusion of the tour. "Now we must return to our ship. Will you come visit us again first thing in the morning?"

"Certainly," Tony said. "There are several other sights well worth seeing. Our Clamarang Mountains, for example, which soar almost four hundred feet into the air. And the River Mote, mean depth of ten feet, nearly three hundred meters wide at its widest point."

"We are not interested in your mountains or rivers," Anna said.

"And who could blame you for your disinterest?" said Tony, smiling miserably. "After all, it should be obvious that we are not a prosperous people, nor are we inventive or even intelligent. But we'll try to show you a good time before you depart for more promising places."

"I don't know why you run yourselves down so," Anna said. "There's nothing wrong with you Eleroians that vitamin supplements and a good education won't take care of."

"Vitamins might not be a bad idea," Tony said. "I suppose you could drop some off before you leave."

"We are not going anywhere yet, Tony," Anna said firmly.

"Tomorrow we look forward to meeting with your leader and explaining to him the advantages, both physical and spiritual, of joining our Alliance."

"I have no doubt that Aftenby, the lord of Khasara, will be interested in your views."

"As well he should be," Anna said.

"But frankly, I'd better warn you in advance, we Eleroi really aren't joiners."

"That will have to change now," Anna told him. "All over the universe humankind is engaged in a desperate war. Our very survival is at stake, and so is yours. You are going to have to choose sides. You are going to have to join our Alliance."

"I'll tell Aftenby," Tony said. "But he's not going to like it."

XII.

"But what did she mean, *her* alliance?" Aftenby asked. "I mean, it wasn't literal, was it?"

"I think she was referring to an alliance of which she is a representative," Tony said.

"It's obvious that she means a group of planets," Denton said. "It's the sort of things barbarians do: form alliances among themselves in order to overturn other alliances. Obviously they want us to join. That's how they get members, you see, by forcing people to join them."

Aftenby shuddered at the thought of joining an alliance. It was precisely the sort of thing the Eleroi had avoided throughout their long existence.

These aliens weren't convinced of the worthlessness of the Eleroi people and the planet they lived on. It was time for the most extreme measures.

XIII.

"No, I don't want any more curry," Brodsky said over breakfast. "And I don't want any more of your high-handed ways, either."

Anna stared at him. "What are you talking about?"

"We were sent here to explore and report back. Not to coerce people into joining the Alliance."

"You have your orders and I have mine," Anna said.

"What is that supposed to mean?"

"Wake up to reality, Brodsky. There really *is* a war on, you know. Do you think anybody can sit on the fence? What happens to these people if the Khalia or their allies find them before we have time to station a garrison?"

"It's their own decision," Brodsky said, "whether to join or not."

"They can leave the Alliance any time they want," Anna said. "Those are the rules. But they have to join first before they can quit."

"There are no standing orders to that effect."

"It's a field decision, left to the discretion of the officer on the spot."

"I'm an officer, too," Brodsky pointed out.

"Yes, but I've held my commission longer than you have. That makes me senior and gives me the right to make a ruling."

Just then there was a heavy pounding at the spaceship port. Brodsky got up to answer it. As he undogged the hatch, he said to Anna, "I don't know why we're quarreling. Our views aren't so far apart. I think the Eleroi ought to be in the Alliance, too. But you're going about it in the wrong way."

"You think you know the right way? Since when have you become an expert on Eleroian psychology? Brodsky, I'm warning you, let me handle this."

"Be my guest," Brodsky said, opening the lock. "Come on in, Tony."

Tony entered, followed by two men. Brodsky knew even before being introduced that these were the lord of the planet and his right-hand man.

And anyhow, there were no introductions. Aftenby, the lord of the planet, said, "So you're the aliens? I understand that you have a flying machine. Please take me aloft so I can show you what damage your visit has brought about."

XIV.

From the air, you could see that the green fields of the Eleroi had turned brown overnight. Rivers that had been green and swift-moving just the previous night had now dried up. A scorching wind blew from all directions. For as far as the eye could see, the desolation was complete.

"I regret this very much," Anna said when they had returned to the ship. "I don't know what happened to cause all that destruction. But it surely was a natural catastrophe of some sort, and no fault of ours, though we will certainly be willing to help you put matters straight again."

"Very kind of you, I'm sure," Aftenby said bitterly. "Come here and wreck our planet, then offer to tidy up afterward. No, thank you very much, please just go away, and we'll do our own tidying."

Anna looked uncertain. She wasn't sure what to do. And she was starting to get flashes of a court-martial ahead if this whole thing weren't handled carefully.

"Brodsky," she said, "what do you think?"

Brodsky looked surprised. "You want my recommendations?"

"If you don't mind."

Brodsky walked across the cabin and stood in front of Aftenby, Denton, and Tony. They looked at him with grave, grief-stricken faces. Brodsky began to laugh.

"All right," he said. "You can turn it off now."

"What are you talking about?" Denton said. "Turn what off?"

"I am referring to the psycho-physio-biological interface you Eleroi have with your planet and with all its energetic systems. I'm talking about your ability to control every process on this planet."

"You think we did this ourselves?" Denton asked.

"Of course. It's obvious to me that you Eleroi have not cultivated defense in the accepted meaning of the term. You have cued your body chemistry into that of the plant life. When you feel bad, the whole planet feels bad. Crops fail. Water pollutes. The air turns foul. The invader at last leaves in disgust. That's the scenario. No doubt it's worked in the past. But it's not going to work this time."

"How did you know about us?" Aftenby asked in a low voice.

"I was able to infer it because I'm just like you. Too clever for my own good, but not particularly skilled at anything."

"You are like us," Denton said. "I suppose you know that all life is founded in contradiction but one does the best one can.

But there's no escaping the inner flaw. Intelligence works to minimalize the occurrence of conditions that would activate the destructive mechanisms which the flaw represents. Or am I going too fast for you?''

"Not at all,'' Brodsky said. ''You're saying that no matter how smart you are, it takes a little luck. And you Eleroi have been lucky so far. But how you do in the future is going to depend on the choice you make right now.''

"Still trying to make us join your beastly Alliance?'' Aftenby muttered.

"No, I'm not,'' Brodsky said. ''My colleague and I will leave the choice up to you. If you decide not to join, we'll go away and leave you alone. Whether the Khalia and their friends will do likewise, I can't say. But I can promise for us. Can't I, Anna?''

Anna looked puzzled. She'd never thought Brodsky could take charge like this. So definite, so sure of himself. She decided that his commanding officer had assigned him to the exploration program for reasons a little better than just getting rid of him.

"Yes, I'll abide by their decision,'' Anna said.

"Well, that's very nice of you,'' Aftenby said. ''Sporting, very sporting. We'll think about all the things you've said, and give the matter our best attention. But for the present, why don't you nice people just go away, and we'll get back to you as soon as we've invented transspatial communication.''

"Aftenby, stop talking for a moment,'' Denton said. ''Can't you see he's laughing at you? The alien knows something we don't know!''

Brodsky nodded and turned to Denton. ''You're so clever, Mr. Prime Minister. Surely you've inferred already what I'm laughing about?''

"I know, I know!'' Tony said, jumping up and down.

Denton said, with dignity, ''What, pray tell, are you laughing about? What do you know?''

Brodsky said, ''I know what you Eleroi are really afraid of.''

"Yes, yes,'' said Tony, who loved to out-infer grown-ups and was very good at it. ''Tell them, Brodsky! But begin at the beginning!''

"Right,'' Brodsky said. ''But the beginning was so far back that probably even you Eleroi don't remember when it began. So let's pick an arbitrary time, maybe a million or so years ago, when you Eleroi discovered that you could live peaceably with each other. I'll bet none of you even knows when you had your last war. You are the only intelligent cooperative society I've ever heard of. How did you do it?''

"Some of it was luck," Denton said. "We had the good fortune to be smart enough to decide to make several key modifications in the genetic engineering of our race. We opted for biological altruism within a game-playing frame."

"You opted for stagnation. You froze your development. Maybe you picked the perfect point at which to stop growing, but stop you did. You turned your back on the universe, pretended it wasn't there, but unfortunately for you the universe hasn't forgotten you. Fellow Eleroi—for I count myself one of you—it's time to try another tactic."

"Join your Alliance, you mean?" Aftenby said. "That's what it comes down to, doesn't it, all your specious argumentation?"

"Of course. But it isn't specious. I could be wrong. But it's what I feel would be best for you. I also feel that you agree with me but are looking for a graceful way of claiming the idea as your own."

"Well, damn it all," Aftenby said. "If you're going to put it that way, what can we say? Eh, Denton?"

"Yes, I suppose it's time," Denton said.

Anna couldn't stand it any longer. "You're actually going to join the Alliance? Just because *he* advised you to?"

"Actually, Brodsky had very little to do with it," Denton said. "Historical necessity throws up its mouthpieces when and as they are required. Not to take anything away from you, old man. But it was inevitable that a race of our intelligence would figure out the next step for itself. Join the Alliance. Yes. I have only one slight remaining fear about that . . ."

"Set your mind at rest," Brodsky said. "I can assure you that what you fear will never happen."

"Will you all stop being so goddamned clever and tell me what you are talking about?" Anna cried. "What do you fear, Denton? And Brodsky, how can you be so sure it'll never happen? What is it?"

Denton smiled, the peevish smile of a man-child too clever by half. "No sense even discussing it," he said. "Perhaps you could tell me how one joins this Alliance of yours. Are there forms to fill out? Does it matter that we don't have any spaceships? And could I possibly bother you for a cup of tea?''

''I'll get it,'' Brodsky said.

''No, I'll get it,'' Anna said and went past him into the galley. She put up the water, fuming. Those Eleroi were really insufferable. And so was that smart aleck Brodsky. Trouble was, she was beginning to get used to him. She decided, quite spontaneously, to make him a really nice curry dinner that night. But what was it that the Eleroi feared?

XV.

''I'm back,'' Leo Huue the Watcher called out as he approached the hut of Ottoline Guaschi. ''Where's your daughter?''

''Hah!'' cried Guaschi, coming out the door with a revolver leveled at Leo. ''You fool! There is no daughter, only miserable death which awaits you on this windswept hillside.'' He leveled the revolver.

Leo wasn't really convinced, but he closed his eyes because if he was going to be shot, he didn't want to watch it happening.

''No, I was just kidding,'' Guaschi said, putting the revolver down on a rock. ''Come out, Chloe!''

From his hut came a small, delectable bright-eyed girl with strawberry curls and a smile that could melt granite.

Leo took one look at her and knew that they were going to be very happy together. And he also knew, or at least inferred, that she had set up this whole thing herself, since the girls of Eleroi did this sort of thing, going in for fantastical forms of courtship once they decided on who the lucky man was going to be. But he also knew, or was pretty sure, that there was one thing she didn't know.

''We can get married whenever you like,'' he said, ''but perhaps it ought to be soon because I've joined the expeditionary force, and there's no telling when we'll have to leave.''

''What expeditionary force is that?'' Chloe asked.

''The one that we're going to send to the Alliance. We've joined the Alliance, you know. Don't you listen to the tree reports?''

"I don't understand," Chloe said. "Why are we sending men? What can we Eleroi do? There's not a man on the planet who even knows how to fix a washing machine."

Leo exchanged looks with Ottoline Guaschi. Ottoline understood. It was a masculine thing, perhaps.

"We'll give them what help we can," Leo said quietly.

He and Ottoline both knew that this could be the beginning of the end, for the Eleroi were so superior to other creatures that the other leaders would inevitably put them in charge of the war effort. And that was the Eleroi's secret fear—that someone would discover their superiority some day and ask them to take over the leadership of everything and everybody. That would be a dilemma, because the Eleroi had a built-in problem about leadership. Their biochemical altruistic programming defaults wouldn't let them refuse; their intelligence wouldn't allow them to accept. A choice like that could be Armageddon for a race like the Eleroi.

But they had Brodsky's word that it would never happen. In fact, Brodsky had been very definite about it.

"Are you kidding? The presidents and generals of the most advanced civilizations in the galaxy turning over control of their destinies to you simply because you're more intelligent and capable than they are? Forget it." Brodsky had told them. "You don't know how it works. Believe me, it'll never happen."

The Eleroi had to be content with that. It was a relief to know that they wouldn't be given too much responsibility in Alliance affairs too soon. But it was also a little irksome to know that they'd never even be asked. For after all, who was more suited to running things than the Eleroi?

Too bad it would never happen.

Or would it?

It occurred to the entire Eleroi race more or less simultaneously that there might, in fact, be a way for them to take over control of the Alliance, then the Fleet, and, finally, the universe.

Such thoughts occur to semitelepathic races who have mastered the bioenergetic interfaces that confer control over environment.

It was an interesting option. The Eleroi would look into it later.

INTERLUDE

The image of Hawk Talon, his gauss rifle smoking, freezes and then is replaced by the almost equally familiar visage of Herb, the spokesman for Telemax. Nearly all of the omni stations in the Alliance are dependent on advertising revenues. Telemax and fewer than twenty other multiplanetary megacorps supplied over half of this advertising. Perhaps that is why the tens of thousands of Independent Merchants are invariably presented on the omni as fast-talking opportunists.

Then again this prejudice may be due to the awkward fact that most of the Indies actually *are* fast-talking opportunists.

INDIE

by S. N. Lewitt

"IDEALLY YOU SHOULD have two months, maybe three," Sein had said when he was briefed for this task. "But you managed to pass once before, and we'll just have to say our prayers. Because no one knows how long anyone stays in the Rat."

That had pleased him at the time. He had had visions of the Rat, the Indie central nexus, as a place full of mystery. After all, according to his father the admiral, the independent merchants were little better than pirates. According to his mother the admiral, pirates were more honorable. So he had expected something like the cantina scene in *Carmen,* with dancing girls and jewel-encrusted goblets kept full of wine, a brooding pirate-king overseeing the division of the spoils, and long afternoons spent under the Chola-range lamps being seduced by the legendary Chola priestesses.

So far only the Chola-range lamps had been true, and that was because the Rat had managed to get particularly favorable prices. Otherwise life as an Indie was not very much different than his experience on the Tobishi lines, and in the seven union halls he had seen since going under cover. At least not on the surface.

"It wasn't just the rateri," Sein had gone on in the briefing, in a room that wasn't very different from the simple Indie registration office. "Although that helped. We followed the lead Jurgen gave us, and more and more it begins to look as if there's something untoward, to say the least, about the Indie business. At least some of the business, especially on the edges of the empire. Since they don't pay taxes and don't report income, we have no idea how well-off they really are, but captures in recent years indicate better ships and the latest technology. Sometimes things that the Fleet is only using in prototype. What do you think?"

"According to the news, the Indies are legal. On the edge sometimes, but basically independent entrepreneurs. I admire people like that. If they're pirates, though, that's a different story," Diego answered.

Sein had shaken his head so that the shaggy thick hair flew into his eyes. "Most of them are legal because we don't know what else they're doing. The information you brought back indicates that they may not even be aware that they have been selling Khalian goods to honest colonies. After all, they deal through the free traders, and if one has a consignment and the fee is high enough, they'll take it."

"But what can the Khalians produce that anyone'd buy?" Diego wondered aloud. "I mean, they're getting their equipment from *somewhere*, but from what I've heard about Weasel technology, they're lucky if they can produce toothpicks on their own."

Sein snorted impatiently. "The point isn't what they can produce, it's where they're getting what they've got. Officially, of course, it's assumed that there's some advanced species that's been conquered by the Khalians and is supplying their technical know-how. Personally, I have an open mind."

"And you want me to see if the Indies have anything to do with this technology transfer, sir." There was no need to make it a question.

It wasn't good enough to rate a smile from Sein, but he did get a curt nod. "Precisely. We don't know exactly what is going on there, but I have a hunch. And in this business we take our hunches very seriously."

Diego had licked his lips in that briefing room. To penetrate the Indie Rat, sealed as tight as a pharaoh's tomb, that would definitely be worth something in his personnel file. To say nothing of seriously impressing his parents. They hadn't been exactly overjoyed when he passed up the opportunity to join the Fast Attack Wing and stayed with Intel. Diego didn't particularly cherish the memory of the elegant family dinner when he had made his announcement.

"Of all the idiotic, self-destructive things to do," his father had yelled so loudly that his mother's heirloom Waterford wineglasses had shaken. She hadn't yelled, but then Diego couldn't remember her raising her voice in his entire life. Generally he wished she would.

"Obviously you have decided to shame us in front of all our colleagues," she said, her tone cold and bitter, turning what had been a tempting meal into a nightmare. "Intelligence is worse than becoming a civilian. I assume you are doing this to assert your independence. As the youngest, I suppose you think that sabotaging your career will gain you our attention. I expect you to return to your senses when you find that this humiliation has not gained you anything at all."

He couldn't possibly explain to them—both of them admirals in the Fleet, children of admirals in the Fleet—why he found undercover work so important. When he had been tapped the first time he had found himself making decisions pivotal to the future of humanity as a whole. For the first time Diego Bach had taken full responsibility and had won his own victories. And suffered for it as well.

Besides, Sein had pointed out, not unkindly, that the career in question was his own. "And in Intel," his superior had continued, "cracking this assignment will make you a name player. Marked for the big time, if you want to take it all the way. Intel has its own career service, you know, and our people don't do badly."

That was an understatement. There was more than one admiral, more than one division head, who had come up through the shadow services. Those on the inside knew, and those outside were kept carefully ignorant. Diego was not so innocent that he didn't recognize that that very factor was part of what enticed him to stay. In the Fast Attack Wing there was nothing at all he could do to keep every minute of every day from his parents' scrutiny, should they so desire to exercise it.

But so far the Rat had been very tame. No public orgies, no drug dens, no ecstasy suicide bands, no executions in Colonial Hall, commonly known as the Hole. At least not yet.

Diego Bach had been in the Rat long enough to have taken on all the characteristics of an Indie. His skin had gone from white to nearly translucent and his blond hair was streaked with silver from the Chola lamps. More than that, he hadn't noticed his eyes narrowing and constantly scanning the scene no matter whom he was talking to or what work he was doing. It was precisely that shift that marked him as a true Indie and no longer an engineer, second class, for the Tobishi lines. That he didn't wear the distinctive colored belt of an Indie here meant only that he was available for any free captain who would meet his requirements. Fifteen days in the Rat was longer than he wanted to spend building the layers of identity that might take him into the Khalian Empire, and it was not nearly long enough.

He had been here fifteen days, and for the fifteenth time he was on his way to the Hole. Overhead, so distant that he could barely make them out, were the warehouses and cargo centers. In the residential section of the environment, shrubs had been planted to block the view of the curvature, so that the whole place looked like a vast park. Unexpected pleasantries had been carefully placed—the stone carving of some obscure god, an artificially weathered bridge, a lantern of filigreed iron hanging from a low branch.

The Indie costumes had ceased being interesting after the first few days. For once his tattooed snake and the heavy, gold Saint Barbara medal around his neck were simply ordinary adornments, neither gaudy nor uninteresting, but merely on the same order as most of the Indie sign-ons in his age and experience bracket. And the commercial behavior he had seen in these fifteen days had been as untoward as the clothing, and as legal.

In fact, Diego had almost resigned himself to filing a no-joy on this Rat and maybe moving on. There were at least three, and if rumor was to be believed this was the tamest of the lot.

"But that's exactly why we're sending you there," Sein had said with a perfectly blank expression. "If there's anything we want to know about, they are certainly going to try to throw us off the scent. Remember, the worst criminals blend best into society on the smaller matters."

Diego hadn't known that at all. Criminal behavior was quite definitely not one of the areas covered at the academy. Still, the situation irritated him. This gentle environment and well-governed public administration were far more prototypical of a good Alliance colony than of a pirate den.

At the Hole he hesitated at the door, scanning the labor log in the viewer. It listed day work in the warehouses on the other side. He'd signed up for day labor on two occasions to get his hands on shipments, but both times he had seen only the most mundane cargos. Still, it was habit to check the board.

"Commers is looking for crew." A hand grabbed Diego from the darkness inside the vast hiring hall and pulled him inside.

He blinked twice before he recognized his assailant, another second engineer called Tai Jummakan, who had been regularly on the work beat herself for as long as he'd been in the Rat. Tai was one of the reasons he had adjusted so easily. She had been born Indie and didn't think twice about spacers who chose her way of life. After all, if she hadn't been born Indie, she would have jumped the first time she'd been within hailing distance of a Rat, that was sure. And she said it every time they talked, every time she poured herself another of the warm, deep brown beers favored in this place.

"You think you'll sign on?" Diego asked casually, knowing that he wanted to find something and despairing of ever crossing the line.

Tai looked at him squarely, her dark eyes narrowing exactly the way they had when he had "jumped" from the Tobishi Lines *Lodestone* on Kariel. That suspicious squint was the only hesitation she had ever shown about him, and Diego realized just how lucky he had been to contact Tai instead of her shipmates, ex-liners who would have scrutinized him a little more closely than his background could stand.

"I'm not sure," she said after a moment of thought. "What about you?"

"I don't know Commers," Diego reminded her quickly. "And you're the one who read the position board, not me."

Tai shrugged and pointed to one of the large boards in the back, the central one that had been blank for days. The crew board. Now it had a single entry, twenty lines long. Diego edged around groups discussing various work options until he was just under the announcement.

It looked perfectly ordinary. Commers's ship, the *Matilda*, had been back-Rat for nearly a month, completely overhauled. The *Matilda* took a crew of twenty, and only four from their last trip out were signing back on.

Something about that nagged at Diego, although he knew it was perfectly normal among Indies to change ships more often than they changed their underwear. So the *Matilda* had made a good run with top profits. Any Indie crew would lay ashore after that, with enough money in the till for a nice long vacation and maybe enough to take the family on a tour of the planetary playgrounds. That was always popular. A month was a very short lay-over, especially after a good run.

Or, Diego considered, it might have been not such a good run. Which could be why Commers was going right back out and why most of his crew didn't want to ship with him. He hadn't met an Indie in the Rat who didn't believe in ''bad luck ships'' and ''ghost riders'' and a whole host of other nonsense that Diego dismissed as simply traditional, foolish, or both.

As he considered it, something else about the entry seemed strange. Diego scanned it again and stopped cold. The third column was blank; no destination was listed for the *Matilda,* no ports of call.

''So,'' Bach whispered through his teeth.

''Yeah,'' Tai agreed. ''You see what I mean. Commers has a rep, you know? He likes to play it close to the edge.''

Diego felt a lump of cold lead in his stomach, his hunch meter going off at max. Like Sein's hunch about the Indies in general, this was one he couldn't really back up, but he *knew.* Reading the anomalies was like reading it written plain on the wall.

His rational mind rebelled, gibbering away about probabilities and lack of data. He could not, it screamed at him, sign on here without more detailed information. Not unless he wanted to blow this job completely. Not unless he was ready to fail.

Diego bit his lip contemplating the board. His hand went by habit to the heavy, gold Saint Barbara medal around his neck. Somewhere, here, he was going to have to take a chance. There was nothing in the Rat, nothing to do but go out and pray. That was the best there was. That was all there was.

He thought momentarily about his family who had raised him in all the Fleet's finest traditions and had expected his career to follow the traditional path, all the way back to his Fuentes forebearer who had fought with Bolívar. He had struck out on his own. Now, had he stayed, he would have been maybe a lieutenant j.g. in the Fast Attack Wing. Sexy, sure, and with plenty of the kind of flash that decorations and personnel files were made of. But there, like in his parents' home, the decision would not have been his, nor the responsibility either. *How long did it take you, Mom, Dad, to get where I am now?* Diego wondered. *Or did you ever? Or do you still sit around and execute orders that you find idiotic? How much do you ever do on your own? How do you know that your decisions count?*

"What's the matter? Your eyes freeze shut or something?" Tai asked teasingly.

Diego grinned at her, the grin he had spent weeks perfecting on the *Lodestone* that pretended intimacy. Then he walked up and pressed his palm to the board. Hell. Might as well make it official before someone else took the berth. This was as good as it was going to get.

"All right," Tai said, exhaling strongly. "Now that means that I have to buy."

Diego grinned again, a little more evilly. He'd heard of that custom, among others, but hadn't expected to be treated. He didn't really know anyone here well enough to drink with. Including Tai. But it was impossible to refuse.

They left the hiring hall and took the main avenue through the administrative district to where it met the small entertainment quarter. A large public theater dominated one side of the street, and expensive shops selling all the loot of the universe lined the other. The shops he had expected, richly appointed and filled with soft-voiced salespeople who never pressed and always treated spacers with respect. The theater had been a surprise, even more so the varied schedule listed outside, not what he had expected from a forbidden, hidden pirate stronghold. *Ruddigore* and *Patience* were being presented in repertory for one more week, followed by two bands with unfamiliar names, Chekov's *The Cherry Orchard*, and a Sunday noon presentation of Mozart's Prague Symphony. Not to mention two recitals, a poetry reading, and a public execution.

Tai sighed as they passed the colorful poster advertising *Ruddigore*. "Last year I was in the chorus of *Princess Ida*," she said wistfully. "And I really wanted to do *Ruddigore*. But I was out when auditions were held. Anyway, maybe next year, if I get a good enough run to pay for the audition."

They turned down a side street and into their usual pub. It was Tai who had introduced him to the place and Tai who held court at their usual table, second from the back on the left. Only this afternoon she waved away all the other regulars and concentrated on Diego alone.

"I have a funny feeling about this," she began softly, her voice nearly drowned out by the sound of other conversations and some ungodly sentimental tune. "Commers has a rep, like I said. His runs are generally very profitable, but like I said, he plays it close to the edge.''

Diego watched her very carefully. ''What, exactly, do you mean by that?''

She shrugged and stared into her beer. ''I'm not sure how to explain it. His operations aren't always, well, what you would call well inside Alliance territory. That's for one thing. For another, his background. He was an officer in the Fleet once, at least that's what the scuttlebutt says.''

Diego felt the lump in his stomach grow. His hunch mechanism was working overtime, and part of him wanted to bolt this place, take out a scooter, and run to the first Fleet ship he found. *But there's no hard evidence,* he told himself. *Less than worthless without data. Besides, you could be wrong. It has happened.*

It had happened on precisely four occasions Bach could count, and he didn't like recalling any of them. Only this was different. This time he knew.

Suddenly Diego had a vision of himself, of Sein, and they were the same. Sein knew things and then sent out people like Diego to prove them. Not because of the hunch, but because of the times he'd been wrong. Because it mattered.

''Well,'' Tai was saying, ''since you went and did it, I guess I don't have too much choice. You've got yourself a shipmate.''

She smiled and Diego noticed, not quite for the first time, that she was really very pretty. Very pretty indeed. And she was going to ship with him. The implications of that were very pleasant. And very, very dangerous. Diego reminded himself to remain aware of the threat. And he even remembered all the way to report on the *Matilda.*

The ship lay outside the habitat, visible through the sectionals in the port sector. *If the* Lodestone *was a ration can, this thing is foil-wrap,* Diego thought when he saw the *Matilda* and tried to suppress a shudder. Flimsy was not exactly the word to describe the appearance of the ship. It wouldn't stand up to a ship of the Fleet, not even to the smallest scout. Maybe there was a good reason that most of Commers's crew didn't sign back on.

Well, he'd printed the board and taken the red-yellow-violet belt that went with the job. By Indie honor there was no turning back now. With a resignation that masked something akin to fear, Diego boarded the *Matilda* through the port tunnel. Tai took the lead and brought them to the galley where the eighteen other crew members waited for their captain.

Gar Commers entered at exactly noon, *Matilda* time, took one of the wire-mesh seats with no ceremony, and leaned forward on the stained plastic table with his elbows. He was younger than Diego had expected, and small, but he moved with the compact grace of a trained fighter.

Diego braced himself. He knew the type; one had graduated ahead of him at the academy. Diego had never been pleased with that second place, and even though the Chola lamps had bleached out the captain's hair and skin to a dusty pale beige, his features bore enough resemblance to those of Midshipman Cheng Lo-Sen that it was almost déjà-vu. Cheng had what Diego was convinced was a Napoleon complex; he liked to play it faster, dirtier and harder than anyone else. Someone had once dubbed him the Weasel; hell knew he was mean enough for one. Only the name never stuck, not after the joker ended up with two broken legs in a sparring match.

Commers smiled at them. Diego knew it was all over. There was nothing of pleasure and only private humor in that expression.

"Welcome to the *Matilda*," Commers said in a voice that was shocking in its richness. "I have been through the manifest, and I must admit I'm delighted by the experience and skills you represent. Perhaps the biggest question is the lack of a destination on the board. The reason I couldn't list one was that we are going to rendezvous with a ship, a human ship, let there be no mistake, to take on cargo. We should reach the rendezvous point in two days. Any questions?"

Commers flashed the smile again. This time everyone knew that the request for query was merely form. If Commers wasn't talking about their rendezvous or the cargo up front, it was because he didn't want them to know.

"Well, that's why we're Indies," Tai said finally when they found a moment to discuss the business that evening over coffee. "You think Tobishi Lines would meet a stranger ship or carry unnamed cargo?"

Diego shook his head firmly. "Not possible. You sound like stranger ships aren't that uncommon. I never heard of one before."

Tai just shrugged. "I don't know. There are a few. Humans,

free traders, Indies, I guess. Only they port in at the Rats, not that anyone knows. Maybe they're all descended from the *Atlantis* complement. That's what most people think, anyway.''

Diego groaned. ''Don't tell me you really believe that. Next thing is they'll be the lost tribes of Israel,'' he said, hunching over the dull galley table that was now spread with an abandoned game of solitaire. The *Atlantis* had maybe existed sometime in the primordial days of space travel, a generation ship that had been lost forever behind the reaches of time and space. It was not the only lost ship, only the most famous because of its ill-fated name.

Tai, however, had lost all interest. ''You're Indie now, Diego,'' she insisted again. ''More danger, more profit. Sure, it would be nice hauling innocent, unassuming produce around well inside the Alliance, but that doesn't cut our shares.'' She laughed and tugged him up. ''Come on. Like I said, you're Indie now.''

Bach came out of his seat and followed her. Once upon a time he would have kept his distance, kept apart. Sein had told him it was the most sensible thing to do, and he had tried. Only it had been so very long and she was very lovely and he had been cut off for too long. So he followed her to the tiny cabin she shared with a navigator on the late watch and prayed that she wouldn't press him too far.

He had forgotten about the snake. Stupidly. Even in one-quarter light it showed against his pale skin, a violet tattoo that ran from his knee to his shoulder, a memento of his first assignment. And his first kill.

Tai traced the path of it on his skin, looked at him with a sad knowingness, and said nothing.

When they docked with the *Hansa,* Diego was already impatiently waiting on the shift lines. Only Commers wouldn't be involved in transferring cargo. Even the first mate was assigned a position, although it was not exactly the heaviest job in the lot.

By the time the red docking light had stopped blinking madly, the bos'n was handing out padded brown gloves and masks. Diego pulled the mask over his face and drew on the gloves with a sense of accomplishment. Only when handling something very dangerous or sterile would cargo handlers be required to wear protective garments.

Then the link line opened and there wasn't any time for thought. They were herded down into what seemed to be only one of several cargo bays. Diego tried to catch information on the way as they raced through the ship. The people were human, all right, at least from the look of them. But he couldn't identify the language they spoke together, nor did the writing—which looked like a child's scribbling—on the various doors help.

"In will you here find your cargoes," their chief shepherd had informed them through a heavy accent.

Seventeen members of the *Matilda*'s crew—each reluctantly —took a crate. They were small and solid, with tiny holes on the top. And they were amazingly light, Diego realized, far too light to carry the prefabs he had hoped to find.

But there had to be some connection. He could feel it. He could taste it. Sein had a hunch, and the man was almost never wrong. Damn it, the Fleet needed the information on where the Weasels were getting their equipment, and these were only humans trading with other humans for something . . . well, Diego didn't know what, exactly.

He followed the rest back to the *Matilda*'s hold. The crate in his arms shifted weight suddenly and there was a scratching sound. Animals? As he set the crate down near the others and returned to the *Hansa* for more, Diego cornered the bos'n on the way.

"Sam, you know what's in those things?" he asked in a hushed whisper.

The oversized handler chuckled. "You bet, kiddo. Them there's sables."

"Huh?"

The bos'n shook his head. "Sables. Animals. Close relatives of the weasel, if I have my facts straight. Best fur in the universe, though. Get enough of them to breed 'em, and you got the softest fortune ever walked on legs."

"And where are we taking them?" Bach insisted.

The bos'n just shook his head. "Should have asked that before you signed on, boy. We're headed back home. Hannibal Crane wants these critters real bad. And when he wants something bad he gets it. And he pays for it, too, don't you worry. You are looking at one long vacation if you want to take it."

Only pure will held Diego Bach from screaming a slew of curses in every language he spoke. He had managed to get this far, to make it into the Rat and farther out of the territory, only to get pets for the richest man in the Alliance. As the bos'n turned, Diego pounded a fist against the bulkhead. If it weren't for his protective gloves, he might have broken a knuckle. As it was, even that action didn't give him any satisfaction.

That's why you had to come. Sometimes hunches don't work out. The logical portion of his mind gloated while the rest of him wondered furiously how he could have been so wrong. And something inside kept screaming that he wasn't really wrong, just not looking in the right place.

"Problem?"

Diego cursed again. He hadn't heard Tai come up behind him, hadn't even bothered to check the corridor before he tried to vent his rage. "No. No problem at all. That's the problem," he hissed.

Tai studied him very carefully for what seemed to be forever, but it couldn't have been more than a couple of seconds. Then, carefully, she slipped something from her belt into the palm of his hand, stood on tiptoe, and kissed him quickly. "Too bad. I was getting to like you," she whispered.

Diego blinked in confusion, and by then Tai was gone. He turned back to the stranger ship, knowing that the *Matilda* held no more promises. Maybe these strangers, though, maybe, if only he could figure out how to make it all work. Somebody around here was involved in empire technology transfer. It was just a matter of who and where.

He looked at what Tai had given him, and this time managed to restrain a whistle of surprise. It was a jamcaster. He'd seen only two of them before, both of them prototypes sitting on Sein's desk. A new kind of space-signaling device that couldn't be traced by the Weasels but locked right in on Fleet ident beams, the jamcaster was the perfect Intel toy. He wondered briefly where Tai had gotten hold of one and decided he'd rather not know.

He slipped the jamcaster into his pocket and made his way back to the cargo holds on the *Hansa*. Pure guesswork, now. He wasn't even sure if he recognized the door that led to the animals. If he were found out, the excuse would be perfectly genuine. Two humans, both dressed in what appeared to be some kind of crew overalls, were talking at the end of the hall. Neither of them spared a glance in his direction. He ducked in the first door he found.

And Diego Bach really smiled for the first time since Sein had tasked him. Pay dirt, all right, and right here. This cavernous storage bay made the whole *Matilda* look like an afterthought. Crates were stacked as far as he could see, huge ones in sealed wrappings and stamped in red. He couldn't read whatever was written, but so far the size at least was right.

Heart pounding from sheer elation, Diego slipped behind one of the piles of crates and past another. When he was sure he was covered, he tried to pry the heat seal on one of crates. His fingers didn't even make an impression on the hardened plastic. Licking his lips and feeling mightily superior, Diego unclipped his Swiss Army knife from his utility belt. It had been a present from his father when he had completed his wilderness merit badge in the Scouts more than ten years ago.

Now the memory of that warmed him. "Be prepared," wasn't it? And his father had insisted that with the best knife with the most gadgets in the universe he would be prepared for anything. Exactly what anything would entail had never entered anyone's mind at that time, but then that's what being prepared was all about. Diego flicked the knife open to the microlaser blade and sliced a neat panel out of the heavy-gauge packing.

This time there was no surprise. Inside, exactly as he had envisioned it, was a prefab unit. All ready to plug a repair hole. Standardization. Henry Ford would have been real proud of these folks, Diego thought with contempt.

Evidence. And not quite what he had expected, either. It wasn't so much that his hunches were off, but that they didn't piece together the way he thought they did. And still there was not enough evidence. Diego replaced the panel and used the laser again, this time on a lower setting to fuse the plastic. The seam was ugly and obvious, but he didn't have the tools to do better. With any luck they'd believe that it was a factory problem.

Only knowing what he knew wasn't enough. These were humans, but he didn't know from where. Who was supplying the Khalians, and could he in fact prove that they were? What if they had simply stolen a shipment meant for the Weasels? or were buying from the same source? The possibilities multiplied in his head, feeding a curiosity that got the better of his sense.

But he had been so quick to assume that now he hesitated. Diego Bach hated only one thing that he counted less than dishonor. He hated to be wrong. And, most of all, he hated to look young and foolish.

If he had any brains at all, he would report back to the *Matilda* at once and report directly to Sein as soon as possible. Maybe the Indies were still worth pursuing, but there were these other humans as well. Someone else would take the job, or maybe Sein would task him again in three months after he'd had a reasonable vacation.

But that wouldn't do his personnel file any good, wouldn't win him any medals or commendations from the Big Board, wouldn't enhance his career or life or self-respect one iota. And, after all, that was what the game was all about—winning. And Diego Bach meant to win at all costs. If the risks were higher, the rewards were well worth the price. And, besides, he couldn't afford to be less than perfect whatever the cost. The most likely to succeed from the academy, Cheng notwithstanding, he had his reputation and the reputation of his whole family on the line. What would the Fuentes have done, those righteous iron-fisted ancestors who had first established freedom on one continent of Earth before branching out to the Fleet and all of space? No matter what, he would make those ancestors proud.

Besides, the *Hansa* was just asking for it, lying open and begging. Here was a nice big cargo bay filled with cartons and packing materials. He could hardly ask for a better place to hide. And there was the old saw about not being found if no one was looking. Quickly Diego toyed with the idea of taking a pair of overalls and trying to pass as one of the crew, but he dismissed the idea just as rapidly. He didn't speak their language, and besides, they probably all knew each other at least well enough to spot a stranger. Still, the cargo bay was pretty well equipped to keep him hidden for a good long time, so long as he could find food and sanitary facilities.

Besides, he had the jamcaster. The thought warmed him, and Diego made a nest in the packing materials and settled down to sleep.

He had lost track of the day when the red docking lights started flashing again. It couldn't have been too long, not when he'd managed on a couple of fish sandwiches and cold fried potatoes he had stolen when two crew members interrupted their lunch to entertain themselves in a manner that those who had assigned a man and a woman to a task on an isolated part of the ship might have foreseen.

Whoever these people were, they certainly were efficient. The head and water fountain were convenient, and Diego ascertained from the plumbing structure that there were similar facilities on every level. He didn't risk an investigation, though. Enough time for that when he found out their destination with the prefabs. Besides, he thought the two tapes he had lifted from the corridor control (also during the convenient diversion that had yielded dinner) might give the self-appointed demigods over in Analysis something to do instead of gossiping over the coffee machine.

He had spent most of his time in the bay, although he had opened a panel in a carton containing a control unit. It had taken several tries, and more than one plastic container held the scars of his Swiss Army knife. There should still be enough charge left for him to seal this one last carton behind him when he climbed into the crew couch. Good thing that the knife was the genuine article and not some cheap knockdown that wouldn't hold a full charge for more than a couple of years.

Then the red light came on, just as it had flashed when the *Matilda* docked. Diego had practiced his movements mentally hundreds of times and had even folded himself into the control unit's acceleration couch more than once to make sure he could stand it for more than a few moments. Still, he was almost surprised at his rational calm in the presence of the docking light and at his own ability to dispose of all traces of his presence before entering the unit and sealing the panel back shut, leaving a few openings for air.

Now, in the dark, all he had to do was pray that the cartons would be transshipped inside. Maybe the packing would hold and the air holes were small enough that he could survive a two-second vacuum transfer, but he'd prefer not to chance it.

Diego tried to listen, waiting tensed and ready for the off-loading. The inside of the carton was dark, darker than eternity, darker than even his worst nightmares. Dark and dull, and the packing material muffled whatever was happening outside. Tension could hold only so long before boredom set in, and to his eternal chagrin Diego Bach fell asleep.

The Weasel barks woke him to full awareness. They sounded very far off, and even if he had been able to understand Khalian, he couldn't have made out any words. Not that he needed to. Now he had enough evidence. Just the sound of that harsh inhuman voice gave him all the information he needed. Whoever these folks were, they were responsible for the Weasel ships. They had brought them, maybe manufactured them, it meant humans were indirectly fighting against their own. Indignation mingled with contempt in Diego's cramped chest as he considered the situation.

Then the carton moved. Jolted by the sudden lift of what he surmised must be a crane, Diego hit his head soundly on the back panel behind the headset before he managed to brace against the prefab sheeting. The couch had been designed for a Khalian and was only about half as long as Bach, and the safety straps were equally useless and more dangerous, swinging around in the confined space with their clasp-weighted ends. He tried to gather the straps in his hands, missed one, and tensed as the carton was placed somewhere else.

This time the movement was smooth. Diego swallowed the panic that knotted in the back of his throat. *Leaving the* Hansa, he thought, *and entering Khalian territory*. He heard more muffled barks, more than one voice, and the low-pitched sound of human speech. Then there were two more hard jerks, and the straps flailed around him. He never did know whether it was one of the safety clasps or his own hands vainly grabbing to hold them that turned the jamcaster on.

There was an island of stability. Diego couldn't tell if he was still in transit or had been transferred to a Khalian vessel or base. One thing was for certain. He had heard a lot of Weasel barking and not much that sounded human for a long time. Things settled and time stretched again. Diego began to consider seriously exactly how he was going to extricate himself and, incidentally, his information from the carton and get back to friendly space.

The carton began to tumble violently. Diego had no idea what was happening. He was aware of voices, of things hitting the packing crate, and of himself helplessly trapped inside. The spinning grew crazier, stopped, began again. Bach was sick. He was glad that he hadn't eaten in so long that his uncontrollable heaves brought up only pain. That he could live with. Anything else in this closed environment would have choked him.

Then blessed stillness. Diego gulped air convulsively, trying to steady himself, when he smelled plastic burn. Fumes filled the small space. Diego held his breath and fingered his knife. One more charge, he hoped and prayed, one more. It was amazing how calm he felt, clear and cold holding the small red knife near his chest. He knew with perfect serenity that he was about to die. What was important was to go with honor, to show no fear, to make at least an attempt to defend himself so that his people would not be humiliated. Strangely, he felt very distant from it all, as if the whole lacked solidity. And he knew with complete certitude that it was more than real and that he was not going to survive.

Suddenly the fumes lessened, and a patch of light showed. Diego readied himself and tried to spring out, laser knife held aggressively the way he had been taught as a child. No matter how bad he looked, no matter how hopeless, the point was not to concede. He focused on that thought alone and lunged.

Only to be caught by two oversized humans in marine uniforms.

"I damn well hope what you've got is worth this," the one with a lieutenant's bar spat at him.

Diego said nothing. For the first time in his entire life, he was speechless.

He was on the *Haig*. That was as much as the destroyer's Intel officer, Manning, would tell him when he reported to the situation room. "Is that it?" she asked after he had finished debriefing. "Just that you saw the prefabs, heard Khalian voices, and can't identify the humans involved?"

"And the tapes," he reminded her. "At least we've got a lead on where the Weasels are getting their ships. It's better than what you had twenty minutes ago."

He wanted to ask again how the *Haig* just happened to be in the region and monitored the jamcaster and sent a marine rescue squad in after him. He really wanted to know. But Manning hadn't answered the first time and wasn't the sort to take kindly to being asked again. Instead, she fingered the tapes lightly before locking them into her porta-base.

"I'll get on the stick to Sein on this," she informed him.

"And we'll try to get you on something home. Although there is a war going on out there." She gave him an unpleasant look and opened her mouth to speak when Jason Padova, the commander of the *Haig,* walked in.

Diego stood and saluted in perfect academy form before Manning had time to react. It never occurred to Bach that, dressed in his Indie overalls with his long Chola-streaked hair and the violet snake visible on his shoulder, he might look just a little out of place.

"We were just about finished, sir," Manning informed the commander.

Padova looked over Diego as if he were some alien art form and then took a seat. "You're free to go if you want to, Johanna," he said to the harried-seeming woman. "I hope it's good news."

Johanna Manning hesitated, considering. "I'm not sure what it is, sir, or what it means. And if we're very lucky, Analysis will have some real data by the time we win the war."

Padova snorted. "Might as well give them a head start on it, then."

Manning nodded and left. The commander turned his attention to Diego, who maintained an attitude of midshipman's formality.

"Sit down, Bach, and stop playing tin soldier," Padova said softly. "You did your job and the marines did theirs. And you got to field-test one of our newest toys. Not bad."

Diego sat stiffly and struggled to keep the surprise off his face. "I don't understand, sir," he finally said.

"There isn't anything to understand," Padova waved a hand. "The cavalry came over the hill on time. Just like in all those fun flicks. I just wanted to meet the infamous Bach junior. Having heard some scuttlebutt on the fit your folks pulled when you went Intel, that is."

Diego blinked once. "Excuse me, sir, but this is real life. I think. And the cavalry doesn't come over the hill, and I had planned an escape route. But it seems like a whole lot of coincidences that you're in the area and monitoring the jamcaster and everything. It sort of strains the odds, sir."

Padova's eyebrows went up, then he smiled. "If it were only coincidence, probably. But then, Gar Commers told me that he had set up a meet with the *Hansa,* and he'd been suspicious for a long time. And that little nonreg toy, well, we did have to test it out under authentic conditions. Not that Commers had you fingered particularly. He just hoped there'd be one of Sein's professional spooks around to do the job. Otherwise he might have to ask the bos'n to take on the task, and somehow I got the impression that wouldn't exactly fly.''

This time Bach did smile, shaking his head in response. "Right, sir. Too big to fit inside, anyway. And he hadn't been a Boy Scout. But you know Commers, sir? Was he a Fleet officer? And how did the marines manage to get me out of that Weasel trap, anyway?''

"Ensign, it's a good thing that you are in intelligence, otherwise your curiosity would get you into serious deep shit rather than just plain killed. You ever hear the story of the man who was too pissed to die? That's Commers. As for the last, well, let's just say I've got more than one trick in my bag.'' With that the commander stood and grinned and turned to leave.

"Excuse me, sir,'' Diego called before Padova disappeared out the door. "Excuse me. I have one question.'' The commander turned to face him, and Diego's voice dropped. "Does it matter? Did this mean anything?''

Commander Jay Padova raked Diego Bach with his ice-blue eyes. "I don't know. What I do know is that how you do it counts. Winning counts. You done good. The rest you just have to take on faith.''

Diego Bach watched Padova go and in the silence, reached for the medal around his neck. Faith. His parents would only think that he had humiliated himself and them, having to be rescued by Padova's marines. But not only had the commander told him, but he knew it was true in his heart, that there was no shame. He had done it right. *Diego Carlos Sergio Fuentes y Gomez, I think you would understand.*

INTERLUDE

Family shows, commonly referred to by omni insiders as famcoms, have long been standard fare on all omni channels. Considering the variety of forms that have evolved for the family itself, some of these shows can be quite exciting. The sexual activities of the feline Morrisons are considered suitable for younger viewers only on ten of the several hundred inhabited worlds of the Alliance. One more acceptable popular show, "The Claremorts," is based upon the permutations of the eight member marriages found on Altair Prime. This famcom being known for its innovative programming in an era when everything has been done before. Billions waited in anticipation to see who had actually shot J. B. Even more popular on the inner worlds is "Banemere," the adventures of a detective whose eighteen wives actually solve the crimes.

Still, most human families still are formed on the old nuclear structure of parents and offspring. Unfortunately everyone in the media knows what dull programming this makes.

A FAMILY BUSINESS
by Karen Haber

STEVE LOOKED AT the check the Thalassian weapons merchant had just handed him: 150,000 credits—enough to pay off the repairs on the *Sargasso VI,* with a little left over for discretionary activities.

He shook the creep's hand. It was a bad idea. Too late, Steve remembered why Thalassa was known among scavengers as the slime planet. He wiped his palm against the wall. Then he threw in a business plug.

"Don't forget, Sargasso Salvage can meet your needs anytime, anyplace in the known galaxy."

"*B-z-z-z-z,*" the Thalassian said, blurring and spreading like a balloon about to pop.

Then Steve woke up. He almost would have preferred to be covered with pieces of slime merchant.

"Goddamn it! What time is it?"

The buzzing chronometer read 1300. But as far as Steve was concerned, whenever he awakened was morning. And he hated morning. The best things in life happened at night. Late. He slapped off the alarm and punched the intercom access.

"Sandera—you were supposed to wake me up two hours ago!"

Instead of his sister's usual distracted reply, he heard only the faint hissing of the open intercom line. Where the hell was she? The bathroom? There was a comlink in there that usually worked. The armory? Like any other mechanical engineer, she loved to tinker with weapons. She'd blow them both into subatomic particles one day.

"Sandera, this is Steve, your only brother. Remember me?"

Silence. What was she up to? She couldn't have gone for a walk outside. Especially if they were still in FTL drive. He listened for the engines. Silence. That meant they were only one day out from the Delta Station base near Trinitus.

Steve dressed, relieved himself, and checked his reflection in the bathroom's plasteel mirror. His long, dark hair needed combing, and his blue eyes were so bloodshot that the color was almost camouflaged—he should have stuck to beer last night. He shook his head, trying to clear it, and went in search of his twin.

She was not in her bunk. He usually could find her there, updating her personal weapons log, keeping tally of all the killing machines that passed through her hands. Ditto the armory. Well, what about the pilothouse? She had to be in the pilothouse.

He climbed up the old-style suspended staircase that was serving as a makeshift entrance until the lift was fixed, then walked into the pilothouse. It was deserted. A blinking light in the corner caught his eye: a vid screen that flashed his name urgently. He keyed up the message:

**HAVE GONE ABOARD ALIEN SHIP TO INVESTIGATE SCAVENG-
ING POTENTIAL. MEET ME THERE.**

What alien ship?

Steve switched on external views and gasped. A cruiser of unfamiliar design was anchored off the *Sargasso VI*'s starboard. It had a strange, boxy shape, antennae bristling from it like the limbs of a square, inverted spider. It dwarfed their own cigar-shaped vessel. He cursed silently and tried to raise Sandera on the ship-to-suit hailing frequency. No answer. He would have to go over there and get her.

His twin's appetite for adventure had brought them plenty of trouble in the past. However, it also paid the bills whenever she stumbled across a profitable cache of guns or armor. Thanks to the Fleet's ban against selling weapons, there was a thriving black market in arms of all kinds.

But what did she think this was, the Fleet? She didn't have a platoon of combat-ready troopers waiting to back her up. All she had was Steve.

Sighing, he checked the autopilot setting and grabbed his saber. He strapped on two laser pistols for good measure. If there were Fleet personnel around, all he'd get was a fine for carrying illegal weapons. Better a live scavenger in debt than a dead one for want of his gun. Steve suited up for the transport between ships. He hoped his twin hadn't gotten them in over their heads.

As soon as the scuttlebutt had reached them about the decommissioning of the Delta Station base, he and Sandera blasted away from Freeborn, heading for the Trinitus system. That was two solar days ago.

Steve didn't like to go scavenging with so little crew, but Hrif and Tol, their regular freelancers, were visiting family and weren't available. Sandera was adamant.

"This will be a solar breeze," she declared, setting the coordinates into the board.

"You always say that."

"Steve, you know it's not every day that the Fleet decommissions a base. Of course, it's expensive for them to maintain all these outposts, and I guess this one was just too far outside the regular shipping lanes. Besides, that asteroid's orbit is getting pretty unstable. Soon it won't be safe to land on it."

Her words didn't reassure him. One of the last things he wanted to do was go visit a wobbly asteroid.

"So why are we rushing over there?"

She assumed her I'm-being-patient voice. Just because she was three minutes older, she thought she knew everything.

"Any Fleet base is a gold mine for us. And we won't even have to risk waiting for the end of a battle or a bounty hunter to kill someone. We can sell Fleet materials right back to Fleet dealers. This is an invitation to make an easy fortune!"

He grudgingly agreed. "I hope you're right."

There probably wasn't much that the two of them couldn't handle together, he thought. They'd been coping on their own since age six, when their mother had left Freeborn for an extended vacation with somebody other than their father. Since then, they'd done all right looking out for themselves—and each other.

And there were bound to be plenty of fat pickings at a decommissioned base for smart scavengers who knew where to look. Any bulky equipment could be handled by mechanicals.

So they'd headed out from Freeborn. When they stopped to fuel up at Kate's Rock, the market was loud with space talk about Delta Station. At least three suppliers asked Steve if he was going to the base. Every scavenger in the quadrant would be picking over that place.

Steve fought his impulse to race back to the ship. The base would still be there when they arrived, and he never went anywhere before checking the "daily" on Fleet activity. The last thing he wanted to do was blunder through a military maneuver and get the *Sargasso* riddled with puncture wounds again. Those repairs had almost bankrupted them, and they still weren't in the black.

Scavengers followed Fleet battles like hyenas behind a pride of hunting lions. At a safe distance. Steve liked it that way. He knew it was not only dumb, but dangerous, to get too close to the action.

On the other hand, Sandera would happily carry a plasma converter right into the front lines. She'd say she was carrying on the family tradition or some other foolish rationalization. The fact was, his twin thrived on excitement.

Besides, Dad had only been a lieutenant anyway. And now he was dead, thanks to a bad business deal.

His legacy was his Fleet pension, which barely covered the groceries, and a declassified Fleet scoutship, refitted for scavenging, the result of a lucky poker hand. So much for tradition. The only tradition to which Steve adhered was that of preserving the flow of his own blood through his own veins.

He had to stoop to keep from bumping his head in the low-slung, gunmetal corridors of the alien ship. It was dark, the winding corridors dimly-lighted by red wall units mounted at shoulder height. There was a strange acrid-yet-musky odor that set his teeth on edge.

He thumbed the key to his suit's communications system and received a faint, answering beep: at least Sandera's tracer was on. But she refused to respond to voice contact. Odd.

He scanned the hall right to left. The first door he came to was locked, as was the second and third. Cursing, he pressed the entry panel on the fourth door. With a low whine, the door sprang open.

Inside, Steve saw a wide, bay-like room with an observation

window and a wall covered with gauges and buttons—controls of some kind. He peered through the window in the murky light. The hold was deep. It spanned several floors. But all he could see were canisters of some kind. Weapons? Well, Sandera wasn't in here.

He stepped back out into the corridor, taking care to duck his head. What was this place, a ship for elves?

The next doorway led to a ramp that sloped upward and downward in a continuous spiral. He took the ascending path and almost tripped over a small body in partial armor, sprawled across the floor, a dark stain on its chest. A pool of blood fanned out under it, drifting downhill. Steve prodded the body with his toe. No response.

He crouched down, yanked off the helmet, then dropped it when he saw what it had protected. He stumbled backward, heart pounding. The acrid stench was overpowering.

The corpse's head was that of a large rodent: dark-furred, gray-lipped mouth pulled back in death's grimace, displaying rows of cruel, pointed teeth.

A Weasel dead from a gunshot wound.

Suddenly, the low ceilings and dim lighting made more sense. Sweat pasted Steve's suit liner to the back of his neck. Sandera had led him aboard a Khalian ship!

The Weasels were small, but they fought like devils. Their response to human trespassers was sure to be quick and deadly, which could account for Sandera's silence.

Steve didn't want to think about that. He checked the tracer; the yellow homing beacon was getting brighter. She was nearby. But was she still alive?

He pulled the safety catch from his handgun and made for the direction of that beacon, running uphill as fast as he could.

The lights on the control panel blinked purple-and-green patterns. They were hard to ignore in the dim room. Besides, they were the only friendly looking thing on the bridge. Sandera watched their random patterns and thought she might get more sympathy from the electronic equipment than she would from her alien captors.

The musky smell on the bridge almost choked her. She wondered what significance scent had for these rodents. Was it another defense system, like a skunk's scent? Whatever it meant, the smell was potent.

Since she'd come aboard, she'd found this ill-smelling, dark ship a baffling riddle. She was almost sorry she'd decided to board it. But her father had always told her to trust her hunches. And when the *Sargasso VI*'s viewscreen had picked up this unexpected blip, all of Sandera's personal alarm systems had gone off. She just knew it was a gold mine for her and Steve. And now, here she was, a captive of the Khalians, thanks to her intuition.

The Weasel commander came toward her, holding an evil-looking gun at her chest. She glared angrily at him.

"What are you doing here?"

Sandera lowered her eyelids, feigning indifference, and pretended that she didn't care if he shot her point-blank. She shrugged.

"I could ask you the same thing. You know you're violating Fleet territory."

"Our navigation device misfired."

Sandera smiled nastily. "I'm sure you want me to think that. Well, what I really think is that you're on a spy mission. The Fleet has probably detected your ship already. They should be here soon, and they'll blast you into pieces so small that nobody could find you with a microscope!"

"By then, you will be dead. You are the spy! Explain what you are doing on our ship!"

She ran her hands through her short brown hair, leaving it standing on end, then shook her head in irritation.

"I've already told you. I thought you were a derelict. You didn't respond to my hail. So I figured there was nobody home. And in space, that means finders keepers. I'm in the scavenging business."

"This is no concern of ours. If, as you say, you mean us no harm, why did you shoot our junior officer?"

"What else was I supposed to do? Stand there and let him shoot me? He shot first, before I could speak. So I returned the compliment." Sandera's voice grew shrill with impatience.

"Human, the only reason we have allowed you to live this long is to discover your true mission and how many other spies are aboard your ship. We will discover this with or without your help. The only choice you have now is to work with us or die.''

"That's an easy choice.''

Sandera started to reach inside her chest guard for the dagger she always kept there. It had gotten her out of more than one after-hours party. Maybe it would get her out of this one.

But the other Khalian said something in a strange language, and her interrogator turned toward him. They both gestured toward a red light blinking on the control console, conferring in guttural barks which echoed off the walls of the bridge.

Sandera left her knife where it was; she could always pull it out later. She could have sworn she'd felt Steve's presence on the ship; she'd turned on her suit intercom for his benefit. So where was he?

She ground her teeth with impatience. How satisfying it would be to pull out her pistol and blast both Khalians and their control panel. But they'd confiscated her gun. Besides, her soul recoiled at the thought of ruining all that nice merchandise.

The engineer in her eyed the alien hardware greedily, while her scavenger side computed potential earnings from it. But even that got boring. She was sick and tired of these overgrown rodents. If they were going to kill her, they were certainly taking their time about it.

She turned her head to check on the Khalians. They were still barking at each other over that red light. She hoped it meant that their nuclear power plant was going critical.

Reaching behind her, she felt a metal knob on one of the wall panels. She turned it gently. It gave. Carefully unscrewing it, she pulled it free and sidled slowly toward the door. When she was almost there, she tossed the knob into the far corner of the room. It clattered noisily, and both Khalians stopped their arguing to turn in that direction. Sandera made her move.

"Halt!'' An imploder shot rang out, missed her, hit the door frame.

She ducked out the door and hit the lock coordinates, scrambling them for good measure. Behind her, she heard furious pounding. She wondered how long they'd need to get out. That lock wouldn't hold forever. And she couldn't wait around for her brother to show up.

Steve bolted through the next exit, keeping a sharp eye out for Weasels. The first door he came to was locked, and his twin nowhere to be found. He had listened with growing horror to Sandera's interrogation by the Khalians. The sound of that shot almost froze his blood. Who had fired it? Was his twin hurt? Dead?

The door popped open, and a Weasel nearly bowled him over on his way out. He spun and fired, blasting the Khalian into the far wall of the corridor. The Weasel landed hard, twitched a couple of times, and did not get up.

He felt something brush past him and turned to see another Weasel rushing down the hall, firing wildly over his shoulder, then vanishing through a doorway. Strange behavior for a ruthless warrior, Steve thought. Cursing, he followed the Weasel. The door led to a ramp. Empty.

"Steve?" He heard a muffled voice in his helmet.

"Sandera! Where are you?"

"On the floor below you. Check your tracer."

"I shot a Khalian. Another one got away."

"He must be down here somewhere. I'm directly below you. Hurry!"

Steve scurried down the ramp. Sandera was waiting for him at the bottom. He was so relieved to see her that he almost forgot that she was responsible for getting them into this mess. He restrained himself from giving her a lecture, even if she did deserve it. But first things first—there were Khalians prowling the halls, hunting them.

An imploder shot cut short any greeting Sandera might have made. The twins jumped back inside the ramp doorway as a short figure raced past them down the corridor and around a corner.

"Spies! I'll kill you both!" the Weasel shouted as he ran past them. His footsteps receded.

Steve poked his head out the door. The hallway was empty. Where had the Weasel gone?

"I thought they had some fancy sense of smell," he said. "So how did he miss us?"

"I think our suit filters it. Or maybe he has a cold."

"I'd like to give him something more serious than a cold." Steve glanced down at Sandera's suit-holster. It was empty. "Where's your gun?"

Sandera looked sheepish. "They took it away. But that was after I killed a crew member."

Steve pulled out his spare. "Here, take this. It should be more effective than that nasty little shiv you carry."

"Thanks." She placed it in her holster and peered out into the hallway. "They've probably got the airlock guarded—we'll never get back to the *Sargasso* alive unless we get rid of these Weasels. I guess we'd better go looking."

They entered the hallway cautiously. Every door they came to was closed. The first door they tried was locked. So were the second and third.

When they reached the fourth door, which was unlocked, they heard the sound of footsteps behind them. Sandera shoved Steve through the door and jumped in after him. They flattened themselves against the wall and waited.

The Khalian raced past their hiding place, imploder blasting. "Cowards! Show yourselves!"

The twins held their breath and waited until the hallway was silent again.

Sandera checked her laser pistol impatiently.

"C'mon, Steve. Let's go."

Steve was making a leisurely inventory of his remaining personal arsenal. He seemed to be in no hurry to resume Weasel hunting.

"I'm getting tired of chasing him while he chases us. Maybe if we sit here long enough, he'll come back around again, and then we can just shoot him."

Sandera was about to reply that her twin was being silly when a sudden sharp movement from him silenced her.

"Uh, San, turn around." Steve sounded peculiar. She did as he said and gaped.

An odd-looking being sat cross-legged on the floor of the room they were in, oblivious to them, apparently in some sort of trance. He wore a blue robe, tied at the waist, that covered his knees. He was barefoot.

Looking around, the twins saw that they had invaded what seemed to be living quarters containing a low bed, a blue furred rug, and a wide, flat-based wooden chair.

The being had not moved the entire time they'd been there. He sat, cross-legged, on the rug. His head was down, revealing an unusual pattern of fine, feathery scales where his hair would have been. The room was silent.

Then Steve and Sandera exchanged incredulous glances. Was

this yet another strange enemy?

Sandera cleared her throat. "Excuse me."

There was no response.

She tried again. "I'm sorry to bother you, sir . . ."

Silence.

Steve strode over and grabbed the alien's shoulder.

"Steve, stop it. You might hurt him!"

As Sandera spoke, the alien uncoiled in one fluid movement and, taking what appeared to be a lunging dance step, gracefully used one slim, muscular foot to kick Steve across the room. He bounced off the wall hard.

"Steve, are you all right?" Sandera's voice was so high she sounded like a little girl.

"I'm not sure," he said, gasping for the breath that had been knocked out of him. What a blow! He sat up and shook his head to clear it. "What was that you were saying about me hurting somebody?"

The alien faced them impassively. He had a pointed chin, high cheekbones, a thin nose, and dark, unreadable eyes.

"Disturbing *seiza* is a poor idea, *ganyi*. Quite dangerous," the being said in clear, fluting tones. He looked ready to repeat his dance, balancing on the balls of his feet, slim-fingered hands describing small arcs in front of him.

"I see what you mean." Steve picked himself up gingerly.

"Many have learned the dangers, too late," the alien said with grim satisfaction. He punctuated the comment with a slashing, kicking movement.

"Listen, I'm convinced. Sorry to disturb you. No hard feelings, okay?" Steve was beginning to get nervous.

He could hear Sandera unlatching her pistol behind him. The alien appeared to understand that sound as well. He stopped his dance, pulled back, and stood several feet away, watching the twins silently, waiting.

The alien was taller than the Weasels, almost human height. *A biped who was both scaled and feathery? Well, the universe was full of strange sights*, Steve thought.

"You seem to speak Galaxan standard," Sandera said. He nodded.

"Who are you? Where are you from?"

"I am Ndege."

"Is that your name?"

"No. My people's. I am Egri, of the Hinc Illae nest." He seemed to be waiting for some response. His imperious manner melted a bit as the twins remained silent. "Have you not heard of Nest Illae?" he asked finally, almost sheepishly.

"I'm sorry. No."

The Ndege seemed a bit crestfallen. When he spoke again, it was with less arrogance. "I would know your names and nests."

"We are Sandera and Steve Hayes. We're from Freeborn."

"Ah, then Hayes are your people?"

Steve shrugged. "I guess so. That's our family name. Which may be what I think you mean by nest. But our people are humans."

Egri nodded. "I have heard of these humans. But you are neither so large nor so clumsy as the *Panya* would have us believe."

"Panya?" Steve and Sandera looked at each other in confusion.

"The overlords—the ones you call Khalians. I am the personal slave to the *Panya* commander."

"You're a slave?" Sandera asked.

"Yes. The Khalians conquered our home planet long ago."

"It looks like they want to do that to the rest of the galaxy. Where is your home?"

"I believe humans call it Target."

The twins exchanged glances again. That was the reputed home world of the Khalia.

"Does every member of the crew have a personal slave?"

"Crew? There is no crew. Only the four overlords. And the sleepers."

"Sleepers?"

"Yes. They sleep in the steel pods. In the ship's hold."

Steve cursed silently. So he and Sandera could have left the ship at any time. With only four crew members awake, the Khalians couldn't possibly have guarded the airlocks. Unless they had mechanicals. And Steve had not encountered any robot defenses when he came aboard.

If this was a sleeper ship, then those metal canisters he'd seen must have been sleep pods. He'd been a fool not to notice. And the entire crew was in suspended animation. Until such time as needed. The Ndege's voice broke into his thoughts.

"Be aware that the overlord commander has gone to summon

his comrades from the sleep.''

''Are you saying that a Weasel is trying to awaken other Weasels from sleep pods?'' Sandera sounded frightened for the first time.

''Indeed.''

''We've got to stop him! Can you take us to this sleeper room?'' The Ndege hesitated. Sandera motioned with her imploder. Their eyes locked. Then Egri nodded and beckoned them to follow.

The Ndege led them down a dark corridor and through a hatch into the hold of the ship. Through a window of the hold, Steve and Sandera could see row upon row of gray metal sleep caskets. And a Khalian, with his back to the window, was busy at the control panel.

Steve reached for his gun, but somehow, the Weasel saw him and spun to face him, imploder in hand. The Khalian fired a wide scatter burst that broke the observation window into a thousand sparkling splinters.

The twins dropped to the floor. Steve glanced up to see Egri standing frozen, in fear or shock.

''Get down, you fool!''

The Ndege didn't move. Steve tackled him, trying to cushion his descent. Egri's eyes were open, the pupils dilated. He remained where he'd fallen, immobile.

''So much for the cavalry,'' Steve muttered. ''Cover me, San.''

''Right.''

He crawled toward the hold door. There was no response from the control box. The Khalian had locked the door shut. Well, if he couldn't get in to see the Weasel, he would have to bring the Weasel out to face him.

Steve pulled a sonic grenade from his belt, keyed in his countersonics, and watched as Sandera did the same. He set the device to detonate in ten seconds, then lofted it through the open window and waited. He could feel the vibrations building up and imagined the Khalian holding his ears.

The grenade exploded, the door flew open, and the Khalian stumbled out, badly wounded, shooting blindly. Steve cut him down quickly and remained in position, awaiting any newly awakened Khalian reinforcements.

Two minutes later he was still waiting. Where were they? He

could have sworn he'd seen movement in the sleeper chamber.

He cut off the countersonics so he could hear.

"Come out, come out, wherever you are," Steve muttered, squinting through the viewfinder on his pistol. Behind him, Egri was stirring, shaking his head as if he was clearing away some invisible fog.

Steve took a look into the hold. The grenade had blasted a hole in the far wall. The sleeper controls looked ruined. There was no sign of other Khalians.

A dreadful ammonia smell was seeping into the hallway. Steve tried to breathe through his mouth.

"Sandera, can you do anything with that control panel?"

He turned to look at his twin. She lay on the deck like a crumpled rag doll. An ugly red-brown stain was spreading across her chest from just below her right shoulder. One of the Khalian's last wild bullets had caught her.

"Sandera!"

Steve punched every button on her suit's med program, trying desperately to stabilize her vital signs. But he was no doctor—he couldn't even begin to judge how badly she was hurt.

A calm voice intruded on his frenzy. It was Egri.

"May I give assistance?"

"What kind of assistance?"

"I am of the Sinsei Guild; the healers. My people have many healing arts, some of which may help your sister."

"How do I know I can trust you?"

"Why would you not trust me?"

"You weren't very helpful when we were under fire. And you kicked me pretty hard a few minutes ago."

"I regret this. You touched me in *seiza,* and my instincts reacted before my intellect. As for a moment ago, well there is an explanation for that, but we do not have time. Your sister is dying. I may be able to save her. With your permission?"

"Go ahead. But I'm watching every move you make."

The Ndege knelt and opened Sandera's suit. He prodded her chest, her arms, felt her pulse, then covered her head with his hand and closed his eyes. A moment later, he nodded as if confirming a diagnosis.

He reached into a pouch at his neck and removed several strange geometric objects that glinted with a dark, metallic glow. He placed them in a circle around the unconscious young woman, sat back on his haunches, and bowed his head as if in prayer.

As Steve watched in amazement, Sandera's breathing rate aligned with that of Egri, and her bleeding slowed. After a few minutes, the Ndege came out of his trance and produced another pouch which yielded ingredients for some kind of salve. This was pressed against the wound and formed a dressing and bandage. The birdman again checked the patient's vital signs and nodded one last time.

"She will sleep now and awaken healed."

Steve knelt down and felt his sister's pulse. It seemed steady. She was breathing regularly. Maybe she would be all right after all. He stood up and turned to Egri.

"Thank you. Could I learn how to do that? It would sure come in handy."

The thinnest hint of a smile passed over the avian's face. "Perhaps. It is a difficult discipline to master. Few among our people manage it."

Steve got up, helped the Ndege to his feet, and watched as he sadly inspected the damaged sleep pods.

"You have saved yourself, but at great cost," Egri said quietly.

"What cost?"

"The most precious of all."

"Huh?"

Egri shook his head sadly.

"Young human, we are speaking here of life."

"We are?"

"The sleepers will now sleep forever."

"You mean they're dead?" Steve felt dismayed. But only for a moment. "Well, they were Khalians."

"Not all."

"What do you mean?" Steve watched, his uneasiness growing as the avian fell silent. "Tell me!"

"Some were my people. And yours."

Steve felt like he'd been punched in the stomach.

"I thought those caskets only held Weasels!"

"Some of them, yes. But the rest were slaves."

Steve staggered away from the alien, blinded by guilt. So those stories of slavery were true. He and Sandera had blundered upon a Weasel slaver, brimming with "cargo," which he had managed to dispatch without hesitation.

He and Sandera had intercepted a Khalian slaver, heading for home. But where had it come from? And how long a journey would require sleepers?

Steve didn't feel like asking those questions. He felt like jumping out the nearest airlock. He had killed human captives. And this gentle being who had saved his sister . . . *his* comrades were now dead as well.

"I—I'm sorry. I didn't know . . ."

"Khalians. Humans. So wasteful of life."

Egri shut his eyes in grief, slowly opened them, and turned toward the canisters. "Come. Some may yet live."

"How?"

"I made contact with them before the explosion. In trance state."

Steve didn't want to leave Sandera alone, but his guilt compelled him to follow the Ndege into the ship's hold.

As awful as the smell was, Steve preferred it to the sight of the dead. They had not died peacefully, and their death throes had left their bodies twisted, teeth bared in grimaces of pain.

He and Egri spent a grim hour inventorying the sleep capsules. Most of the sleepers had perished when the controls were destroyed. The Khalians were particularly contorted. Steve was privately grateful not to have met them in life.

The human and Ndege casualties were worse. Some had obviously come awake in their canisters and fought to escape as the support systems failed. They had suffocated.

Steve watched sadly as Egri turned away from the sight of his dead fellows. Only three of the Ndege sleepers had survived. These he helped out of their canisters, embracing them in a curious manner, rubbing nose to neck.

Although he was relieved to see that no Khalians were among the survivors, Steve was sick at heart over the carnage he'd caused. He could imagine how Sandera would feel. He remembered that he'd left her alone and unconscious. He felt twice as bad.

"Egri?"

The Ndege turned to face him.

"I must go see about my sister."

"I believe that she will awaken soon."

"You saved her life. I owe you for that."

The Ndege shook his head.

"No debt. You have freed me from the overlords. A terrible price was paid, yes. But you have freed the others as well. Khalian slavery is not pleasant, and Khalian slaves do not live long."

"Do you want to return to Target? You can take the ship."

"No. That would only mean enslavement again. I would prefer to make a home with my fellow outcasts away from the concerns of the Khalians and their war with the humans."

"So would I, but I'm afraid that there's no place in the known galaxy where you can remain untouched by Fleet activities. Or Khalia. Why don't you come back to Freeborn with us? We're about as remote as you can get this side of Port Tau Ceti."

The Ndege nodded slowly.

"We will consider your offer. Perhaps you should see to your sister now? We desire to mourn our comrades privately. And the rest of the innocent dead."

Steve could not find his voice. He left them in silence.

When he entered the hallway, he saw Sandera sitting up, wide awake, resting her back against the corridor wall.

"Hi. My shoulder's sore." She smiled. Steve almost hugged her. She pointed to the bandage. "Did you fix this?"

Steve shook his head and sat down next to her. "No. That's Egri's handiwork. Turns out he's some sort of doctor, too."

"I thought so. This bandage looked too strange to be something you would cook up."

"How do you feel?"

"Shaky, but all right."

"That was close. You'd better practice ducking, or learn to shoot faster," he said, teasing her.

She punched him weakly in the arm and smiled. "Did you get rid of the Khalians?"

He nodded. "Egri said there were four crewmen, but I've only seen three. All of them are dead. There may be one more hiding out. I doubt it."

"You look upset."

Steve took a deep breath before replying. "That grenade I tossed? It blew away all the sleepers in the hold."

"So what? They were Khalians. They would have killed us first if they could have."

"They weren't all Khalians, Sandera. Some were Ndege, like Egri. And humans." He watched her eyes widen as the impact of his words hit home.

"Humans? How?"

"San, this is a slave ship! No wonder they didn't respond when you hailed them—they didn't want anybody to know they were out here. The Khalians probably sneak around in Fleet territory like this all the time."

Sandera fell silent. Her eyes glistened with tears.

"I didn't know. . . . How could I have known . . ."

"I'm not blaming you. I guess it's better that they're dead than enslaved in some Weasel city. But I wish we'd never seen this ship. And what are we going to do with it now?"

Sandera's eyes stopped glistening with tears and started narrowing—a clear sign that she was thinking about business. She stood up abruptly.

"I'll bet this ship could make us rich, Steve. The Fleet will want to study her. And there's all kinds of weapons in the armory here. We'll make more than we ever could have made on that scavenge run to Delta Station."

"What about the Ndege?"

"They can come with us, or we'll drop them off wherever they'd like to go."

"Maybe we'd better go ask them what they want to do."

They walked back into the battered hold to find the Ndege emerging from the sleep chamber. Egri brightened when he saw Sandera walking next to Steve.

"I see the patient has recovered."

Sandera smiled. "Thanks to you. I owe you my life."

The Ndege shook his head. "As I have told your brother, you owe me nothing, Sandera Hayes. You have given me and my fellows freedom. And with that freedom, we would like to accompany you to your home world. If you will have us. We have nowhere else to go." His comrades nodded sadly.

"Of course we'll have you. And welcome!" Sandera hugged Egri, then pulled back, blushing. The Ndege looked pleased, but stiffened suddenly and turned to Steve.

"You have not killed all of the Panya."

"How do you know?"

"I sense one hiding among the dead."

Steve pulled his pistol out. "None of us will be safe until we find him. Come on."

They moved cautiously into the sleep bay. The air was still filled with choking fumes.

Steve thought he saw movement at the periphery of his vision and turned to shoot, but found Egri in his sights instead of a Weasel.

Before he could speak, there was the sound of scrabbling footsteps behind him. A Weasel leaped out of the shadows and jumped on Steve, choking him. His vision swam as he began to black out.

"Steve!" He heard Sandera shouting from a great distance. Then he felt the hum of the imploder, and the Khalian released the grip on his neck. Strong Ndege hands helped him to his feet.

Steve looked down at the dead Weasel. Its face was contorted in rage, even in death.

"Sandera, remind me not to criticize your shooting anymore."

"It's a deal."

"What is to be done with the dead?" Egri asked.

Steve turned to his sister. "Think you can rig some sort of cold storage in there? We should probably deliver the corpses to the Fleet."

Sandera looked at the sleeper controls briefly, then nodded. "It looks like we can flood the chamber with liquid nitrogen, then seal it off. Shouldn't take too long if you help me." She opened the tool pack on her suit and set to work.

Steve sat in the *Sargasso*'s pilothouse, watching the stars blur into the strange white haze of the FTL drive. They would be home in two days. He yawned, then smiled sheepishly at his sister.

"Well, I'm pretty beat. You sure you don't mind taking the first watch?"

"Don't worry about me, little brother. I can't wait to log in some of those Khalian weapons. And the best time to do it is when you're in dreamland. That way, you won't pester me.''

"Well, if that's all the thanks I get for rescuing you from the Weasels, so be it.'' Steve stood up and made for the doorway. "Buzz me at 2000. And San?"

"Yeah?"

"The next time you decide to jump ship and check out some derelict, do me a favor. Wake me up first.''

INTERLUDE

Chief Petty Officer, retired, Rejih Rameriz slammed his fist against the panel built into his chair and switched off the omni. Minutes before his four grandchildren had sat fascinated at his feet, while watching Hawk Talon once again singlehandedly save the Alliance.

The conversation that followed had been quite annoying. It had begun when the youngest had asked him what he had done in the Fleet. Before Rejih could answer, the oldest had explained in a disgusted tone that their grandfather had worked on a freighter. "The kind of ship real Fleet guys had to save all the time."

After fifty years of service, Rejih could think of no way he could explain that someone had to bring the bullets for the "real" good guys to shoot. He was proud of his five decades in the quartermaster corp, but he simply knew of no case where a quartermaster had singlehandedly saved the Alliance.

PROMOTION
by Bill Fawcett

SOME PROMOTION, Auro Lebario, recent recipient of the Silver Star Cluster for courageous actions under fire, thought to himself. He winced as the *Red Ball* rattled violently around him, dropping the shiny new lieutenant's bars he had been polishing and braced himself against the sink. The freighter shuddered a second time as her FTL drive began to wind down. Mumbling deprecations, Auro threw his rag against the grimy wall of his cabin and retrieved his bars from under his carefully made bunk. Then the young officer glanced self-consciously at the cabin intercom. It provided a two-way video link with the bridge. He was relieved to see it was off. Once more he fought down rising resentment—at the Fleet, at Meier, even at Buchanon.

With a theatrical sigh, the dark, handsome cadet forced himself to relax. There was no time for anger now. The ship would be there soon.

Making an effort to steady his hand, the young lieutenant trimmed a stray hair off his beard, which was now cut in the same style as Commodore Agberea's. Agberea commanded the escorts that guarded the swarm of merchant ships, of which the *Red Ball* was the flagship. Auro couldn't decide whether to laugh or cry at the designation. This so-called flagship should have been retired from any respectable fleet and sold to some desperate Indie freighter before he was born. It contained one gun: an underpowered laser cannon, smaller than the one used on most marine landing craft. This alone severely limited the opportunities that ambitious young lieutenants had for glory.

Auro's real frustration was that he had, once more, volunteered.

When asked by Captain Buchanon what station he desired, Auro had simply expressed an interest in any station where he had his own quarters. Feeling at that time very much the hero, he knew this was an appropriately humble request. On something as crowded as a Fleet task-force cruiser in hostile space, he should have known better.

The young lieutenant pulled on his dress jacket, trying not to scrape against the oily walls of his "private" quarters. The grease obviously was the only thing holding the rust in place, and rust was the major element of the *Red Ball*'s hull. On the one spot Auro had cleaned, he discovered that the cabin's former resident had scratched the crude image of a Tripean doing something obscene, but impossible, to a Gection bisexual. Auro was afraid to find out what was hidden under the rest of the grease.

Fleet Tactician Buchanon had answered Auro's request for private quarters by asking if he was willing to accept the position of executive to another recently decorated officer, Commodore Abraham Meier. Auro had recognized the name as belonging to the grandson of Isaac Meier, Admiral of the Red. His politician father had taught him that it was always a good idea to keep track of the major Fleet families. When offered the chance to work with a Meier, Auro had felt that his efforts in doing so were finally paying off. Members of high-ranking Fleet families tended to get promoted more quickly than normal, as did those around them. When the cadet had learned that the position included the brevet, and probably permanent, rank of full lieutenant, he had volunteered without further questions.

It was only as he had shuttled over to report for duty that Auro discovered this Meier was a quartermaster. His father was fond of quoting an old Yiddish saying: Fool me once, shame on you; fool me twice, shame on me. Auro had volunteered twice, this time he should have known better. He could only be mad at himself. Captain Abraham Meier's "fleet" consisted of two dozen recently commandeered freight haulers and a hospital ship. The newest ship in this "fleet" was twice Auro's age. The smallest was over five times the size of a cruiser and had half the gravitic thrust of a scout.

Even the six scouts escorting the freighters were only

technically under the pudgy commodore's command. In his five days on duty Auro had not seen one communication from Meier to Agberea, though several had come in from the scout wing's commander. Most of those messages were worded more like orders than acknowledgments. Scuttlebutt had it that the two officers had been feuding since early in the war.

Hesitating at the door, Auro wondered if he should bother to wear the silver and gold medal he had been awarded the week before. Being the Hero of Bethesda seemed a bit pompous for the bridge of a freighter. Still, within minutes they would at least be near a space battle, and he had not had any other excuse to wear it. Finally pride (not vanity Auro assured himself) won, and Lieutenant Lebario pinned on the gaudy decoration just as the intercom warned that it was five minutes to drop back.

Auro tried to convince himself he couldn't be the nervous lieutenant who looked back at him in the mirror. Then he frowned at the reflection of his cadet uniform. Despite his promotion, there had been no way for him to obtain a proper uniform. The flagship's quartermaster had curtly informed Auro that officers supplied their own uniforms. Then, laughing, the chief had estimated the nearest tailor to be about fifty-seven light years behind them. The noncoms' obvious amusement had caused the painfully rapid deflation of the Hero of Bethesda's ego.

Bending low to squeeze out of the hatch that led from the *Red Ball*'s galley, Abe Meier was, if anything, even more upset than his new executive officer. Recently, every time he received a new command he felt helpless and overwhelmed. Even his victory over the Tripeans now seemed a matter of good luck and blind chance . . . a fluke unlikely ever to be repeated.

A year after the Tripeans had joined the Alliance, Meier had become eligible for rotation. The Tripeans had taken his deceptions with good grace and were busy exporting their goods to hundreds of nearby Alliance planets. When the transfer request had arrived the papers had already been completed; without a doubt Abe's grandfather's doing. They had been accompanied by a permanent appointment as commodore. The quartermaster had expected a desk job on Port to accompany that promotion. That was the normal reward. Instead, Commodore Meier found he had requested the command of a small

squadron of pursuit ships. A request that had already been
approved.

This new command hadn't exactly worked out. The commodore grimaced at the memory of his one and only combat
command. Abe's squadron was placed too far from the action to
take part in most of the battle. His sole decision had been to
order one ship to maintain its station. The lieutenant commanding that ship had disobeyed and later been awarded a spiral arm
for valor for what had followed. No official mention had ever
been made of Meier's order to return to station, but it had kept
him from sharing any of the glory.

A month later Commodore Abraham Meier had been quietly
transferred to the command of a scratch formation of support
ships. His grandfather's heavy hand was apparent in this
assignment as well. It was his way of being helpful. He had
never understood why his grandson had chosen ordnance over
one of the combat arms. The old man had always felt there was
no other place for a real officer but in a combat wing. If
Abraham had been a nobody without important relatives, his
indecisiveness at Dead Star would have grounded him forever.
Instead, his grandfather must have viewed this assignment as his
chance to avoid being grounded permanently.

At that moment, being grounded sounded very appealing.
His orders were to drop back at X-plus fifty minutes and
maintain a station twenty minutes flight time from Bull's-Eye.
That was pretty close considering how slow the haulers accelerated.

His force was to be ready to assist as needed. There was no
explanation of how a squadron of ships that was outgunned by a
single Khalian frigate was going to assist a two-hundred-ship
Fleet battle group.

As he approached the bridge, Fleet Commodore Abraham
Meier felt fresh out of miracles and suspected it would take one
just to survive the next few hours. He also felt vulnerable,
exposed, and defenseless. They were emotions it was hard to
discourage since that was exactly their situation. Daring probes
by individual scoutships had identified Bull's-Eye as the main
repair center for the entire Khalian fleet. In the immensity of
space it was nearly impossible to bring to battle an opponent
who didn't want to fight. Anytime the Fleet had arrived in
overwhelming numbers, the Khalians had simply fled into FTL.

Bull's-Eye had been consciously chosen as a location the Khalians had to defend. Once they dropped out, his freighters would be drifting minutes from what promised to be the largest space battle of the war.

During the marine landings on Bethesda, a shortage of ammunition had developed. The support fleet had been scheduled to arrive late enough to avoid being caught in the initial battle; and also too late to support the first troops after they were down. This time Dynamite Duane had decided to bring everything in at the same time, assuring his ground forces that supplies would be available when needed.

Ignoring the fact that the virtually unarmed freight haulers would be helpless if they were attacked by even one Khalian warship. When the freighter's masters had pointed out this possibility, the admiral's response had been to infer their reluctance was cowardice. He had assigned a protesting Agberea to guard them, but it hadn't been enough to soothe the owners' concerns. When the ship's masters had formally protested, Duane's response had been to send them back to Port on a message courier and place Commodore Meier in command.

Hurrying down the corridor, Meier nearly collided with Lieutenant Lebario. The boy—it was hard for the commodore to think of the twenty-year-old officer in any other terms—had worn fatigues every day since reporting for duty. His commander's first impression was that he was wearing some sort of dress uniform, perhaps that of his planet's militia. He vaguely remembered reading that Lebario was some sort of noble, or from an important family back home. Then Abe realized his new executive officer was wearing a Port academy cadet's uniform. And not even a cadet officer's uniform, at that. It wasn't very reassuring.

There was a confused moment while they sorted themselves out. Finally, the younger man gestured for his commanding officer to lead. Both tried to look relaxed as they rushed to the bridge, and both failed.

Meier hurried across the freighter's small control room, weaving past the officers already on duty. With the addition of two command consoles the bridge was cramped almost beyond functioning. There simply wasn't room to command a squadron of ships from the bridge of a freighter. The commodore had been forced to argue the refit team out of cutting off the artificial gravity and placing his command consoles upside down. There were few things more disconcerting than having to address officers who are hanging from the ceiling.

It was vital for everyone to be ready before they dropped out. Radio communications were impossible while using FTL drive, since you were literally traveling faster than radio waves. No matter how carefully you dropped up or back, the formation was always scattered and would have to be re-established. With any number of Khalians nearby, a stray ship was almost certain to be lost.

The rest of the crew on the bridge were obviously tense. Most were ex-merchant marine or Indie officers who had been virtually shanghaied for Fleet duty. None had ever been within a parsec of a Khalian. Indies who got close enough to see a Khalian warship rarely were available for further duty.

Auro glanced at Remra. When he had first come on board, the Hrruban pilot had been the first to befriend him. Auro had never met a Hrruban before, and the alien's sleek form and soft fur had added a pleasant novelty to the friendship. Then one day the chief engineer had kidded him about his "girlfriend."

Dark nebulas! The young officer blushed at the memory. She didn't even look female. He had just assumed Remra was another male. Somehow that knowledge had spoiled things, and he found himself avoiding her. Now they were all jammed together, and Auro realized that he didn't have an answer to the Hrruban's obvious question. Auro didn't know why he had been avoiding her. To his relief, Remra was preoccupied with the controls.

Dropout followed a wrenching shudder. The ship creaked, a long groaning that reverberated along its three-hundred-meter hull. The young lieutenant had never heard a ship make a sound like that before. It reminded him how thin the hull of a merchant ship was. You could shoot through one with a hand-held slug thrower. Auro's stomach protested, and bile burnt the back of his throat. He wished for a tube of water, but there were none on the bridge. The warning roar of proximity Klaxons followed. As planned, the battle for Bull's-Eye had already begun. That was obviously the only thing that had gone as expected.

Admiral Duane had briefed them all over an omnilink. Their intelligence, he had assured the listening officers, was less than a week old. It gave them a three-to-one superiority in the number of combat ships and over four-to-one by weight of fire. Admiral Duane had then explained how their biggest problem would be not defeating the Khalians but keeping them from escaping into FTL the moment the size of the battle group became apparent. His solution was a three-dimensional pincer maneuver, requiring split-second timing.

In theory the first wave was to be just sufficiently large to pin the Khalian ships near the planet. The rest of the Fleet ships were to drop back on the far side of Bull's-Eye and swing around the planet, trapping and then overwhelming the Khalians.

The flagship was broadcasting the combat briefing, so when they dropped back, Auro keyed in a quick review of the fighting on the command console. The first wave had entered the system in near-perfect formation. Their use of the double globe had proven to be a completely effective mobile defense. According to the briefing there were fifty-six ships in Force One, including seven heavies. As predicted, a large number of the lighter Khalian ships swarmed toward them. Too large a number.

Meier's twenty-seven freight haulers and a hospital ship had dropped back several AUs above the system, halfway between her sun and Bull's-Eye. This gave them a complete view of the battle. Closer to Bull's-Eye, Agberea was organizing his scouts. Below them the first shots were just being exchanged between the Force One and the lead Khalian ships.

The first readout at the edge of his display caused Meier to think it had malfunctioned. It showed two hundred seven Khalian ships rising to meet Force One. This was over twice as many as Fleet intelligence had predicted. When he hit the recheck, the console's computer confirmed there had been an error. There were now two hundred twenty-seven ships.

The command frequencies filled with frantic orders. Duane himself began issuing orders committing the ships of the pincers as soon as they dropped back behind the planet. On the display Meier could see them plunge into the battles by individual squadron and wing. Ten minutes later the entire area around the planet was filled with ships swirling in no particular formation, each tearing at each other with beams and missiles. Only Force One had retained its globular formation, providing a safe harbor for damaged Fleet ships. Both sides were taking heavy losses.

As Meier watched, one spark—representing a Fleet heavy—glowed yellow as its screens dropped and then disappeared. As that battlecruiser died someone tripped her FTL engines to overload, and three Khalians were trapped in the explosion. Even this far from the battle, the *Red Ball*'s tiny visual monitor went black.

The *Red Ball*'s scanners could detect the massive spaceport at the planet's equator. Meier had time to be astonished by its size. The quartermaster in him calculated that half of the Fleet could be serviced by it. The Weasels had no choice but to defend Bull's-Eye with desperate courage. After fifteen minutes they still had a numerical advantage of twenty percent. If things continued as they were, the Fleet would probably win, but only after crippling losses.

Hovering over the battle, his freighters could do nothing but watch the swirling melee. As another heavy disappeared from the console, Meier swore in frustration, the Yiddish phrase echoing off the walls of the freighter's small bridge. Lebario spun, startled, and then hurriedly turned back to his own console.

"I'm getting a call from Admiral Duane, sir," announced the young exec. With nothing to do, the former cadet watched Meier as his thoughts raced. Auro's duty was to issue any actual combat orders to the freighters. To the youthful hero this was a humorless parody of what his duty had been on board the *Morwood*. Then the memory of the decapitated body of a cadet who had sat beside him there intruded. Auro remembered just how vulnerable, thin hulled and poorly screened the *Red Ball* was and shuddered. After nearly being smashed by debris meters inside the thickly armored hull of a heavy cruiser, he was keenly aware that less than a centimeter of steel stood between the bridge and vacuum.

"I'm already monitoring the Fleet command frequency, Lieutenant Lebario." Commodore Meier corrected him in what he hoped was even tones. He was aware that the young officer had won his decoration in combat. Abe wondered if this made the boy feel superior. It certainly made *him* feel inferior. Still, he couldn't allow the young man to hear voices. Perhaps Lebario should be relieved? But what did it matter; they were just spectators. Earlier the boy had been nervously fingering his silver cluster. Now he seemed to exude confidence, and Meier

found himself jealous. Would he be this calm in his next battle?
Would there be a next battle? So far they had not been noticed.
Breathing deeply to force calm, Abe turned his attention back to
studying the combat display.

"Sir, the admiral," Lebario corrected him. "He's on your
personal frequency."

Immediately the captain switched over, avoiding the younger
man's eyes. "Meier here."

"I'm going to have to pull your escorts," the admiral
announced. "We need every ship that can fight. I'd throw your
freighters in, if they had more than popguns." The commodore
could barely understand Duane. The roar of static from the
exploding plasma blasts nearly overwhelmed the signal.

His eyes were riveted on the battle display. There was no way
he could deny the urgency of the situation. Meier agreed: Duane
needed every combat ship and needed them minutes ago.

"Aye, aye, sir. And good luck."

Seconds later Agberea sounded jubilant as he acknowledged
the change of command. As always, there was a controlled air of
superiority when he addressed the quartermaster who kept being
assigned as his superior. "We'll get a few for you," had been
his closing comment. Keyed up as Agberea must be, he
probably hadn't even meant to taunt me, Abe rationalized.

By the time Meier looked back at the command console, their
escorts were diving toward Bull's-Eye at maximum acceleration.
Meier could hear Agberea ordering them into a tight formation.
Meier envied him. In seconds they would be in combat, able to
salve their frustration with blazing cannon. He could only
cower, hoping to be unnoticed.

The commodore found himself splitting his attention between
Lebario and the console. The lieutenant was staring at the
command display, his hands clenched tightly. Behind him their
Hrruban pilot hissed a low oath. Abe studied the console for a
few seconds, but the battle was too confused for Meier even to
figure out what had provoked the outburst.

Seconds later, when a dozen Khalian ships managed to
overwhelm a Fleet heavy cruiser, the younger officer visibly
flinched. Then Abe swore as well, as they watched, unable to
help, while a Khalian ship overtook a damaged Fleet destroyer
and blasted the wounded vessel into scrap. Then both tried not
to show their relief when that same Khalian turned, ignoring

them, and rejoined the battle.

Meier himself was torn between being glad he wasn't part of that deadly melee and the desire to do something, anything, to help his comrades. Lebario's thoughts echoed the commodore's. Somewhere down there Buchanon and his fellow cadets were fighting for their lives. Yet there was nothing he could do but cower up here, ready to supply the mud troops after the real fighting had ended. If they won.

As if summoned, a new mass of ships appeared at the edge of the command console. They had to be the troop transports. Flipping to maximum range, the lieutenant quickly confirmed. Then something glimmered on the far side of the screen.

If Meier had stationed their force any closer to the battle, Auro wouldn't have seen anything. Or if the transports hadn't caused Remra to change screen scales, again they would have missed them. But because those very long range scanners were engaged, they had warning of the new Khalian fleet as soon as it dropped back.

There were almost fifty ships in the Khalian formation. Most of them were large for Khalians, destroyer class and above. Their formation was ragged, even for ships dropping back after a long journey. It didn't take them long to recover. Even as they accelerated toward Bull's-Eye, the Khalians formed themselves into a tight wedge.

Without being asked, Lebario began programming in the readouts for this new Khalian force. Meier noticed his executive officer's sudden activity. Rising nervously in the cramped control, he watched over the former cadet's shoulder, staring at the screen and trying to force the new Khalians to disappear by sheer force of will.

They didn't.

Lebario's projection superimposed itself on the monitor. The Khalians had dropped back on the far side of Bull's-Eye's sun. Now they were accelerating toward that star. They would whiplash past and slice through the Fleet globe at a fantastic speed. Even without warheads, their missiles would be traveling fast enough to rip through even a heavy cruiser's screens.

Duane had to be warned. No other Fleet ships were in a position to pick up the menace, nor were any likely to be using long-range scans. Meier keyed the emergency frequency and then tore off his headset, half deafened. The earphones filled the control room with the roar of static from tens of thousands of plasma blasts. Communications must now be limited to tight beams at short range. There was no way to warn them. Meier remembered his ominous orders to "render assistance as needed." But there was nothing he could do against twice his number, even if he had commanded real warships, not rusty freight haulers and a hospital ship.

On the display, the red blips of the Khalian reinforcements drove relentlessly along Auro's projection. Their course appeared as a red line, cutting between his freighters and Bull's-Eye's sun and ending where Force One defended the damaged ships it sheltered. When the Weasels hit, the globe would disintegrate and the battle would be lost.

To complicate matters, more troop transports began dropping back twenty AUs in the other direction. They would be unaware of the danger. They were supposed to be at a safe distance, but now they were situated almost exactly where the new Khalians were likely to end their deceleration after slamming through the battle. It would take the underpowered, bulky vessels nearly an hour to recharge their FTL drives. If even one of the Khalians smashed past the Fleet ships intact, thousands of marines and militia would be slaughtered.

Both officers stared at the other in silence. Each realized the other was hoping for a suddenly announced solution. Between them the red blips of the Khalian reinforcements crept across the display. Finally, Lebario, sweating visibly in the cool cabin, felt he had to say something.

"I was just following Captain Buchanon's plan." The young officer referred to his sole bit of glory defensively. *Don't ask me,* he thought. Out loud Auro added, "You are in command."

"In command of a mountain of supplies," Meier commented ruefully. "Pity I can't win this battle with paint too." He was in command, it was up to him to assist as it was most certainly needed. Then his voice trailed off. There was nothing left to say. No more miracles.

The silence that followed seemed long.

"Maybe if we spray 'em pink, the Khalians would retreat in embarrassment." Lebario interrupted the silence, trying to relieve the almost unbearable tension. He referred to Meier's famous stunt against the Tripeans. His voice almost cracked, and the young officer felt giddy with unused adrenaline.

Instead of giving the nervous laugh Lebario expected, the commodore looked solemn.

"Well, paint worked before," Meier said to the air while spinning back to his own command console. Moments later a manifest of the hundreds of supplies they carried replaced the battle display.

No one on the bridge recognized the smile as the short, heavyset officer stopped the scrolling readout at ARMAMENTS. The cargo had been distributed almost evenly among the freighters, a measure which maximized the chances of at least some of each needed supply surviving the battle. Turning to Lebario, Abe Meier gave a stream of orders that began with the surprising command to "have all ships prepare to jettison cargo."

At first the lieutenant thought his commanding officer simply had lost his nerve. He braced himself mentally to assume command, then hesitated. This was Admiral Meier's grandson. Not the person to make *that* kind of mistake with. He studied his commanding officer. There was something about his smile. Auro would wait. In another hour it might not matter. If the Fleet warships were defeated, the *Red Ball* and its escort were too slow to escape the Khalians.

Auro Lebario barked a short laugh as he relayed the seemingly nonsensical order. A year ago he had been bored by the regimen of training at safe, comfortable Port. Now he was getting in the habit of being in battles where there was little chance of survival.

Remra looked over at the two officers, her concern evident. The battle below was as good as lost, and instead of ordering the FTL drives charged, Meier had just ordered full power to the gravity drive. Now they were diving rapidly toward Bull's-Eye's sun.

What the Hrruban saw was hardly reassuring. Commodore Meier was still grinning broadly. The young lieutenant was keying in commands but looked confused. He still reminded her of one of her favorite kits. Studying the readouts, the pilot grew even more concerned. They were on a collision course with the approaching Khalian ships. Did Meier expect them to fight it out?

Relentlessly, the two forces accelerated at each other. The captains of the other freighters now were protesting all over the command circuit. It went against their every instinct to dump valuable cargo. That complaint alternated with those from the captains who realized they were on an intersecting course with fifty Khalian warships. They were getting pretty adamant.

Twice Meier had a captain relieved and ordered those ships' executive officers to continue. On a third vessel Meier got all the way down to the third officer before they found someone who would obey the seemingly suicidal orders.

On board Hrenter's *Falcon*, Krestek was quite pleased with the situation. Seated in the place of honor overlooking the control room, he allowed himself the luxury of a twitching tail. He had been afraid they would arrive too late to take part in the battle. The captains of the raider fleets he had gathered were the most independent of all Khalia. He had spent too many hours forcing the captains of the other ships to accept his command. Only by the threat of actually firing upon the final holdouts, an act which all knew would have them both banned from receiving replacement modules, had finally convinced the last.

They had emerged from the formless sea quite distant from Goldenfield. At first this had seemed a disaster, and his growl had cowed everyone else on the bridge. Khalia had lost ears for lesser errors. Then Krestek had recognized the opportunity. He was going to lead an attack which would be sung of by the bards in all forty systems, or at least the thirty-one the Khalian empire still occupied.

Without hesitation, the darkly furred Khalian had ordered all ships to accelerate at full toward the only remaining large formation of Fleet ships. His guiding bard was to draw his line carefully so that they would be pulled ever faster by the attraction of Goldenfield's star. They would smash through the furless animal's globe before there was time for the sheared ones to react.

The other ships fell in behind the *Falcon* until they were in the formation of the clenched jaw. The hairless cowards would break and flee. It had been this way in other battles. So it would be again. Only this time he would be the hero. Females would offer themselves, just to be able to say they had been known by him. After such a victory no one would dare contest his replacing his father as clan chief.

Around Krestek, the fur was rising on every crewman's

shoulders as they prepared for combat. The familiar rhythm of
the guide bard's chanting helped soothe them only a little. Every
few seconds one of the bards would meet his eye and gesture
that they were still on course.

"There are many ships descending at us," a nervous youth
screeched. Ears went back, and everyone on the bridge studied
the symbols and sparks dancing about the screen in the front of
the control room.

"Turn to meet them." Krestek's annoyance was obvious.
This would disrupt his attack. Where had the sheared ones
gotten more warships? "No, wait, fool!" the Khalian captain
admonished. "They are freight carriers, unable to harm us. We
go to win honor and fame, not to race foolishly after defenseless
prey."

A junior officer leaned forward and nipped the ear of the cub
who had screamed the warning. The notch would remind him
always to check the nature of his enemies in the future.

To the Khalian commander's surprise and delight, the
freighters neither fled nor jumped into the protection of FTL.
Instead they foolishly continued to accelerate on a course that
would bring them to within cannon range. Their destruction
would be a bonus. It would add to the glory of his victory. And
with so many ships' captains trailing behind to witness it.

"Order the other captains to leave the freighters to the
Falcon. No other ship is to fire," he commanded. There would
be grumbles, but it was his prerogative.

A touch of doubt entered Krestek's thoughts. Perhaps the
freighters hoped to delay him. The humans, too, could be
awaiting reinforcements. He would let nothing prevent him from
having this hour of glory.

"Every ship is to maintain maximum speed." Krestek sensed
this victory would be warm and bloody. "We can let nothing
slow or turn us." Anxiously he watched as the foolish human's
freighters continued to plunge directly into their path. Minutes
later the Khalian was reassured when the freighters began to turn
away. Soon they had turned tail until they were running directly
ahead of his own ships.

The navigator signaled that they would actually pass through
them several minutes before reaching the real battle. Good.
They would have time to swat them aside at his leisure.

"Maintain course," he demanded of the chief bard. He

wanted to be sure they would be the first to smash through the human formation. "And more speed!"

"Sir, they may have dumped their cargoes." It was the same cub as before. This time his voice was hesitant. The hairless one's ships were lighter now. Krestek studied the screen, watching for any sign of lifeboats. If they meant to ram, most of the crew would have been abandoning ship. Nothing. The sensors the techlords allowed them were unable to observe anything smaller than a warrior. It must have been cargo. They must have just noticed his ships. The Khalian could picture the panic on the humans' faces.

"Have you never chased a Fofoul?" Krestek answered in knowing tones. "They too leave behind offal when panicked. These humans are sacrificing their cargo to gain a small amount of greater speed with which to flee before us. For a few seconds more of life. They have no honor.

"Does it not make you proud to be a Khalian?"

Everyone on the bridge bared his teeth in pride. The points of light which represented the human ships grew closer. The star was beside them now, and in a short time they would be able to observe directly the rest of the battle. Minor adjustments would be needed if they were to strike exactly where Krestek desired.

Their first warning was when the small screen of the visual scanner was suddenly useless, the camera's lens blotted when they passed through a cloud made up of globules of pink paint.

"They leave their spray behind like the pruss," his second in command joked, pointing at the useless screen. The visual screen was unnecessary in battle. It was the battleconsole that guided them.

Then the explosions began.

The commodore held his breath when the Khalian formation began to edge toward them. If they changed course his plan would fail. After what seemed a very long time, the Weasels returned to their original course. The Hrruban pilot on Meier's left muttered to herself, having realized the Weasels had just taken their measure and discounted them. Her pride chafed. Even to primitive sensors their helplessness must be evident. There weren't enough guns on all twenty-seven freighters to constitute a threat to even one Khalian raider.

Six minutes remained until the freighters and the Khalian

reinforcements met. Meier ordered half of the nearly four hundred thousand plasma artillery shells they carried jettisoned. Duane would be irate that there were fewer shells for his marine's artillery, but if these Khalians reached the battle intact, there wouldn't be any landings. There wouldn't even be any Fleet.

Varying their course slightly, Meier ordered over five million rounds of explosive rifle ammunition dumped next. Two minutes later this was followed by a million small repair parts, nuts, and bolts. With three minutes left they jettisoned twenty-three tons of ball bearings and, just for luck, six thousand five-gallon cans of paint. These cans, containing mostly red-and-white hull paint, burst most impressively when exposed to the vacuum of space.

Finally, the still-clumsy freighters altered course until they had curved around and were running directly ahead of the Khalians. The fur on Remra's back stood upright as the pilot watched the Weasels draw closer. Without thinking, Auro reached over and squeezed the Hrruban's shoulder. Their eyes met, and both relaxed slightly.

Two minutes later Meier ordered the remaining artillery shells cast overboard. His uniform was drenched in sweat, and Auro noticed the commodore had begun rocking slightly back and forth as he studied the command screen on his console. They had formed the freighters in a nearly flat arrangement with the Red Ball in the center. A textbook maneuver designed to ensure that no ship collided with another ship's cargo. Now Meier ordered Remra to allow the rest of the freighters to ease ahead of them a few thousand klicks. For a moment Auro wondered if the pudgy officer was bent on suicide.

Khalian shells began to burst, creeping rapidly closer to the Red Ball as the faster warships overtook them. Lebario threw the switches arming the laser cannon. Abe Meier tensed even more, unsure what he would do if his plan failed. Then the leading Khalian ship struck his impromptu mine field.

The combined velocity of the shells and the still-accelerating raider was massive. It was far greater than the normal speed at which the shells are fired. The kinetic energy alone of several dozen shells hitting was enough to overwhelm the shielding of many of the smaller Weasel ships. Every one of the five-kilogram plasma shells that came into contact with a ship's screen also exploded, often setting off others. The resulting chains of explosions were visible as distant sparks on the *Red Ball*'s rear visual scanner. Remra purred something under her breath. Within seconds the entire screen lit up as if a skyrocket had burst.

When the first Khalian ship disappeared off the screen, several of the bridge crew cheered. They began to slap each other, laughing wildly, when the leading Khalian ship burst apart after continually colliding with thousands of rifle rounds. Trapped by their own velocity, it took less than a second for the entire Khalian force to slam into the deadly cloud of hardware and jettisoned ammunition. Those who survived scattered in a vain attempt at revenge or at avoiding the unexpected hazard. Many of these slammed into the second batch of cannon shells Meier had ordered jettisoned. More ships became hulks, and the few that remained dropped back to the safety of FTL space.

After eleven seconds the only functioning ships remaining in the area were Fleet ships.

When it became apparent they had succeeded beyond their wildest dreams, Lebario stretched luxuriously. For a few satisfied moments Auro simply sat at his console. Then he turned to face his commodore.

"May I have permission to paint, um, *thirty-seven* kill symbols on the hull, sir?" he asked, after reviewing the displays of the last four minutes. And that was just the confirmed count. The rest of the bridge crew smiled at his request. Remra turned back to her console and rolled the ship in a victory maneuver older than even the Fleet.

"If you can find any more paint, Lieutenant," Abe Meier replied solemnly.

INTERLUDE

The image of the Hrruban ambassador flickered as the camera-man adjusted his angle. Gleaming behind her was the battlecruiser *Reg'nethrim*. The sun glistened off his fur as she smashed the traditional bottle of Napa red across the warship's bow. The assembled officials applauded politely.

"That was the scene off Altair as yet another ship joins the Fleet." The announcer's voice was professionally enthusiastic. "Demonstrating not only the Alliance's growing might, but also how all member races have joined together to face the common enemy."

"Yeah, officers," the marine growled to his buddies. That was one of the problems with shipboard duty. After a few months you ran out of new omnidisks. They had been in space fifteen months and were down to rewatching year-old omnicasts.

"I'd almost welcome some action," the medic agreed, ignoring the fact that he was an officer, of sorts.

"Don't even hint at that," Miguel hissed vehemently swatting him with a Khalian tail pelt. But every man in the room knew the gods had been challenged.

CROSSING THE LINE
by Jody Lynn Nye

THE TECHNICIAN SHOT a glance at Mack Dalle's breast-pocket adornment and snickered.

"Stop that," Dalle snapped sulkily. "I didn't ask for the damned assignment, and I didn't want the damned medal. It's not my fault Iris Tolbert wants me to wear it for the PR department."

"Did I say anything?" Technician Tretta Marx asked innocently, handing him a humming cylinder. "Your viral scanner, Doctor."

"Thanks." Dalle ran the device over the ruptured tissues in the chest of the corpse on the examining table. The hum wowed, and he reached behind him for a slide. "Here, fix this sample, will you?"

"Anything for a war hero." Then, catching Dalle's frosty glare, "Sorry! Sorry!" Tretta slapped a coating onto the plastic strip with one hand and flipped up the switch on the ancient and arcane two-D intercom unit with the other. "Bio lab." She caught herself staring and cleared her throat. "It's for you, Mack."

With a sigh, Dalle moved around to her side of the table. Tretta tossed her head meaningfully at the screen. Curious, Dalle looked, and then pulled himself up from his habitual slouch into a crisp salute. "Good afternoon, Commodore."

"It's all right," Commodore Abraham Meier told him, looking out of the three-by-three screen. "At ease. Dr. Dalle, I need a medic for a delicate mission, and your dispatcher, Commander Tolbert, has given me leave to ask you to help."

Dalle ignored the crow of glee from Tretta behind him. "Mind if I ask what it is, Commodore?"

Meier's eyebrows went up, but his jocular tone didn't change. "Caution is not a bad thing. Why not? We have a situation, Doctor, in which a Khalian ship is drifting crippled several AUs farther out. Their engines are gone, no power beyond life support according to sensor readings. They claim to have two hundred human slaves on board. Prisoners. That's the only reason that they haven't been blasted yet, and they know it. Now, if we claimed to have two hundred of *them* on board, they'd blow us up without a tear, but they're counting on what they call our 'weakness.' Do you follow me?"

"Yes, so far."

"So, I don't think it's so long before they might blow themselves up anyway. I'm sending in a company of marines to neutralize the Khalians on board and rescue the human prisoners. And the best way to get them there is on a medical scooter. Looks harmless. Hard to even detect. No outward armament, but moves very quickly. The Weasels will even consider it reasonable for us to send a doctor to look at the prisoners. And so I come to you."

"Let me guess. Tarzan and the Apes."

Meier peered myopically at him through the pickup. "I beg your pardon?"

"Was my participation specifically requested by Marine Sergeant Alvin Shillitoe?"

"Yes, that's right. Can you report immediately, Doctor? Those prisoners can't wait very long. If the air and heat are running short, we both know our people will suffer first."

Dalle looked sadly at his half-begun research, then at Tretta, who was mashing her lips together trying not to laugh out loud. "Yes, sir. I'll be right there, sir."

Dalle squeezed through the door into the conference room aboard the *Red Ball* and made his way through a forest of hands slapping his back to the only remaining empty chair. He stood behind it for introductions to Commodore Meier and his aide, and then slid into the seat, looking around him at the room full of enormous humans whose faces he knew. These were the Apes, and Tarzan himself was sitting across from him grinning out of a face which Mack had personally reconstructed.

"Howya doin', Doc?" Sergeant Alvin Shillitoe winked.

"Hi, Tarzan," Mack replied cheerfully. He hadn't bothered to change out of his lab tunic, since it actually bore his insignia of rank, not to mention the tiny gold button which substituted for the despised medal, but the apes ignored it. Most of them had several of the bronze stars he was wearing, plus other citations which required more blood, theirs or the Khalian's.

"Told ya we wanted you as our medic," Shillitoe said. "Good pay, cushy hours, great chow . . ."

"*May* I have your attention, please?" Meier interrupted patiently and waited until the room quieted. He nodded to his aide who touched the controls on the holotank in the middle of the table. A star field shimmered into view, with the image of a Khalian planetary raiding ship centered in it.

Colored sensor lights flicked off statistics in the lower corners of each side of the cube: temperature, placement, movement, the time. According to these, the ship had been there less than two hours. Mounting a subterfuge such as this in lightning-quick time was nothing less than a miracle for the Fleet. Mack decided it had to have been Meier's influence. The man's grandfather was Admiral of the Red, and the Commodore had a reputation for bloodless miracles.

"It's very simple," Meier was saying. "The longer we delay, the greater the chance that the Khalians will just kill the prisoners. *Especially* if they think we're sending in a rescue party. Any Khalian would rather go out fighting. I think all of you know that. That's why we're using a med scooter as transport. There's no glory in killing an unarmed doctor. Too easy."

Mack gulped.

"So how are we supposed to get in there, supposing they fire across our bows and tell us to keep our distance?" Sergeant Shillitoe asked briskly.

"With a diversion," Meier smiled. "Of course. The scooter will arrive first. For a while the other scrap and ionized debris will hide you. When you are a few kilos out, the *Red Ball* will close in on them. We'll stop just within firing range. Auro here can practice up on his gunnery skills, using their turrets for targets." The commodore gestured toward the young aide who had been sitting quietly at the far end of the table. He was wearing a cadet uniform.

"That kid? While we're approaching his target area?" Mack almost asked out loud, then thought better of it. The marines all looked suddenly restless and uncomfortable.

"Let them think we're coming closer. When they turn their attention to us, the more obvious threat, all of you will board their ship."

"How," Mack squeaked, his throat closing up unexpectedly, "will they get there?"

"Behind you on a mechanized pulley line," Meier said simply. "The marines will be wearing camouflaged environment suits."

"What's to stop them blasting us out of space when they see you?" Alvin asked, narrowing an eye.

"They'll be too busy," Meier promised. "Besides, we believe their guns are out of commission, too."

"You *believe*, sir?"

"And I wait for their signal to pick them up?" Mack asked hopefully.

Tarzan smiled again.

"Oh, no, Doctor. You're going in, too," Meier corrected.

"What?" Mack barked. "Why?"

"Well, one, there are humans on board that vessel that might need your help; two, we need an experienced pilot in the med scooter . . . and three, they might blast you out of space when the marines enter their ship."

"Oh." Mack considered. "I guess I'm going in, too."

The small cabin of the medical shuttle was cramped. The company of Apes, dressed in the standard dark blue under their deep-space gear except for their helmets, sat on benches, operating tables, the mobile gurney, the inducer bed; anything that was flat.

"Sorry the accommodations aren't more comfortable." Mack apologized over his shoulder from the control panel. He was suited up as the marines were, except his gloves and helmet lay on the floor under his seat. "Most of my company is lying down when they visit."

Deep-space gear was camouflaged in what Mack's old friend Patrick Otlind called "early optical illusion." The black matte coating of the sensor-neutral shells had the effect of drawing the eye away from it, as though it were uncomfortable to look at.

The helmet faceplates were the only part of the suits that shone, but matte glass had been tried and found wanting for clarity. Insignia was supposed to be displayed in navy blue cutout on the side of the helmets, but since the Fleet's pride was in their admirals' colors, this prohibition was largely ignored. Alvin's men wore inch-long crescents of yellow next to their faceplates. Yellow was for Admiral Duane, and something else. Mack could tell without looking closer that those crescents were in the shape of bananas.

"You ought to have one, too," Alvin argued, picking up the doctor's headgear. "As an honorary Ape."

"No, thanks," Mack said. "We're supposed to be as invisible as possible. Remember?"

"It's a mark of honor," insisted Pirelli, the language specialist, a dark-skinned man as tall as Mack himself.

"Betcher afterburners," agreed Zanatobi. He came from the same system as Iris Tolbert did and had its characteristic blue hair.

Alvin grinned and affixed the banana decal under the medical cross symbol. "There you go. You're one of us now."

"Thanks, guys," Mack said, rolling his eyes.

The blue-gray scooter halted ten kilometers from the cigar-shaped Khalian vessel, and the marines studied its image in the medical ship's screens.

"By Krim, that doesn't look big enough to have two hundred people on it," Jordan opined. His armor clanked as he got up for a better look.

"You think they in luxury cabins?" His buddy, a golden-skinned female named Utun, jabbed him from behind with a gloved hand. "They packed in like we are."

Alvin chuckled and then ordered everyone to seal up.

The red LED indicating that the scooter had reached its exact destination went on at the same time the speaker exploded with a burst of angry interspace chatter from the Weasel ship.

"You get any of that, Pirelli?" Shillitoe asked.

"Yessir. They want us to halt and be destroyed."

"You mean *or* be destroyed, don't you?" a nervous voice asked.

Pirelli shook his head in disagreement. "I call 'em as I hear 'em." Foxburg and Zanatobi exchanged amused glances.

"At least they're talking to us. Meier's hearing this, too.

Okay, lights out.'' Tarzan gestured to Mack. The marines picked up their helmets and popped them on.

Uncomfortably, Mack obeyed, plunging the control room into darkness. That didn't sound like the Weasels' weapons weren't functional, then again, they were still here and were kilometers inside the range of even a small laser. He bent double to grab his gauntlets, helmet, and diagnosti-kit from under the pilot's seat. Alvin probably already knew that Mack was afraid of the dark, but he wouldn't mention it if the doctor didn't. That marine tradition was even older than the Fleet itself. As long as a personal foible didn't interfere with the mission, it didn't matter.

Mack leaned into the audio pickup. ''I am a medical vessel. Our concern is for the welfare of the humans you carry on board. I am unarmed.''

The speaker continued its furious chatter. Mack put on his helmet and breathed a sigh of relief when he heard the vacuum hiss and saw the internal LEDs go on, indicating that his space suit was operating perfectly.

''Suits sealed? Equalize pressure, Doc. We don't want them to notice a heat trace when we open the lid.''

The door slid across its track, unveiling starry space, interrupted only by the black, cigar-shaped mass of the Khalian vessel. On the speaker, the alien began another series of threats, ending suddenly with a squawk as the raider was bracketed by pale beams from the *Red Ball*'s lone turret. For a moment Mack watched as the beams danced off first the bow and then the stern of the Khalian ship. It appeared Lebario was an expert gunner— if that was where he had been aiming.

''Let's go.'' Tarzan's tone was level, deceptively relaxed.

''We're working for Meier,'' Foxburg said as he moved into place beside the hatch. ''Shouldn't we be carrying a can of paint?''

There was no sound as the pulley charge shot across space and impacted with the side of the Khalian raider. It was like watching a trivid without audio. Mack filled in his own sound effects, the *hiss* and *thunk*, followed by a *twang!* as the pulley cord went taut. From Mack's perspective the raider's often patched hull appeared to hang over the scooter. One by one, the marines took hold of the knots spaced five feet apart and were drawn slowly out into the night. Pirelli went first, yanked up as smoothly as a spider on its dragline. Shillitoe hung back, tapping each marine as his or her turn came up. Mack followed Jordan, his shoulder resting against the man's leg, and concentrated on looking only at the man's back, not at the vast emptiness around them.

"Radio silence." Alvin's voice came softly. Each of the marines' suits was in contact on either side with another one which provided a sort of tin-can communication system up the line.

The end of the line shook now and then as the raider's failed engines shuddered, trying to start, sending out ripples that Mack could feel under his gloved hands. It must be one of the Weasels' pseudoengineers chanting instructions over the controls, no doubt trying to coax life into the machinery. If he ever succeeded, the entire platoon of Apes would be whiplashed into space.

The doctor knew he was being flung back and forth, but with the exception of visual clues, his body was unaware of the movement. Space was frictionless, and all Mack's actions had an air of unreality. His fellows were nearly invisible ahead of him, darker shadows against the scorched hull of the raider, except when silhouetted by bright sparks when the *Red Ball*'s laser dug into the Khalian ship.

"Kitchy koo!" Utun snickered, detaching one hand from the rolling line and reaching for Jordan's armpit.

"Goddamn it, stop that!" the marine muttered, the sound conducted along the metal ribs of their combat suits. Flinching away from her, the marine found himself riding the line upside down and flat out like a paper doll in the wind.

"Minimize your target profile and stow your chatter," Shillitoe hissed from the back of the line, risking a radio squirt.

Jordan twisted until he was once again directly behind Utun and clamped a hand onto her ankle. Cautiously, Mack shifted to make room for him. This caused yet more disruption as the tiniest shift caused the line to sway.

When they reached the raider, each marine activated the magnets in the soles of their suit boots and attached their boots with gentle clanks to the hull.

"We're on." Shillitoe spoke into his microphone. "Breaking communications with *Red Ball* now."

They couldn't hear it, but they knew that on the other side of the Khalian ship, the *Red Ball* was drawing closer and closer to the Weasels' weapons range. Every one of its lights was ablaze. Mack could see that the blue-gray scooter across kilometers of space was lit up like a brand, reflecting the *Red Ball*'s glory. The Weasels would be able to tell that the hatch was open, but now it didn't matter. To get rid of the marines, they'd have to depress their turrets low enough to fire onto their own hull, or blow themselves up. And there was no doubt the Weasels were capable of doing something that suicidal if they were technically able to do so.

Utun blew the airlock open with a shaped charge, a little nasty issued by ordnance that Fleet boarding parties used when no one answered the door. The charge was small enough to leave the inner lock intact. If there were humans on board, they couldn't afford to breach the hull. The Apes piled through the hole, covering one another as each one came through. The second lock, as usual, opened easily. The inner door wasn't meant to keep anyone out. Shillitoe popped in last and started giving orders as soon as the airlock door had whooshed shut behind him. The tasks had been set out and gone over a dozen times with Meier and again on the scooter. Every marine knew already what had to be done, except for Mack.

"Dockerty and Ellis, engineering. Utun, Jordan, life support. Pirelli, Marks, Inez, Sokada, the bridge. The rest of you follow me. We secure the prisoners. Doc, come with me or stay out of the way. Up to you."

A grim expression on his face, Mack followed the marine sergeant. Reality had reasserted itself the moment he had removed his frosted-over helmet in the warm ship air. They were on a Khalian ship, and they were looking for two hundred live human prisoners, in who-knew-what physical condition. He worried that the tiny diagnosti-kit would be insufficient to treat the damage he would find. Experience had taught the Fleet marines that their greatest danger was just before they had secured the ship. It was then that every remaining Weasel stopped fighting and tried to cause their ship to self-destruct. Mack realized that attending to the prisoners could probably wait until they had complete control and until the *Red Ball* could safely come alongside—otherwise his services would become entirely and permanently unnecessary.

The other marines waited only until the condensation had evaporated before putting their gear on again. Each man was armed with a needle gun or projectile-firing pistol and a camouflage-tinted saber. Mack stripped off his gauntlets and slung them defiantly into a matte-painted corner as he trotted after the marines.

Zanatobi threw him a glance through his mask. "Don't leave 'em there. You'll never see 'em again. The Weasels'll use 'em for condoms."

Mack started to explain the facts about Khalian biology, then realized his leg was being pulled.

"What about the helmet?" the young doctor asked, determined to keep the mood light. Anything to keep from having to face that he was scared hollow.

"Eh, they'll use that for a head."

"Why not?" Mack reasoned. "That's what *we* use it for." But he attached the helmet to the snaps at the nape of his collar and let it bump along behind him so he could hear the mike chatter.

The party trotted along through the impact-padding lined tube that was the corridor. The insulation hullward was a shiny silver to deflect laser fire, as the inner walls were painted a flat black matte to absorb the high-intensity beams. It was the cheapest way in space to ensure against breaching the hulls by accident with a laser. Their heavy footfalls were no more than soft pok-pok-pok sounds on the cushioned floor.

"*Down!*"

A spatter of explosive pops echoed in the corridor behind them, and the party flattened itself on the deck.

A rebel yell of triumph from Dockerty rattled over the headset pickups. He and his partner reported seconds later that they were successful in breaking through to engineering. "We mopped 'em, Sarge! Surprised 'em good. Five dead. One bastard hit an alarm before we croaked 'em, though. We're looking for the cutoff for the self-destruct mechanism before someone triggers it from the bridge."

"So they know we're here." Shillitoe accepted the report with carefully controlled optimism. "Don't let anyone in there who looks like he hasn't shaved."

"Sure, Sarge," Dockerty acknowledged.

* * *

The Khalian vessel shook faintly in space as Auro Lebario's carefully aimed salvos scored on first the bow, then the stern. Auro realized that if he kept alternating hits in just the right places, the slaveship would windmill off into the night like an alien juggernaut. He had to keep reminding himself that he was a serious part of the rescue effort, but from his unprotected position in the gunnery bubble, his view still looked like the screen of a video game. His constant computer readouts even gave him a running tally of how many hits he'd made. Unfortunately, if the Khalians ever got their lasers powered up, he'd be an easy target.

"Game over." Auro mused uncomfortably, shifting his shoulders under his cadet's tunic. He took careful aim on the glinting metal of one of the dormant gun emplacements and pressed his fire control. Sparks shot satisfyingly off into space from the edge of the Khalian ship.

"Goddamn it!" Shillitoe exclaimed to the ceiling as his group dashed through the corridor. "This isn't blasted target practice, Lebario!" As if in answer to his comment, the floor ahead of them chattered with little puffs of smoke. "Hostiles ahead! They must be desperate if they're risking laser fire in here."

The tracer in Mack's diagnosti-kit lit up as they dodged between structural pylons for cover and returned fire. "Tarzan, there's one of ours ahead."

"We're not shooting at our own guys, are we?"

"No. I have a vital-signs signal. It's weak; probably one of the prisoners is captured Fleet personnel. There's a door and electronic interference between the signaling unit and us."

"And those overgrown rats want to keep us from getting to them," the sergeant growled, peering over the edge of a bale. "How many of them are there?"

"I count five flashes, Sarge," Zanatobi called from behind a long container. "Might be just three or four moving around. Nope, five. I was right the first time."

"Something funny about this," Foxburg mused. "How come they're already fighting with lasers? They couldn't have known there'd be a boarding attempt. These critters just don't think that far ahead. This is a last-ditch attempt of some kind."

"Maybe they're out of bullets," a marine named Viedre offered, flattening himself next to Shillitoe.

"Maybe it's a mutiny," Mack suggested. "They were already fighting when we arrived."

Mack's guess proved to be the right one. When at last the Apes broke through, the bodies of the Weasels lay before a barricade protecting them from what lay behind a sealed hatchway on the opposite side from the marines' approach. The sole Khalian remaining alive hissed his terror as he saw that his opponents were fully-armed marines. His defiant death cry rang in the hall as Zanatobi shot him down.

"We weren't what he was expecting," Shillitoe said, turning over the body with a foot. "No communications device. On any of 'em. This lot was cut off."

"He was calling for a bard," Pirelli noted with amusement, gathering up the lasers.

"We'll tell 'em he died fighting later," the sergeant said.

"Just before we space 'em," Viedre added.

"Betcher afterburners," Zanatobi smirked.

A curt nod from the sergeant sent his men into combat position ranged around the sealed door. Viedre attached a charge to the locking mechanism in the wall next to the portal and looked up at his commander for his signal.

"Sarge"—Dockerty's voice shouted over the helmet pickups —"that alarm brought six more Weasels. We're trying to hold 'em off. They've been making suicide leaps for the self-destruct controls!"

"Hang in there," Shillitoe commanded. "We'll be with you ASAP. All units," he called to the other parties of marines, "all units join Dockerty's in engineering, or we're going to be space rubble!"

"Aye, Sarge." "Right, Tarzan." "Okay!" came from the other advance units.

"We can't find nobody, but they shooting at us," Utun's voice spat. "Jordan and I gotta stay."

"All right," Shillitoe said, moving his chin away from the mike control and listening to the hum of Dockerty's giving commands. "Let's get the prisoners out. We don't know how many Khalians are on the other side of the door, and we're running out of time." He hefted his projectile thrower. "On my signal. . . . Now!"

Yelling war cries, the Apes burst through the sliding door as soon as the charge blew out the lock and found themselves confronting bloody and mutilated remains. It took Mack a shocked thirty seconds to realize that the bodies were not human, but Khalian. One of them was wearing a Fleet-style white medic's tunic. Mack recalled that there were some Khalian medics. But he was still on guard because he was being watched. Staring with equal surprise at the marines were the two hundred humans, looking thin and showing evidence of ill-treatment, but alive.

Sergeant Shillitoe popped off his helmet and looked around the cold, steel-walled room at the prisoners. "What happened here?" Several of the strongest-looking men and women were stained with blood to the elbows. The room appeared to have been a communal dormitory. Evidently, the Khalians believed that the locking hatchway was secure enough to keep the humans imprisoned. There were no chains or rows of holding pens, as the marines had seen on other Khalian ships.

"We caught them off guard, Sergeant, is it?" one of the men said proudly, stepping forward. He wore the remains of a Fleet uniform from which his insignia dangled. "I'm Captain Pollock. It was pretty bad for a while—no food, no medical supplies—but we soon realized we outnumbered the bastards more than ten to one. We made our plans and struck. In no time, we would have been in command of the ship." He drew himself up into a stiff stance of attention, but it was clear he was exhausted.

"Too bad you couldn't have let us know," Shillitoe said with dry humor. "We wouldn't have had to come. Of course the ship isn't going anyplace right now. The engines are shot."

Many of the prisoners nodded to one another. "So that's why they were going crazy," Pollock acknowledged. "We heard the thrumming stop just before we attacked the guards."

Dockerty's voice broke in, automatically augmented in volume from the detached helmet's speaker. "Sarge, they're rolling in a laser cannon. If they fire that, they might breach hull integrity, and it's all over!"

Foxburg was disgusted. "They're stupid. They *want* to blow the ship up, right? If they were smart, they'd turn the cannon around the other way and blast through the bulkheads."

"—And I can hear them cutting through a wall behind us," Dockerty interrupted. "They're determined to get to that self-destruct mechanism, Sarge. We can't hold out much longer.''

''—Caught one trying to set off a missile warhead,'' another voice interrupted.

Crisply worded reports came in from the rest of the assault team. At least two dozen Khalians remained, spread all over the ship in twos and threes. Shillitoe was beginning to realize just how many meters of twisting corridors a ship this size had. There was no way they could eliminate all of the remaining Khalians before one got lucky and blew them all to pieces.

''Dockerty, cut off all power sources,'' the sergeant commanded. ''That'll take care of the laser cannon. Utun, maintain life support. Go over to emergency power if you have to.''

''I can't read these controls, but I'll try, Sarge,'' the woman's voice crackled on the pickup.

A concerned hubbub arose from the prisoners.

''We have to go help him!'' Dalle exclaimed, his eyes wide, pulled between his concern over the condition of the prisoners and Dockerty's ability to hold off the enemy.

''Not yet,'' Shillitoe said, glancing at the crowd of humans clustering around them. He raised his hands for attention. ''Listen up. Hey. Hey! Quiet down!'' The powerful voice which had earned him his nickname carried over the combined murmur of the assembled humans and bounced off the rear bulkhead. Mack winced. ''You heard the man. They're trying to blow this ship up with all of us aboard. We could use your help. You want to get revenge on the damned Weasels?''

The cheer of agreement proved to Shillitoe that the question was rhetorical.

The marine sergeant's voice rang off the metal walls. ''Together we're an army—unstoppable. Hunt down every single Weasel you can find and kill them! But we've got to hurry! Follow me!'' The building roar from 208 voices finally drowned out his commands.

Shillitoe and his men tossed some of their spare weapons over to their makeshift army and ran out of the door. Like a wave, the prisoners forgot their exhaustion and hunger and surged after Tarzan. Mack glanced over each man and woman as the crowd passed him. The chance to vent some of their frustration and anger at being held prisoner had given strength back to them. It wouldn't last long, but this way they had a chance. He unholstered his projectile thrower and followed in the wake of the furious mob.

"You'll all go forward and take out any Weasels left on the bridge," Shillitoe ordered as they came to the engineering section. "And look out! I've got two marines up there. Don't mistake 'em for bald Khalians!"

Half of the crowd of prisoners followed Zanatobi up the passageway, bursting past two surprised Khalians who were unrolling the power cable for the laser cannon inside engineering. The prisoners tore both the raiders and the cable to pieces with their bare hands before the Khalians could react.

The tidal wave of human bodies overwhelmed the few Khalians who were attempting to break through to engineering. Behind its plate-glass window, Dockerty's sweating face broke into a relieved grin, which changed into astonishment as the prisoners swarmed in the door, led by a screaming Zanatobi. Dockerty took the opportunity to shoot a couple of the nearest Khalians as they gaped in surprise. Ellis, on the floor with a laser burn through his thigh, rolled over and over to get out of the mob's way.

If a Khalian fought back, using its formidable teeth or talons, another human took the place of the wounded human, and several more assaulted the enemy from behind. In a few breaths, the last remaining Khalians had been throttled, stamped on, and clawed. Sounds echoing down the corridors signaled the discovery of those Khalians who had spread out inside the spaceship. Shillitoe, hurrying toward each new roar, was unable to break through the crowd or even prevent the Weasels' bodies from being pulled apart.

"On the other hand," he muttered to Mack as they forced their way through to Ellis's side, "they had it coming. Why should I spoil their fun?"

"Hey, Tarzan, we're all through here," Zanatobi's voice coming through on the headset interrupted them. "You wanna tell someone to pick us up now?"

"Just as soon as I figure out how to recommend two hundred civvies for medals," Shillitoe shot back. "You lazy bastards let them do your job!"

INTERLUDE

Most humans would be surprised to discover that Omnilar, the most popular and most influential of all omni stations, is owned solely by Louawisa 34, an Alertian. Since the Alliance is predominantly human, this fact is neither hidden nor emphasized. Instead, the only executive that ever appears on screen is the charismatic, and well-constructed, Dee Vinate. For most human viewers this is quite enough.

There is no information as to the source of the immense wealth which Louawisa 34 used to obtain his majority interest in Omnilar. What is known of the reclusive trillionaire are his fervently pacifist views, views reflected in his company's constant calls for an end to the conflict and a rapprochement with the Khalia.

Not surprisingly, Omnilar's viewership diminishes as you approach the frontier sectors.

BAD LUCK
by Janet Morris

"YOU WANT US TO *what?*" Captain Tolliver English of the 92nd
Marine Reaction Company (Redhorse) shook his curly blond
head as if he couldn't believe his ears. The impassive, can-do
facade he assumed when confronting strangers and navy brass
slipped, revealing naked emotion: anger, frustration, and open
revolt. "You're out of your mind. Sir."

English squinted at the stranger in dark civilian clothes as if at
a distant target suddenly in his line of sight. The marine
captain's hips jutted and his hands rested there, where his
equipment belt would have been if they'd been groundside
instead of parked high above Bull's-Eye (MCA-1187) in the
Haig along with half the damn Alliance Fleet, shaking off the
effects of the recent space-to-space "victory" and getting ready
for the Bull's-Eye operation's next phase.

"Toby!" cautioned Jay Padova, the *Haig*'s paunchy commander, taking the cigar from his lips as he hurried around his
desk to put himself physically between the two men.

The civilian put out his hand, fingers spread, stopping Padova
in his tracks. "At ease, sailor," he ordered the ship's commander absently. "I'll handle this." His head half turned, but
his flat stare never left Toby English as he called over his
shoulder, "Manning, get us some coffee, or something."

English had nearly forgotten about Johanna Manning, the
Haig's staff intelligence officer, over behind Padova's desk with

237

her porta-base hooked into the auxiliary com console.

He braced himself for the inevitable explosion from Manning, who was prickly at best. There wasn't even the slam of the porta-base's lid. Manning slipped by in English's peripheral vision without turning a short-cropped hair, her thin face expressionless, as if the stranger's command had turned her into a stewardess.

Nobody spoke until long after the door to Padova's office had exhaled her and sighed shut again, which gave English more than enough time to reevaluate the civilian. Shoehorned into maddeningly tight quarters on an Alliance navy destroyer with his fifty marines still mourning the loss of three of their company on Bethesda, English had become so attuned to detecting one kind of deadliness in a man that he'd failed to recognize another in the stranger.

English's men tended to cook off like the Bethesda spaceport had, with plenty of warning glow and noise and heat. Violence close to the surface was one thing the Redhorse captain had learned to spot; his marines were made that way—it kept them alive.

But this man was a different sort of dangerous, the kind that gave no warning, no signal, unless the sheer absence of display was warning enough. And it hadn't been, not to Toby, not when Padova hadn't seen fit to brief him beforehand. *But I should have known,* he chided himself. What the hell was a civilian doing in Padova's inner sanctum in the middle of strike prepositioning?

Looking over the "civilian observer" again, English saw everything he'd missed because he really hadn't been looking for it. The flat expression on a face that might have been handsome if there was any human emotion on it; the perfectly groomed home world haircut and clothes on a body too fit for a noncombatant and too relaxed for a soldier. The weird little tics that didn't quite fit: a red silk cord knotted on one wrist in an intricate pattern, an expensive universal chronometer on the other; the belt too wide to be there only to hold up his pants and a jacket cut to accommodate concealed hardware; the predatory, attentive amusement that came from nowhere and everywhere but his eyes.

But then, none of that would have meant anything unless you'd seen the way he ordered Padova and Manning around. Slouchy guys with nothing much to say, who didn't flap no matter what, weren't the sort you worried about unless you'd been somewhere like Xeon where, after they'd come and gone, you found some of your own guys floating face-down in the Purple River—the ones who'd been asking out loud the sorts of questions everybody wonders about, but most have more sense than to ask.

Just when it all cycled for English and he muttered "damn" under his breath, the stranger said, "Let's take it from the top, Marine. We want you to take some NDI—nondevelopmental items—down to Bull's-Eye on your sortie against that Khalian naval repair facility, instead of the antiquated tech you've been using. This isn't a field test; this equipment's going to upgrade your Redhorse's effectiveness by thirty percent. Since you're at half-strength compared to, say, the One-Twenty-first, and doomed to stay that way as long as you're hitching a ride on this navy tub, you ought to thank us, not bitch."

"Thanks. Sir. But no thanks." English crossed his arms.

Padova opened his mouth to speak, changed his mind, shoved his cigar into it, and lumbered heavily back to sit behind his desk, shaking his head slowly where Toby English couldn't help but see.

"You're under the mistaken assumption that I'm asking, Captain," said the civilian. And now there were deep lines around his eyes as he looked past English, to where the bulkhead door was. "So let's get that straight. I'm a civilian observer, you bet. My name's Grant. I'll be dropping with your Redhorse to see how you boys perform with your new toys."

"We're not guinea pigs. We're not paid to provide burn-in time under fire for some technospook program—" The severity of Padova's headshake warned English to shut it down. English jammed his hands into his pockets.

Grant said, "I just told you this was NDI, not experimental, hardware. Are you calling me a liar? Because if you are, don't. I'm going to be your best friend or your worst enemy for the duration of this Bull's-Eye vertical insertion, mister. Unless, of course, you want to sit up here in Padova's brig while I put Redhorse through its paces. Who's your senior lieutenant?"

"I—" English's mouth was dry. They'd lost Manning (no relation to Johanna Manning), along with Tamarack and Louis, on Bethesda. "We're waitin' on command replacements, not that we need 'em . . . we're at by-the-book full strength. Right now my old recon first, Sawyer, has that slot." And Sawyer was a couple rounds shy of a full clip lately. "Look, Grant, sir—changing gear just before a drop's bad luck. Everybody knows that. Don't back me into a corner on this. My guys are real short fused, and the last thing they need is changes just before they're supposed to secure eight klicks of dry dock on a world where Khalians are the indigs."

"Don't you think we know what you need, Marine?" said the purported civilian.

"You want to give me some idea of who the hell you are and where you come from, talkin' to me like this?" English turned to Padova, hand out as if for help. Again, Jay shook his head, and the look on his face was sour, as if his cigar tasted real bad today.

"How's OPSCOM suit you?" asked the stranger.

"It don't suit me at all. Not with you runnin' around in a funny suit givin' orders to a naval destroyer commander and me both like you was tasked for it." OPSCOM was military. "You got some sort of—?"

The man in civilian clothes reached into his jacket pocket, and English stiffened reflexively.

Grant tossed a holographic ID at him.

Even before he caught it, English wished he hadn't seen the insignia on the back. "Okay," he said, after flipping the ID in his fingers. He'd about guessed; he was just hoping he was wrong. Interagency Support Activity personnel sat wherever they wanted, and right now this one wanted to sit beside Toby English's 92nd while it secured an area twice the size it should have to secure. At least, for once, their intelligence would be current. "You could have saved lots of time, tellin' me this in the beginning, sir," he said to the GS-15 from Eight Ball Command. "Let's go see this so-called NDI of yours."

Out of the corner of his eye, as he handed the ID back to the Observer, English could see Padova wipe his forehead with the back of his hand. He couldn't figure what Jay had been worried about. English never would have let push come to shove, not with a mission thirty-six hours away.

On the way out, he thought maybe he understood what was bothering Padova after all: as he was leaving with the Observer, Manning came back in with a tray, a coffee pot, and an opaque glare on her thin face.

"Hey there, Bushbaby," said the man called Grant to Padova's chief of intelligence. "Just in time. Come on, you

ought to see this stuff before you have to use it. There's no place
on this little boat to do much in the way of familiarization: the
run-through I'll give you is all you'll get until we're on the
ground. Unless you want to bunk in with the 92nd for the night,
that is, which would be one hell of a waste.''

English had never dreamed that Manning might go
groundside with them. He'd never dreamed he'd see anything
like the look on her face at that moment—not from Manning,
not ever.

She went chalk white; her lips turned blue and her eyes got
very bright. Slowly and deliberately she set down the coffee and
poured herself a sipper full. "Let's go, then," she said to the
Observer without looking up at him, although he was a big man,
English's height. "If you'll excuse me, sir?" she called past
them to Padova, very professionally, very controlled, through
still bloodless lips.

"Dismissed," Padova replied with evident relief. English
began wishing he was going to wake up from this weird-ass
dream sometime real soon.

The so-called NDI was about as nondevelopmental as something you could spray on Weasels to make them lose their fur.
The whole point of NDI gear was that it would work: it was
supposed to be pretested, field-proven, off-the-shelf technology,
maybe packaged or combined some new way, but generally
familiar.

English had been hoping for something simple, or something
noncrucial at least. How much could Eight Ball Command want
to change just before an insertion? If it worked, you didn't go in
and muck around with it, and the gear that the 92nd was using
had been keeping them alive and dangerous to the enemy's
health well enough to suit anybody who had to use it.

But now here was all this new shit, with no time to train, let
alone get up to speed, with it. English had trucked two full kits
from the resupply pod down to the 92nd's wardroom so that he
and Sawyer could shake the stuff out with everybody watching.
But you couldn't shoot the damned APOT (A-potential) guns in
here, and you couldn't try the modified scanners, or they'd
screw up the ship's astronics. Same for the Associate-assisted
helmets. So there was no way of knowing whether the beam
weapons would really freeze and/or explode the Weasels in their
tracks (so long as you kept the weapons in contact with your new

suit like the manual said), or whether the hand-helds would give you any better lock-on than conventional direction finders, or whether any of the new electronics would integrate with the 92nd's conventional systems, or just jam things up.

They shouldn't be worrying about integration, English told the horror-struck men of the 92nd; anyway, they had whole new hard suits coming, and field packs as well.

"Why are you doin' this to us?" somebody wanted to know.

English looked up from the pile of gear he wanted to touch about as much as he'd have liked to stick his bare hand in between a mother Weasel and her nursing pup, and saw that it was Trask, the new field first, who'd spoken.

"Wouldn't want you to get bored, Sergeant. You think these goodies are neat? Wait till you put on that helmet and hear your Associate electronics telling you what they think you should do in any and every combat situation. Ain't technology wonderful? Now we don't have to think at all—just carry the gear from one place to the next and do what it says."

Sawyer, who had been up all night in the resupply pod alongside English, working with the NDI, rubbed a shadowed jaw. He'd saved English's ass on Bethesda, and probably everybody else's in the wardroom, some time or other. Good recon specialists were like that. He could exude confidence like a tranquilizer spray, and there wasn't a scar on him after fifteen years in the field, which helped you believe he knew what he was doing.

He turned on that aura of invincibility and said with an easy, gap-toothed grin, "Come on, girls, what's the damned difference what we kill 'em with, so long as we kill 'em? We're looking at one-type-kills-all weaponry, here. OPSCOM thinks this is what we need, then this is what we need. Intel thinks maybe there's so many Weasels down there that we aren't gonna want to change clips." He really did look like he believed what he said, even though he knew the part about OPSCOM wasn't exactly true.

Demonstrating, he shouldered the power pack for the APOT rifle. "You just spray 'em like this, just like hosing down a perimeter with defoliant. You want the tails for your coup-coats? You set it to low. You want to blow 'em to smithereens? You set it to high. You want to stun instead of kill? You set it to mid position."

"How much does it weigh?" A corporal named Bucknell asked the inevitable question.

"We've been through that with the technical Observer who's going to drop with us. It's all well within milspec," English said very quietly, suddenly drained of energy now that it was clear the men weren't going to be as balky as he'd been—thanks to Sawyer. Having slipped that data in so that nobody'd be surprised about the Observer, he said, "I'm going to leave you with Sergeant Sawyer. Just remember—it's not too heavy and it'll jump, so we don't have any reason to bitch about it."

"Unless it don't work," said Corporal Bucknell.

Sawyer threw an APOT rifle at him, and the corporal lunged to catch it. "It works better than you do, Nellie, and that's for sure."

As he left them to their own study of the new equipment, English heard Sawyer telling the men in a low voice meant to be comforting that this mission was "so slick, so Priority One, so black that the Observer *and* the ship's Intel officer are going down with us. Not only that, I heard that Padova's own feet might touch the ground on this one—that if we need, we've got . . . even the *Haig* sittin' on her ass on Khalian turf waitin' for us."

As long as nobody was sure English had overheard Sawyer, English didn't have to deny the rumors. For all Toby knew, what he and Sawyer had overheard passing between the Observer and Manning might be true.

But there was other stuff passing between the Observer and Manning that English didn't want to think about, personal stuff—especially because there was something similar going on between Manning and the 92nd's line lieutenant, which was why Sawyer had been so testy lately.

For the first time in the whole damned war against the Khalians, English really wished he could sit this one out.

At least he didn't have to ascertain personally that every one of his marines had exactly the suit fittings and fit that could mean the difference between victory and defeat. Sawyer would handle that. It was going to take all night.

Sawyer had *begged* for the duty, even though it wasn't really either man's job, by the book. By the book, there was nothing scary about all this new equipment on the eve of a major engagement. If Sawyer hadn't volunteered to oversee the refit,

English would have felt obliged to stay.

This way he could try to get some sleep, something Sawyer felt compelled to avoid for reasons that probably had way too much to do with Manning and the on-board Observer and that, unless and until they impaired his lieutenant's performance, were none of English's damned business.

If they had been, he'd have told Sawyer days ago that fooling around with one of Padova's ranking officers was a bad idea. Sawyer knew that, and knew that English knew what was going on and didn't like it. And that hadn't stopped him.

The only good thing to come out of this whole mess was that, for reasons of his own, Sawyer had decided to shape up just when English really needed him. But then, that was the way of it with the marines of Redhorse.

"One more time, girls," said Sawyer to the jump-ready troops in the free-falling APC lit with strobing red light: "Our orders say we take prisoners, if possible, remember. That's what the 'game bags' "—the sergeant bared his teeth—"and the tape is for. But them orders also say don't lose none of these goodies, which includes the suits we're wearin'. So we ain't takin' any casualties, neither."

There was a general mutter from the marines in the ready bay, too subdued for English's liking.

"So what it cuts to," Sawyer continued in a voice that bounced around like sliding gravel in the APC's belly full of bare-headed marines, "is we don't leave nothin' behind—not a scanner, not an ELVIS pack, not a Weasel with a breath o' life in 'im . . . and sure as shit none of these APOT rifles." Sawyer glanced at the A-potential weapon in his hand with all the affection he'd have showed an Eirish python. "Now let's go over this e-quipment one more time. E-L-V-I-S stands fer electromagnetic vectored integrated scalar, which means it powers the rifle you're holding. Lose the pack, this multibuck piece of hardware's good maybe for a bayonet or a club. Your suits and gloves, once they're sealed to the suit, are part of the weapons system: they feed the energy from the pack into the rifle. Keep the rifle in contact . . ."

English was worried about that. There was no way to explain the APOT system to the men any better. They didn't know anything more than they needed to about superconductivity, zero-point potentials, or Aharanov-Bohm effects in currents conducted through composite-metal rings. And all they needed to know was, if you kept the APOT rifle in contact with the suit and pulled the trigger, the gun would kill what you were pointing at, vegetable, animal, or mineral.

English knew a little more, enough to be worried for more than superstition's sake; enough to guess how come the Observer was making the drop, if not the jump, with them. The APOTs, driven by the forty-pound ELVIS packs and modulated by the "Associate" electronics in the 92nd's new helmets, punched virtual holes in space-time to get at the unlimited energy under the surface of what English and his men knew as reality.

What that might do to the man inside the superconductive suit who was holding the rifle discharging that energy and wearing the transducer-management system . . . that was another of those questions you just didn't ask somebody from Eight Ball Command who'd come along to log the answers when he saw them.

In the time-honored jargon of English's trade, it sucked. One guy strutting around some lab somewhere shooting pop-ups in a fun house was a whole lot different from fifty men whacking away at the enemy at will and random in an eight-klick strike zone. Nothing English had seen in his briefing material (which had said on its back cover, before he'd incinerated it personally, PLEASE DO NOT RETURN THIS DOCUMENT/EACH ACTIVITY IS RESPONSIBLE FOR DESTRUCTION OF THIS DOCUMENT ACCORDING TO APPLICABLE REGULATIONS) had treated items such as minimum distance between ELVIS packs, or what would happen if one suit-wearer-weapon system took friendly fire from another. No mention had been made of overload or malfunction conditions, either.

English shifted in his new hard suit gingerly, wishing it didn't make him so nervous. In seven and a half minutes, they were going to put on their helmets at Sawyer's signal and start jump check. Then the queasiness he felt would probably disappear. Like as not, his unsettled stomach and back-brain headache had more to do with the way command had fallen out than his hardware.

Sure. As soon as he couldn't see Grant and Manning, huddled forward of the dropmaster, his gut would settle down. Then all he'd have to worry about was whether the Associate electronics in his helmet would override his damned all-com or his suit would short-circuit in a puddle and fry him where he landed. It was a rainy night down there on Bull's-Eye, moonless, dark as a black hole, Manning had told them.

Nothing could have been darker than the look on the Intel officer's face as Manning sat beside the Observer, watching Sawyer out of the corner of her eye.

English had done his best to alleviate the tension between her and Sawyer by separating them. Hadn't helped. Maybe it would when they got on the ground. English was jumping with Sawyer and the 92nd, Manning was staying with Grant and the dropmaster and the pilot of the APC: the big Observer was along to drop, but not jump, with the grunts.

The APC was a "no-see-em" (NOCM: Nocturnal Operations Clandestine Module); it would sit at the pickup point, safe as its multisignature countermeasures could make it on a grid square designated Ten Ring, and from there the intelligence officer and the civilian observer would watch the whole thing via everybody's in-suit collection electronics.

If you had a problem, this time, or some nonreg little glitch, you couldn't just synchronize your helmets and wipe the data strip. This time, the whole go was on the record. Eight Ball Command wanted to see and hear everything that happened when the APOT system met the enemy for the first time. But it bothered English that the Observer wasn't wearing the system and making the jump with them. Given the nature of the man and his provenance, it said more about the dangers involved than had the manual English incinerated.

If the Observer had been old, lame, fat, blind, or somehow not-jump qualifiable, it wouldn't have felt so wrong to English, and he knew it. Not that the jump was standard, either. Nothing about this mission was standard. Grant didn't want anybody hanging in the air in a chute—that was understandable. The insertions were per grid square, without the room for error you needed using chutes.

That *wasn't* understandable.

But Grant had insisted, and English was in enough trouble already with the Observer. If he'd refused to lead the 92nd, somebody else, probably Sawyer, would have had to take his place. Grant had made that clear enough.

So two- and three-man teams were jumping with jet-packs, or

on rappelling lines, in order to meet the surgically precise logistical requirements of Eight Ball Command's hand-delivered orders.

English wasn't sure the order of command would have held if he tested it up the line or in court, but he didn't have any way to do that, and Padova had flat refused to let him query any marine brass on ship-to-ship frequencies. "Just do the operation, Toby, and don't ask questions. You know better than this." Padova had been positively paternal, squeezing his arm and giving him full-bore, concerned stares.

Damn, English just hated drop phase, and it never got any better, he told himself. If it wasn't this screwy mission with its fuzzy parameters and last-minute command shake-ups, it would have been something else.

The APC was dropping free, vectored to masquerade as space junk burning into atmosphere on a self-destruct trajectory from the recent space battle above. The Khalian repair facility would be on heightened alert, but not for something dead and crashing.

Intelligence said the facility didn't have enough muscle left operational to blast them out of existence during coast phase, unless it powered up one of the ships it had been repairing, which might have escaped the blanket of electronics-frying beams the Alliance had thrown over Bull's-Eye when the space battle began. But you never knew for sure.

Sitting ducks sweat, and English's 92nd was no exception. Usually, you had your helmet on by now. But these new systems had powerful magnetos, and nobody knew what-all powered up when the Associate helmets made their connections with the suit. So they sat exposed, everybody looking as ready as he could manage.

Maybe that was why the talk was so sparse and the edge on his men seemed so dull.

Or maybe it was all English's imagination. He had more data—so he had more reason to worry—than anyone else except Grant and maybe Manning, who weren't expecting to leave the safety of the APC.

Just as he was thinking about her, Manning got up from beside Grant and made her way aft, bent over in her old-style suit, through the gauntlet of armored knees and stowed gear between them.

When she stopped before Sawyer, she was only a few meters

from English, but he couldn't hear what she whispered in Sawyer's ear. English saw the black hard case she handed him, though. You couldn't miss it.

English made a command decision to ignore whatever the hell it was that was going on. Sawyer would tell him if it was any of his business, once they got out of this damned can.

He went back to worrying. The Associate AI was preset to detect Weasels—Weasels at a thousand meters; Weasels twenty meters belowground through solid concrete; any Weasel with a heat signature or a heartbeat. But English had no real familiarity with how that targeting was going to look through his heads-up visor display. He fingered the helmet between his knees, playing with the retractable faceplate, trying to wait patiently for the drop light to stop strobing, which would mean they were on-site for the first jumps.

But when Manning quit huddling with Sawyer, English couldn't resist the temptation to try and do some damn thing to better the 92nd's odds. "Hey, Manning," he called softly, and everybody else shut up.

She straightened as best she could and said, "Captain?"

"You get me some wheels down there, Manning. I'll carry your books."

"We called for them, Captain," she said, taking a cautious, backward step along the aisle of armored knees, "but you know how it is . . ." She trailed off; English couldn't see her face.

The civilian observer's voice carried effortlessly all the way from the bulkhead separating the flight deck from the troops. "Your trucks are down there somewhere, marine. But knowing the Fleet's efficiency," Grant added, "the chances of them being within twenty klicks of where we're going aren't the kind I'd bet my life on."

It wasn't really what you wanted the men to hear, but English had started it. Still, smart-mouth critiques from an outsider just before going into combat . . . English came up off the jump bench.

Sawyer's big arm slapped him across the chest. It seemed like it could have been an accident, two men moving at the same time in the APC, both trying to get clear field of vision on somebody up front. English's butt hit the bench again.

Sawyer was half out into the aisle and already saying, in a voice he reserved for body count and interrogation, "Bein' our civilian observer, sir, we was hopin' you might know if it's true that Weasel technology is really a hundred years behind our own?" It wasn't a question; it was a lateral escalation.

But the remark was alchemical: English slumped in his seat (forcing his hand away from his equipment belt and the good old-fashioned kinetic kill pistol nobody was going to take away from him), thankful for Sawyer's intervention. If English was going to smoke Grant the Observer, there was plenty of time, and he needed either the confusion of battle or a better reason than not liking Grant's critique of Fleet efficiency.

English wasn't the only one whose mood was abruptly changed by the line lieutenant's remark. His old squad started swapping recon jokes about Weasels, and everybody began to loosen up.

Which was a goddamn gift from the Almighty, wherever He was billeted, this close to point and shoot.

Two minutes later, the red light stopped strobing. English came half out of his seat, marked the time, and reminded the 92nd, "Remember, we take the facility and hold it, with whatever prisoners we've got, until the militia from Bonaventure relieves us—that's Plan A. Plan B's the same, but we hose it down and reform at Ten Ring—"

"*With* the prisoners," Grant added from forward.

"You heard the man," English said and didn't know he was smiling as he spoke. "The rest is through your all-com. Let's get those helmets on ASAP when we've got burn . . ."

Burn kicked in, and English let himself be pushed back onto the bench.

Controlled descent gave way to radar underflight in a matter of seconds. Every head was in its helmet now. Every hand checked its gloves and its gear bag and its APOT rifle and ELVIS pack and webbing.

Inside the Associate helmet, the world of the APC looked real different, but English could live with it. The left-side display gave him numbers and plot points for each of his men, voice actuated and voice identified: color-coded call signs that couldn't be misconstrued.

The low-light filter made it seem like dusk in an Eirish glen. English ratcheted the filter through his settings and then began on his privacy channels and dual-coms, checking his presets.

"Sawyer?" he said, without a single convention. The Associate shunted him onto dual-com.

"Yo, boss," came Sawyer's reply, and a yellow bead above

the digital number two, shining from the com status grid projected onto English's visor display, told the captain that his lieutenant had invoked privacy, as well as, because that dot was blinking, ISA encryption. "How 'bout that? This Associate really can read my mind. Cut a tenth of a second off my decision to tell you that Grant bastard's due for a whole very uncomplimentary sentence to himself in my after-action report."

"Delta Three, we're on the record all the time," English reminded his first officer formally. "That don't mean I disagree with you."

"Delta Two, sir," Sawyer came back. "Let's get these dogies movin' . . . if you're ready, sir."

All-com came up so fast that English wasn't sure he'd actually had time to toggle it; could be, like the book on this equipment had said, the Associate took its cues from his neural firings.

And then English heard a voice he didn't know, a voice he'd never heard in his life and wished to hell he'd never hear again. It was clear, uninflected, and it sounded more like a computer information system giving him an old girlfriend's new phone number on-planet than anything else he'd ever heard.

But it wasn't giving him data he'd requested; it was giving him orders. And it wasn't coming from a planetary source; it was coming from the Associate (Command Pull Down) module in his helmet. It said—on all-com to everybody under English's command—"Delta One to Redhorse. Deploy Alpha Team One-One, sixteen seconds. Fifteen. Fourteen . . ."

"Shit," said Sawyer, in the dual-com through which they could both talk at once without the primary speaker overriding the contactee. "That's *my* job—"

English swore and said, "It's not me; it's the damned Associate." Delta One was the call sign reserved for the APC, through which could come orders from off-planet, the Observer's comments, and possibly critical Intel reports from Manning. He slapped the privacy toggle to make sure it was engaged, too rattled to deal with the complexities of his new visual displays. "Let's ride this out till we get groundside, Sawyer. Every damned piece of equipment this man's Alliance makes has got an override."

"I hope to hell so," Sawyer said with a grunt as he rose to check the rappellers. The dropmaster opened the bay door.

"Nobody wants a commander he can't frag if it comes to it."

English said nothing. He was working on his own group of unwelcome reactions. He didn't want to hit the ground so spiked. He told himself that the Associate wouldn't have entered the circuit if he and Sawyer had been up and running, doing their jobs to the split second as they should have been. Then he concentrated on lowering his pulse rate and staying a full two seconds ahead of every step in the deployment of pairs and three-teams that remained to be executed before he himself jet-dropped into whatever Bull's-Eye had to offer.

Jumping with jet-pack assist and heavy gear from a low-flying APC had never been English's choice for a thrill. The gravity of Bull's-Eye was an eighth lighter than home world standard, so that was some help. It was also as dark as the inside of a Weasel's belly, so English was going to give Manning one point.

Was, until he and Sawyer landed spot-on where they were supposed to, and nothing resembling a command jeep was there or anywhere within the Associate's sensing range. Or range of the hand-held scanner, either. So he took away Manning's point.

That left the score on touchdown: Weasels, zero; Redhorse, zero; Fleet Intel, zero; and Eight Ball Command, one (since they'd done one hell of a job positioning the strike force, as far as grid coordinates went).

English and Sawyer had been in constant contact with the 92nd and every pair and three-team spread out over the five-klick grid was exactly where it was supposed to be, and seeing precisely what it was supposed to be seeing. The only bitch was that the damned Associates were keeping the men on schedule with inhuman precision, and the voices in their ears were spooking marines who just didn't spook easy.

There'd been nothing in the manual about the distracting effect of having some machine tell you when to duck and when to run, when to turn to the right and when the left, and when to sight down your weapon's barrel.

By the time Omega got into a shooting situation, everybody was so tense that English had decided to take back the point he'd given Grant on his mental scoreboard.

He and Sawyer were working their way through knee-deep mud that looked like sludgy blood in his night-enhanced vision, listening on all-com and dual-com at the same time, so they could hear everybody's heavy breathing and swearing and hear when it stopped dead because Omega had walked right into a social situation.

All this tech, and the Associate couldn't project a better holo of Omega's situation than English's old and trusted gear could have done. He flipped through the logistical and tactical grids and couldn't find what he wanted. At last, he asked generally, "Can't this damned system show me what's happening at Omega's plot point?"

And *wham!* Up came a split-screen view of what the two Omega marines were seeing through their helmets that entirely blocked out little items like the ground in front of English and where the hell he was and what was happening with the rest of his men.

Blind and surprised, he stumbled on something and went to his knees.

"Captain, you all right?" came Sawyer's voice in his ears.

Conscious that everything he said would be on the permanent record for some subcommittee somewhere to ponder, English spoke very slowly. "Delta Three, I'm fine. Except I can't see a damned thing except what Omega's seeing as they engage the enemy, and that's mostly trees and muzzle flash that screws up the video. I'm going to disengage this system and go back to as close as I can get to what my old, low-tech stuff would have given me—something a man can use and has got a right to expect in combat."

He was sitting on his ass in the mud now, breathing heavily and shaking with suppressed emotion. He could hear his heart beating, and it was louder to him than the sounds being shunted to his helmet from the twenty other locations his command system was monitoring.

When his trembling fingers had found the right toggle and banished the holo display from his faceplate so that he could see what was in front of him, Sawyer said, "Hey sir, did you hear what Omega said about that firefight?"

"No, I was too busy with my goddamned toys," English growled.

"They said they couldn't pinpoint the enemy. It was like the shooters were invisible or robots or something. Plenty of bang, plenty of muzzle flash, but no Khalians."

"What the fuck?" English came to his feet, sliding in the mud. "Invisible?"

Through a clear faceplate overtraced with grid lines, English saw Sawyer shrug fatalistically, a huge and ominous shadow against the electronically paled night, which seemed to be burning in the distance. "Don't know, sir. What say we go get into some trouble and find out?"

"Soon as we can call this quadrant swept for the record, Sawyer." Elaborately, English circled in place, tapping scans on his overqualified snooper gear. When he'd done his 360, he enunciated clearly, "Well, would you look at that, Sergeant—I mean Lieutenant, Sawyer? The Associate program pronounces this section of the grid clear of Khalians. Proceed, mister, to Square Thirty-eight, by the fastest route."

English, APOT rifle at chest height in front of him, began to trot in that direction—the direction of the flashes he could see in the sky, the direction in which Omega had engaged an invisible enemy.

Sawyer, beside him, was overriding the push chatter with a prioritized "man, I don't like this one shit bit. How come we don't call the APC for a recon?"

"Cause they're hearin' us, big fella," English answered with a savage satisfaction that devalued everything but what must be going on in the APC. "They know what's goin' on better than we do. You want me to ask for overflight? If we need it, how come my Delta One Associate ain't asked for it already?"

A purple bead flashed on the com status block in the upper-left-hand corner of English's faceplate: Sawyer, he realized, knew this equipment better than he did. *Purple Priority better be a recording defeat,* he thought when he heard Sawyer's next transmission.

"Toby, Grant's a pig-bastard; he'll let every mother's son of us go down here to make his point about this system he's testing. And we don't know what result he's lookin' for—good, bad, or indifferent."

"I can't make that colored light you've got work on my set," English said, a warning and a guarded reply.

"Here." Sawyer reached over and tapped it on. His gloved hand stayed on English's chest. "Manning slipped me a plasma gun, reg issue. Ain't that strange?"

Chancing that the lit purple diode was all Sawyer assumed it to be, English said, "She wants you to shoot him for her?"

"Nah, she wants me to come back alive. You know, she don't say nothin'; she's a good soldier."

"I'm not trackin' this, Sawyer."

"Yeah, well, I'm not sayin' it's right. He's bustin' her butt, more than command ought to push stuff."

"Easy, Sawyer. Anything can happen out here. And he's busted my butt, up where Jay Padova could see, so I sympathize. But they're like that, so's she, and don't forget it. They ask more than any manjack can deliver, like it's their due or something."

"She wouldn't 'a given me this plasma gun if somethin' weren't real wrong."

"Hey, man, this a fucking war zone. *Everything's* real wrong, or we wouldn't be here. Now, you want me to call them into the field, is that it?"

"Manning? Hell no. I just think that, since it's the Observer's project, he ought to be out here risking his tail with the rest of us, observing."

"I'll see what I can do. But I gotta tell you, I hope to hell you know what you're doing with this purple bead."

"There's no spook-generated system in this man's arsenal that doesn't have a safety net."

"Disable it for now—we can't hear the chatter unless it's off. Just show me how you did it, and let's get back to the war."

English then called in on Delta One's freq that "given the reports of invisible enemies, we think we've got technical difficulties. Request Ten Ring Observer on the spot."

Manning's voice answered, so distinctive she didn't need the call sign she used. "He's on the way, Delta Two. You find those wheels?"

"Nosiree, ma'am. But they'd probably have stuck in the mud anyhow, and then we'd be worse off. Delta Two, out."

They were headed toward a stand of trees which looked strangely thick where they bunched when unfriendly fire belched out from among them, gouts of red and green and yellow-white that taxed his faceshield's imaging ability.

English was down in the mud before Sawyer's yell to hit the deck, or his Associate's calm "take cover, take cover; return fire, return fire" penetrated past his reflexes to his conscious mind.

The Associate, intent on preserving itself or him, had wiped all discretionary scans. He couldn't see the 92nd's field-of-fire grid, only his own.

"Damn, I hate this thing. That's for the frigging record, if anybody cares," he told his recorder. "Thing thinks I ain't got enough sense to return fucking *fire?*"

Sawyer was already blasting away at the woods, firing at ground level.

And that was the first moment that Toby English thought about what the fire characteristics of the APOT system would be when you and the suit it depended on were lying in a mud puddle.

He had his own rifle butted against his shoulder before it occurred to him that the conducting characteristics of water might not be the best thing for a human inside a suit whose partial function is to act as a conductive circle. Then he told himself, *They would have thought that out.*

He said, "Hey, Sawyer? Sawyer? Ain't that enough, man?" while beside him Sawyer lay on his trigger like there was no end to the amount of firepower the APOT could dispense, blasting away at one spot where there'd been trees but now was just a white-gray-brown haze with a hot center you couldn't describe in any report because it . . . fluxed. It seemed to phase. It was so bright that his faceplate was blacked everywhere else but where it was, trying to deal with it.

English knew he should do something: shoot his own rifle, maybe. Maybe Sawyer was just not going to answer until he'd got his target. You don't talk and aim, that's for sure. But English really didn't want to shoot his rifle, especially because his Associate wasn't saying "return fire" any longer. As a matter of fact, it wasn't giving him any kind of target in those trees.

Thinking back, and then scrolling back with his hand-held, English realized that it never had—given him a target, that is.

It had told him to return fire, but it hadn't targeted any Khalians in those trees.

"Sawyer, man, stop goddamn shooting," he said in his com. Then he decided that maybe the mud and water they were lying in was somehow screwing up helmet-to-helmet transmissions, and he wriggled over, still aiming his APOT at the trees, to put his helmet into contact with Sawyer's.

When he did, it was as though the world dissolved under him. Everything went funny: his whole body felt like a low-level electric shock was bathing it. He couldn't see anything. Then he could see lots of things but nothing you could talk about in tactical, or even human, terms. He could see swimming things like giant sperm with toothy mouths, things like electric eels, and all sorts of squiggly foamy stuff. And he could see things moving in the background that maybe could have been people or, more exactly, could have been heat signatures or infrared images of people.

Then he used every bit of willpower he had, broke contact, and repeated his original motion, this time slamming his helmet against Sawyer's.

Sawyer's head went sideways. His shoulder came out of contact with the APOT; his finger eased off the trigger. Still holding the rifle, he turned slowly and lay on his back, one leg bent at the knee, in the mud. The APOT pointing skyward, he let off two more bursts of fire.

It seemed like a twitch, not anything premeditated.

Given the circumstances, English got the hell out of the mud puddle. Pointing his own APOT down at his lieutenant with one hand, the stock butted against his hip, he reached for his service pistol. All he had to do was thumb the safety off and pull the trigger, and Sawyer would be a memory. Nothing to do with field effects or conductivity, just a nice clean slug in the face or up under the chin, depending on luck and which shot was most likely to go through the armor and kill his friend cleanly.

But first, you had to be damned sure you were looking at that kind of problem.

Both weapons at ready, English went down on one knee and said, "Sawyer, talk to me, man. Associate, give me some kind of feed to Delta Three, now!"

He held his breath. The dual-com bead lit in his peripheral vision. He could hear the other man breathing. The breathing was ragged, but calm. *Please God, don't make me have to shoot him.*

Not with some enemy out there, maybe even now drawing a bead on Toby English, a damn-fool officer making a perfect target of himself, the only thing standing in a whole field of Bull's-Eye's blood-red mud.

"Hey, Toby, what . . . ? What the hell?"

Sawyer came up out of the mud onto his elbows real fast, so fast that the APOT rifle Toby was holding seemed to slam itself against the other man's faceplate.

Both men spoke at once.

Sawyer's voice said, very softly and calmly, "You want me to lie back down? Drop my weapon? Tell you what I think just happened?"

English nearly shouted, "Hold it, man! Just fucking freeze, okay? Drop the APOT and—"

Sawyer's rifle splashed into the mud.

English sat back enough to use his own APOT, his revolver still trained on Sawyer, to push the other rifle out of Sawyer's reach. "Now talk to me, buddy."

"I started shooting at those trees, you remember that," Sawyer said. "Then time just sort of stopped. I couldn't get disengaged. It was kind of like an electric shock, but it was more like being stuck. I was stuck shooting at those trees, and my AI—that damned Associate—couldn't give me a target. It wanted me to return fire, but it couldn't give me anything to shoot at, so I was going at them by their muzzle blasts. . . . Then you hit me, and I could make my trigger finger lay off. That's it."

"Sounds pretty good to me." English thumbed the safety back on his kinetic pistol and said, "Probably the mud. Shorted something in the system, what with you lyin' belly down for all your length. Sorry about hittin' you." His own neck hurt, now that he thought about it, from the force of their helmets' concussion. "But I had to do something."

"I'm real grateful you didn't shoot me. Little headache's nothin' to sweat. Think I'll get up right now, real easy . . ."

Sawyer had to pick up his APOT next; English had to shoot him or let him. He let him.

They got the hell out of the mud and headed downslope to where Sawyer's fire had dried everything for half a klick, crouching halfway to the fallen trees that seemed to have exploded.

"Well, it's a test system," English offered lamely.

"Yeah, I guess. You with me, Captain? We got men out there. We got targets we maybe didn't smoke. We got lots of ground to cover . . ."

"Yeah, it's okay, Sawyer. Just don't shoot that APOT when

you're lyin' in the mud, and I promise I won't either."

Sawyer, motioning to him, pointed to the hard case he'd shouldered at jump time, the one Manning had given him. "Remember we've got an alternative if you want to issue an order to use it, sir."

Damn, Sawyer was twitched and so was he, over what had almost happened.

"Let's get back into the 92nd's circuit and see if there's any tails up there that we can cut for our coats," English said more heartily than he felt.

English's head was still aching, and Sawyer was reeling slightly as he climbed the hill. The instinct to keep the other man a little ahead of him was too strong for English to offset it, so he lagged behind rather than give Sawyer a shot at his unprotected back, even though the recon specialist was the last man you'd ever distrust . . .

What the fuck had that been, *back there?* English told himself to forget it, to wait until he viewed the mission transcript. If Grant would let him.

That reminded him, and he called in for a check. Then he got real busy, seeing as how he found that Manning had a half-dozen queued reports of no-contact with hostile fire to shunt to him, and that Grant was on-site at a concrete building they'd designated 23A, waiting for him and generally directing the mission because English had been "out of contact, presumed MIA."

He wasn't going to argue about it. He wasn't going to ask how the Observer had gotten himself into the middle of the Khalian facility while Delta Command was still hiking in from the periphery.

But as he listened to stale, unit-status reports shunted from the APC, he remembered the whispers that Padova might make landfall on this one, which didn't necessarily mean that there was air support at Grant's disposal and not the 92nd's, but probably did.

And, more immediately, there wasn't a dead Khalian among what was left of those trees. Sawyer pulled out his scanner when he saw the nature of the debris and the size of the explosion, saying, "Damn, that looks hot."

But it wasn't hot. Not at all. It was cold as death. And that was all a field scanner was going to tell you, even though, if you looked up into the paling night, you could see what looked an awful lot like a mushroom cloud just beginning to disperse.

"I'm liking this mission less and less," Sawyer said, then stepped gingerly into the twigs and toothpicks and kindling that crumbled at your touch—all that was left of the stand of trees he'd hosed down with the APOT.

Well, not quite all, it turned out. "Look at this!" Sawyer's voice was real flat. His helmeted head turned toward English as English came to take what his lieutenant was holding, and he could see his own reflection distorted in Sawyer's polarized face shield.

His image was as anonymous as what he picked gingerly from Sawyer's hand: a frozen, blue, human finger with a gold wedding band gleaming at its root. Below the band, there was nothing. The finger was hard as stone. But it wasn't stone: when English prodded the bone centering it, the bone itself crumbled away.

"Damn, this is from a human shooter. That's why we couldn't get targeting fixes. The Associate was looking for Khalians, not humans."

"Why didn't it give us the humans as friendlies?"

"We didn't ask it for humans; they weren't ours—at least I hope to hell they weren't our logged soldiers or the Bonaventure militia's. Nah. It couldn't have been friendly fire, man. It couldn't."

"Get a head count," said English, already beginning to trot toward his rendezvous with the Observer, already in the center of the complex. "And current status reports. We need to make some command decisions. While we're moving."

His voice was totally controlled, he thought, but Sawyer said, "Take it easy, sir. We don't know what kind of problem we've got, yet."

"Maybe you don't," English told him, trying to pace himself. He had to run nearly two klicks through hostile territory before he could confront the real enemy.

Sometimes you really wish you were wrong about people. Skidding into the damnedest firefight in Marine Corps history, English kept wishing he'd been wrong about the civilian observer, Grant.

Then he could have been wrong about the APOT-Associate

system he was lugging into battle like a technological albatross hanging on him. But he'd known in the back of his mind, ever since Grant had started that "don't let this equipment fall into enemy hands" shit, way back when they were spaceborne, that the program was experimental, X-class in the jargon, which meant that the marines testing it were liable to become ex-marines.

He couldn't even get his damned command back, not really. On the way into the Khalian complex, he'd had one nasty exchange, via his com circuits, with the Observer, who told him tersely that "your Delta-One Associate's running this mission, buddy, not me. Like it's supposed to, when human frailty becomes a command liability."

The purple bead that wasn't supposed to be there was blinking in English's face when Grant said that, way off the record. Now the troop deployment weirdness made sense: command group of two, not the regulation three, way out in the boonies, as far as possible from the action. There was no way that Grant hadn't set English up to take a fall so the Delta-One Associate could strut its stuff. The negative points English was going to pick up on this one were real enough—he shouldn't have let this happen.

But ahead of him were problems more real than reprimands and demotions. You had to stay alive for those. You had to get your men off-planet alive, more to the point, to worry about how it was going to look later.

Right now, it wasn't looking like anything English had ever seen, and he and Sawyer were running all-com and dual-com and yelling themselves hoarse, without the vaguest notion whether anybody could hear them, were listening if they could, or if it even mattered.

The big concrete-and-steel shipyard was coruscating with light, like it was on fire, which it couldn't be. Buildings kept shivering, shimmering. Once in a while a whole wall would fall, coming down like melting icebergs.

In between the buildings, his marines were firing at will upon the enemy.

And there wasn't a Khalian to be seen. Nobody was sure when it became clear that the opposition in the Khalian facility was uniformed-human opposition.

It just was. Consequently, there was more confusion in Toby

English's ears than he'd dreamed in his wildest nightmares could occur in combat.

"Can't see the fuckers. Jesus God, what's the matter with this shit gear?" somebody screamed in his ears on all-com.

"Shoot the weapons, fool," came Corporal Bucknell's recognizable voice through the audio melee while, beyond English's helmet, the sky seemed to come apart, men phased in and out of his helmet display as if they were using revolving doors, and reality itself came apart.

He knew it was the A-field effects, in close proximity.

But he shot his own APOT anyhow, wherever he found unfriendly fire, and each time he did, the whole world shifted under him. At one point, he and Sawyer found themselves holding hands like a couple of schoolgirls, stepping over half a human body which kept shifting: first the trunk would be there, then the legs. Only the blood in the mud was consistent.

Sawyer was locked on privacy com with Grant, trying to find out how the hell you got the Associate syscom to recognize human adversaries and blip them on-screen for you, while English yelled himself hoarse arguing with Delta One and talking to his men by name.

You had to stabilize them some way. They were well trained; they were good soldiers. They were working with the data they had, and it was the data that was fucked up. Shit, it was the damned space-time that was fucked up.

English had never cared about physics, except for the sort necessary for dealing with foot pounds per second and quantifying your bang per buck. He didn't now. But whenever he shot that APOT, he saw weird stuff: he saw trees instead of concrete, he saw big bugs, he saw what looked like munching dinosaurs. He saw everything but the fire zone he was scrambling through, on his knees, toward the low concrete administration building where Grant was holding forth from the roof.

Finally, Sawyer rejoined his circuit and overrode the yelling and cursing and pleas for orders with his dual-com: "Okay, sir, we've got the glitch fixed. We'll get human target blips. But we gotta be careful; no way to tell when the Bonaventure militia's going to show up. Associate's got equipment-related targeting data, but—"

A blast of conventional firepower pulverized the corner of a building to English's right. They were pushed back and down by the concussive blast and showered with bits of hydrastone.

When his faceplate cleared, English was already talking to the 92nd. "You've got targeting, Redhorse. Repeat, equipment recalibration complete. Fire at will. Remember, you've got stun settings. These are human, repeat, human shooters. Take prisoners if you can but not at excessive risk. Watch for Bonaventure militiamen. Repeat, possibility of friendly fire."

Bucknell's voice came right back. "Beta Two here. What about the rifles? I keep seein' shit that's not there when I fire. Any—" Bucknell's transmission ended abruptly.

A flash blossomed from the general direction that English's display grid placed Beta.

Sawyer was yelling into his dual com. "Nellie? Hey, Nellie! Come back, damn you."

English reached out to touch his lieutenant. When Sawyer turned his helmeted head, English went to purple com. "Look at your grid, Sawyer." Beta wasn't reading on the grid at all, not any of them. "Let's go join Grant at the command station. Better view than from here." Nice and ambiguous, in case the purple band was monitored, after all.

Sawyer's head was still turned English's way. He motioned to the shouldered hard case that Sawyer was carrying. The lieutenant nodded and got the weapon out.

English thumbed his APOT onto stun and stepped out into the rubble-strewn street, oblivious to the crap showering him and the phase effects screwing up his electronics every time someone from the 92nd discharged an APOT rifle.

He was going to get one prisoner, like he was supposed to. Then he was going to go shoot Grant, and damn the recording capabilities of his suit. They were probably perfect, like its armor's protective capabilities were better than anything he'd ever encountered. Had to give Eight Ball Command one point for getting something right.

Too bad armor hadn't been enough to keep Beta on his display grid. Too bad Fleet Intel had gotten its signals screwed up one more time and put them down to fight Khalians on a purported indig world where the enemies weren't Weasels at all, but human collaborators of some kind. Too bad the Associate system was pisspoor at detecting targets when those targets weren't what it had been preset for. Too bad everything went wrong with this mission all the way down the line. He'd told the civilian observer at the outset that it was bad luck to change gear just before a drop.

He got a fix on a muzzle flash in some rubble and dropped to one knee before Delta One could tell him to hit the deck. He was squeezing his APOT's trigger at the gun emplacement before the damned thing put up its targeting blip, because it had to compare the shooter with its template for nonfriendly and nonmarine humans and make a determination.

English didn't. He had to shoot whatever was shooting at him. This he did, on his stun setting, teeth gritted. The damned world shook under him; the sky beyond his visor turned noontime blue, and birds winged across a marsh where buildings ought to have been; there was no gun emplacement, no shooter, just a pretty scene that wasn't there.

English held his finger on the trigger and sprayed what looked like cattails, because he knew that was where the shooter had been.

When he finally stopped firing, the world switched back to the one his mind knew he inhabited. He slapped at his suit's climate control because otherwise the sweat rolling down into his eyes was going to blind him.

In front of him, the gun emplacement was a particulated heap, as if it had melted or frozen. A little mushroomy wisp of greasy smoke was rising from it. "Crap, I know I set it for stun," he muttered.

"Maybe you did," came Sawyer's voice. "I was on the same target. Sorry."

"It's them that're sorry." There wasn't enough mass left there to bother checking for a survivor.

"If you don't mind me saying so, sir," said Sawyer, slipping the APOT rifle onto his shoulder after unslinging his plasma gun, "we ought not to both be shooting these APOTs in such close proximity."

"For the record? Yeah, I just figured that out. Unless the stun setting flat doesn't work, like the rest of this junk. The hell with this. Somebody'll get prisoners." He pointed to the roof where Grant was hunkered down. "Let's go take care of our other problem."

Sawyer ran with him. They dodged what they could of the conventional fire. They jumped some frozen bodies, some half-melted ones, and they jumped what looked like the remains of Beta. If remains was what you could call a couple of bits of twisted armor and a half a scanner.

As they approached the intersection beyond which the administration building's blown doors loomed, English realized that there was less chatter in his ears.

There was also, he noted as he flipped his helmet to visual only for a what-you-see scan, less munitions flash—almost none. And the sky was looking like it should, for the most part: dirty, predawn, smoky light.

At his signal, Sawyer called for another head count and status report.

As English scuttled with his lieutenant across the empty street to the administration building, nobody shot at them. Almost absently, he calculated the results of the head count. Alpha had seven uniformed human hostiles who'd surrendered. Beta was absent and unaccounted for. Gamma had met up with Bonaventure and was executing a building-to-building sweep. Epsilon had secured one shipwright's bay and was certain the ships there were brand new, not in for refit.

"Don't sweep that area yourselves," English told them. "Wait for reinforcements." He and Sawyer went through the rest of the roster and detailed two other three-teams to assist Epsilon in sweeping the ship bay and the ships themselves.

The remaining units were ambulatory, having sustained only minor injuries so far, but bitchy as hell and saying their stun settings were killing the enemy.

The news didn't surprise English, coming as he and Sawyer darted to the blown doors and began making their way up the administration building's exterior stairs. "You got prisoners, Redhorse, bring them in to Admin, 23A; the rest of you have your cleanup orders." Groans and complaints came over the all-com.

But what happened next did surprise English, and Sawyer as well.

A shadow fell over them. A big, ominous shadow of pitch black in the lightening sky above. Both men crouched on the catwalk stairway. They were clear targets for air support. They'd been so close to winning this thing, English was plain shocked. Somebody had let a Khalian ship get up and running. But that couldn't be. They would have seen it, wouldn't they? Was the Associate system so stupid that it would blind and deafen them to anything as deadly as a whole spacecraft lifting off?

There'd been all those weird effects, though—moments when English was seeing and hearing and acquiring data that had nothing to do with who was shooting at him and from where . . .

"Holy mother, it's the *Haig!*" Sawyer said in disbelief.

English sank down on a stair and flipped up his faceplate. He didn't trust the visor display not to shuck him. It sure looked like the *Haig*'s belly. He squinted for ID numbers and got them. Something in him seemed to unravel. He couldn't do what he wanted to do on the roof, not with the *Haig* overhead, acquiring minutely accurate photo-returns of everything below.

English rubbed his face with a gloved hand; it felt numb. He slapped down his visor and said to Sawyer, "Well, that's that."

Sawyer knew exactly what he meant. "Another time, another place."

"I guess," said English doubtfully, feeling the adrenaline he wasn't going to be able to use start messing with his motor control. A shiver racked him; his head hurt worse. He said, "We'll go up anyway, and see whether that bastard thinks we've secured his goddam area for him."

"Yeah, well . . . We won this one, anyhow."

"That's what you call what happened here?"

Sawyer didn't answer. English got his legs under him, which wasn't all that easy in his private adrenaline aftermath, and they climbed wordlessly, listening to all-com confirm that resistance was nil, to someone whoop occasionally when he took a prisoner and could come directly in, skipping the nasty and often dangerous cleanup phase.

On the roof, under the shadow of the destroyer as if she were his personal umbrella, sat Grant, cross-legged in a semicircle of electronic black boxes.

Grant was wearing one of the new hard suits; he wasn't wearing a helmet. An Associate-type helmet lay discarded by his side.

He stood up when English and Sawyer approached. "Nice job, Captain. Lieutenant," he said.

English thought, I could still shoot him. His gloved hand shifted from his APOT rifle to the kinetic pistol on his hip. "You know, I don't know what you mean. This stuff don't work worth squat. The stun settings are a joke, and if you were down there in the thick of it, you'd know that strange stuff happens when two or more men discharge these APOTs in close—''

"Later. I'll take your report later, Captain. Now your job is to make sure that every piece of this equipment is accounted for. And I want to see every prisoner, personally. Put them together and then call me.'' His gaze flickered above his head, and then back to English. "Too bad about your lost men, but that's what this job is all about.''

"Tell that to Nellie's widow and kids, when she finds out we're testin' X-class equipment without proper briefing.''

"Now, how would she—or any civilian—find out something like that?'' the civilian observer wanted to know.

English's hand cramped on his pistol butt. And froze there. It wasn't worth it. If he shot Grant, Sawyer would have to shoot him, or be a part of something that wasn't his doing.

"Aw, you know word just leaks out, sir,'' said Sawyer through his faceplate's speaker grille, and it sounded so raw and so threatening that English's head swung to look at his lieutenant.

Sawyer had that plasma rifle in his hands. It was trained on Grant, unwavering.

English mentally kicked himself. Nellie had been one of Sawyer's recon pets. English should have realized that, as bad as he felt, Sawyer would feel worse.

He never made a conscious decision to intervene; he hardly heard his asshole Associate program telling him that "target is misaquired! Do not fire. Repeat: target is friendly. Do not fire!'' in the dual-com. He simply stepped in and slapped the plasma rifle's muzzle upward.

Then he grabbed the gun and twisted it from Sawyer's unresisting grip as he said, on purple-com, "Come on, man. This pig-bastard isn't worth any more of our lives.''

In his helmet's silence, English could hear Sawyer's labored breathing. Then the recon specialist said, "Maybe not today.''

Grant's voice was coming in on English's audio band, telling him that there wouldn't be any problem about this. He, Grant, knew how wired men could get in this kind of action.

"Just take those helmets off, boys, so we can all relax and talk about this until your men are formed up.''

There were orders, and there were orders. English and Sawyer turned to go back down the stairs as if they'd planned it.

Grant's hand came down on English's shoulder and spun him around—fast, hard, and professionally. The plasma rifle was out of his grip and in Grant's hands before English knew what was happening.

And Grant said, holding the rifle, "You're dismissed, gentlemen. I want prisoner review in fifteen minutes, right where you're standing."

There was no way around following your orders in this man's corps.

When the 92nd Marine Reaction Unit had brought all its prisoners together, there were nineteen all told. They marched them up to the administration building's roof, and Grant stood there looking at the bunch of sorry humans in unfamiliar uniforms who Sawyer and some of his recon boys had already started interrogating.

Sawyer was on Grant's far side, detailing what little he'd learned. These were humans who had been staffing this shipyard, and in general this world, for the Khalians for nobody would say how long. The prisoners didn't act like conscripts. To them, the Alliance was the enemy, which made them less than cooperative, and was one of the reasons that the 92nd had been able to take so few alive: these men were suicide commando types.

"They admit to shooting their own people, women and children first," Sawyer told Grant, "rather than let us take them."

Grant nodded and took a step forward. He still had Sawyer's plasma rifle slung over his shoulder, and then it was in his hands in a shooting grip.

Everybody was bareheaded, and English saw comprehension dawn in Sawyer's eyes just as he himself realized what Grant was going to do.

There was just enough room to do it, too, without endangering any of the 92nd who were guarding the prisoners.

The four plasma charges that Grant fired, squinting, into the prisoners were so bright that the prisoners seemed to be enveloped in green-white light as they died.

The marines all turned their heads away, anyhow. So did the man doing the shooting. You didn't watch a plasma burn without a polarizing visor between you and it, not if you wanted to use your eyes for much of anything for a while after.

When Grant lowered it, the weapon was sputtering and empty. The slag it had left where the human prisoners had been wasn't pretty, but neither was the thought of humans collaborating with Weasels against their own kind.

Blinking, Grant tossed the rifle toward Sawyer, who caught it reflectively before it hit him in the chest, one gloved hand on the hot barrel and one on the stock.

"Thanks, Sawyer," said Grant. Sawyer didn't answer. The Redhorse guards were staring. The civilian observer turned to English and said, "Don't forget: all this equipment has to be turned in once you're back on the destroyer. All of it, accounted for. Anything you lost in combat better be well documented. And keep in mind what you saw here today. We really don't want any wild rumors spreading of what this system can and can't do."

"Yes, sir," said English through clenched teeth.

"Dismissed, mister," replied Grant, and from above their heads, the sound of a lander coming to pick the Observer off the roof began to grow loud in the predawn air.

Given the circumstances, English decided to take away the point he'd given Eight Ball Command for the quality of the new hard suits. That made the Bull's-Eye vertical insertion a zero-sum game, since English never gave Redhorse points for winning when winning got his marines dead.

INTERLUDE

Children from three races hurry out of a MicBurald. Each is happily eating a different form of soy. Overhead the sign reads, 50 TRILLION SOLD WHEN WE LOST COUNT.

"Ready to eat in just eleven nanoseconds," a voice promises.

Fade and bring it up as:

The silvery form of Hawk Talon's brain ship and trusted companion swoops toward the distant peaks. The jagged terrain spins dizzily as the viewer is given a ship's-eye view of the approaching mountain. As they get closer, explosions and flashes can be seen.

Cannons roaring, *Derv* guides their ship in over the mountainside, knocking a Khalian slave ship from the air. Below, a dark mob is closing in on the last Khalian fortress on the planet.

Inside the ship, the Fleet captain watches the battle as he dons his combat suit.

"Who do I shoot?" The brain ship sounds worried. Below, thousands of former slaves and Khalians are fighting. Dozens of races are represented. It is hard to tell friend from foe.

Striking a noble pose, Talon surveys the chaos.

"The bad guys," he replies while slapping a clip into his plasma rifle.

"Which ones are the bad guys?" the *Derv* asks her valiant captain.

"Only the Weasels," Talon explains, preparing to dive out of the airlock and join the battle. "No real sentient will fight for the Khalia."

TEAM EFFORT
by David Drake

MOST OF THE Headhunters were experienced enough to know that the *Bonnie Parker*'d been hit—that bone-jarring *clang!* wasn't just reentry turbulence.

"Instead of coming in on the deck—" Kowacs said, continuing with his briefing. Barely identifiable holographic images wavered in front of his helmet and the helmets of his troops, poised at the cargo bay doors, "—the Jeffersonian militia we're supposed to bail out managed to drop straight down into the middle of their objective, a Weasel air-defense installation."

The *Bonnie Parker* was still under control. Not that there was a damn thing the 121st Marine Reaction Company in her belly could do if she weren't. The Headhunters crouched in two back-to-back lines, ready to do their jobs as soon as their ship touched down and her long doors opened.

As it was, there wasn't half enough time for Kowacs to tell his troops exactly what their job *was*.

There wasn't half enough information, either.

The landing vessel bucked. The hull screamed with piercing supersonics like those of a gigantic hydraulic motor, then banged again into the relative silence of reentry.

Not another hit: a piece tearing loose as a result of the first one.

Not a good sign, either.

Corporal Sienkiewicz, Kowacs's company clerk—and bodyguard—was nearly two meters tall and solid enough to sling a shoulder-fired plasma weapon in addition to her regular kit. She grinned in a close approximation of humor to Bradley, the field first sergeant, and murmured, "Bet you three to one in six-packs, Top: we don't ride all the way to this one."

"They figured they could keep the Weasels' heads down with suppression clusters until they landed," Kowacs said as he watched the gray, fuzzy holograms his helmet projected for him. Instead of a Fleet hull, the Jeffersonians had used their own vessel—and crew; *that* was bloody obvious, but their cameras and real-time links were to Alliance standard. "And then the missile launchers couldn't depress low enough to hit their ship."

The air-defense installation was a concrete pentagram of tunnels and barracks, with launchers at each point. The crisp outline danced in the holograms with the electric dazzle of antipersonnel bomblets going off. A red flash and mushroom of smoke marked the Khalians' attempted response: as soon as the missile left its hardened launcher, shrapnel exploded it.

In synchrony with the detonating image, the *Bonnie Parker*'s hull banged.

This time it *was* another hit.

"Cockpit to cargo," rasped the PA system, distorting the voice of Jarvi, the command pilot. "Three minutes to touch-down."

The Jeffersonians—those dick-headed *anarchists*—must have been carrying five times the normal load of suppression clusters; that and luck were what had saved their asses during the drop.

The extra weight was also why the image of the ground beneath their landing vessel was expanding at such a rate.

"They made it that far," Kowacs continued, his voice cool, his guts cold and as tight as his hand on the stock of his assault rifle. "They landed with the bay doors open, and about half their assault company jumped before the boat was stabilized."

Blurred images degraded a stage further as the editor—an artificial intelligence aboard one of the orbiting support vessels—switched to the feed from the helmet of one of the ground troops. Shouting soldiers, very heavily equipped and logy with the weight of their hardware, lurched to the ground and sprayed streams of tracer into Weasels popping from hatches in the surrounding concrete walls.

The installation had been hardened against air attack. It wasn't intended for defense against infantry landing in its interior.

A shadow fell across the tumbling holograms. The viewpoint changed as the Jeffersonian looked over his shoulder and saw his landing craft balloon away from him with half the troops still hesitating at its doors.

The men who'd jumped weighed at least five tonnes. That sudden release had caused the pilot—already fighting excessive descent speed—to let his craft get away from him.

The ship bounced up ten meters on thrust. Before the pilot could get it back on the ground, one of the launchers had belched a line of smoke. The missile was still accelerating when it hit the landing craft, but its warhead didn't need the boost of kinetic energy to do its job.

Tendrils of burning metal trailed from the edges of the hologram where glare hadn't blanked the camera. Then the entire picture went dead.

"There's a magazine in the middle of the installation . . . ," Kowacs said, continuing with the briefing notes assembled from panicked, scrappy messages received in orbit after the landing craft and its booster link were lost.

The light banks in the *Bonnie Parker*'s bay went out. The yellow emergency system came on, and the forward doors, port and starboard, started to clam-shell upward. They opened about half a meter, enough to let a frigid, high-altitude wind scream and blast the marines. Then they jammed.

Somebody started to pray in Kowacs's earphones. Because the system was locked for the briefing, the voice had to be one of the platoon leaders he'd known for *years*, but he didn't recognize it.

". . . in which many of the friendlies have holed up awaiting rescue," Kowacs continued as if his palms weren't wet and icy, as if part of his mind didn't wish a flash like the one that ate the Jeffersonian craft would *end* this.

Sergeant Bradley slipped between the lines of marines and patted one on the shoulder. The high-pitched prayers stopped in midsyllable. It didn't matter who it'd been, didn't matter at all.

For a moment, Kowacs had thought it might be his own voice.

"We'll land—" he began, speaking louder instinctively, though he knew the system would compensate for the wind rush by raising the gain in the Headhunters' earphones.

The *Bonnie Parker*'s emergency lighting flicked out, then back. The starboard rear door, the one which the Weapons Platoon faced, cycled upward without stopping.

"Cockpit to cargo," said the PA system in O'Hara's voice. If O'Hara was speaking, it meant the command pilot had her hands full.

Or was dead.

"Rig to jump in sixty seconds. I say again, rig to jump."

"Headhunter command to cockpit," Kowacs said, tripping his helmet's liaison channel. The four platoon leaders had stepped out of line without needing the orders there was no time to give, checking their units' newer members who might never have made a wire-discharge jump in combat. "Will we be in guidance range of the target?"

There was a clatter as Weapons Platoon jettisoned its belt-fed plasma weapons and their ammo drums out the hatchway. The guns were too heavy to be supported by the emergency wire-discharge packs that were all the Headhunters had available now.

"That's a rog, Headhunter," O'Hara bellowed, his words broken either by static or by the sound of an electrical fire in the cockpit. "Some of you, at least. But you'll need to find your own way home."

First and 3rd Platoons were reporting ready in the holographic heads-up display in front of Kowacs's eyes. The green dot for weapons appeared as he switched back to the unit push and said, "We've got one door so we'll jump by sticks, Delta first, then Gamma—"

Second Platoon winked READY, but Kowacs continued with what he'd intended to say—"then Alpha, last Beta. Your helmets have the coordinates downloaded. They'll guide to the intended landing zone—"

"Jump!" screamed the PA system. "Jump, damn you!"

"Go!" said Kowacs.

Weapons Platoon cleared the doorway, one marine holding back a microsecond until Bradley shoved him from behind. Third Platoon was already pushing into position from the opposite side of the bay, hunched forms fumbling with the reels of wire attached to their equipment harness.

Nobody'd expected to jump until seconds ago. They'd been

ready to throw their jump gear away as soon as the *Bonnie Parker* touched down. Now they realized that if the reel unhooked, they'd freefall while the thirty-meter wire floated in the air until its power-pack could no longer polarize the charges at its opposite ends.

"Gamma, *go!*" snapped Lieutenant Mandricard, and 3rd Platoon was in the air before Kowacs had thought they were ready. A couple of the men were a step behind the others. They dived for the opening, so graceless and massive in their loads of combat equipment that they looked like pianos tipping over a balcony.

He only hoped they'd get their tumbling under control before the dischargers deployed. If two wires fouled, their charges shorted and—

"Alpha"—ordered Lieutenant Seeley over the command net. She was muscling to the hatch one of her marines who'd stumbled when the *Bonnie Parker* bucked; as the ship did again, making the whole platoon wobble like tenpins but without falling until Seeley completed—"*Go!*"

The jump door was empty. The bay of the *Bonnie Parker* lighted with crackling brilliance as one of 2nd Platoon's newbies hit his manual deployment switch while checking his jump reel one last time.

The wire lashed about like a demented cobra, shorting its juice every time a coil touched metal. Within two seconds, the sparks vanished into a net of purple afterimages. The marine stood stricken—and his wire lay limp and useless.

"I'll get him, Placido," Kowacs said, stepping to the newbie before the 2nd Platoon lieutenant could. Kowacs let the sling hold his assault rifle. His right hand slipped his own jump reel from his belt, fingers working the catches with the ease of smooth practice, while his left stripped the newbie's dead unit.

"*Go!* Beta," Kowacs ordered. Placido hesitated between the door and the newbie. Not all of his platoon was in position; those who were, jumped, and the remainder followed raggedly, each Headhunter lunging out as soon as there was open space before him.

The newbie would have jumped too, jerking himself away from Kowacs before the fresh reel was in place. Instinctively the kid preferred to die rather than be left behind by his unit.

No problem. Corporal Sienkiewicz gripped the newbie's equipment harness, and nobody she held was going anywhere. Kowacs finished hooking the reel, slapped the kid on the shoulder, and shouted, "Go!" as he turned to take the spare unit Bradley had snatched from the equipment locker five meters away.

Sienkiewicz flung the kid across the *Bonnie Parker*'s bucking deck, putting her shoulders into the motion. He was bawling as he sailed through the hatch with Lieutenant Placido beside him.

"Here, sir!" Sergeant Bradley shouted, lobbing the replacement discharge reel toward Kowacs because the *Bonnie Parker* had begun to vibrate like the blade of a jackhammer. Kowacs raised his hands, but the gentle arc of the reel that would save his life changed into a corkscrew as the landing vessel tried to stand on her tail.

One of the bay doors torqued off into the airstream. Kowacs couldn't tell where the discharge reel went because all sixteen of the bay's emergency lights blew up in simultaneous green flashes. Kowacs was tumbling, and when he could see anything it was the great cylinder of the *Bonnie Parker* above him, dribbling blazing fragments of itself as it plunged through the dark sky.

The *Bonnie Parker*'d been a good mount, a tough old bird. To the marines she carried into one part of hell after another, she'd been as good a friend as hardware could be to flesh and blood. But this was a business in which your luck ran out sooner or later. The *Bonnie Parker*'s luck had run out; and the only difference between the landing vessel and Captain Miklos Kowacs, dropping unsupported through the atmosphere of a hostile planet, was the size of the hole they'd make when they hit the ground.

"Location," Kowacs ordered, and his helmet obediently projected a hologram readout onto the air rushing past. Three kilometers from the intended target area, which didn't matter now, and according to the laser altimeter, forty-seven hundred meters in the air.

Very shortly that wouldn't matter either, but the numbers weren't spinning down as quickly as Kowacs would've thought. Spreading his arms and legs slowed him enough that, even with the weight of his gear, he might not be traveling more than, say, thirty meters a second when he hit.

The commo still worked, though there was a hash of static from jamming, other communications, and the band-ripping petulance of plasma weapons.

"Six to all Headhunters," Kowacs said on the unit push. "We're going to be landing south of the target, most of us. Attack the south face. See if you can get some support to knock down a section of the wall. I don't want any unnecessary casualties, but remember—unless we move fast, the Weasels won't've left us anybody to rescue."

Kowacs took a deep breath without closing the communication. Then he said the rest of what he had to say. "Delta Six, I'm passing command to you. Acknowledge. Over."

"Roger, Six," said Lieutenant Woking in a voice as calm as Kowacs had tried to keep his own. He wasn't the senior lieutenant, but he'd been in the 121st longer than the other three, and Weapons Platoon would be on the ground first.

Nobody was going to argue with Kowacs's final order, anyway.

"Everybody get an extra Weasel for me," Kowacs said, unable to see the useless holograms for his tears. "Headhunter Six out."

Somebody grabbed his right hand.

Kowacs twisted. Another marine, anonymous with his face shield lowered, but Bradley beyond doubt. The field first hadn't deployed his own static discharger yet. It wouldn't support two, not heavily equipped marines. That'd been tried, and all it meant was that the guy who'd fucked up took his buddy with him.

"Let go!" Kowacs shouted without keying the commo. Bradley's muscles were seasoned to holding his shotgun ready for use through the shock of combat jumps; Kowacs couldn't pull his hand free.

Corporal Sienkiewicz grabbed Kowacs's left hand. As Kowacs looked back in surprise, the noncoms popped their discharge reels simultaneously.

When the long wires were powered up, static repulsion spun them off their reels in cascades of purple sparks. They acted as electrical levers, forming powerful negative charges at the top of the wire and in the air beneath the reel itself. Their mutual repulsion tried to lift the man to whom the reel was attached—

for as long as the power-pack could maintain the dynamically unstable situation.

Static dischargers weren't perfect. Jumping in a thunderstorm was as surely suicide as it would have been with a conventional parachute, though because of lightning rather than air currents. Still, a marine—or the artificial intelligence in the marine's helmet—could angle the wire and drop at a one-to-one slant, regardless of wind direction, allowing as much precision as a landing vessel could provide.

It wasn't safe; but nobody who volunteered for a Marine Reaction Company figured to die in bed.

"This isn't going to work!" Kowacs shouted over the wind rush.

"It'll work better than remembering we didn't try," Sienkiewicz shouted back. "Start pickin' a soft place to land."

The noncoms were taking a calculated risk which they felt was part of their job, just as Kowacs had done when he gave the newbie his discharge reel. Not much he could say about that.

What the hell. Maybe they'd make it after all.

Vertical insertions were scary under the best conditions, and a night drop was that in spades. Though the laser altimeter gave Kowacs a precise readout, his eyes told him he was suspended over the empty pit of hell—and his gut believed his eyes.

Dull orange splotches lighted three sections of the blackness, but there was no way to judge the extent of the fires. Burning cities, burning vehicles—or the burning remains of landing vessels like the *Bonnie Parker*, gutted in the air by Weasel defenses.

Occasional plasma bolts jeweled the night with a sudden intensity that faded to afterimages before the eye was aware of the occurrence. Even more rarely, a secondary explosion bloomed at the point of impact, white or orange or raw, bubbling red. Even the brightest of the blasts reached Kowacs's ears as a distance-slowed, distance-muted rumble, barely audible over the rush of air.

They seemed to be plunging straight down. "Top, are you guiding?" Kowacs demanded as his altimeter spun from four into three digits and continued to drop.

"Are you nuts?" Sienkiewicz said before Bradley had time to reply. "We got enough problems keeping the wires from tangling as it is. Sir."

"Oh—roger," Kowacs said in embarrassment. *He* should've thought of that. When he gave himself up for dead, he seemed to have turned off his mind.

And that was a *real* good way to get your ass killed.

They were low enough to see a pattern of lights beneath them, half a dozen buildings within a dimly illuminated perimeter. A vehicle with powerful headlights carved a swath through the darkness as it drove hell-for-leather toward the compound. For good or ill, the three marines were going to land within the perimeter at about the time the vehicle entered by the gate.

"When we touch down—" Kowacs started to say.

His altimeter read 312 meters one moment . . . and 27 a microsecond later as a starship glided beneath them, blacked out and covered with radar-absorbent resin.

Somebody—Bradley or Sienkiewicz—swore in amazed horror. Then both noncoms twisted, fighting to keep their lines from crossing and shorting out in the roaring airstream.

Kowacs, hanging from his friends' hands, watched the ship make its landing approach. His mind took in details of the vessel and the movement around it, considering options coolly—

Because otherwise he'd think about a crackle of energy above him and a sickening drop for the last hundred meters to the ground. Dead as sure as five kilometers could make him.

"Ready!" he called. The ship had crossed under them, then slowed to a near halt just above the ground. They were slipping over it again on the opposite vector, neither descent quite perpendicular. Steam and smoke rose from the center of the compound, swirling violently in the draft from the ship's passage and her lift thrusters. The vapors formed a tortured screen where they were cut by the blue-white headlights of the ground vehicle that had just raced through the gate.

The ship was Khalian. Her vertical stabilizer, extended for atmosphere travel, bore the red hen scratches that the Weasels used for writing.

"Now!" Kowacs ordered. The three marines tucked out of the pancake posture they'd used to slow their descent, letting the ground rush up at a hell of a clip. They sailed over a metal-roofed building and hit rolling, short of a second structure—a warehouse or something similar, windowless and austere.

Bradley's line still had enough of a charge to splutter angrily when it dragged the roof and grounded. Sienkiewicz was thirty kilos heavier than the field first, even without the weight of her plasma gun and the other nonstandard gear she insisted on adding to her personal load. Her line popped only a single violet spark before it went dead.

Close. Real fucking close.

And it wasn't over yet.

Kowacs had been as prepared as you could be to hit the ground faster than humans were intended, but Bradley had released his right hand a fraction later than Sienkiewicz had dropped his left.

Kowacs twisted, hit on his left heel, and caromed like a ground-looping airplane instead of doing a neat tuck-and-roll as he'd intended. His left knee smashed him in the chest, his backpack and helmet slammed the ground, and when he caught himself, his rifle sprang back on its elastic sling to rap his hip and face shield.

Pain made his eyes flash with tears. His hands, now freed, gripped and aimed the automatic rifle.

Pain didn't matter. He was alive, and there were Weasels to kill.

"Helmet," Kowacs said, "translate Khalian," enabling the program against the chance that he'd hear barked orders soon.

"Clear this way," whispered Bradley, pointing his shotgun toward one end of the five-meter alley between warehouses in which they'd landed. He spoke over Band 3 of the radio, reserved for internal command-group discussion. The low-power transmission permitted the three of them to coordinate without trying to shout over the ambient noise.

Which, now that they were down with no wind rush to blur other racket, seemed considerable.

"Clear mine," echoed Sienkiewicz, covering the opposite direction with her rifle while they waited for their captain to get his bearings.

"Are there doors to these places?" Kowacs asked, pretending he didn't feel a jabbing from his ankle up his left shin and praying it'd go away in another couple steps. He slouched past Bradley to a back corner. The two males curved around the warehouses in opposite directions, like the hooks of a grapnel, while Sienkiewicz covered their backs.

In the other direction, the starship's lift jets snarled and blew fragments of baked sod into the air. A siren, perhaps mounted on the vehicle the marines had seen arriving, wound down with a querulous note of its own.

The buildings backed up to the perimeter fence. None of the inhabitants had interest to spare from the ship that had just landed in the center of the compound.

"No door here," Bradley reported from the back of his building. He spoke with a rising inflection, nervous or just quivering with adrenaline, looking for a chance to kill or run.

"We'll go this way," Kowacs muttered to his team as his left hand switched on the forty-centimeter cutting blade he'd unslung in anticipation. The unloaded whine changed to a howl of pure delight as its diamond teeth sliced into the corrugated metal wall of the building.

This was the sort of job for which the cutter was intended, though the "tools" wouldn't have been as popular in Marine Reaction Companies had they not been so effective in hand-to-hand—hand-to-paw—combat. Kowacs swept the powered blade in a wide arc while the noncoms poised to rake the interior if anything moved when the wall fell away.

Kowacs's mouth was open. To someone outside his head, he looked as if he were leering in fierce anticipation.

In reality, he was stiffening his body to absorb a burst of shots. Weasels inside the warehouse might decide to fire into the center of the pattern his cutter drew, and the first *he'd* know of their intention was the impact of bullets sparking through the sheet metal.

Three-quarters of the way around the arc, Kowacs's blade pinged on a brace; the section wobbled like a drumhead. Sienkiewicz leaped at the wall behind the heel of her right boot, burst into the dark warehouse, and sprawled over a pile of the furniture stored there.

"Bloody *hell!*" she snarled as she rolled to her feet, but their helmet sensors indicated the warehouse was cold and unoccupied. Kowacs and Bradley were laughing as they clambered over the accidental barrier.

Kowacs swept his eyes across the clutter, using sonic imaging rather than white light. Sienkiewicz had tripped on a sofa. Like the rest of the furniture stored in clear film against the back wall, it was ornate, upholstered—

And quite clearly designed for humans. Short-legged

Khalians would find it as uncomfortable as humans did the meter-high ceiling of a Weasel bed alcove.

"Let's go," Kowacs said, but he and his two marines were already slipping down the aisle between stacked cubical boxes of several sizes. The glare of whatever was going on in the center of the compound flickered through the louvered windows at the front of the building.

Sergeant Bradley's load of combat gear bulked his wiry form, changing the texture of his appearance in a way that it didn't his heavily built companions. He was taking shorter steps with his right leg than his left, and the twitch of his pack amplified the asymmetric motion.

Kowacs glanced at him.

Bradley looked back, his expression unreadable behind the face shield. "No problem, Cap'n," he said. "We ain't holdin' a track meet."

He pulled a five-unit grenade stick from his belt, poising his thumb above the rotary arming/delay switch that would tell the bombs when to detonate.

Kowacs didn't have to see Bradley's face to visualize the smile that was surely on it.

The sort of smile a cat wears with its teeth in a throat. The sort of smile Kowacs himself wore.

The windows were narrow but the full height of the front wall. They flanked a door whose crossbar had a manual unlocking mechanism on this side. Sienkiewicz worked it gently, holding her plasma weapon ready, while Kowacs and Bradley peered through the louvers.

The only light in the warehouse was what trickled through the windows themselves. There was no possibility that those outside would notice the Headhunters preparing for slaughter.

The Khalian vessel was small for a starship, a cylinder no more than sixty meters in length; but, unlike the *Bonnie Parker,* it wasn't designed to land outside a proper spaceport. The pilot had given up trying to balance on his lift jets and had dropped to the ground. The narrow-footed landing legs, intended to stabilize the ship on a concrete pad, carved through the flame-blackened sod like knife blades; the belly of the craft sank deep enough to threaten an explosion when the jets fired again on lift-off.

The hundred or more waiting humans crowded close, some of

them yelping as those behind pushed them against still-hot metal. Vapor puffed from the starship as an airlock started to valve open.

A big air-cushion vehicle with polished brightwork, its wheeled outriggers lowered for high-speed road travel, pushed close to the airlock with a careless disregard for the clamoring pedestrians. As a ramp extended from the starship, the car's door opened and a plump, self-important man got out. His multicolored clothing was as rich and obviously civilian as the vehicle in which he'd arrived.

"Say when," Sienkiewicz demanded, her foot poised to shove open the door and fire her plasma weapon. She had no view of what was going on outside. "Say *when!*"

"Sir, what the *hell* is going on?" Bradley whispered. "These aren't—I mean, they're . . ."

"Sie," Kowacs said in a calm, soft voice, "fire directly into the airlock, then flatten yourself. Top, you and I will throw grenades with three-second"—his own thumb armed a bundle of minigrenades just as he knew Bradley was doing with his own—"delay, airburst."

"And duck out the back, Cap'n?" asked the field first.

"And rush the ship, Top," Kowacs corrected with no more emotion than he'd shown when going over the munitions manifest three weeks earlier in Port Tau Ceti. "There won't be time for anybody aboard to close the lock. Not after Sie lights 'em up."

The man from the car strode up the ramp. The rest of the crowd—all males, so far as Kowacs could tell—jumped out of his way as if he were still driving his vehicle. The starship's inner lock had opened, because when the fellow reached the top of the ramp, a human in a black-and-silver uniform appeared from inside the vessel and blocked his way.

For a moment the two men shouted at one another in a language Kowacs didn't recognize. The man in uniform unexpectedly punched the civilian in the stomach, rolling him back down the three-meter ramp. The crowd's collective gasp was audible even over the hiss and pinging of the ship's idling systems.

"Sir," begged Sienkiewicz, staring at the blank panel before her. "*Sir!* When?"

The plump man got to his feet, shouting in fury. A figure stepped from the ship and stood next to the man in uniform.

The newcomer was a Weasel. As it barked to the man in uniform, the translation program in Kowacs's helmet rasped, "What are we waiting for? Don't you realize, even *now* a missile may be on the way?"

"Ready," said Kowacs, his rifle vertical, gripped in his left hand, and the stick of grenades ready in his right.

The uniformed human turned to the Khalian and *barked*.

"Shoot that one," the helmet translated, "and we'll cram the rest aboard somehow."

The Weasel raised a submachine gun. The plump man leaped back into his car with a scream.

"Go," whispered Kowacs.

Sienkiewicz kicked the warehouse door thunderously open an instant before the lightning flash of her plasma bolt lit the night.

The jet of plasma spat between the two figures in the airlock, struck a bulkhead inside the ship, and converted the entrance chamber into a fireball. The blast blew the Weasel and the uniformed human ten meters from the lock, their fur and hair alight.

Anybody inside the starship had burns unless they were separated from the entry chamber by a sealed door. As for the crowd outside . . .

Kowacs's and Bradley's grenade sticks arced high over the crowd before the dispersion charges popped and scattered the units into five bomblets apiece. The bomblets went off an instant later with the noise of tree limbs breaking under the weight of ice.

Shrapnel ripped and rang on the front of the warehouse; the crowd flattened like scythed wheat.

Kowacs was up and moving as soon as the last bomblet went off. There was a spot of blood and a numb patch on the back of his right wrist, but nothing that'd keep him from functioning. The grenades spewed glass-fiber shrapnel that lost velocity fast in an atmosphere, but it wasn't completely safe even at twenty meters. Closer up, it—

Sienkiewicz slipped on bloody flesh as she tried to fire a burst from her rifle into the men at the fringe of the grenade explosions. Her shots went off into the night sky, but that didn't matter. The survivors who could move were running away, screaming; some of them blinded; some scattering drops of gore as they waved their arms in terror . . .

The dispersion charges had spread the bombs well enough

that most of the crowd wasn't running.

The Khalian from the ship thrashed in its death agonies on a sprawl of humans. Kowacs's rifle burped three rounds into it anyway as he passed, and Bradley, half a step behind, blew off the creature's tusked face with his shotgun.

They weren't so short on ammo that they couldn't make sure of a Weasel.

Kowacs hit the ramp first and jumped it in a single stride despite the weight of his gear. His team faced around reflexively, just as he would have done if one of the others had been in the lead. Bradley fired at the backs of the survivors to keep them moving in the right direction. It was long range for the airfoil loads in his weapon, but one of the targets flung up his hands and dropped a meter short of shelter.

Sienkiewicz put surgical bursts into the windscreen, then the engine compartment of the ground vehicle. The idling turbine screamed, then the fans died and let the skirt flatten. Yellow flames started to flicker through the intake gratings.

A solenoid clacked behind Kowacs as a survivor in the starship's cockpit tried desperately to close the airlock, but the jet of plasma had welded something or fried part of the circuitry.

Kowacs rolled into the ship-center room the plasma bolt had cleansed. A meter-broad circle'd been gouged from the hull metal opposite the lock. Anything flammable at sun-core temperatures was burning or had burned, including a corpse too shrunken to be identified by species. Open hatches led sternward, toward two cabins and the sealed engineering spaces, and to the left—forward, to the cockpit.

Kowacs fired right and jumped left, triggering a short burst that sparked off the ceiling and bulkheads of the passageway it was supposed to clear.

None of the bullets hit the Khalian running from the cockpit with a submachine gun in one hand.

Kowacs hadn't expected a real target. He tried to swing the muzzle on, but his right side slammed the deck so his shots sprayed beneath the leaping Khalian. The only mercy was that his opponent seemed equally surprised and tried clubbing the marine with his submachine gun. The Weasel had sprung instinctively on its victim instead of shooting as reason would have told him to do.

"Nest-fouling ape!" shouted the translation program as the

submachine gun's steel receiver crashed on the dense plastic of Kowacs's helmet. The creature's free hand tore the marine's left forearm as Kowacs tried to keep the claws from reaching beneath his chin and—

Bradley fired with his shotgun against the Weasel's temple.

Kowacs couldn't hear for a moment. He couldn't see until he flipped up the visor that'd been splashed opaque by the contents of the Khalian's skull.

The hatch at the other end of the short passageway was cycling closed. Kowacs slid his rifle into the gap. Its plastic grip cracked, but the beryllium receiver held even though the pressure deformed it.

Bradley cleared a grenade stick.

"No!" Kowacs shouted. He aimed the Weasel submachine gun at the plate in the center of the cockpit hatch and squeezed the trigger. Nothing.

"Sir, they'll be protected by acceleration pods!" Bradley cried. *"This*'ll cure 'em!"

The grenade stick was marked with three parallel red lines: a bunker buster.

There was a lever just above the submachine gun's trigger, too close for a human to use it easily, but just right for a short-thumbed Weasel. Kowacs flipped it and crashed out a pair of shots.

"We need the ship flying!" he cried as his left hand reached for one of his own grenade sticks and the hatch began to open. He tossed the stick through the widening gap and leaped through behind them.

The bundle wasn't armed. The Khalian pilot was gripping a machine pistol in the shelter of his acceleration pod, waiting to rise and shoot as soon as the grenades went off. He didn't realize his mistake until Kowacs's slugs ripped across his face.

"Get the stern cabins," Kowacs ordered. "The cockpit's clear."

Kowacs glanced behind him at the control panel: undamaged, no bullet holes or melted cavities, no bitter haze of burning insulation.

No obvious controls either.

"Fire in the hole!" Bradley's voice warned over the helmet link.

Kowacs stiffened. Grenades stuttered off in a chain of muffled explosions; then, as he started to relax, another stick detonated.

"Starboard cabin clear," Bradley reported laconically. He'd tossed in a pair of sticks with a two-second variation in delay. A Weasel leaping from cover after the first blast would be just in time for the follow-up.

Ruined the pelt, of course.

The cockpit's four acceleration pods were contour-to-fit units that, when activated, compressed around the form within them. Three of the pods were shrunken tight to hold Khalians like the corpse in one of them, but a side couch was still shaped for a human.

"Port cabin's locked!" Bradley shouted, his voice from the helmet earphones a disconcerting fraction of a second earlier than the same words echoing down the passageway at merely the speed of sound. "Sir, want I should blast it? Can you back me?"

Humans *could* fly the damned ship.

It was just that none of the humans *aboard* could fly the vessel. And if Kowacs understood the implications of what that Weasel cried a moment before the plasma bolt gave him a foretaste of eternal hell, the ship was their only prayer of surviving the next—

"Cap'n," Sienkiewicz reported, "I got a prisoner, and he says—"

Kowacs was already moving before the radio transmission cut off in a blast of static, hugely louder than the *crack!* of the plasma weapon that caused it.

Sergeant Bradley crouched at the corner of the stern passageway. Bradley's shotgun was aimed at the stateroom he'd found locked, but his head craned back over his shoulder as he tried to see what was going on outside the vessel.

Kowacs skidded in the blood and film deposited on the deck of the central cabin when plasma-vaporized metal cooled. He made a three-point landing, his ass and both boot heels, but the captured submachine gun was pointed out the airlock where Sienkiewicz stood.

The plasma weapon was on Sienkiewicz's shoulder; a glowing track still shimmered from its muzzle. One of the warehouses was collapsing around a fireball. A surviving local must've made the mistake of calling Sie's attention to him.

"Move it! Move it, dog-brain!" she bellowed to somebody

beneath Kowacs's line of vision. "Or by God the next one's in *your* face!"

As Sienkiewicz spoke, the translation program barked in Weasel through her helmet speaker. She couldn't've captured a—

Kowacs stepped to the corporal's side, then jumped so that the fat civilian scrambling up the ramp in blind panic wouldn't bowl him over. It was the gorgeously clad fellow who'd strode up the ramp before—and been knocked down by the human in uniform, with a promise of death if the Headhunter attack hadn't intervened.

"Waved his shirt from the car, Cap'n," Sienkiewicz explained. As she spoke, her eyes searched for snipers, movement, *anything* potentially dangerous in the night and sullen fires. "I thought. . . . well, I didn't shoot him. And then he barked, you know, that the place was gonna be nuked, but he could fly us out."

"Sure, you did right," Kowacs said without thinking it even vaguely surprising that Sienkiewicz apologized for taking a prisoner alive.

"Quickly, the cockpit!" the machine voice in Kowacs's ear demanded while the prisoner's mouth emitted a series of high-pitched barks. "They'll surely destroy this base any moment. They can't allow any sign of our installations!"

The fellow was still in a panic, but the way he brushed past Kowacs proved that he'd regained his arrogance. He looked clownishly absurd: he'd ripped a piece from his shirtfront to wave as a flag, and at some point recently, he'd fouled his loose, scintillantly blue trousers as well.

"Sir!" Bradley cried. He'd enabled his speaker along with the translation program, so barks counterpointed his words. "This cabin! We can't leave it!"

"Watch it, then, for chrisake!" Kowacs snarled as he strode with the prisoner into the cockpit.

The prisoner slipped as he tried to hop over the Weasel in the passageway. He muttered what must have been a curse, but the words were in the unfamiliar language in which he and the uniformed human had argued before the Khalian appeared.

Somebody fired at the ship with a machinegun—from the side opposite the airlock, so there was no response from Sienkiewicz. The light bullets were no threat to hull plating, but the *clang-clang-clang, clang-clang-clang, clang-clang-clang* wound Kowacs's mainspring a turn tighter with each short burst.

The prisoner flopped down into one of the center pods. It conformed to his body like a workpiece in a drop forge, spreading sideways and upward to support him in an upright position. Kowacs knelt on the deck beside him, holding the muzzle of the submachine gun near the prisoner's ear.

Holographic displays curtained the blank consoles, meshing unexpectedly with a kaleidoscopic fragment of Kowacs's memory.

When he'd dived into the cockpit, aiming and firing before the hunched Khalian could respond, there'd been similar flickers of light over the plastic consoles. They'd died with the seated pilot, but they came up automatically as soon as a living intellect sat before them again.

The prisoner's finger twitched. Six columns of red light mounted higher. The ship rocked gently, dispelling Kowacs's doubt that an obvious civilian would be any better able to fly the damned thing than the Headhunters themselves were. The prisoner was shaking them loose from the soft surface instead of powering-up abruptly and blowing one or more of the blocked nozzles.

Clang-clang-whing-*spow-ow-ow!*

The machine gunner had shifted to a position from which he might be able to accomplish something. Kowacs hunched lower, but the bullet zipping through the airlock buried itself in a bulkhead on the third ricochet. The sniper had moved.

Sienkiewicz was all right: her plasma weapon crashed out its last charge. The blast that followed was much too great for a belt of ammunition or a few grenades. The machine gunner must've taken cover in a warehouse, without considering what might be in the cases around him.

"The Weasels are going to nuke this place?" Kowacs demanded of the man beside him. His speaker's barking translation was almost as irritating to him as the bullet impacts had been.

"Not them, you fool!" the prisoner snapped, rocking the ship up ten degrees to port. Kowacs clutched the back of the pod for support. "*They* don't have brains enough to be concerned. It's the clan chiefs, of course, and they're right"—the ship rocked back to starboard—"but *I* don't intend to die."

"Sir, we're gonna blow the hatch," Bradley reported flatly. Sienkiewicz could back him up, now. The holographic display that took the place of cockpit windows showed one whole side of the compound mushrooming upward in multicolored secondary explosions.

But a charge heavy enough to blow a bulkhead still wasn't a great idea in the confined space of a ship this small.

"Hold it, Top," Kowacs ordered. "You—prisoner. Can you open and close the door to the port cabin from here?"

"Yes," the prisoner said, grimacing. One of the red columns abruptly turned blue. All six disappeared as the man's finger wagged. The ship settled at a skewed angle.

"Wait!" Kowacs ordered. "Open it a crack for a grenade, then close it again?"

"Yes, yes!" the prisoner repeated, the snarling Khalian vocables seasoning the emotionless translation from Kowacs's headset. "Look, *you* may want to die, but I assure you that your superiors want *me* alive! I'm *the* Riva of Riva Clan!" He made a minuscule gear-shifting motion with his left hand.

"Top! Here it comes!" Kowacs shouted.

Bradley and Sienkiewicz had already been warned by Kowacs's side of the cockpit conversation and the *clack* as the hatch's locking mechanism retracted.

The corporal cried, "Got 'em!" Her automatic rifle fired a short burst to keep Weasels clear of the gap while Bradley tossed in the grenade. The hatch hadn't quite cycled closed again when the scattering charge momentarily preceded a quintet of sharp pings—not real explosions.

"Shit, Top!" Kowacs cried, squeezing his helmet tight to his knees and clasping his forearms above it. "Not a—"

The bunker buster went off. The starship quivered like a fish swimming; the holographic display went monochrome for a moment, and flexing bulkheads sledged the vessel's interior like a piston rising on its compression stroke.

"Think we oughta give 'em another, Top?" joked Sienkiewicz with the laughter of relief in her voice.

They were okay, then, and both the ship and its controls seemed to have survived the blast. Kowacs could even hear the hatch start to open again, which said a lot for the solidity of the internal divisions on Weasel ships.

"Idiots!" said the prisoner—the Riva, whatever that was;

"clan" might only be as close a word as Weasels had to the grouping the Riva headed. "Suicidal fools!"

Kowacs didn't know that he could argue the point. Thing was, doing the job had always been the Headhunter priority, well above concern for side effects. Bradley's bunker buster would sure as Hell've done the job.

Its bomblets sprayed fuel, atomized to mix completely with the surrounding air. When the igniter went off, the blast was somewhere between a fire and a nuclear explosion. If the hatch *hadn't* resealed the moment before ignition, the pressure wave could've pulverized more than the contents of one cabin.

The Riva's hands wriggled. Four of the flat-lined red holograms blipped upward as he fed thrust to selected jets. The starship lifted a trifle, though not as much as it had when the bunker buster went off.

Sergeant Bradley stepped into the cockpit. Kowacs turned with a smile to greet him. They'd survived thus far, and they were about to shake clear of ground zero as the prisoner played the ship with the skill of a concert pianist on a familiar scherzo.

The ship wasn't going anywhere serious with the airlock jammed open, but they could shift a couple kilometers and start hollering for recovery. A captured ship and a human prisoner who'd thought he could give orders to Weasels—that was enough for anybody, even the Headhunters.

Bradley was a man of average size who looked now like a giant as his left hand lifted the Riva from his seat and jerked his face into the muzzle of the shotgun. Bradley had killed often and expertly. There was utter cold fury in his face and voice as he whispered, "You son of a bitch. Why didn't you tell me? Why didn't—"

"Top," said Kowacs, rising to his feet and making very sure that his own weapon pointed to the ceiling. He'd seen Bradley like this before, but never about another human being. . . .

"—you *tell* me?" Bradley shouted as his gun rapped the prisoner's mouth to emphasize each syllable.

Sienkiewicz had followed the sergeant; her face bore a look of blank distaste that Kowacs couldn't fathom either.

The ship poised for a moment with no hand at its controls. When it lurched heavily to the ground, Bradley swayed, and Kowacs managed to get between the field first and the prisoner who was the only chance any of them had of surviving more than the next few minutes.

"I got 'im, Top," Kowacs said in a tone of careless command, grabbing the Riva by the neck and detaching Bradley by virtue of his greater size and strength. "Let's go take a look, you."

He dragged the prisoner with him into the passageway, making sure without being obvious about it that his body was between the fellow and Bradley's shotgun.

Didn't guarantee the sergeant *wouldn't* shoot, of course; but there were damn few guarantees in this life.

The cabin door opened inward, which might've been how it withstood the explosion without being ripped off its hinges. Smoke and grit still roiled in the aftermath of the blast.

Kowacs flipped down his visor and used its sonic imaging; the ultrasonic projection sources were on either side, and the readout was on the inner surface of the face shield. Neither was affected by the fact he'd forgotten to wipe the remains of the Weasel off the outside of the visor.

The cabin'd been occupied when the grenade went off, but Kowacs's nose had already told him that.

Five bodies, all human. They'd been huddled together under the bedding. That didn't save them, but it meant they were more or less recognizable after the blast. Two women—young, but adults; and three children, the youngest an infant.

Weapons would have survived the explosion—stood out against the background of shattered plastic and smoldering cloth. There hadn't been any weapons in the cabin.

"You son of a bitch," Kowacs said in a soft, wondering voice, unaware that he was repeating Bradley's words. "Why did you do that? You knew, didn't you . . ." The sentence trailed off without a question, and the submachine gun was pointing almost of its own accord.

"Why should I save the heir of Kavir bab-Wellin?" blurted the prisoner, spraying blood from lips broken by the sergeant's blows. "Kavir would have killed me! Didn't you see that? Just because I became the Riva over his father, he would have *killed* me!"

Somebody shot at the hull again. Either they were using a lighter weapon, or anything seemed mild after the bunker buster had crashed like a train wreck. Sienkiewicz eased to the airlock with her rifle ready, but she wouldn't fire until she had a real target.

"I'll . . . ," Bradley said in a choked voice. He pulled another grenade stick from his belt.

Kowacs was so calm that he could visualize the whole planet, nightside and day, shots and screams and the filthy white glare of explosions.

"No, Top," he said.

He was aware of every one of the ninety-seven marines in his Headhunters, the living and the dead, even though only Bradley and Sienkiewicz were within range of his helmet's locator. He was walking back to the cockpit, carrying the Riva with him; ignoring the chance of a bullet nailing him as he stepped in front of the airlock—ignoring the burst Sienkiewicz ripped out at the target her light amplifier had shown her.

"Cap'n?" said the field first, suddenly more concerned than angry.

Kowacs dropped the prisoner into the chair out of which he'd been jerked.

"Fly us," he ordered flatly. Then he added, "Helmet. Project. Course to target. Out," and a glowing map hung in front of the ship's holographic controls, quivering when Kowacs's helmet quivered and moved the tiny projection head. The pentagonal air-defense site shone bright green against a mauve background.

"Fly us there. Land us in the middle of it with the airlock facing the pit in the center."

The Riva's hands made the same initial gestures as before: raising thrust to alternate jets, making the holographic map shiver in wider arcs. He didn't speak.

"Sir, have, ah . . . ," Sergeant Bradley said. He was too good a soldier—and too good a friend—to let anger rule him when he saw his commanding officer in this unreadable mood. "Have our boys captured the place? Because otherwise, the missile batt'ries . . . ?"

He knew Kowacs hadn't gotten any report. Knew also there was no way in hell the 121st was going to capture the hardened installation, not after they'd been scattered by the emergency drop and left without the belt-fed plasma weapons that could've taken apart the concrete walls.

The ship seesawed free with a sucking noise from beneath her hull. All six thrust indicators shot upward. A streak of blue flashed as the vessel shook violently, but the hologram cleared.

They began to build forward speed. Air screamed past the open lock.

"Their computers'll identify us as friendly," Kowacs said.

His eyes were open, but they weren't focused on anything in particular. His left hand was on the prisoner's shoulder, as if one friend with another. The muzzle of the submachine gun was socketed in the Riva's ear. "There'll be a lockout to keep 'em from blasting friendlies, won't there, Riva old buddy?"

"There is, but they can override it," barked the prisoner nervously. He was too aware of the gun to turn toward the Headhunters as he spoke. "Look, I can take us to a safe place, and you can summon your superiors. I'm very valuable, more valuable than you may dream."

"Naw, we gotta pull out what's left of a Jeffersonian assault company," Kowacs said calmly. "We'll do it fast. Weasels don't think about electronics when you surprise 'em."

"This is madness!" the pilot shouted. "They'll surely kill us all!" There were tears of desperation in his eyes, but his hands kept the ship along the course unreeling on the holographic map. In two minutes, maybe three, they'd be there. No longer'n that.

"If we can't do it, nobody will," Kowacs said. "The Weasels'll finish 'em off, every damn one of 'em."

Light bloomed with dazzling immediacy a few kilometers behind the ship. The two marines braced themselves; their prisoner squeezed lower in his acceleration pod.

The vessel pitched. Cabin pressure shot up momentarily as the pressure wave caught them and passed on to flatten trees in an expanding arc.

They were still under control.

Sienkiewicz stepped into the cockpit, moving carefully because of her size and the way the open airlock made the ship flutter in low-level flight. The empty tube of her plasma weapon, slung at buttocks height, dribbled a vaporous fairy-track of ionized metal behind her.

"I just take orders, Nick," Sienkiewicz said, marking the words as a lie by using Kowacs's first name. "But it was them decidin' to do it their own way that got 'em where they are. I don't see why anybody else needs to die for some anarchist from Jefferson."

"Because it's our *job*, Sie!" Bradley snapped, his anger a sign that the big corporal spoke for at least part of his own mind as well.

"Two *karda* to your goal," whispered Kowacs's earphones, transforming the Riva's nervous chirps without translating the Khalian units into human ones.

"No," said Kowacs. "A job's not enough to die for."

He pulled the submachine gun from the grip of the Weasel he'd killed in the next pod. They'd need everything they had to give covering fire while the Jeffersonians scrambled aboard.

Bradley took the weapon from his captain. "Better range to the wall than a scattergun," he said.

"I want you to watch our pilot," Kowacs said.

Bradley dropped his shotgun into a patrol sling with its muzzle forward beneath his right arm. He smiled. "Naw, our buddy here knows what I'll toss into the cockpit if the ship starts acting funny before you tell 'im to move out. A bunker buster'll work just as good on his type as it does on little kids."

"Right," Kowacs said without emotion. "Let's move."

"We're Alliance troops," he went on as they filed down the passageway to their positions at the airlock. "So're the Jeffersonians, whatever they think about it. Maybe if we get this crew out, they'll tell their buddies back home that it's a big universe."

He took a deep breath. "If the Alliance don't stick together," he said, "somebody sure God's going to stick it to all of us. One at a time."

Deceleration stresses made the Headhunters sway. A stream of red tracers—Fleet standard, not Khalian—flicked from the ground and rang on the starship's hull.

Their target's broad concrete rampart slid beneath the airlock.

What Kowacs didn't say—what he didn't have to say—was that there'd always be men who acted for safety or comfort or personal pique, rather than for their society as a whole. The five burned corpses in the cabin behind them showed where that led.

It wasn't anywhere Miklos Kowacs and his troops were willing to go.

Not if it killed them.